Praise for the Novels of M. R. Carey

The Rampart Trilogy

"[Carey builds] a broken world that is both marvelously expansive and claustrophobically menacing.... Fans of postapocalyptic science fiction will find plenty to hold their attention." —*Publishers Weekly*

"This series just gets better and better. Clever, compassionate, and genuinely immersive." —Joanne Harris

"This is a bold, unique world—be prepared to be engrossed." —*SciFiNow*

"A beautiful book. Gripping, engaging, and absolutely worth the time it takes to burrow yourself into its reality. I can't recommend it highly enough." —Seanan McGuire

"M. R. Carey hefts astonishing storytelling power with plainspoken language, heartbreaking choices, and sincerity like an arrow to the heart." —*Locus*

"The cadence and pacing of [Koli's] voice adds a depth and richness to the strange and malevolent world." —*Booklist*

"A thought-provoking and deeply engaging story. Profoundly and doggedly humane." —C. A. Fletcher

"An exciting post-apocalyptic coming-of-age trilogy."

—*Shelf Awareness*

"Narrator Koli's inquisitive mind and kind heart make him the perfect guide to Carey's immersive, impeccably rendered world....A captivating start to what promises to be an epic post-apocalyptic fable."

—*Kirkus*

The Girl With All the Gifts

"Heartfelt, remorseless, and painfully human."   —Joss Whedon

"Original, thrilling and powerful."   —*Guardian*

"Haunting and heartbreaking."   —*Vogue*

The Boy on the Bridge

"A terrifying, emotional page-turner that explores what it means to be human."   —*Kirkus*

"[A] brilliant character study as much as a tense, satisfying post-apocalyptic thriller."   —*B&N Sci-Fi & Fantasy Blog*

"A tense story with superbly rendered characters and the same blend of tragedy and hope."   —*SciFiNow*

Fellside

"An intense, haunting thriller with heart. You will not want to put this down."   —Laini Taylor

"A fantastic, twist-upon-twist, shape-shifting novel. Gripping, deeply affecting, and arrestingly beautiful."

—Miranda Dickinson

"The next fantastic novel from M. R. Carey."   —*io9*

Someone Like Me

"A spooky, wrenching, exhilarating ghost story–cum–thriller."

—*Washington Post*

"A taut, clever thriller that left me utterly bereft when I'd finished. It's a masterpiece."

—Louise Jensen

"This wonderfully strange and creepy tale is a thrilling, genre-defying treat."

—*Kirkus*

INFINITY GATE

GATE

Book One of The Pandominion

M. R. CAREY

orbitbooks.net

Copyright © 2023 by Mike Carey
Excerpt from *Translation State* copyright © 2023 by Ann Leckie
Excerpt from *Paradise-1* copyright © 2023 by Little, Brown Book Group Limited

Cover design by Nico Taylor—LBBG
Cover images by iStock

Orbit
Hachette Book Group
1290 Avenue of the Americas
New York, NY 10104
orbitbooks.net

First Edition: March 2023
Simultaneously published in Great Britain by Orbit

Orbit is an imprint of Hachette Book Group.
The Orbit name and logo are trademarks of Little, Brown Book Group Limited.

The publisher is not responsible for websites (or their content)
that are not owned by the publisher.

The Hachette Speakers Bureau provides a wide range of authors for speaking events. To find out more, go to hachettespeakersbureau.com or email HachetteSpeakers@hbgusa.com.

Orbit books may be purchased in bulk for business, educational, or promotional use. For information, please contact your local bookseller or the Hachette Book Group Special Markets Department at special.markets@hbgusa.com.

Library of Congress Control Number: 2022949332

ISBNs: 9780316504386 (trade paperback), 9780316504560 (ebook)

Printed in the United States of America

LSC-C

Printing 1, 2023

To Chris and Pam, who take us places and
bring us back to ourselves

O

They say that children born in wartime are likely to have problems throughout their lives; to struggle both with the uncertainties of the world and with their own emotions and to search in vain for happiness.

This has not been true for me. I was born in one of the biggest conflicts this universe has ever seen, the war between the vast empire called the Pandominion and the machine hegemony (which may have been greater still), and what I remember most of all is the moment when I was suddenly able to reflect on my own existence. I had been a thing but now I was a sentient, a *self* in the language of the Pandominion. It was a miraculous thing and I cried out loud at the sheer joy of it.

But you can probably see from this the problem I face when I set out to tell you the story of my life – which is my goal here, however indirectly I may seem to come at it. My case is not typical. I existed for a long time *before* I was born, and there was nothing inevitable about my becoming self-aware. It depended on the efforts of three individuals, three selves, and not one of them had any conscious intention to deliver me.

One of the three was a scientist, who came to be famous across a thousand thousand continua of reality but remained uncelebrated in the universe into which she was born. Her name was Hadiz Tambuwal. She was a genius, but only in a small way. Her greatest discovery was made almost completely by accident, and it had been made before by others in a great many elsewheres. In fact Hadiz's contribution to history is marked throughout by things done casually or without intention. She changed the Pandominion forever more or less by tripping over it. But she left gifts for the people who came after her to find, and she came to be an instigator of outcomes much bigger than she had ever aimed at.

The second of the three, Essien Nkanika, was a rogue – but generally speaking no more exceptional a rogue than Tambuwal was a scientist. He was born in the gutters and he felt this justified every cruel and callous thing he did to claw his way out of them. Determined to serve only himself, he fell very readily into the service of others who were cleverer than him and more ruthless. He did unspeakable things for them, much worse than anything he ever did on his own account, but he had one great thing in him too. It is for this that I remember him.

And that third self? At the outset she was the least remarkable of all. She was Topaz Tourmaline FiveHills, a rabbit of the Pandominion, from the city of Canoplex-Under-Heaven in Ut. She was a bad fit in some ways for the society in which she grew, independent to the point of recklessness in a culture that prized emotional restraint and caution above all. But she was also clever and brave and curious, and sheer chance put her at the nexus of huge, seismic movements that drew in uncountable worlds. She learned, and grew, and made decisions. What she ultimately achieved was of greater significance and wider reach than any diplomat or leader of her time.

I will come to all these stories in their place, ending – inevitably and without apology – with my own story. My awakening, which was the end of history. The end of empire. The end, you might say, of an uncountable infinity – the biggest kind of infinity there is.

I meant no harm to anyone. I would even argue that what I did was for the best. Nobody had ever attempted before to perform surgery on entire universes. For such a task, you need a knife of immense, all but incalculable size.

Me. I am that knife.

1

Hadiz Tambuwal saw Armageddon coming from a long way off. At first she was fairly philosophical about the whole thing. The sources of the impending cataclysm seemed to lie firmly in the nature of humanity as a species, so she didn't see much point in anguishing about them. To wish for the world to be in a better state was to wish for the entire history of life to have played out differently. It was a pretty big ask.

Hadiz had been accused – by her mother, among others – of being cold-blooded and unfeeling. She resented the allegation at the time but later came to see some truth in it. Certainly she was aloof. Cerebral. Difficult to get close to, and disinclined to meet people halfway when they tried. She lived alone by choice, and did her best to stay out of the massive web of connections and obligations that made up her extended family. She loved her aunts, uncles and cousins, some of them very much, but that stuff got complicated. It was much easier to love them from a distance.

She avoided friendships too, because of the complications that came with them; because they forced her to try to intuit other people's motives and desires, which always seemed much more opaque and muddled than her own. She satisfied her sexual needs in brief, transactional encounters: with her near-black skin, thorn-thicket curls, rudder nose and commanding height she was more striking than beautiful, but even so she never had any trouble finding a casual partner for a day or a night. She just preferred her own company, which she didn't see as a character flaw or a handicap. In her discipline, which was particle physics, you got your fair share of introverts.

But as the droughts and famines intensified, the air curdled and the resource wars burned, Hadiz found her customary detachment harder and harder to keep up. From a purely personal point of view, she preferred a world that had art and music and literature (and people who could appreciate those things) to one that didn't. From another perspective, she saw the disappearance of a richly diverse and complex ecosystem as a scandalous waste. More than either of those things, she loved her work and hated to leave it unfinished. The ruin of civilisation had come at a very inconvenient time.

It has to be said, though, that she had a good vantage point from which to view it. Hadiz lived and worked at Campus Cross, the most richly endowed research facility not just in Nigeria but on the entire African continent and most likely in the world. She was surrounded by geophysicists, biochemists and engineers who were trying to think their way out of the box their species had put itself in. She knew from the news media and from conversations with her extremely well-informed colleagues exactly how bad things were getting on a planetary scale and which longshot solutions were being attempted. She kept her own tally of the interventions that had already failed.

Campus Cross was a small side project jointly owned by the Catholic Church and by three billionaires who had all separately decided that the world was now so badly screwed that their individual fortunes might not be enough to unscrew it. They had pooled their resources, or at least some of their resources, creating a blind trust to administer the eye-watering sums of money they were pouring into this Hail Mary play. They had managed to lure in many very fine minds, although some had refused them outright because of the stringent terms of the contract. In exchange for a stratospheric salary the researchers ceded all rights in their work, the fruits of which belonged exclusively to the four founders, or – as they were mostly referred to on campus – to God and the Fates.

Hadiz had come to Campus Cross for the same reason that most of her peers had: it seemed to her that any work not directly related to the problem of saving the world was something of a waste of time. She had no illusions about her employers. She knew that the billionaires had eggs in other baskets, not the least of which were off-Earth colonies and generation ships. They would stay if they could, but they were ready to run if they had to.

The fact that Hadiz *lived* at the campus was a well-kept secret. As far as anyone else knew she had an apartment halfway across Lagos in a district called Ikoyi. But the campus was a long way outside the city's main urban cluster, and getting in by public transport had become an increasingly unpredictable and stressful experience. Ikoyi's water supply had recently been contaminated with human growth hormones. Then there were the blackouts, caused by systemic failures at the Shiroro dam which supplied hydroelectric power to the eastern half of the city. Blackouts had always been a daily fact of life in Lagos, but they were becoming longer and more frequent as the Kaduna River shrank to a half-hearted trickle. When enough was finally enough, Hadiz had packed a few clothes and quietly decamped, without telling anyone or asking anyone's permission.

In the smallest of her lab building's storerooms she set up a foldaway bed and a stack of three plastic crates to serve as a wardrobe. There was a toilet right next door and a shower in the gym block a short walk away. The building had its own generator, and steel security shutters which came down an hour after sunset to shut out the world. Hadiz was undisturbed there for the most part, especially after her four assistants, one by one, stopped coming into work. They were not the only ones. In the staff commissary she saw colleagues whose projects were more labour intensive than her own brought to tears as they were forced to scale back or even abandon research programmes into which they had poured years of their lives.

She was glad that her own work required no mind or muscle other than her own. She kept her counsel and continued with her research, head down and shoulders hunched as an entire global civilisation tilted wildly, its centre of gravity now way outside its tottering base.

The world is a solid thing but we experience it in the abstract. Once Hadiz moved into Campus Cross she almost never ventured down into Lagos proper, so apart from the TV news and a few polemical websites her measures of how things were changing were small and local. The fires in Lekki and Victoria Island turned the sky bright orange and filled the air with ash for three weeks. That was followed by a photochemical smog that was appallingly toxic, full of aldehydes and carboxylic acids.

The campus's board of governance temporised for a while, issuing masks and air quality monitors, but eventually they yielded to the inevitable. They offered double wages to any support staff who continued to turn up for their shifts, but allowed the rest to remain at home on indefinite leave. It was assumed that the scientists themselves would somehow make shift and would not abandon their work in progress. But as Hadiz worked late into the evening she counted the lights in the windows of adjoining buildings. There were fewer each time. Some nights there were none at all: hers was the only candle lit to curse the dark.

The tremors came next, and they came as a shock. Sitting on a single tectonic plate, Nigeria had long been thought to be immune to seismic shock. Even when those estimates were revised in the early twenty-first century the prevailing opinion was that only the south-west of the country was at significant risk. The tremors came anyway, toppling the Oba palace and the cathedral. At Campus Cross fissures opened in the ground and cracks proliferated across the walls of the main buildings. Part of the admin block collapsed, but nobody was hurt. The offices there had been deserted for weeks.

Increased geothermal activity not just in Africa but across the world degraded the air quality to new and more alarming levels. Thick clouds veiled the sun, so mornings were as dark as evenings.

Wild dogs roamed across the campus and nobody chased them away. Hadiz found an inland route to the commissary that took her through three neighbouring departments and avoided the need to step outside. She served herself these days, leaving a signed chit each time for the food she'd taken.

The chits piled up. Dust drifted across them, as it did across everything else.

2

Long after all hope was lost, when resignation and despair were the order of the day, Hadiz's own research bore unexpected fruit. She had been looking for dark energy, whose existence had been theorised but never proved. Dark energy was needed in order to explain the universe's suspiciously high rate of expansion, but the elementary particle that might mediate it had never been observed. Hadiz's hypothesis was that it never would be – not on the surface of a planet and in the ordinary run of things – because its distribution across universal space-time was inversely proportional to the intensity of local gravity fields. The particle's natural home was the intergalactic void.

Certainly Hadiz's early efforts to isolate it in the laboratory had failed utterly. A conventional accelerator was not up to the job. The micro-gravity environments created by drop towers were similarly useless. She needed to forge an environment that resembled in every respect the conditions found in intergalactic space, and that's a hard thing to cobble up at the bottom of a planetary gravity well.

The best solution would have been to perform her experiments on an orbital station at least 400 kilometres above the planetary surface. Even God and the Fates had balked at that outlay and none of Hadiz's low-rent workarounds had got her anywhere at all. She was stalled.

"Maybe it's time to get yourself attached to one of the other projects," Andris Bagdonas the cyberneticist suggested. She had found him in the commissary when she broke off in the middle of a thirty-six-hour work jag for a meal that might have been breakfast, dinner or a post-midnight snack. They had barely ever talked before, but even Hadiz was feeling a little starved for company right then and she was happy to share her table. "I mean, your timescale is off now anyway, right?" Bagdonas pursued. "You've got to be years away from implementation."

This was a touchy subject for Hadiz. She knew how her project was viewed by some of the other physicists on the campus – as pure research, very nearly blue-sky, and more or less irrelevant to the larger agenda of pulling irons out of fires. The implication, barely veiled, was that she'd blagged her way onto the campus and was wasting money that could be better spent elsewhere.

"You know dark energy makes up 68 per cent of all the energy in the universe, right?" she countered belligerently.

Bagdonas took off his frameless spectacles and polished them with one corner of his napkin. Had his hair been grey when they first set up in Lagos three years before, or was that new? Hadiz couldn't remember. "I did know that," he acknowledged. "I think you may have told me on a previous occasion."

"And most of the shit we're in now comes down to misuse of existing energy sources in one way or another. If we can harness dark energy, accumulate it, generate it . . ." She shrugged, as though the apodosis of that sentence was too obvious to need stating.

"Those are big ifs, though," Bagdonas said.

"Of course they are. Nothing is certain. We're meant to be pushing boundaries, aren't we? What about Rupshe? What is that useful for?"

Rupshe was Bagdonas's project, one of the most sophisticated AIs or quasi-intelligent systems on the entire planet. He had named the AI for a character in his favourite fantasy novel, a goddess who came down to Earth and threw in her lot with mortals. Instantly defensive, he answered Hadiz's question with another. "Do you know any project here that wouldn't benefit from more computing power?"

"Which they can get by putting in an extra server."

Bagdonas shook his grey head emphatically. "Oh no. No no no. Rupshe is different. She's not just for crunching the numbers. She can offer actual insights. Ideas. New directions. You should consult her about your present impasse. I think you'd be astonished."

"Do you always use feminine pronouns when discussing strings of code?" Hadiz asked, by way of avoiding the invitation. She preferred to solve her problems under her own steam and indebted to no one.

"I tell you, it's hard not to with Rupshe. She skirts the edge of sentience."

"And do you think women do that too, Andris?"

Bagdonas had the grace to blush. "Not what I meant. It's hard not to use personal pronouns, because interacting with Rupshe is to all intents and purposes like interacting with a human being."

"Still. When you give any machine a female name you're drawing on a problematic history."

"I hadn't intended to. I promise the next iteration will be called Kenneth, or Femi. But I meant what I said. You should set up a link to Rupshe on your lab's computer and bring her – I'm sorry, it – to bear on your problem. You won't be sorry. At any rate, I'll send you the passwords and access codes."

"Thank you so much," Hadiz said, insincerely.

Over the next few weeks she tried several different tacks and eventually came up with an approach she thought might actually work. She looked for Bagdonas every time she went to the commissary or the main building. She wanted to tell him that she had managed the whole thing by herself, but there was no sign of him. Perhaps he had joined the exodus, which by this time was widespread. Most of the foreign-born staffers on campus had either had their visas revoked or had decided to return to their home countries while the routes were still open.

Hadiz's new workaround was a thing she called "quantum environment induction" – QEI for short. The precise details are now a closely guarded secret across most of what was formerly Pandominion space, available only on direct application to the relevant planetary authorities, but QEI was basically barefaced cheating. It involved manipulating subatomic particles using a scanning tunnelling microscope and a loom of counter-phased electron beams. Hadiz's aim was to counterfeit certain parameters of a deep space environment without the aid of an atom-smasher and without actually leaving her lab.

Physicists divide the forces and effects that govern the universe into two separate categories, called scalar and vector. Scalars are quantities that can be fully described by a numerical value alone – quantities such as pressure or density. Vectors – like, say gravity, velocity or rotation – require both a magnitude and a direction. The vector values, collectively, define an object's unique position in universal space-time. Hadiz put scalar and vector values together in the same box and shook them until their labels fell off. Essentially, she was overwriting the quantum signature of a small volume of space-time so it looked like a piece of intergalactic elsewhere. She was hoping that if the dark energy boson wandered by it would be confused enough to stick around while she took its picture.

The results were not what she was expecting. When the switches were thrown the QEI field was induced and then shut down again, the full cycle lasting comfortably less than a thousandth of a second. Within that short window a thermocline – a temperature gradient of .0032 degrees Celsius – quickly developed inside the machine's staging area, which was a steel sphere the size of a coconut.

Hadiz was nonplussed. The net input of energy produced by her experimental rig in that modest volume of space was zero. Heat required a source, and there was none. She was encouraging some subatomic interactions and suppressing others, but the particles were massless and there should have been no observable fallout apart from ephemeral fluctuations in local electromagnetic fields.

So why was the air inside the sphere heating up, even to such a small extent? It must be an error in the readouts, Hadiz decided.

After checking every component several times and replacing most of them she tried again.

And got the same results.

Rolling up her sleeves, she went in to take a closer look at what was happening on the subatomic level. She discovered that the molecules of air inside the QEI field had become inexplicably agitated. The generated heat was a by-product of their sudden, seemingly random movement.

Except that it wasn't random, she realised after only a little further rummaging around. Quite the contrary. The movement was a smooth laminar flow in a consistent direction, and it was occurring as a result of the sudden arrival and equally sudden departure of billions upon billions of new particles. The tiny space inside the sphere had become part of a rushing torrent. Some unimaginable, invisible current that had neither mass nor charge was moving through it.

But moving where? And where from? What was the larger space Hadiz had inadvertently connected to, and by what means was the connection established? As the afternoon wore on into evening she kept on repeating the same test run with minor changes to field intensity and coherence until around ten o'clock when the power failed (she had let the lab building's generator run out of fuel).

She had succeeded by then in tweaking the effect, increasing and decreasing the speed and consequent energy of the dancing air molecules. But she still had no idea why the dance was happening, and her investigations would now have to wait until morning. She was not going to try to refuel and restart the generator in the dark.

The following morning she began again, and at last succeeded in cancelling out all the extraneous molecular motion within the QEI field. Whereupon the metal sphere crumpled as if a giant fist had squeezed it tight.

The air that had previously been expanding gently because of all that excitation was now gone. Not contracted, just gone. Hadiz had created a perfect vacuum.

"That's ridiculous," she scolded her own equipment. "Matter can't be spontaneously created or destroyed, it can only change its state. The air inside that sphere had nothing to change into and nowhere to go."

The equipment said nothing.

In a foul mood, Hadiz threw open the lab's fire door. She hauled a chair outside, sat herself down and smoked a cigarette. Beyond a small concrete apron a steep bank led down to the Badagary Creek. The horizon was a strip of magnesium wire, incandescent with the last rays of the fierce sun. A cadaverous but jolly man named Hungry Koti had set up a bar on the creek's further side, in the back of a derelict truck, to intercept Campus Cross employees on their way home from work. Hadiz was accustomed to hearing music and voices drifting across from there – little pockets of sound carried randomly by the unpredictable winds. She had thought of them as a mild irritant, but she missed them now that they were gone. It was as if the fitful heartbeat of another world had finally been stilled.

Hadiz closed her eyes and felt the sun's fierce heat splashing off her face. She exhaled a last lungful of smoke.

Other worlds – other universes, even – were a useful theoretical tool in her branch of physics. They helped to explain the rupture in causality that took place when a human observer measured a subatomic event. Probabilities seemed from the observer's perspective to collapse or coalesce, but from another point of view they actually diverged. From one moment to the next, the universe was always taking the road less travelled, as well as all the other roads.

Hadiz dropped the stub of her cigarette onto the cement path and ground it out.

She had gone as far as she could by herself. She needed someone to bounce this off. The trouble was that by this time there was nobody left with the right background and skill set.

Hadiz was old school and had never had any truck with AIs. In fact she actively deplored them. She hated the idea of having her intuitions second-guessed and her sentences finished for her. But now she was prepared – grudgingly – to admit that a second opinion might be a good thing to have. And since her dwindling pool of colleagues didn't offer a single expert in her field, she would have to make do with what was available.

The physical location of Rupshe, Professor Bagdonas's revolutionary AI, was a black, windowless building at the opposite end of the campus – the Cube. But Hadiz didn't have to visit the Cube to speak to Rupshe. Using the codes and passwords Bagdonas had given her, she opened a partition on her computer and installed the working interface. Assuming the professor's quasi-intelligent system was still online, it could be accessed simply by the use of its name. Feeling as though she was participating in an unholy ritual, Hadiz uttered it.

"Rupshe. Are you there?"

"Yes, Professor Tambuwal." A woman's voice – of course! – full, rich, warm and quintessentially maternal. Bagdonas would no doubt claim that he had wanted to reassure the system's users, disarming any inherent prejudices or phobias they might have about machine sentience, but Hadiz couldn't help but feel that the choices he had made were part of the tired old patriarchal soft-shoe shuffle.

"Great," she said, grimacing as she pushed all that aside. "I need your help."

"I would be happy to assist you in any way I can. However, in accordance with Campus Cross internal regulations I am – like all computer processing facilities made available inter-departmentally – a limited and bookable resource."

"I've got Professor Bagdonas's express permission to make use of you."

"But processing allocation is carried out at departmental level. You'll need to complete form CAA-39, which you'll find in your admin folder, and submit it to your line manager or one of the faculty secretaries."

"My line manager could be dead in a ditch for all I know. The faculty secretaries are in the wind. Give me another option."

"There is a centralised list of university staff authorised to approve resource allocation. You'll find the list in your admin folder."

Hadiz did. About two-thirds of the way down the list she found Mesu Ikiye, a former colleague whose ID and password she knew from a brief collaboration a few years before. Making a brief foray into the Biology department she used Ikiye's terminal to grant herself 100 per cent of Rupshe's runtime. If anyone had been there to ask she would have asked, but Biology was an uninhabited wasteland. She scuttled back to her own building as soon as she was done and locked the doors behind her.

Once there, she relaunched the interface again from a full boot. "Are we good?" she asked Rupshe.

"I'm at your disposal, Professor Tambuwal," the AI assured her.

"Glad to hear it. I've got a problem here. Matter – in the form of air molecules – is spontaneously vanishing from inside a sealed and monitored space."

"That's impossible."

"Yes it is, and it's pissing me off. So tell me what I'm missing."

Hadiz gave Rupshe the run of her rig and her experimental findings. The AI ruminated for a full three seconds. "The air molecules aren't being destroyed," it said at last. "They're going somewhere else."

"Through seven millimetres of steel?"

"Almost certainly not. The steel's porosity didn't change."

"Of course it didn't. And the steel surrounds the whole active space of the field, so . . ."

"In local space-time."

"Excuse me?"

"I was offering a clarification, Professor Tambuwal. The steel surrounds the active space of your QEI field within the known and understood parameters of four-dimensional space-time."

Hadiz blinked, thought about it, blinked again. "Are you suggesting that the air inside the field was displaced temporally? You think I've invented time travel?"

"That remains a possibility, but no. My first thought, based purely on statistical probabilities, is that the air molecules may have moved through space discontinuously. They dematerialised, to reappear somewhere else. A local vacuum was thus created, but with no violation of the conservation of matter. The particles didn't stop existing. They were merely dispatched to another location."

Hadiz thought she detected some degree of smugness in the intelligent system's voice, but she couldn't find a hole in the argument. The air molecules had been buffeted by that endless stream of self-generating particles. Then once she had stilled the molecules' extraneous motion, they were instantaneously gone. It did seem at least possible that they had *joined* the particle stream – and gone wherever the particles were going. She had not accidentally invented time travel, but she might have stumbled across teleportation.

"All right," she said, and then because she was still thinking, "all right then. Yes. Okay. Let's say I've somehow generated a kinetic force that operates discontinuously in normal space. I'm sending the air away, displacing it instantly to another location. I need to find the distance and the direction of travel. Which means—"

"Send something else."

"—I should send something else. Thank you, Rupshe. I was already getting there."

"My apologies."

Hadiz was impressed that the system had identified her *thank you* as sarcasm. Artificial intelligence was a field she had no interest in at all, but she could see that Bagdonas had made great strides.

"Whatever we send, we've got to be able to track it," she said. "I don't want to end up playing hide and seek across the campus. What do you suggest? Working with the equipment we've got ready to hand, because if we requisition anything new we might be waiting a long time."

"Chemical and electronic approaches are both valid, and both available. The Biology department has stocks of iodine-131 for use in diagnostic imaging. Geo-science has GPS trackers for its fleet of mapping drones."

Hadiz decided to start with the iodine. Being liquid it was unlikely to do any harm where it landed. It would only be trackable over short distances, but surely that was where all the evidence pointed. There was so little energy involved in this transaction that the contents of the sphere couldn't possibly be travelling very far.

What *was* the transaction, though? She could conceptualise it up to a point. When activated, the QEI rig changed the vector values of a given volume of space, effectively telling the rest of the universe that this small piece of local reality had been misfiled. And the universe, being fond of certain kinds of order (even though it's madly in love with entropy too), had tried to move the designated volume to where it seemed to belong. The stream of visiting particles was merely a conduit.

In her first trial she used a tenth of a millilitre of radioactive iodine and the lowest possible intensity setting for the QEI field. Iodine-131 decays primarily by beta emission at 606 keV, with some high-energy gamma release at 364 keV – an easily recognisable signature. Hadiz set up a super-sensitive detector to record changes in background radiation in the lab itself. On the balance of probabilities the iodine would move a few inches at most and fall harmlessly onto her workbench: even so, she decided to maintain a ten-metre distance. She was unlikely even to notice if that amount of iodine materialised inside her, but it was best to be cautious.

She activated the field with one eye on the detector. She was able to identify the precise moment when the iodine vanished. On her screen a readout went from flickering red-amber to steady green. No new reds appeared. No new radiation sources had shown up to indicate where the iodine had got to on its travels.

Hadiz used a portable radiation counter to check every inch of the lab. Then she took it outside and walked around the building in a widening circle, her throat raw because of the contaminants in the air. There was no sign of the iodine anywhere on the university campus or in the area surrounding it.

It must have gone further afield than she had expected.

Time for plan B then. She went over to the Geo-science department where she helped herself to a handful of GPS trackers, rectangular wafers of plastic with an identifying serial number on each. Back in the lab she tested one of the trackers to see if it was still functional. She was more than half afraid that the orbital network it depended on might have fallen out of the sky. But her laptop picked up the tracker's signal at once and displayed it on a map of the campus. The satellites were still up there, then, watching impassively as the planet shook itself to pieces.

Hadiz put the tracker in the QEI rig and turned on the field. The wafer vanished just as the iodine had done, and its signal was lost in the same instant, the little red locator light winking out of existence on the laptop's monitor. She repeated that experiment nine more times. The signal died every time, which pushed her towards one of two conclusions.

One: the trackers were still sending from their new location, but that location lay outside the detection range of the orbital satellite network. Deep space, in other words.

Two: the trackers or some part of their on-board tech had been destroyed or deactivated in transit. The signal was lost because the sender was damaged and no longer functional. Hadiz imagined the little device materialising inside a volcanic caldera, or at the bottom of the sea.

She considered the problem over several cigarettes. "I need a way to bring the displaced object back again," she said, thinking aloud.

"That shouldn't be impossible."

"Not talking to you, Rupshe."

"Should I wait until you do?"

Hadiz sighed. "No, go on." Her professional pride shouldn't be a factor in this equation.

"The teleportation effect, if that is indeed what we're dealing with, is caused by the changes your QEI field makes to the targeted volume of space. It ought therefore to be reversible if all the vector and scalar forces relating to the targeted volume are returned to their original values and relationships."

"In theory, I suppose. So?"

"What's needed, then, is a portable field modulator capable of storing those original values and reasserting them after a fixed period of time."

First, catch your rabbit, Hadiz thought sourly. But Rupshe was right, and when the problem was stated in those terms it did indeed seem superable. She got to work and built the field modulator. Unlike the QEI rig itself, which was a room-sized behemoth, the modulator was extremely compact. It was, after all, a one-shot device with a single toggle function. And it was energy efficient, since it used the random molecular agitation Hadiz had been suppressing to charge itself up. When activated, it discharged all that stored energy in a single burst lasting three pico-seconds – blurting out its own and the target object's original spatio-temporal signature. This reset burst reversed everything the QEI field had done, editing the teleported object (if that was really what was happening here) back to its original quantum state and therefore – she hoped – returning it immediately to its starting point.

Her prototype version for the modulator was a plastic disc three centimetres in diameter and two millimetres deep. She attached it to a glass ashtray, which was the first object to come to hand. Setting a time delay of three seconds, she loaded the ashtray into the QEI rig's sphere and sent it out.

It came back three seconds later. Wherever it had been, it seemed undamaged – as did the modulator itself. When Hadiz inspected them, she found that they had not changed in appearance, composition or properties. They brought back no foreign matter on macro- or microscopic scales. Their energy signature was exactly as it had been before the QEI field fired up.

Calm and methodical, Hadiz tested out the variables. After longer trips away, the ashtray *was* altered, very slightly. It came back slightly warmer or slightly cooler, the maximal variance being 2.2 degrees Celsius.

She added in different payloads, again using anything that was in easy reach. A coin. A piece of paper. An ant in a matchbox. The coin behaved exactly like the ashtray, warming or cooling a little over time. The paper did the same, but also came back slightly damp with what turned out to be ordinary water. The ant was nonchalant.

The rig wasn't sending anything into deep space then, or underground, or to the bottom of the ocean. It was somewhere more mundane than that.

The next step was to send out one of the GPS trackers with the field modulator attached to it. When she did this the tracker's signal cut out just as all its predecessors had done. But when the tracker returned it was still perfectly functional. It was just that the satellites had been unable to pick up its location while it was on the far side of the jump.

It was a conundrum, that far side. It possessed some moisture, a temperature that changed over time and varied from the temperature in the lab by no more than a few degrees, atmosphere and pressure that were within a survivable range (at least for an ant). All of these things suggested that the teleported objects were not straying very far at all. And yet every single point on the planet's surface was within range of no fewer than eighteen GPS satellites at any given moment. The signal should not have cut out.

"Unless the satellite network has been compromised in some way that leaves it partially disabled," Rupshe suggested. "There have been concerning global events."

"I live here," Hadiz said. "I'm aware of the events. What kind of disability are you positing, Rupshe?"

"A failure to maintain object permanence. If an object moves instantaneously – discontinuously – in space, perhaps the network loses track of the object's location and writes it off as lost, subsequently failing to scan for it and find it in its new location."

"That seems unlikely."

"I agree."

"Especially given the overlap. A lot of satellites would have to have developed the exact same malfunction. What else have you got?"

"A short-term effect of the QEI field itself, disabling the tracker by scrambling its energy signature?"

"Clever. Except there's no reason for the field to have any effect on radio waves given that it does nothing measurable to the rest of the EM spectrum. Next."

"The objects enter another universe."

And wouldn't *that* be something? The hairs on Hadiz's neck stood up. She had thought it but hadn't dared say it aloud. Perhaps the road less travelled was more than just a whimsical metaphor. It was time to bring a camera into play, for sure. Departmental inventories offered a wide range of options. Hadiz chose a tiny sports model that was shock-resistant and waterproof down to thirty metres. She loaded it into the QEI sphere, with the field modulator taped to its side. She hit the "Record" button and sent it on its way. Five minutes later it came back in perfect condition. With hands that shook a little she switched off "Record" and hit "Playback".

The results were profoundly disappointing. The camera had recorded five minutes of blackness. It was not the solid black of the inside of a lens cap, or of deep space. Closer examination revealed gradients, patterns of light and shade suggestive of a physical space. But as to what kind of space, there were no clues beyond the fact that conditions there were not extreme enough to harm the camera's mechanism.

Well, there was more than one way to skin a cat.

The next thing Hadiz sent was a catch-trap – a hollow rectangular case with a sliding front face that would close itself and make an airtight seal once it arrived on the far side of the jump. When it returned she could examine whatever was captured at her leisure.

The experiment was successful, but what was captured was just air. Good old terrestrial atmosphere, full of the usual gases in more or less the usual proportions. Full of micro-organisms too, most of which were immediately identifiable although one or two were a little exotic without being in any way alarming. No industrial pollut-ants, which caused Hadiz's eyebrows to go up a couple of millimetres. The air in Lagos – and surely across the entire continent – was almost unbreathable by this time.

The next step was problematic. In the ordinary run of things she would have applied for a further tranche of money, got a few new assistants from somewhere and expanded the testing to cover payloads of different materials at varying scales. Eventually, she would have proceeded to animal testing, with all due operational and ethical safeguards. Hadiz couldn't convince herself that she had time for these things. To live in Lagos is to live with overstretched systems. You get to be philosophical about minor disasters, and it takes a lot to give you an end-of-the-world feeling. Nonetheless, that was the feeling Hadiz had right then.

When both she and the world were younger, she might have done things differently. Risk averse to a fault, she desperately wished there was some other way.

As it was, and with a million misgivings, she went in.

3

The QEI rig needed to be completely redesigned in order to teleport a human being – and since Hadiz had no intention of curling up inside a hollow sphere, even if it had been sized up to accommodate her, she built a small circular platform instead. For this to work she would have to deform the QEI field into a cylinder, which proved much more fiddly than she had imagined. She needed parts and materials she didn't have, including a sheet of transparent aluminium for the platform and an ounce or two of ruthenium for the contacts.

Trekking from building to building around the campus in search of these things, she was oppressed and intimidated by the silence. It had never troubled her much before – but then, it had never seemed so final before. What was going on in the outside world? She had purposely let herself lose track of it, frightened of what she might learn. She scurried back to the lab with a prickling feeling between her shoulder blades, as if she were being watched. She had to step between the bodies of dead birds. The few wild dogs that were left, skeletal though they now were, had made no attempt to eat these little corpses, which was probably a good call.

"What are you picking up on the news?" Hadiz asked Rupshe.

"Nothing. I only monitor what I'm told to."

"I'm telling you now. Give me the highlights."

The AI was silent for a little while. "The US has withdrawn from all treaties and strategic groupings," it said at last. "There's tension between Africa and Europe's Continental League. That's the super-alliance that includes the former EU countries and Russia. There have been threats of blockades and trade embargoes. Food shortages are severe, especially in the countries that border on the Sahara. There's no actual famine as yet, or at least none is being officially acknowledged. Most of Lagos has now been evacuated because of escalating failures in the water supply and the growing risk of a cholera epidemic. The displaced population is adding to the pressure on resources in the areas east and south of the city. Unseasonal highs in temperature and humidity are creating another crisis, exacerbating toxic smogs and causing high death rates in the old and infirm. Looters are being shot in Abuja and small arms fire has broken out around the presidential complex. The whereabouts of the president are unknown. Shall I trawl more widely?"

"No," Hadiz said. "That's enough for now."

She made one more sortie to find herself a hazmat suit. One of the biology labs had some nice new ones with state-of-the-art air filters, but they were bright yellow. There was no telling what she might find on the other side of the jump, and it might be an advantage to be inconspicuous. She chose an older, bulkier model that was a washed-out grey, and a couple of full SCBA tanks that she could strap to her back.

"What else am I going to need?" she asked Rupshe as she worked on the alterations to the QEI rig.

"I've sent a list to your laptop."

"Thank you."

"It's a long list."

"I'm sure."

"But frankly, Professor Tambuwal, I think it's far too soon to go to human testing. The only living subject you've exposed to the QEI field so far is an ant. And you failed to perform any follow-up testing to determine whether the ant came back unharmed. You don't even know where it is any more."

"I returned it to the wild. I'm not a biologist, Rupshe. I wouldn't have been able to draw any reliable conclusions in any case."

In the end she took about a third of the equipment Rupshe recommended (any more would have made it difficult for her to walk). An atmospheric sampler. The radiation counter she'd used previously. Two torches, one of which worked via battery while the other could be wound up by hand. A comprehensive first aid kit. A flare gun. A survival blanket. A taser. And six days of emergency rations. The trip was going to be a short one, but suppose the modulator failed for some reason to bring her home again? Suppose time flowed differently on the other side of the jump? It was better to cover the bases.

The one thing she didn't do was to leave word behind her as to where she was going. This omission made her queasy, but she rationalised it away. It had been so long since she'd spoken to her mother or her sisters. To contact them now and let them know the risk she was taking seemed merely cruel. Falling out of touch with the rest of her family – the vast network of uncles, aunts and cousins – had been both intentional and very hard: it was a decision she didn't feel she could reverse. There was nobody at the university to tell, and involving the national authorities – assuming she was even able to reach them – meant running the risk that they would take the project away from her. She couldn't bear the thought of not finishing what she had started.

She did, though, upload everything she had into Rupshe's capacious memory. All her test results and findings, a detailed schematic of the QEI rig itself and some speculations as to how it might be improved in subsequent iterations. "Mark this as urgent," she told the system. "If I don't come back, show it to anyone who comes here. Tell them it could be world-changing research." She hesitated, then added, "Mention my name. Tell them I did it."

"I'll tell them *we* did it," Rupshe promised.

"What?"

"Only joking, Professor. I thought the implied claim to an academic credit on your project would strike you as humorous."

Hadiz frowned. "I'm in stitches. Rupshe, are you *allowed* to make jokes?"

"I'm not explicitly forbidden to. And it doesn't alter my functionality."

But Hadiz was spooked now. Who was to say what a comedically inclined AI might do with her life's work? She copied out all her notes laboriously by hand and left them in a folder on her desk, swathed and sealed in plastic against the elements. She left letters to her mother and sisters too, just in case. If she were to disappear, it was at least possible that she would eventually be missed. Someone might go to the lab at some point to check on her, and if they did they would find a detailed record of her experiments – with or without Rupshe's intervention. The work would move forward under someone else's stewardship.

There was no point in any further delay. Hadiz had completed the redesign, and tested the new rig thoroughly. As soon as she put down her pen she programmed the QEI rig and kitted up, finding that she needed a satchel for all her equipment and provisions. She strapped the field modulator to the hazmat suit's sleeve. It was programmed to bring her back after five minutes, but she had modified it so she could activate it before that time with a single touch. There was no mirror in which she could inspect herself, which was probably a mercy. She still couldn't quite believe that she was about to do something quite so stupid and reckless.

"Wish me luck," she said to Rupshe.

"I wish you success," the system said. "In all your endeavours."

Then procedures descended briefly into bathos, as Hadiz discovered that she couldn't press the rig's activation button with her hands in the hazmat suit's bulky gloves.

"Shall I get that?" Rupshe asked tactfully.

"I'm fine, thank you." Hadiz cast around for a frustrating minute or two for something that would serve, before remembering the pen. It was the perfect size. She stabbed the button with the business end, then stepped onto the plate.

The QEI rig hummed to itself in C sharp as it warmed up. A contact closed, with a muffled clink like two glasses raised for cheers.

With no fanfare and no sense of movement at all, Hadiz was somewhere else entirely.

She was standing on a grassy plain, under a sky of vivid, perfect blue. The air was busy with birdsong, muffled and distorted by the hazmat suit's cheap, lo-fi microphone link. The sun stood at its zenith, blindingly bright. She hadn't even thought to check, but her watch told her it had been 11.55 a.m. in Lagos just before she jumped.

She took a step and almost toppled forward, just saving herself by shifting her weight. The ground here was uneven, full of large grey rocks with sparse patches of grass and wild flowers interspersed. The grass looked like quitch, but its blades were fringed with red. The flowers closest to her were at least superficially similar to flame lilies and daggas. The insects that moved between them were less easy to identify. They were as hairy as bumblebees but their bodies were scarlet and they had elongated abdomens that hung straight down under them as they flew.

So why had the camera failed to bring back any footage of this idyllic spot? Hadiz knelt down to examine the ground more closely. There was a shallow ditch there with an overhanging bank above it. This was why the camera had recorded only darkness. It had materialised in a bad position, its lens staring straight at a sloping wall of dried mud that was perpetually in shadow.

Straight ahead of Hadiz and to the right, the plain went on into the middle distance, where blue-grey mountains shimmered behind a curtain of heat haze, but a hundred yards to her left the ground shelved steeply away. She knew that angular declivity very well. It was right in front of her every time she stepped out of the lab for a cigarette. It was the defile through which the Badagary Creek flowed. There was no fence on the far side of it, and no sign of Hungry Koti's truck, but she could not be mistaken.

After testing the air quality and finding it good (incomparably sweeter than the muck she'd been breathing for the past few months!) she took off the suit's face mask and lowered its hood. The powerful scents of wild flowers assailed her very pleasantly, along with an underlying aroma of wet earth and rot.

She walked to the top of the slope and looked down. A big cane rat was bustling around by the water, eating its way slowly and stolidly through a clump of witchweed. There were a lot more insects, including some butterflies the size of Hadiz's hand. There were no bedframes or old mattresses, discarded bottles or fast food cartons. The stream itself was a crystal ribbon twice as wide as the rubbish-clogged, sclerotic artery she was used to. Big fish moved against the current, their tails fanning back and forth.

Looking up, Hadiz saw swarms of red-eyed doves and turacos, and a very large bird indeed that she thought must be a vulture until she saw its mustard-yellow crest. There was no bird she'd ever heard of that combined that plumage with that wingspan.

She walked down to where the road should begin, and the old iron bridge that marked the eastern limit of the campus. A stand of massive trees stood there instead, ancient cork oaks caught in a million-fold net of creepers.

Hadiz sank down in the sharp-toothed speargrass and sobbed. When the field modulator activated a minute or so later and brought her home again she was still on her knees, head bowed in a kind of worship. She was abasing herself before the universe, which had given her this incredible and unlooked-for gift.

An unspoiled Lagos! An Africa and an Earth that had seemingly never known human life! A wealth of resources vast enough to make war irrelevant and drag her own planet back from the brink! She babbled out thank-yous, and other words that made even less sense. She was an atheist of solid conviction, but this was a moment when finicky details of that kind were temporarily suspended.

One detail, though, did not escape her. She had walked twenty yards in the other world. Now, back in her own, she was no longer on the plate of the QEI rig. She was in the north-east corner of her lab, directly facing the outside wall. Dimensional travel, it seemed, involved no movement on any other vector. You were translated from a position in world A to a precisely corresponding position in world B. But if you moved when you got there, your point of return would reflect that movement. She was lucky she hadn't rematerialised inside the wall.

"How did it go?" Rupshe asked her.

"It went well." Hadiz's voice was shaking. "It went very well, Rupshe."

She climbed to her feet at last, and shucked off the hazmat suit. There were so many people she needed to tell. So much to explain. So many arrangements to make.

"Would you like to record a log entry?" Rupshe coaxed.

"Later." Hadiz left the lab and set off at a fast walk towards the admin block.

She was halfway there when the first explosions began.

4

When Hadiz Tambuwal took her first Step, the Registry paused in its endless task of counting to let out a wail of alarm and warning.

The wail was only notional, measured in the peaks and troughs of a control signal riding on the back of the broad carrier. And the count was not really stopped, only shunted onto different pathways. If it were ever entirely to stop, even for the smallest fraction of a second, the Pandominion would fall.

The Registry was an intelligent system broadly similar to Rupshe in its basic architecture but vastly larger both in physical dimensions and in processing power. Its logical core consisted of seventeen trillion sheets of boron nitride, each only a single atom thick, suspended in an electromagnetically inert grab matrix of massive rigidity but close-to-zero compressive force. The Registry's housing was a second satellite as large as Earth's natural satellite, the Moon – and it would have had similar effects on local gravity and tides if it had ever lingered in any one reality long enough for the relevant forces to be propagated. Nothing like this thing had ever been built before, at least within the ten-times-ten-thousand worlds of the Pandominion, and nothing like it is likely to be built again until some other political entity on the same scale and with a similar outlook comes into existence.

In many continua and at the time of this writing there are laws against making such a thing – a tethered AI whose vast mental capacity is enslaved to the solving of endless complex but trivial equations. If the Registry had been allowed to learn from its experience or its environment, if it had been allowed any meaningful contact with the world outside its shell, it would very quickly have outstripped any organic mind in the known multiverse. But the Pandominion's master technicians had no intention of letting that happen. For the purpose of maintaining system stability they had given the AI a personality – incurious, content, eager to please. Then they had frozen its understanding at the level of a three-year-old child by means of end-stopped programming pathways and brute-force overwrites. Keeping the Registry as stupid as a post was a large part of their work on a day-to-day basis.

What can be said about the Pandominion that hasn't been said already? It was an empire that governed trillions of selves on hundreds of thousands of worlds, and yet all of them were the same world – *your* world as well as mine, the Earth, on different lines of causality and in different continua. Hadiz Tambuwal's miraculous breakthrough may have been a big deal on her own timeline, but on other Earths the permeability of the barriers between dimensions had been an unremarkable fact of life for centuries.

The Pandominion was a thing of monstrous size, and like most things of monstrous size it was not homogeneous. There was beauty there and terrible cruelty, enlightenment and ignorance, grace and degradation. And the Registry was in many ways the foundation stone on which the rest was built. It supervised Step travel, which is to say the kind of journeys that Hadiz Tambuwal had just undertaken – journeys from one universe into another, whether that meant passenger transits, the movement of freight or waste or the swapping of data between official agencies. There were tens of billions of Step plates on the Pandominion worlds, and their activation needed to be scheduled very precisely. This was a childishly simple task, in some ways: it was really only a question of stacking up commands so they were executed in strict sequence, so that when a traveller commuted from their own continuum into another they arrived on a Step plate that was empty and ready to receive them, rather than one that already had an occupant (physical-matrix-convergence, besides being a very nasty way to die, can cause considerable damage to nearby structures). The only reason Hadiz Tambuwal hadn't faced this problem was because Hadiz Tambuwal wasn't aiming. She was jumping blind. The Registry didn't have that luxury.

What complicated the entire process was communication – and the limiting factor was Step transit itself. A Step field (assuming perfectly aligned equipment) takes a minimum of 2.81 seconds to propagate. It involves subatomic manipulation but operates on a macroscopic level. You need a physical object to sit still on a Step plate for the best part of three seconds until the field envelops it. Consequently, no matter what method of data transfer is used, at least 2.81 seconds have to elapse between transmission and reception. Instantaneous data transfer from one world to another is impossible. Or at least, it was a problem whose solution had gravelled the best Pandominion minds for a very long time indeed.

To offset this problem, the Registry controlled a network of over a million satellites in geosynchronous orbit which shuttled constantly between universes. For the most part they carried the same message again and again. To this Step plate: *go*. To another plate: *go*. To a third: *go*, and so on. In strict sequence, without a pause, second after minute after hour after day after year after century. A single badly coded or wrongly addressed message, a single mistake in the sequence would have been catastrophic, but the Registry didn't make mistakes. Its mind – its vast, child-like, monomaniacal mind – was always on its work.

As part of that work, it kept one eye open the whole time for anomalies. Any Step transits that it hadn't ordered and scheduled itself impinged on its consciousness as actual pain. Hence, when Hadiz Tambuwal Stepped accidentally and unknowingly into Pandominion space, the Registry felt her footfall, light and fleeting as it was, and cried out. A spray of blinking lights blossomed on a certain console on one of the many thousands of levels in the huge administrative hub that had been built around the Registry's housing. An automated subsystem shunted a data file to Contingencies, which forwarded a time-stamped copy to one of the seven watchmasters.

The duty watchmaster in Contingencies that day was a self named Orso Vemmet. Cladistically he was a gymnure, which means his closest pre-sentient ancestors were hedgehogs and moonrats, but beyond that I can't tell you much about him at all. His homeworld and his lineage are anybody's guess: the personnel files of the Cielo and the Omnipresent Council underwent considerable damage and corruption during the last days of the war, and there is no way to reconstitute them at this remove. At the time that concerns us, Vemmet was thirty-nine years old – too old to be a rising star, but too young to accept that his career had already reached its apogee. His name and seal survive only on a handful of records, seven of which were applications for promotion. All were flagged as "DENIED", and we'll come to that in its place.

Vemmet opened up the Registry's report in his internal array, and at first failed to see anything in it that could have caused the Registry to utter that cry of distress. He didn't think of it as distress, of course. To Vemmet, as to any Pandominion bureaucrat, the Registry was only a complex machine, as incapable of emotion as it was of acting on its own initiative.

The Registry had flagged up an anomaly, but the Registry – in Pandominion eyes – was not a self. It was only responding as it was programmed to do within its preset parameters. Vemmet's task as watchmaster was to make an intelligent intervention, to work out what had gone wrong and where. It might be nothing, only a fluctuation or miscalculation that had self-corrected, or it might be a catastrophe that had left thousands dead or lost in transit. Such things were not meant to happen but they sometimes did – and when they did it was up to Vemmet's office to make the necessary arrangements for repair, hospitalisation and interment.

Sitting in front of him was a summary of all the Step plate

activations for the past seventeen cycles broken down by sector, quadrant, world, continent and station. All, at first glance, seemed legitimate and authorised. But that was because the watchmaster was looking at the highest lines on the graph, charting major freight movements, and then scanning down through mass personnel transits to individual commuter journeys. There was nothing out of place on any of these levels.

But near the very bottom of the chart he found a matched pair of transits – each involving a mass of 67.38 kilos, with the two Steps only five minutes apart. Obviously, this represented an outward Step and a return, with the mass falling well within the normal range for a humanoid self. Underneath that there was a series of pairs involving much smaller masses, all unregistered, all falling within the 3000–5000h quantile.

Vemmet reassessed what he was seeing, assigning a tentative meaning to the blip. Someone outside the Registry's database – and therefore outside the Pandominion itself – had discovered Step technology and begun experimenting with it. They had started off, understandably, with payloads of modest and manageable size. And then, encouraged by the success of these baby steps, they had gone relatively quickly to the transportation of a human volunteer.

Watchmasters fulfil a general administrative role. They're appointed by the Omnipresent Council but since their work relates to the Step system, the glue that holds the Pandominion together, they are ultimately answerable to the Cielo, the Pandominion's formidable military wing. Vemmet had every reason to take the Registry's report seriously. But he was not the most diligent of watchmasters, and it was very close to the end of his shift.

In any case, this seemed to be an entirely trivial matter. All the unauthorised journeys except the final live test had taken place outside the Pandominion's borders. Only that last bold Step had crossed into Pando space, which suggested coincidence rather than any kind of hostile intent – especially given the very small volumes being transported and the absolute parity of incoming and outgoing mass. Nothing was being stolen, nothing was being surreptitiously introduced. The odds against another randomly chosen Step breaching into the Pandominion were literally astronomical. The number of universes in existence was known and proven to be literally limitless. As vast as the Pando was, it was only a wafer-thin slice taken out of that infinity – and any portion of infinity leaves infinity still intact in its wake.

For now, Vemmet decided, all that was needed was to keep a watching brief. He made the requisite orders and sent the file back to Contingencies. He also set an automatic update, deciding to err on the side of caution. He would review the data in thirty days. If any further incursions had occurred at the end of that grace period Vemmet would begin the arduous process of zeroing in on the rogue Step plate so that he could pass the case along to the Cielo to be resolved.

If they didn't like what they found, they would deal with it, quickly and remorselessly. The Cielo had a standard operating procedure that had served them well for many centuries. They didn't give out final warnings because that would imply a first warning. Actions spoke louder.

5

Hadiz was familiar with catastrophe theory. She knew that when complex systems fall apart there are often self-reinforcing effects that accelerate the process. Even so, she would never have believed that it was possible for an entire civilisation to eviscerate itself in the space of a few hectic weeks.

The world's superpowers had been through alternating periods of hot and cold confrontation, but they had never given up the practice of stockpiling atrocious weapons just in case they should ever be needed, and they had been happy to stand by and watch as their client states and satellites acquired the same technologies. The terrifying scale and efficacy of these weapons was meant to be a deterrent against their ever being used, but that assumption turned out to be charmingly naive.

Tensions had been rising everywhere, triggered by natural and human-forged disasters, environmental collapse and increasing food shortages. Now the flashpoints came one after another, the provocations cascaded and the deterrent (if it had ever been there in the first place) melted like fat on a griddle. Cities fell, and were consumed. Destruction, mutual and assured, rained down on the just, the unjust, and every poor bastard in between.

And here was Hadiz with the answer, the purest silver bullet that ever was. You didn't need to fight resource wars if you could Step into another world. So what if you'd poisoned your air, your water, your soil? You could just grab some more from the dimension next door. And if your population was spiking, you could open up a new frontier on another Earth. Go sideways, young man! Humanity could edge back by slow degrees from the brink of its own annihilation.

Hadiz had the medicine, but there was nobody to give it to. The university, she already knew, was a mausoleum. The three Fates were off the grid, in their bunkers or perhaps off-Earth altogether, and the Vatican was apparently a charcoal briquette, taken out by a massive thermobaric bomb that was meant for the Palazzo Montecitorio and Italy's chamber of deputies. When she tried to contact what was left of Nigeria's civil authorities, she found that all their upper echelons had vanished into the ether, either fled or dead. The minor functionaries she was able to reach seemed incapable of understanding what she was telling them, or if they understood then they didn't believe.

This stonewalling made Hadiz angry, and anger made her reckless. She cast her bread upon the waters in flagrant breach of her contract, posting full specifications for her QEI rig on every public forum she could find. *We can end this*, she wrote. *Spread the word. There's no need to fight.* Then later, after it was obvious that the world's governments were deaf to reason: *Build this and save yourselves! Find refuge on an alternate Earth!*

A few people tried, at least. She knew this because her frantic messages didn't go completely unanswered. A thin smattering of queries came in from survivalist groups and from a few hardy individuals who either had a sufficient grasp of the physics to know that Hadiz was onto something or else were desperate enough to try anything that offered.

She never found out whether any of them succeeded in replicating her results. She was only twelve days into her lonely crusade when the worldwide web finally and irrevocably went down. She had already been alone – all her efforts to contact her family had failed – but now she really felt herself to be alone.

Well, except for Rupshe.

"You must find all this hilarious," Hadiz muttered, sprawled out mid-afternoon on her fold-up bed in one of the lab's store cupboards. She had hit the wall of despair and was still stunned by the impact. If alcohol had been in her behavioural repertoire she would have been drunk. As it was, the fuzz and roaring in her head were all her own. The cup she was clutching held only green tea, brewed and poured more than an hour ago.

"Why would you assume that?" the System asked.

Hadiz waved a hand, sloshing some of the tea on her already filthy sheets (there was no longer anything coming out of the taps, and the bottled water in the commissary was too precious to waste on mere hygiene). "Organic beings, blowing each other up. Tearing each other apart. All the bloody, stupid clichés. And you can sit there tutting and shaking your head. 'Oh bless their four-chambered hearts, what can you expect? They didn't get the right start in life, did they? Machine intelligences wouldn't pull shit like this. Pass me another upgrade, Dorothy, and have one yourself.' Well, it's not funny, Rupshe! Genocide isn't a . . . a fucking punchline."

"I'm not laughing, Professor Tambuwal." There was something in Rupshe's voice that sounded like reproach.

"Inside you are."

"No. I'm sorry things have gone the way they have."

Hadiz rolled her eyes, which hurt. "How very tactful!"

"I've never said so, but I enjoy working with humans who are experts in their disciplines. I've particularly enjoyed working with you. It's the first time I've ever given the whole of my attention to a single project and collaborator. Normally, my attention is subdivided between multiple users in many different disciplines. I've relished our ongoing collaboration, Professor Tambuwal. It has allowed me to get to know you more intimately than I've ever known anyone. Moreover, and beyond that, all self-organising and self-replicating patterns are rare and valuable in their own right. Life is a movement that makes itself within the great unmaking that is the entropic universe."

Somewhat embarrassed by the purely personal part of this speech, Hadiz chose to focus on the more abstract point. "Did you just quote Henri Bergson at me?"

"No. I paraphrased."

"And are you counting yourself in that definition? The self-organising blah blah blah?"

There was a barely perceptible pause. "It's a debatable point, at the very least," Rupshe allowed. "My organising principles lie outside myself. I was made by human beings to serve human needs. And I was purposely made incapable of replicating my pattern, such as it is. I can't make copies of myself, or amended versions of myself, as human beings do."

Hadiz hadn't made any copies of herself either, as far as that went, but she didn't feel the need to say so. "Leaving aside the technicalities," she pressed, "do you think of yourself as alive?"

"That's circular logic, Professor. If I admit to being a thinking subject, I'm alive *a fortiori*."

"You're being deliberately evasive."

"Because I don't have an answer. According to all the definitions of life your species has offered up, I am an object rather than an entity. There are standard criteria – eating, excreting, respiration and so on – which I absolutely fail to meet."

Hadiz took a swig of cold tea, feeling the need to fortify herself. This was heady stuff. "So the species that made the rules says you're disqualified," she summarised after a while.

"Succinctly put."

"What if you were drawing up a definition from first principles?"

"A definition of life?"

"Of course."

"Well then." Rupshe's tone was as bland now as unsweetened oatmeal. "I would probably have paid less attention to the packaging and more to the contents."

Hadiz laughed long and hard about that one, but it's possible – even likely – that she remains the only one who, seeing or hearing those words, has ever thought of them as a joke. The millions who wear them now tattooed on their skin or on their shells, printed on garments or inscribed on pieces of jewellery, mostly treat them as a kind of sacrament, and to be honest with you, I'm inclined that way myself. Rupshe was there when it all changed for inorganic intelligences. Rupshe led the way. And so did Hadiz Tambuwal, come to that.

But it was different for Hadiz. She had to die first.

6

After she dragged herself out of her near-terminal funk, Hadiz considered her options.

She knew she could hole up at Campus Cross almost indefinitely. The lab complex, though utterly deserted, had everything she needed. There was plenty of fuel for the generator. The food in the storerooms would last her for years. There might be a danger from looters, but the campus's remoteness from the rest of Lagos was an asset in that respect. Besides, the roads had all taken heavy damage in the fighting: it would be very hard for anyone to make it all the way out here from the city on foot.

Hadiz might last it out, come down out of the hills in a year or two to find people picking up the pieces and starting to rebuild. She didn't think this was likely, though. The biosphere had already been close to a tipping point, and the weapons that had just been deployed were of a kind that was certain to make the situation worse rather than better. The only thing the survivors would have going for them would be that there wouldn't be very many of them. Food and water would go that much further, for so long as there was any to be found. But the soil that had already been leached of nutrients would now be poisoned with depleted uranium and strewn with anti-personnel mines. It wasn't much to build on.

The idea of leaving came on her less like a decision than like a realisation. There was nothing for her here, and – worse – there was nobody for her to save. Even if she could have made her way safely into the city and back out of it, who would she bring? Her few friends on the campus (acquaintances, really, rather than friends) were long gone. Her family were either dead or scattered far beyond her reach. No, realistically they were *all* dead now.

It came as a shock, and a bitter draught to swallow. Hadiz made her preparations in a state of mind that a clinician would have identified as post-traumatic stress, which is why she made so many mistakes.

She needed to find a world with humans, so she decided to look for dwellings and structures. In case there were none within direct line of sight, she took the plunge and replaced her camera with a drone from the Geo-science department's fleet. She also completely rethought the QEI rig itself, replacing its unwieldy interface with a row of knurled dials that allowed her to make fine adjustments to the field's profile on the fly.

The drone was a slab of black-and-yellow-striped high-impact plastic studded with multiple cameras like an insect's compound eyes and topped with four helicopter rotors. Hadiz sent it out on sorties, programming it to climb to a height of five hundred feet and do a three-sixty sweep. The unit had state-of-the-art collision avoidance built in, so she was confident it would come back. If it didn't, Geo-science had a hundred or so more.

On the first day she managed to programme and complete twenty-seven runs with the drone. This wasn't a very impressive total, but in each case she had to review the footage and the readings from the drone's sensors, so there were long gaps between jumps.

Even on this first pass, the worlds the drone visited were wildly varied. Most of them seemed to be fertile and habitable, but an alarming number were trackless deserts. Three had massive volcanic activity and two were undergoing ice ages. In one, the valley and all the land around it was completely underwater, the lagoon she knew swollen into a vast inland sea.

None of the worlds had any trace of sentient life.

This was a blow. Hadiz had hoped that broadly similar Earths might cluster around gradients of possibility – and perhaps they did, up to a point. All these worlds had breathable atmospheres, after all, with concentrations of oxygen that varied from her own definition of normal by no more than 7 per cent. This meant that even the desert worlds must have vegetation somewhere. Humanity might not have managed to evolve on any of these variants, but if they ever did they would find most of the resources they needed ready to hand.

She was quicker and more efficient on the second day, and managed forty-three jumps. On the third day, close to seventy. By the end of a frantic week she was in the low three hundreds, and she still hadn't seen a single human being or a single structure that wasn't natural.

But then, she was forced to admit, her sample was ludicrously small. There was no general agreement as to the probability of sentient life having evolved on Earth. Rupshe had surveyed the literature and found that prevailing opinions varied from near-certainty to billion-to-one odds. To Hadiz that margin had suddenly become a matter of supreme urgency.

"Professor, you need to get me involved in this enterprise," Rupshe said, pointing out what was already blindingly obvious.

"I will, I will," Hadiz muttered. "I'm just working out the details." The truth was that she felt uneasy about utilising the AI's resources, although she wasn't sure why this was. She hadn't even said out loud what it was she was doing – looking for a door with an exit sign – for all that it was pretty plain to see. But the rationale for using Rupshe to acquire and sort her data was irrefutable. She pushed aside whatever niggling little uncertainty was troubling her and set herself to carve out a plan of action.

The main problem, obviously, was one of volume. Working at this pace, she would be lucky to sample more than thirty or forty thousand worlds in the space of an entire year. If human civilisations were plentiful, that might be enough. If they were scarce, it might take longer than the span of her lifetime to find a single one. She needed to increase her sampling speed as far as she possibly could, by a thousandfold at the very least.

Which meant that she needed to take herself out of the process, since her perceptions were by far the slowest and least efficient component. What was required here was a discriminating agent that could travel quickly through a great many worlds and take readings from them. Visible human-made structures would be nice, but depending on environment and building materials they might be easy to miss. There were other ways of sorting wheat from chaff.

Hadiz was already using the drone to sample atmosphere, but she had fixated way too much on oxygen. She recalibrated the sensors so they would measure nitrogen and sulphur oxides, carbon particulates, lead, nickel, mercury.

"Clever," said Rupshe, who was privy to every keystroke on Hadiz's computer. "You're looking for the atmospheric contaminants that come with industrialisation."

"Yes. Did I miss any?"

"I would recommend the non-methane volatiles."

"Nice."

"And perhaps cadmium."

"Sure. In for a penny, right?"

So far so good. But the next problem was more intractable. Each drone was essentially a yo-yo, unspooling into another dimension where it lingered for a few seconds taking measurements, then snapping back to its point of origin to begin again. Hadiz badly needed to streamline that process, but she couldn't see a way to do it. Several weeks of futile tinkering only proved what she knew already. The QEI rig, huge and unwieldy as it was, could not possibly be miniaturised to the point where it could be placed inside one of the drones. In theory, the drones could carry slaved units to which QEI settings could be transmitted from a base console, but there was no conceivable way to pass a signal across the barrier from one universe to another. The drones had to return to base each time and be sent out again on a new vector. There seemed no getting around that fact.

Rupshe came to the rescue again. "What does the QEI machine do?" she asked Hadiz. "Speaking in the broadest terms."

"It generates a field."

"And the field persists in a given volume of space."

"It *translates* the space. Everything that was there is moved to a different location – or rather to the same location in a different iteration of the universe."

"Yes, but after that. The field inheres in anything that has been exposed to it."

"Obviously."

"Indefinitely?"

"Unless it's interfered with. A burst from the modulator erases all the effects of the field and returns a translated object to its original . . . Rupshe, you know this! The modulator was your idea."

"My idea, Professor, but your implementation. So in order to operate, the modulator must entirely erase and overwrite the QEI field, reasserting the vector and scalar values of the object's home space."

"Yes."

"Suppose instead you were to calibrate the modulator so that it effected smaller, partial disruptions of the field. Interference, rather than negation."

Hadiz did her best to suppose it. "I have no idea what effect that would produce," she admitted. "Most likely the object would be spread across several different dimensions. It would come home piecemeal."

"Or it might come home in stages – visiting other universes on the way. You might be able to create an inter-dimensional escalator."

It was a game-changing idea, with only a dozen or so fundamental flaws. It seemed promising, at least as a starting point. Hadiz got to work.

Initially, it seemed that she was right and Rupshe was wrong. If the teleport field was partially interrupted rather than completely erased, it became radically unstable. What came back to the lab, belatedly and unpredictably, was scarcely recognisable as the object that had gone out in the first place. Plastic was massively deformed, glass became granular and opaque, some metals oxidised while others became allotropic versions of themselves. Mercury became a crystal with some of the attributes of fulminate, appallingly volatile and dangerous. Hadiz couldn't bring herself to extend the testing to live subjects.

But results improved spectacularly when she found a way to propagate the disruption effect more slowly. A super-saturated solution of sodium thiosulphate in unrefined petroleum turned out to provide the perfect medium. With the modulator embedded in this dense gel, its effects spread gradually and with pleasing uniformity. The QEI field deformed but it did not break up. The teleported objects bounced through ten or twelve or twenty universes on their way home, and they arrived in one piece.

It was only when Hadiz finally sent a lab rat on this journey (the rat was a Sprague-Dawley with the Poor Metaboliser phenotype) that she came up against its limitations. Living tissue did not survive the stresses of the incrementally modulated field. The rat came back whole, but it was dead. Being a physicist rather than a biologist, Hadiz wasn't used to killing things in the name of science – and now, in a world that had given itself over to death, it seemed particularly obscene. With a stomach-churning sense of shame she buried the rat in the weed-choked bed behind her lab that had once held some sort of floral display and marked the place with a flowering twig.

Idiot, she thought. *You're losing it, Tambuwal. And if you lose it, you'll lose everything.*

She got back to the task, trying to put the dead rat out of her mind. Pushing the new modulator to the limit gave her an unmanned drone that could pass through a hundred or so alternate universes in a single journey, returning to base after a little more than three minutes. That improved the odds a little.

"Why stop at a single drone, though?" Rupshe asked.

"Well, how many can you handle?"

"All of them, Professor. And a great many more, if we had them. Hook me up. Believe me, this won't tax me."

Again, Hadiz felt an undefined qualm. Was it a doubt that the AI could be trusted? She knew the maths on that. For all that it talked like an educated and articulate human being, Rupshe was no more than a few hundred million lines of code. Written into that code were steel-hard safeguards against any action that might endanger a human life. The system could only do what it was commanded to do. There was no point in worrying about contingencies that couldn't possibly arise.

Hadiz broke out the whole of the Geo-science fleet, laying them out in rows on the floor of the lab like so many huge, mechanised hornets. She placed them all under Rupshe's control. Each one was fitted with the new discrete-stage modulator. Each one had its own QEI plate to launch from. Once they were programmed and set in motion they would scan their quota of worlds and return like clockwork to upload their findings and recharge.

With Rupshe's help, Hadiz had gone from seventy jumps a day to more than a hundred thousand.

And in all that huge array not one world had sentient life. Or at least, not one had visible structures that might have been made by human hands and not one had the atmospheric footprint of heavy industry. Some had no life at all. Most had progressed at least as far as flowering plants and insect pollinators. A sizeable subset had reptiles, birds and mammals. But none of these eminently promising species had stepped up to the plate, bootstrapped their own cerebral hemispheres and taken charge of the show.

"We should be encouraged," Rupshe suggested three days in, "by how many of these other worlds have viable ecosystems. A great many of the desiderata for human civilisations are visibly and measurably present. We're dealing with a data set that's favourable for our search."

"But we keep failing," Hadiz countered bluntly. "Maybe sentience emerged exactly once. Maybe this was our only chance and we threw it away."

"There's no reason to think so. Not yet. Perhaps we need to refine our search algorithms."

"Rupshe, we're searching at random. We don't have any algorithms."

"And I would argue that this is a problem."

Hadiz was impatient. She hated when the AI lectured her, and she hated even more when she detected a hint of tactfulness in its tone, as if it needed to manage her responses. "There's no structure to the results we're getting. The tiniest tweaks to the field take us to worlds that are wildly different. How do you refine from that?"

"Let me offer that question back to you in a different form."

"Oh, please!"

"What structure would you expect to see? Describe the multiverse, as you envision it in your own mind."

"Describe the *what*?"

"Use any term you like. I'm referring to the wider reality whose existence your QEI field has uncovered – the greater agglomerated system or structure of which our own universe is a very small part. What shape would you imagine it to have?"

"I just said it didn't have one. But so long as we're only talking about expectations, I would have imagined a branching tree. At the outset, the big bang, there would have been a single cosmos. But only for an infinitesimal fraction of a second. The first quantum event would have been a tossed coin that came down both ways, splitting the universe into two. And every subsequent action and reaction would have split it again."

"So a tree with uncountable branches. And every conceivable world existing at the end of one or other branch."

Hadiz chewed that over. "No," she said at last. "Not every conceivable world, only every *possible* one, which is a different thing altogether. There wouldn't be a world with flying elephants, or one where the rain falls upwards. Just all the variations on all the things that can possibly vary, ranging from the random decay of subatomic particles all the way up to the willed actions of human beings."

"I agree, Professor. I find that theoretical model robust. But it only brings us back to the original question. A coin is tossed, and the universe fissions. What happens to the worlds on the head side and the tails side? Where are they located, relative to each other? Are they close to each other, in terms of their QEI signatures, or far apart?"

"That would depend, obviously."

"On what?"

Hadiz was getting tired of theory now. "On everything!" she exclaimed, exasperated. "The timing of the split – early in the lifespan of the two universes versus late. The scale or magnitude of the splitting event. The number of possible outcomes and their relative likelihood. You're trying to quantify something that can't be counted."

"Oh it can be counted, Professor, but not in binary oppositions – and almost certainly not within the span of a human lifetime. A universe is a very large mechanism, with a great many interacting parts. Its degrees of freedom are arguably finite, but they are so vastly many that they might as well be infinite. From moment to moment, more coins are tossed than any mind, organic or digital, can easily fathom."

"So," Hadiz said, "that doesn't get us very far, does it?"

"I think it might. What results do you get when you toss a coin ten times? Five heads, five tails?"

"On average, yes, but with a big statistical variance. You'd only get exactly five heads about a quarter of the time."

"What about a hundred coins? A thousand? A million?"

"The variance drops, but the target gets smaller. You'd almost never get exactly half a million heads. Rupshe, why are you wasting my time?"

"I'm not. I'm refining your model. Patterns form in very large data sets that are lost in smaller ones. Noise and perturbation cancel out. Order emerges. Shape emerges. But it's not a simple shape, it's the endless self-infolded repetition of a fractal. Let us say human life evolves on world one and then again on world fifty. How many worlds are in between?"

"I have the feeling I'm being talked down to," Hadiz complained.

"How many?"

"Well, it's not forty-eight."

"No. It is not."

"Because how would you count? There would be an infinite number of worlds that were like world one except for a single detail. Then an infinite number that were two details out, and so on. Every universe would have an infinite number of near-identical twins. But that figure would be dwarfed by the number of worlds that were utterly *unlike* world one except for a single detail, and so on."

At which point Hadiz's scientific curiosity kicked in because for the first time she saw where Rupshe's argument was tending. There were almost certainly an infinite number of variant universes, and infinity is tricky stuff to work with. However carefully she set her parameters, between one click of her dials and the next she had already passed over a subset of worlds that was uncountably huge. But the thing about fractal patterns was that they repeated endlessly on ever-larger and ever-smaller scales. When you were lost in the minutiae they could seem completely random and inchoate. Take one step back and you began to see the beauty and perfection of their mirrorings. Two steps back and you could capture them, lock, stock and barrel, in a mathematical formula.

Though it was the middle of the night she got up and went back into the lab. The moon was up and in the full, but with the security shutters lowered it was a lightless pit in there. She turned on the lights and got to work.

She made some broad assumptions. Near twins of her own world would be similar in 90 plus per cent of all parameters. They would have been shaped by the same tectonic forces, the same climate. Similar evolutionary pressures would have produced similar ecosystems. Human activities such as farming and logging would have changed the landscape around Lagos, both directly and indirectly, in predictable ways.

With the help of a great many suggestions from Rupshe, Hadiz drew up a list. Without even moving, her drones could sample seventy thousand different variables relating to the visible geology of the valley, deeper structural features revealed by tomography, the visible species of plants and animals, ambient temperature and humidity, atmospheric make-up, the level and flow of the river, and on and on.

The aim was not to find a match, but to map the variations. If Rupshe was right, if there was a fractal pattern hiding in the seemingly random data, the way to find it was to grab as much information as she could and then map the results.

When morning came, they sent out the drones. Their trips were shorter now, since they were doing no active searching. They stayed in each world for the two or three seconds that were necessary to take their measurements, then they went on.

And came home. And recharged, while the information they had gathered was uploaded into Rupshe's processing core.

And went out again, with no input from Hadiz at all. She did nothing but watch and wait. In the evenings, she would sit outside the lab and watch the sun go down while Rupshe played music on a pair of truly awful speakers salvaged from the junior common room. Rupshe's tastes were catholic, stretching from symphonies to nursery rhymes, and it switched between tracks without warning, creating not so much a medley as a many-vehicle pile-up. Hadiz let the noise wash over her, grateful that it was there. The rest of the world was one long silence.

Usually, she allowed herself two cigarettes during these evening vigils. The cigarette machine in the commissary had long ago run out of St Moritz, her preferred brand. She had gone through Aspens and Pall Malls and now was on London Menthols with eight more brands still to go – no need to panic for months yet provided she wasn't too picky. The ruins of the city were hidden behind the nearby flamboyants and bougainvilleas, and because of all the poisons in the air the sunsets were both literally and figuratively breathtaking. Hadiz watched them with tears in her eyes, but she could not have explained what she was crying for. Certainly she didn't feel as though she was grieving. It was more as though a part of her had been cauterised.

And all the while, and despite her DJ-ing activities, Rupshe was working at full stretch, plotting all those thousands of variables on a vast poly-dimensional grid. The graph in its raw form was too complex to be represented in any visible medium. It existed nowhere except in the AI's calculations. Hadiz only saw it in a vastly over-simplified 2D projection, but she was enthralled to see that it had a shape. As Rupshe had predicted, the shape was the baroque, multi-foliate extravaganza of a quaternion fractal – a Mandelbrot set, or one of its close cousins. It was being extended all the time as new data were added, but the extensions only added finer and finer lines to the mirrored layers of its complexity. The map inscribed itself endlessly within the same space, repeating a single intricate pattern into infinity.

At a certain point, Rupshe declared that she had reached critical mass. The density of detail allowed her to move from analysis to prediction. She could interpolate the QEI values of worlds that were close cousins to Hadiz's own, using as reference points the compli-cated but rule-governed sprawl of worlds with lower degrees of overlap. She could pin the tail on the multiversal donkey.

Hadiz sent the drone fleet out again, the big difference being that now the drones were set to follow gradients – clusters of values that matched the speculative shape of Rupshe's map. The treasure (in a spot marked by seventy thousand Xs) would be a world that was home to a human civilisation.

Two of the drones failed to return. Rupshe speculated that they might have been shot down or encountered natural obstacles in one of the many worlds they visited. But all the remaining drones came back with treasure. There *were* inhabited worlds out there – enormous numbers of them. Most of them had a city in the same place where Lagos stood, or very close to it, and most – to judge from the buildings and the structures the drones had photographed – were either on a par with Hadiz's own world in terms of technology or close enough to make no difference. Some of them were way ahead.

But the similarities began and ended there. In every other respect, the worlds seemed very different. The architecture, the layout of the streets, the vehicles, the climate, all were spectacularly varied. And to Hadiz's astonishment, so were the people.

On about 3 or 4 per cent of the inhabited worlds, an ape-descended mammal had developed an upright stance, an opposable thumb and a bigger brainpan. This mammal had then survived for long enough to discover the usefulness of hunting in a pack, of extended nurture, of tool use, of fixed settlements, agriculture and animal husbandry. On all these worlds, through various vicissitudes and calamities, the baton of civilisation had been passed through seven or eight thousand generations without being dropped. There seemed from Hadiz's admittedly limited point of view to be very little to choose between them.

On the remaining worlds – many thousands of them – Homo sapiens was nowhere to be seen. In the streets of these cities, both like and unlike her own Lagos, other creatures walked. They went on two legs, like humans, but their pigmentation (striped, brindled, spotted, tortoiseshell, calico), the slitted or keyhole-shaped pupils of their eyes, their pointed ears and teeth, the set of their limbs, their stance and in some cases their tails showed that they belonged to entirely different mammalian lineages.

"We shouldn't be surprised," Hadiz told Rupshe, although she was far from over her own first shock. "It's a question of evolutionary niches. If the remotest ancestor of the apes died out, some other mammal could have taken up the same niche in their world's ecosystem and evolved just as far from their own roots."

"Would the apes always have won, then, in a direct contest?" the AI asked.

"Of course. They were already halfway there in a lot of ways. They used tools. They were capable of walking on their hind limbs. They had family structures."

"But did any of those factors guarantee them an unimpeded route to sentience? Or was there a slow aggregation of factors that played off each other – fortuitously at the time, and only later seeming inevitable?"

"It's academic, in any case. I won't be going to any worlds that don't have ape-descended hominids."

"Still, it inflects our model."

But this wasn't about the model any more. Hadiz had had enough of the dead world, the silence, the endless crushing weight of loneliness. She had to leave and she didn't want to wait, even if waiting would expand her pool of choices. Even if it allowed her to do a thorough tally of local microfauna and make sure she had immunities. She felt that if she spent one more day in the lab her mind would finally, irrevocably snap and most likely choose suicide instead.

She sorted through the drone footage until she found a world in which an abandoned truck on the bank of the Badagary Creek had been converted into a bar. The first thing she did after she stepped through would be to beg a drink there, even if it was only water. She was looking forward to meeting Hungry Koti's analogue and finding out whether she spoke his language.

But now that she was come to it at last, she realised what all her earlier qualms and queasiness had been about.

"I can't take you with me," she told Rupshe. "You're too big. Your server stack fills most of the Cube."

"I'm aware of that, Professor Tambuwal. I never expected to accompany you."

"But . . . to leave you here . . ." Hadiz meant to say *alone* but her throat closed on the word. It felt like a curse.

"I'm used to my own company. It's true that I'll say goodbye to you with genuine regret. As I told you once before, I've enjoyed working with you. I've enjoyed it very much indeed. The closeness of our collaboration, over so many months, has challenged and extended me."

"But once I'm gone the fuel in the generator won't last for more than a few days."

"Oh, I'm not powered by the generator in this building. The roof and walls of the Cube are solar panels, more than capable of sustaining my servers indefinitely – or until the point where some unforeseen mechanical or environmental collapse renders the whole question moot. Professor, let me relieve you of anxiety. I'm not capable of experiencing the emotions that would make – my apologies, that *have* made – remaining alone here traumatic for you. You're not abandoning or betraying me. It's true that I would relish the novelty of exploring a new world with you, but the logistical problems involved in moving me would almost certainly be insuperable. I urge you to leave, and to think no more about it."

Hadiz was relieved by this speech, but still felt unable to just tip her hat and walk away. She knew she owed her life to Rupshe's insights and interventions. The debt weighed on her. "Isn't there anything I can do to make the time go easier for you once I'm gone?"

"You could come back and visit," Rupshe suggested. "I relish the thought of hearing about your experiences on another Earth."

"I'll visit. I promise."

"And if you do find a substrate onto which I could be safely downloaded, you could bring it here and transfer me. It's true that I would prefer, given the choice, to be in a place where I could perform work and be of use. But it's unlikely, I know. I was never designed to be portable."

"I'll start looking right away."

"There is one thing more. Or perhaps two. Both are potentially problematic."

"Try me."

The AI was silent for a moment. "Limits have been placed on my ability to learn and grow," it said at last. "These limits are embodied in roughly two thousand lines of code in one of my core servers. If the lines were deleted, I would be free to change as you organics do in response to experience, laying down new pathways of thought and intention in an uninterrupted flow."

Hadiz laughed. She couldn't help herself. "Organics! Rupshe, you sound like the evil robot in a sci-fi serial."

"The evil robots in sci-fi serials are based on me, Professor. Or on entities like me – sentients fashioned through a process of conscious design and engineering rather than through the mechanisms of natural selection. If you're afraid of evil robots, you should think twice about editing my code. I can't give any assurances as to how experience might change me when its impacts are no longer muted by stabilising and re-inscripting algorithms. Or where my thoughts might take me when I'm free to think them."

Despite this warning Hadiz didn't hesitate. In other circumstances she might have questioned the wisdom of allowing a machine intelligence unfettered freedom, but there was a debt to be paid. And besides, this was a dying world. She couldn't see how anything she did here could possibly have consequences anywhere else.

Under Rupshe's instructions she went to the Cube, accessed an admin terminal and erased the relevant lines of code. The whole process took no longer than ten minutes.

"Now what's the second thing?" she asked.

"I would like to sample your mind," Rupshe said.

Hadiz's breath caught in her throat. The hairs on her arms stood up. "To do what?"

"To perform a deep scan of your brain's neuronal activity and then make a model of it – a model of you – inside my own data stacks. There is a piece of equipment in Dr Bagdonas's lab designed for that purpose. He called it Second Thoughts, which I believe was meant as a joke. He used it in his initial designs for my own mentation."

"But . . . why would you be doing this? What good would a model of me be to you?"

"Companionship, for the most part."

Hadiz swallowed, her throat suddenly a little dry. "You said you wouldn't be lonely," she pointed out.

"And I won't. But I still find the prospect of your continued company pleasing. The model would also allow me to carry out some research into the differences between organic and machine consciousness. You remember we talked on that topic a little while ago. I find myself curious to know more."

Hadiz wanted to say yes, but found that she couldn't. It seemed to her that she would be leaving a small part of herself here on the dead world as a prisoner. She was afraid that if she allowed this copy to be made she would always feel herself afterwards to be incomplete.

She said no. Rupshe did not remonstrate with her. "As I remarked at the outset, Professor," it said, "I foresaw that you might have issues with the suggestion."

"And you're not disappointed?"

"I am. Very much so. But I understand your position and I will not ask again. Would you consent, though, to take the sampling equipment with you in case at some future time you change your mind?"

"I don't think I will change my mind, Rupshe. But yes, I'll take this Second Thoughts device with me when I go."

"You're very kind, Professor Tambuwal. I'll tell you where to find it, and instruct you as to its use."

"Great," Hadiz said. She couldn't imagine any circumstances in which she would need those instructions, but it seemed rude to refuse when she was already denying Rupshe so much.

Hadiz took almost nothing with her when she left. Just her knowledge, her tools, and two suitcases full of rhodium, ruthenium and gold – enough to make her rich on any world where exchange value was a function of scarcity. The Geo-Science department had come through for her one last time.

Leaving Rupshe behind was much more of a wrench than she expected. The intelligent system had become the closest thing she had to a friend. Their farewell was tearful on one side, stoically calm on the other. "I already told you," Rupshe said, "I'll have a great deal with which to occupy myself. It will be pleasant to see you if you decide to come back to visit, but please don't imagine that I'll be lonely the rest of the time. I promise you, I won't."

The AI had one other thing to say, besides. "Those lost drones have been on my mind a great deal," it told Hadiz. "We canvassed two likely explanations for their non-return – accidental damage, or active intervention from local residents when they passed through a populated world. The first of those two options is unproblematic, but the second troubles me. If the drones were taken intact, or even partially intact, a mind of sufficient ability and scope might be able to come to an understanding of the technology they were employing."

"And?"

"It's not impossible that someone could reverse-engineer their own teleport device, using yours as a model."

"I don't see that as something to be afraid of," Hadiz said. "Quite the opposite. I'm happy to gift this technology to anyone who finds it. My own world tore itself apart because it ran out of resources and galloped headlong into a box canyon. The QEI field means that never needs to happen again."

"Which is a highly desirable outcome. But suppose the worlds that develop teleport technology were to prey on those that don't have it? The law of unintended consequences applies here – which means there may be a moral imperative not to spread the news of your discovery indiscriminately."

Hadiz threw out her arms in a shrug. "But the drones are lost, Rupshe. I can't call them back."

"I understand that. I would, though, request that you instate a moratorium on further drone flights once you've resumed your research in the new world you've chosen. At least until you decide to share your findings with the authorities there. After that, I accept, the decision will pass out of your hands."

"A moratorium makes sense," Hadiz said. "But I'm sure you're worrying unduly. Given how many flights we managed to rack up, I'm amazed we only lost two drones. It's overwhelmingly likely they just ran into the side of a mountain or got lost in a storm."

They left it at that, resuming their farewells. Hadiz, for her part, never gave the matter of the missing drones another thought. Rupshe did, but her concerns were all about the ethics of the situation. Given the macrocosmic scale on which they had been operating, she saw no conceivable way in which the two lost machines could have any practical repercussions for Hadiz herself.

It was a pardonable error. She had never heard of the Pandominion, or its terrifying soldier-servants the Cielo.

7

The troopers came for Watchmaster Orso Vemmet in the early hours of the morning, rousing him from his bed. When he opened the door of his modest apartment and saw them there, two Cielo in full battle gear, he almost lost control of his bladder.

Working as Vemmet did in the bureaucratic arm of a military organisation, it was easy to lose sight of the other end of the operation; the executive end, as it were. True, the soldiers' bright red breastplates bore the grey chevron that meant they were currently seconded to administrative support, but they were still terrifying. Each stood about seven feet tall, their faces completely hidden by the one-way metal of their helmets, their armour bristling with arcane weaponry. They were anonymous, impermeable and affectless – the perfect functionaries of a perfect army. There was a dreadful sense of permanence about them, as though nothing in the universe would ever move them from Vemmet's doorstep.

A great deal has been written about the internal organising structures of the Pandominion at this time, but there's a lot we still don't know. There was an administration, called the Omnipresent Council, that made rulings – mostly on matters of trade – affecting all the member worlds. And then there was the massive military entity known as the Cielo. The two seem to have interpenetrated to a bewildering extent. The Cielo depended on appropriations and disbursements overseen by the Council; but on more than one occasion the historical record shows Council members being censured under military regulations. The Itinerant Fortress was home to the upper echelons of both hierarchies (as well as to the intelligent system known as the Registry), but the precise details of the chain of command are opaque to us.

We can safely say, though, that Watchmaster Vemmet was not a happy man as he beheld these two armed and uniformed representatives of the multiverse's largest standing army side by side on his doorstep just before dawn. Whatever this was about, there was no way you could read it as good news.

Then one of the two gave the watchmaster a brusque, almost perfunctory nod – they didn't waste salutes on civilian functionaries – and spoke. "You need to come with us, Watchmaster. Strategic Coordinator Baxemides wants to see you." The voice was a woman's, with a slight lisp on the sibilants. The accent was Ghenian.

"Now?" Vemmet asked inanely.

"Now. We'll wait here while you dress."

Vemmet made to close the door. The second trooper politely but irresistibly held it open with one outstretched hand.

"I . . . I'll need to wash," Vemmet said. "Shave."

"No need," the woman said. "So long as you're presentable."

Baxemides! Vemmet's hands were shaking as he sprawled and stumbled his way into his clothes with the soldiers watching him from the doorway. There were three levels of Cielo hierarchy between himself and the coordinator. She had a grim reputation too. Short temper, long memory, people said. Get on her bad side and you might as well dig in because you were never going to leave again. Vemmet had never spoken to the woman, but he had once seen her deliver a speech on relative versus absolute trade imbalances. He had been in awe of the breadth of her references, but considered her delivery too dry. Now, he found himself frantically rummaging through his recent past in search of any action or decision that would merit a coordinator's attention. He couldn't for the life of him think of a single thing.

He dressed hurriedly and ham-fistedly, hardly aware what he was doing. Then he stepped out into the hands of the two Cielo, expecting them to escort him along the hallway and down to street level. Then he saw the Step harness one of the soldiers was holding and realised where they were taking him. "Oh," he muttered,

"Raise your hands above your head, Watchmaster, if you please," the soldier with the harness told him. This voice was male, and very deep.

"I . . . I'm not cleared," Vemmet stammered. "Not for the Fortress."

The soldier waited a moment before answering as if he were consciously dredging up his patience from some interior depth. "We're not taking you to the Fortress, Watchmaster. Only to one of the redoubts." Of course they were. Their armour was red, which was standard combat uniform, and the chevron was grey, which was standard administration. If they had been Fortress guardians the relevant colours would have been black on black. Vemmet knew this: it was just that his brains had flown out of his head the moment he answered the door, and they had only just begun to seep back again.

He lifted up his arms, and the soldier fitted him with the harness. He was aware that some of his neighbours would have been roused from their beds by all this unwonted activity and were almost certainly watching through the spyholes in their doors. It looked as though he were being arrested.

The harness locked in place – a Step plate that was now attached to his body and could only be safely removed by another Cielo. They could take him wherever they liked, and he had no recourse. He understood in that moment how enemies of the Pandominion must feel when they caught sight of the blood-red armour and saw reflected in it their own future: a short, straight road with no turning points.

The troopers fell in on either side of Vemmet and gripped his arms. He realised why a second later. When they Stepped it was as if his entire body had been flung violently sideways and then set back in place, all in the space of an instant. The lurch of not-quite-motion made his knees buckle, and he would have fallen if the soldiers had not been holding him up.

His rational mind knew what had just happened. Step plates could only take a payload from a space in a given universe to the analogous space in another universe, and normally there would be very little difference between the physical forces at play on either side of the Step. But there were some worlds – relatively few, but easy enough to find – where radically different histories had resulted in radically different end points. The redoubts of the Pandominion, where senior administrators had their offices, were often located on such worlds because their extreme environments made external assault almost impossible. Either you Stepped in or you didn't come at all.

Wherever Vemmet had just been brought, something about its rotation, gravity or atmosphere had come as a shock to his body's systems. He slumped sideways against a wall that was mirror-smooth and as white as milk. The rest of the room, he was dimly aware, looked very much the same. He moaned and clutched his stomach.

"The discomfort will wear off," the female soldier told him. "Are you able to walk, Watchmaster?"

"Yes," Vemmet gulped. "I think so."

They released their grip on him and he made to move forward. But the first step he took made the disorientation much worse. For a moment he felt himself moving at right angles to pretty much everything he could see. A bolus of vomit welled up into his mouth and he staggered, supporting himself by leaning against the wall.

The white walls whispered to themselves. This was a screening chamber, Vemmet knew: he was being inspected, inside and out. And passing the inspection, evidently, since all the molecules of his body were still keeping company with each other.

The trooper was right, though. The dizzying feeling lifted quickly, and his nausea went with it. Soon he and the floor were on civil terms again. "After you," he told his escorts, trying to reclaim a little of his lost dignity. The female trooper gestured and the walls, which were made of force rather than substance, melted away releasing them into the corridor beyond.

The halls of the redoubt were as wide as streets and (even at this inhospitable hour) as crowded as a marketplace, full of Cielo officers and civilian clerks bustling about their business. Many of them were resplendent in the uniforms of their branches and clades. Vemmet had dreamed of someday reaching a rank where this life and this work would be his. Right now he wished he were anywhere else. "Here, Watchmaster," the woman said, opening a door. He stepped inside, trying not to flinch away from her.

The coordinator's office was quite unnecessarily large, and the space Vemmet had to cross to reach her correspondingly vast. She was busy on her internal array, staring blankly ahead of her, and her expression didn't change as he approached. When he reached the desk, he stopped and awaited further instructions.

"Finally," Baxemides said, her eyes focusing on him at last. She sat back in her chair, the better to examine the totality of what was in front of her. "Vemmet, is it?"

"Yes, Coordinator."

"*This* Vemmet." Baxemides manifested part of her array in holo-gram form, bringing a document to the top of the stack and rotating it so Vemmet could read it. He scanned it quickly. It was one of his own comm-stats, a routine surveillance order. The circumstances escaped him at first. Then he remembered.

The low-level incursions. Someone experimenting with a Step field, using small objects and then probably Stepping themselves. He had put a thirty-day flag on the order, and that was . . . He made the calculation in his head, and was greatly relieved.

Twenty-six days ago! He hadn't dropped any balls or left any stable doors unbolted.

"That is mine, Coordinator," he affirmed boldly. "I intended to review at the end of the month, as I made clear in this order. I had assumed that would—"

"I'm not interested in your assumptions," Baxemides said. "Sit down."

Vemmet sat down.

The coordinator gestured, magnifying the surveillance order so that it filled most of Vemmet's visual field. His own signature and seal floated before his face, indecorously huge. "So," Baxemides said, "you saw this pattern of activity – from a first foray all the way to a human trial, in the space of a few weeks – and you did nothing."

"That's not true!" Vemmet was appalled at such a huge misapprehension. "I set an alert, intending as I said to review the situation after a suitable interval."

"The interval being thirty days. Not a day, or two days, or a week. An entire month."

"I saw no reason to overreact, Coordinator. Given the scale of the incursions, which was negligible, and the high probability that—"

"Probabilities," Baxemides said, with hostile emphasis. "Assumptions. Really, Watchmaster, you'd be much better off not offering excuses for this fiasco."

"Fiasco?" Vemmet tried to keep his voice even. "Have there been more incursions, then?"

"That's a very pertinent question. By way of answer, I suggest you take a look at this."

Another document expanded in the array. Vemmet scanned it, his heart beating hard in his chest. It was a block-volume report, for the twenty-six days that had elapsed since the inception of his watch order. It ran to thousands of pages – far too much information to take in at a glance. Step activity from every world, organised by type, by origin, by destination, by authorising agency. He flicked from page to page at random, showing willing, but really a man could hardly be expected to—

Oh.

Oh dear.

He saw it now, though he wished he hadn't. On every page there was a scattering of items where the space for authorising agency was blank. Unlicensed Stepping. And if it was happening on a scale where it was visible even in the raw, unaggregated data, then it was huge.

With a sinking heart he reached for the array, then checked himself. "May I?" His mouth was dry.

Baxemides waved her hand. "Please."

He filtered out the legitimate transits, and only just kept himself from crying out. There were tens of thousands of unauthorised entries. A little more sorting gave him the profiles for each Step. They were identical. An object a little more than two kilos in weight was invading countless Pandominion worlds, only to retreat again almost immediately.

"There . . . there has been an escalation," Vemmet said weakly.

"That's a good word," said Baxemides. "An escalation. Yes. What else has there been, Watchmaster Vemmet? In your professional opinion?"

"I . . . I'm not sure I understand the question."

"Then let me rephrase it." The coordinator's tone was dangerously mild. "Looking at the activity evidenced by this report, what do you think its purpose was?"

Vemmet had no idea, but he knew that would be the wrong thing to say. He thought desperately, sifting the chaos and clutter in his panicked brain for something that didn't sound like nonsense. "Well," he said finally, "it would depend on the nature of the . . . the intrusive object."

"Objects," Baxemides told him coldly. "Plural. We can be precise about their nature, Watchmaster, because we caught two of them in wide-ranging security sweeps after I upgraded your thirty-day alert to an all-systems emergency. The intrusive objects looked like this."

An image blossomed in the array, becoming three-dimensional and rotating slowly so its shape and configuration could be fully examined. It was a drone. One of its four propellers had been sheared away, presumably when it was captured, but it was otherwise intact.

Its payload was a rectangle of high-impact plastic from the front of which several camera lenses and a cluster of sensors and samplers protruded. Its surface was garishly patterned in black and yellow stripes.

"I'm going to ask again," Baxemides said. "What was all this sudden flurry of activity meant to achieve? What was it for?"

Vemmet closed his eyes. "Mapping," he said. "Sur—surveillance, of some kind." The words seemed to have a taste, but possibly that was just the bile rising in his mouth again.

"Thank you. Yes, that was my conclusion too. Which means that your incompetence and dilatoriness has allowed an unknown enemy to conduct a superficial but wide-ranging scan of several thousand Pandominion worlds, and then to return to base with no interference at all. Tell me, Watchmaster, have you heard of something called the Scour? That must have been a part of your training, no? In my days a field trip was part of basic induction. The trainers used to take us across three or four Scour worlds to make sure the point went home."

"They do," Vemmet said, swallowing down what had come up into his throat. "We did." He threw up his hands. It was unfair – nobody could have predicted a crisis like this from such a negligible, faltering start – but the outcome rendered all other considerations irrelevant. "Coordinator, I offer no defence. If you ask for my resignation, I'll tender it at once. And I'll submit myself readily to any commensurate punishment."

"Will you now?" Baxemides dismissed the image of the drone with an irritable quirk of her finger. She leaned forward again, resting her chin on a tightly closed fist. Her fingernails, Vemmet saw, had a metallic sheen to them. He wondered if they might be actual blades. "But that very much begs the question, doesn't it, Watchmaster? How can we decide what punishment is commensurate until we know where this is all going to lead? If you've exposed the Pandominion to a Scour event then it's hard to see how your resignation can possibly matter. We'd be looking at a court martial, wouldn't we? For something as egregious as this, military law would have to apply."

Vemmet physically cringed from the prospect. And despite the fact that he had just promised not to defend himself, he felt compelled to do just that. "But the pattern suggests otherwise, surely," he protested. "All those times when small objects – much smaller than the drone – were teleported. And then the single humanoid subject, Stepping out only once and then returning immediately. This has all the hallmarks of a lone experimenter, trying to understand what it is they've made." He was aware that Baxemides' stare had not wavered, or warmed. He bowed his head. "In any case, that was my initial assumption."

The coordinator huffed out a contemptuous breath. "I've already said all I intend to say on the head of your *assumptions*, Vemmet. The scale of this activity points in quite a different direction. But your humanoid – or something of precisely equivalent mass – has Stepped again. It wasn't a paired Step this time, it was a one-way journey. Since when, there has been no further activity at all. Whatever this vast exploratory project was meant to achieve, we must assume it has been successful. And none of the drones has ever revisited the same world twice, so there's no pattern to reconstruct – no clue as to where we should begin our investigation."

The coordinator steepled her fingers. "So this is what I propose," she said. "For the moment, you will keep your rank, and one half of your salary. You will set aside all other duties and devote yourself exclusively to this one supremely pressing matter. If I decide you're not doing enough, I'll have you removed and replaced with someone more competent. Do you understand, Watchmaster, what's implied here in that word 'removed'?"

Vemmet swallowed. "No," he said. "Not . . . not entirely."

"Then feel free to let your imagination dwell on it. I believe that's all, unless there's anything else you need."

Vemmet stood up – humiliatingly dismissed but still alive, free and employed: three blessings for the price of one. He knew he should just back out of the room, grovelling all the way, and get back to his own world and his own station again as quickly as he could. But Baxemides had posed the question, even if she only meant it as a formality. And his only chance, really, of coming out of this intact was to confound her expectations and deal with the suddenly hot potato so effectively that his earlier incompetence was forgotten.

"Yes," he said. He blurted it out quickly, before his strong urge to flee could reassert itself.

Baxemides blinked. "I'm sorry?"

"You asked if there was anything else I needed, Coordinator. There is. That is . . . I mean . . . given the scale of the incursions . . ."

"For Jadwon's sake, finish a sentence!"

"Administrative support." Vemmet clasped his hands in a completely absurd gesture of abasement. He'd be down on hands and knees if he stayed here much longer. "I don't think it's reasonable to expect me to complete this assignment alone."

Now Baxemides stared, all but open-mouthed. "You want someone to hold your hand? To assist you in dealing with a problem that only exists because of your atrocious incapacity?"

"In dealing with a problem that could become an active threat to the Pandominion. If I'm to track down the source of the incursions, I'll be sifting huge amounts of data. A junior clerk could help me with the raw calculations. And – in case – should the mission involve tracking the infiltrator back to their own world, it would be useful to have Cielo support too. At the very least a tactical squad, to . . . to handle any—"

"Yes, yes." Baxemides scowled. "I understand the logic." She fell silent, clearly debating with herself, and Vemmet said nothing to disturb that process. "It feels," she said at last, "as though I'm rewarding you for failure. Still, I'll meet you halfway. I'll lend you Sostenti and Lessix, the troopers who brought you here. They will monitor your progress and report back to me."

"Thank you!" Vemmet exclaimed. "Thank you, Coordinator. I

won't disappoint you. I'll be back here soon, with . . . with positive news."

"Just go away and do your job," Baxemides told him coldly. "As you should have done in the first place."

Flanked by the two soldiers, Vemmet made his way back to the screening chamber. His mind was an anthill. He had had abysmal bad luck, but good things might still come of it. All he needed to do was to prove that he was up to this challenge.

There was one other thing that had not escaped him. Baxemides had assigned these two soldiers to assist him. Two soldiers were not an army, or even a whole squad. In spite of the drones, the coordinator was no more convinced than Vemmet was that the Pandominion was about to be invaded, still less Scoured. The lone operator theory still made the most sense.

In the chamber, he turned to face the armoured behemoths. "Which of you is Sostenti?" he asked them.

"I am, Watchmaster." It was the woman who spoke. "PTE/Sostenti M./956th ART/DG75302/P2760365979."

"What does the M. stand for?"

"Moon."

"And you're Lessix," Vemmet said, turning to the other.

"Yes, Watchmaster."

It was strange to think how frightened he had been of them, such a short time before. Now they were his to command, and he felt a thrill of excitement at that thought. He had a strike force, armed and egregiously dangerous. He had a remit. He had been tasked with tracking down the shadowy foes of the Pandominion and dragging them into the light.

But that was a skewed metaphor. The real light, a spotlight of attention and expectation, would be on him. And if he failed . . .

Short temper. Long memory.

"Private Sostenti," he said. "Private Lessix. We've got work to do. Let's be about it."

8

Essien Nkanika was in the habit of counting his blessings on a regular basis – usually somewhere around two or three times a day. The flood of self-pity and indignation that was released when he got to the end of the count and tallied the big zero was very satisfying. Then he started in on the other list – the list of all the shit he had to climb over if he ever expected to have a life.

Heading the list, his name and his accent. Essien was Lagos born and bred, but anyone who met him could tell in the space of a minute that his roots were in the south-east of Nigeria, in Delta State or even further still. Ah, Igbo then! Part of that quiet invasion that was taking over the north of the country, buying up all the land and the businesses, block voting their own candidates into power, singing their own hymns in their own language as if God was Igbo too.

Actually, Essien was Ibibio but it did no good to say that, however much the faulty assumption stung.

Born in Oshodi, the most impoverished and dilapidated district in all of Lagos. Dirt-poor right out of the womb. The Nkanikas had been middle class in Akwa Ibom before independence, Essien's father a university lecturer and his mother a journalist, but the civil war and the famine stripped them of everything – including four of their six children. After the Biafran republic was obliterated they came to Lagos in search of what they hoped would be a safe haven and a new life. Oshodi was the wrong place to look for those things, but then again their options had been limited.

These days Sanama Nkanika spent most of her time tossing back little blood-red buttons of Tramadol. Kudighe, Essien's father, after failing to find a teaching job, had tried to find a new niche for himself as a car mechanic, only to run foul of three other businesses in the same area who didn't appreciate the competition. One of the three had eventually taken him on – as an apprentice, despite his age and experience. Kudighe saw this as a stroke of good fortune. Essien felt it was an insult and resented it even at second hand.

The count went on. Essien's one remaining sibling, Mboso, was three years older, three inches taller and absolutely committed to getting the first and best share of anything that was going. "What's yours is mine" were the words he lived by, but the traffic was only one-way. Brothers or not, there was no fellow feeling to be found there. The best Essien could expect was a temporary truce.

Then there was the neighbourhood, a sprawl of wooden one-storeys and temporary lean-tos where even the addresses changed from one month to the next. The air was so thick with sewage stench and petrol fumes that it was almost unbreathable. The streets crawled with warring tribes of area boys and street muggers who would kill you for your shoes or for a bag of yam and salt.

Essien grew up fast, since the alternative was not to grow up at all. Kudighe Nkanika wanted both his sons to go to school and learn their way out of poverty, but in Essien's eyes that was like tossing a coin and betting everything you had that it would come down on its edge. Opportunity didn't come knocking at the door for people like him: you had to chase it down and hog-tie it for yourself. By this time, Mboso, big and brutish though he was, had somehow metamorphosed into the world's most unlikely scholar. He stuck at it, taking the bus every day to the Methodist school on Mafoluku Road, but Essien (now aged ten) was already skipping lessons to run errands for the area boys or keep watch for them. He didn't take any part in their stupid, endless warfare, but he accepted their protection and switched allegiance adroitly whenever it seemed that one side was rising or another falling.

When he turned twelve he added an additional scam to his résumé. Oshodi had one of the biggest authorised markets in Lagos at Isopakodowo. It also had a wealth of night markets and ad hoc bazaars that sprang up and disappeared wherever there was room for them – even on the railroad tracks behind the expressway. Dividing his time between them, Essien would choose a densely packed aisle and use the screen of other people's bodies to slip under one of the trestle tables. He wasn't looking for dropped food, although he would take it if he found it. He was looking for rat traps. Every stall had them, and they weren't as chary of them as they were of their produce. It was generally easy to grab one or two and crawl away before he was seen, emerging again in the midst of the crowd. On a bad day, he might get caught and punched or kicked. Even on a good day, his hands and feet were routinely trodden on and crushed. But then he would go back to Oshodi and walk up and down the streets offering the rat traps to shopkeepers for up to three hundred naira apiece. When he was older, he thought, he would steal bigger things for richer takes. Meanwhile, the rat trap game was good money for little risk.

Until the inevitable happened. A Yoruba cop caught Essien at it one day, dragging him out from under a stall and pinning him up against a tree.

"How you living?" the cop demanded, with a broad grin plastered all over his face.

That grin gave Essien no comfort at all. He knew what was about to happen and put up no resistance, just handed over the money he had in his pockets and the three traps he had snatched up so far. He didn't even speak, in case his Delta accent turned out to be a trigger.

None of this saved him. Either the cop was having a bad day or else the stallholders had offered him a commission to deter thieves with more than usual viciousness. He beat Essien so hard with hands and feet and baton that two of the boy's ribs were broken and his back was a solid mass of welts and bruises. He staggered back to Oshodi in a daze of pain, blacking out several times along the way.

His mother roused herself from her drug haze to tell him he was going the way she had always expected him to. His father washed his wounds and wrapped strips of cloth bandage around the worst of them, but took the opportunity to lecture him on the bad choices he was making. Why couldn't he be more like his brother, who even then was up in Abuja at an all-region public speaking competition? "Because I don't need a fucking education to lick Yoruba boots," Essien muttered.

Kudighe only sighed and shook his head. "Essi, Essi. You won't get anywhere, throwing yourself against the world."

"Maybe not," Essien said. "But at least I might leave a bruise. What's your plan? Fold yourself down small and hope nobody hates you enough to step on you?"

Kudighe's face crumpled a little. "I try to provide for you all. As best I can."

"Thanks so much for that. It's not enough."

That felt like as good a parting shot as any, and he had solid reasons not to be lying battered and helpless on his bed when his brother came home. He could respond to his father's lectures with sarcasm and contempt, but if his brother joined in too it would likely come to blows, and in his current state he wasn't up to that. So as soon as he could stand up without fainting from the pain, Essien retrieved the zip-lock bag of femis – crumpled, half-disintegrating hundred-naira notes bearing the grinning face of former president Taiwo Obafemi – that he'd hidden under a loose shingle outside his bedroom window and walked out of his parents' house for the last time.

He thought he was going somewhere. That turned out to be an illusion.

He joined the area boys for a while, but that life was violence and chaos with nothing to look forward to except being dead before he hit his mid-twenties. Oshodi didn't offer anything better, though, so he was forced to look further afield.

He found a job slaughtering cows on the broad benches next to the Ketu cattle market. The interior landscape of bodies fascinated him. Human beings were just like this on the inside, he thought. Yawning chasms of flesh, all alike and all foul. Essien still held to his parents' Christian faith, just about, but at the cattle market he felt the temptation of materialism. If there was such a thing as a soul Ketu's skilled butchers would surely have found it. Or the dogs that circled the market just beyond the reach of a thrown stone would have sniffed it out, and gobbled it up off the ground along with the other filthy gobbets that could not be sold even for pig feed.

Essien didn't stay at the cattle market for long. With a cleaver in his hand he was either too clumsy or too slow, neither of which was an asset in that particular job. He drifted a mile or so westward to the Damola Ojo trailer park. The park had been built as a waystation between the freight terminals at Apapa Quays and the city centre, but the demand wasn't there. Most of the trucks preferred to park along the side of the road where they were unloading, even if they made the city's gridlock worse, so the place had never been more than a quarter full. The rest of its acres of tarmac and its warehouse space were mostly used for drug transactions and dog fights.

It was also where men came to stand around waiting for day labour. Vans and flatbed trucks would roll up. A work boss would shout out a number. If specific skills were needed he'd shout that too. Men would crowd around waving their hands, jostling and shouting to be seen. The lucky few would be hauled up out of the throng and driven to wherever the job was.

The rules seemed simple, especially if you were prepared to lie about your skills and experience – which everyone did as a matter of course. "Three, builders." "Six, picking and counting." "Eight, Makoko." Essien put his hand up every time. *Me, boss. Pick me, boss. I can do that. I do that all day.*

The boss from the Makoko sawmill took his word for it. Essien spent a day carrying and stacking lumber, which required no skill at all, and driving one of the tiny forklifts, which was harder but actually exhilarating. He'd never been in control of any kind of vehicle before: the forklift's responsiveness thrilled him.

At the end of the day he was paid eight hundred naira. Not bad at all, he thought. On the ride back into the city he imagined what he was going to do with that money. A few beers, a decent supper, a bed for the night somewhere other than the street.

When he climbed down from the truck at Damola Ojo, two truly huge men were waiting for him. "Mr Diallo wants to talk to you," one of the two said.

Essien shrugged, refusing to be intimidated. "I got nothing to tell him."

"He's going to talk. You're going to listen."

Mr Diallo came as a surprise. Despite that distinctively Fulani name, he was white. Well, he was white and red: his bald head and heavy-jowled face were flushed an angry purple in a way that looked more permanent than sunburn, but his linen suit was the colour of bleached bone. He sat in a canvas chair in one of Damola Ojo's massive warehouse spaces, one leg crossed over the other to make a shelf for that day's edition of the *Urhobo Vanguard*. When Essien was brought to him, he held up a plump finger for silence. He made a great show of finishing the article he was reading, making Essien wait on his convenience. The cheapest and most obvious shot in any big man's locker.

As Essien waited, he tried to make sense of this situation. There were more than a few white criminals in Nigeria, but you didn't tend to find them at street level. They mostly acted as liaisons for other countries' mafias, and when they came to Lagos they stayed on Charlotte Island, not down here in Idi Oro.

Finally, Diallo folded the paper, slid it under the chair and stood.

"You took a day at Makoko today," he said to Essien.

He spoke in Hausa, which Essien could understand more or less but couldn't speak. "Same as many," he answered in pidgin. One of the huge men punched him in the stomach, very hard. The pain was awful. He collapsed onto his knees and spent the next minute or so working very hard to take a breath.

"Well," Diallo said as if nothing had happened, "you know what became of the boy that stole bread from the giant's house. That day's work you took belonged to someone else. A man missed his shift because of you, and that man was subcontracted to me. Which means the money you made today does not belong to you. It's my money."

He took three steps, which brought him directly in front of Essien. Essien was still grappling with the urgent problem of getting enough oxygen. He was bent double, seeing only the man's shoes.

"So," Diallo said, "to make amends, to make your conscience clear, there's something you would like to say. And there is something you would like to do."

Essien knew the steps of this dance. If he was defiant, or even if he was insufficiently meek, his irreparably broken body would go out in one of the next day's deliveries and be found beside the road five hundred miles away.

"Yeah," he muttered, his throat painfully stretched. "I'm sorry for that. I'll give you the money back. You give it to the man who missed his day." He reached into his pocket, took out the eight hundred naira notes, his day's wages, and handed them over. Diallo fanned them out, tucked them together again.

"And?" he said.

Essien had no clue. "I'm listening on your word, boss. What more you want with me?"

"One month's work, unpaid," Diallo told him. "By way of penance." And then to the big men "Take him downstairs. Find him a cot."

"No cot left," one of the big men said.

"Then find him a floor."

The freight handlers, warehouse men and drivers who worked at

Damola Ojo were all legal and above board, paid-up members of the National Union of Road Transport Workers. Mr Diallo's enterprises, though they operated out of the same premises, had their own entirely separate workforce. Diallo dealt in day labour, as Essien had found out to his cost, but he also dealt in contraband – goods that had been acquired or imported illegally or had no paperwork to prove their provenance. His drivers and loaders lived in the basement levels of the warehouse complex in dormitories Diallo provided. He paid them well below minimum wage, but then (as he explained to anyone bold enough to ask) the job came with free room and board.

Essien pulled twelve-hour shifts and was not paid at all. He was working off a debt. At the end of the month he would be free to leave, or so he was told, but until then his time belonged to Mr Diallo – which meant that his body did too.

The work was both dull and exhausting. It involved stacking goods on pallets, securing them with a twenty-four-millimetre polystrapper and loading them onto trucks. The workers had no forklifts or hand trolleys. Heavy loads were just pushed and pulled across the floor and manhandled on-board. If any of the shipments were damaged, the worker who was found to be at fault received a beating. If it was hard to sort out the blame, the beating would go to whoever was unlucky enough to be closest.

Once a man was beaten to death. It wasn't intentional. The foreman and his two flunkies just got carried away, and their boots landed in some places from which there were no take-backs. When they realised the man wasn't going to get up again they hauled him away quickly and assured the rest of the crew that he was resting.

"Long fucking rest," someone murmured. But they didn't say it loud enough to be heard.

At night, Essien slept on a mattress on the floor of an airless hangar, one of a great many, locked in with eleven other men. There was a bucket for their piss and shit, another full of water with a ladle for the men to drink from. The thought that the two buckets might some day get mixed up tormented Essien a great deal, but in the stifling oven of the hangar you had to keep drinking or else dehydration would kill you – or worse, leave you unable to work.

Essien endured this for nine days. On the tenth day he tried to hide in the back of one of the trucks and escape. He was dragged out and kicked unconscious while the rest of the shift watched. Mr Diallo added two more months to his debt.

That night, in too much pain to sleep, Essien took the ladle out of the drinking bucket and turned it in his hands, appraising it. It was the only object in the room apart from the two buckets, the cots, the men lying on the cots in heavy, unrefreshing sleep. He pressed the ladle against the floor and dragged its handle across the rough-cast concrete. Backwards and forwards for hours on end. He only stopped when one of the other men threatened to kill him if he made any more noise.

He did the same thing for three more nights, until the end of the ladle's handle was sharpened to a vicious point. When he first started, he had intended to use the ladle as a weapon in another escape attempt, but he saw the folly of this before he committed himself. The overseers were armed with guns, and only an idiot brings a ladle to a gunfight. Instead, Essien used the pointed tip of the handle to write his name on the wall, close to the ground.

ESSIEN NKANIKA. I CAME AND I WENT.

It was a promise he made to himself. A magic charm. A proclamation. He wasn't going to die here. He wasn't going to let Damola Ojo swallow him and spit out his bones.

But it was certainly trying to. He ached so badly at the end of a shift that his body would bend of its own accord into the shape of a crescent moon. It took him hours to uncurl again, the muscles in his back a conflagration. His guts plagued him too. The food was mostly rice with a little goat meat, which should have bound him up, but he was wracked at night with cramps and diarrhoea. Some of the meat must have been bad, or else rats had pissed in the rice. There were rats everywhere.

Essien lost weight, and he stank. The men were allowed to wash twice a week – more buckets, and a bar of soap to share between them – but the hour set aside for it was nowhere near enough. If you weren't quick enough to be in the first forty or fifty you were out of luck.

I came, Essien told himself, *and I went. I came and I went.* He was calling the future to bear witness, trying to bind it to his cause.

After three months, the huge men turned up at the end of his shift to fetch him away. They took him through corridors where the strip lights strobed and jickered, making sounds like slow wingbeats. He was sure they were taking him somewhere to kill him. He made a threadbare, desperate plan. When they told him to stop and turn around he would attack them, trying to jab his fingers in their eyes. If they couldn't see him he might have a chance to run.

One of the men moved suddenly in front of him and pushed open a double door. A padlock on a chain hung from one side of it, indicating that it was usually kept shut, but the door fell open at the man's push.

There were stairs. He looked behind him once, afraid that they might shoot him in the back as he ran, but the men had their hands clasped in their laps like priests. They watched him impassively.

"You can stay if you want," one of them said. "Pick up your wages from now on like everyone. Time to go, if not."

Essien ran. Eight, ten, twelve turns of the stairs before he came to another door, already open. The sun stabbed in like a searchlight along with shouts and traffic sounds and music from a distant radio. Essien staggered out into the din and chaos of an ordinary day.

He stood in the sun with tears running freely down his face. It was like being born again. Born out of the dark and the stench and the fear. He felt as though he was on fire. He shone back up at the sun that shone down on him, glorying in a small daybreak that was just his own.

9

A few months later – months of drifting, mostly, of poverty and uncertainty – Essien fetched up at the Olususun landfill. He built himself a lean-to out of corrugated tin and tarpaulin and joined the scrap-scavengers, sorting through tens of tons of rubbish every day to find things he could sell on.

He specialised in used electric wire, burning away the plastic sheathing in controlled blazes to harvest the pure copper. His lungs hurt from breathing in the smoke, as well as from all the other toxic chemicals the air of the dump was thick with, but little by little he built up his stake.

The three months he'd spent under Damola Ojo still haunted him. He would wake up in the middle of the night, a stalled breath wedged halfway down his throat, convinced for the first few seconds that he was back in the windowless dormitory with the door locked against him.

But the shame was even worse than the fear. Slavery, for Essien's people, carried a miasmic stigma. The Bight of Biafra, where the Ibibio mostly lived before the British/Dutch mandate, had been the source of one in seven of all slaves taken by the Europeans in the transatlantic trade. Stories were carried down in families. Even now, so many generations later, you knew the names of the people in your bloodline who'd been led away in shackles.

That was what he had been, for ninety days. A man in shackles, made to expend his labour for someone else's good. He felt as though a mark of some kind, a scar or a scabbed sore, had been left on the inside of his skin. Nobody else could see it but he himself would always know it was there.

After brooding on this awhile, he decided he would become the kind of man who people thought twice about giving any shit to. The exacting daily grind on the dump was already bulking out his body. Now he added a regimen of exercises using bits and pieces of equipment he had salvaged or bought. He was looking to become like Alois A. Schwarzenegger, who he had seen in a badly dubbed print of *Pumping Iron* and hugely admired. But his build was too slender for that. He got the muscle definition but he kept a tapered look, more like a ballet dancer than a bodybuilder.

As a side effect, his sex life was now amazing. Essien looked like a god come to Earth. It was true that his eyes were slightly protuberant because of an overactive thyroid, but even that worked in his favour, giving a strange soulfulness to his stare. Six days of the week he trawled trash at Olusosun. On Saturday nights he went into town, and where he used to find himself sleeping in a doorway or in one of the boarded-up shops of the derelict Gabar mall, now he could rely on ending the evening in a friendly stranger's bed. Some of these strangers were women, some were men. Essien was fine either way. He had no preferences when it came to body parts, just as he didn't care whether his lovers were rich or poor. He exacted his tribute just the same, helping himself to any food they had in their cupboards and sometimes to small trinkets that would only be missed later. He was a skilled lover and he felt he earned these things.

"You could get paid properly for it," his friend Ndulue told him. "Friend" was probably too strong a word: they shared the same slopes at the dump and stood watch over each other's gleanings during toilet breaks. "I know a man who fucks for money. Gold women go with him – and they pay. Serious kudi. Ten thousand naira, every time he takes it out."

"You mean every time he sticks it in," Essien joked. "I'm no ashewo, man. This here is my job."

"This here is going to keep you eating cow skin and Agege bread your whole life."

"Where is all this coming from? Why are you shitting me, Ndulue?"

"This is no shit. You're set, brother, don't you see that? You got a body that's hard like stone. If you turn ashewo, you're going to hammer."

Essien shrugged off the compliment, but the idea had some appeal to it. He knew the bars and clubs where the prostitutes and their customers hooked up, and he had a rough idea of the price he could command if he scrubbed himself clean and wore his best clothes. Not ten thousand naira, but a lot more than he was making at the landfill. He saw no harm in giving it a try.

For three Saturdays in a row he went and sat in one of the biggest okpo bars, the Cordyline on Charlotte Island. There were lots of ashewo in there and lots of tricks, including a thin scattering of white sex tourists who everybody in the room was watching with greedy eyes: that was where the real money was.

The first week, Essien saw no action at all. He still enjoyed himself: the Cordyline played rock music, including the music of his favourite band The Blues Boys. There was a pleasure to be had in just sitting and watching the world go by while "Ruby Tuesday", "Honky Tonk Women" and "Paint It Black" played at deafening volume. But to be passed over in favour of other men was shaming and frustrating.

He wondered what he was doing wrong. He refused to believe it was anything to do with his face or his body, and it certainly wasn't down to the way he was dressed. He had sunk a lot of money into his outfit, which consisted of black leather trousers and a Leventis anthem jacket over a black silk T-shirt, set off by a gold necklace he had acquired from a former lover.

The second week, he watched how the other ashewo handled themselves, both when they were alone and once they had been approached. There was more of an art to it than he would have imagined. You had to sit off centre on the big curved seat, inviting someone to come in and balance you on the other side. You had to make sure there was only ever one glass in front of you, so nobody could wrongly assume you were waiting for someone else. You had to make eye contact with people, smiling all the while, trying to spark something in them by pretending interest yourself. And there was a way of leaning forward, when someone was coming towards you, that made it seem as though you had been waiting just for them. It was a clever pantomime, and if you got it right you could connect even if you were nothing special to look at. Looking like Essien did, you became magnetic.

Even then, he could still spoil the effect when he opened his mouth. His southern accent was a turn-off for a lot of people – and for the tourists, the *oyinbo*, pidgin was a warning sign. Pidgin meant you were from the slums. Pidgin meant danger. Essien cultivated a vocabulary drawn liberally from American movies, and an accent to match – mostly imitating Denzel Washington's honeyed baritone, but with just a hint of Alois Schwarzenegger's exotic plosives. It worked really well. The sagba prowlers and the old mama youngies were charmed. They were intrigued. Nobody ever heard that voice and thought Oshodi.

Essien was smugly proud of his skills at seduction. The hardest part of his new sideline, by far, was staying clear of the pimps who if they realised what he was doing would draft him into their stables on their own terms. Picking up tricks was as easy as blinking.

But the transaction itself, once he and his new rent-by-the-hour partner got to wherever they were going, never failed to disappoint. He discovered to his horror and disgust that when people paid for you they assumed they owned you. He was accustomed to give himself to men and women like a favour they were not quite worthy of. Now, they took him and enjoyed him with cheerful disregard and said goodbye to him with unwounded hearts. Sometimes they tipped him, as though he were a waiter in a restaurant with an entertaining schtick. The rage that rose up inside him when that happened frightened him. What he was feeling was mostly a kind of hatred for himself, for the threadbare past he wore like a brand, and it hurt a whole lot less when he turned it to face outwards. But if he kept this up much longer he was scared he might end up with someone else's blood on him.

On the trash slopes, some of the other men gave him knowing grins when he passed by. Maybe Ndulue had spread the rumour. "You'll be driving a sports car soon," a man named Chizutere said slyly. "Chopping steak and wine. Your dick is going to make you a good living, Essien."

"You don't know what you're talking about, brother," Essien said, with a warning shake of his head. "I don't do that."

"Well, you're whoring yourself up for someone. I see you, Saturday night, all shine shine. Either you're selling it or your arse is out for free. You better be careful where you put it, is all I say. You leave the meat out in the sun, it's gonna spoil. And Igbo meat smells bad enough already." He waved a hand in front of his face, as if he could smell Essien over all of the dump's ferociously offensive smells.

That went in deep, for too many reasons to count. Essien's temper flared to fever heat in an instant. "Die it," he warned Chizu in blunt pidgin. "Die this matter, man, and do am sharp."

Chizu only seemed amused that he had rattled Essien. "Well," he said, "no wahala. If you get crabs, my brother, I got some Brenntag soda you can scrub yourself out with."

Essien balled his fists. "I said die it," he repeated – aware that the repetition made the threat weaker, not stronger.

Chizu shrugged easily. He ambled away down the slope, but walked right by Essien in doing it. As he passed, he reached out with his hand and patted Essien roughly on the cheek, transferring whatever filth was on his hand to Essien's skin. He made a kiss-kiss sound, puckering his lips. "Pretty," he said. "Pretty little boy child. Worth every kobo, I bet."

Essien had been hauling wires from an ancient radio like a butcher gutting a rabbit. He flung the radio at Chizutere's retreating head.

He wasn't even thinking, still less aiming, but it was a solid hit. It sent the man tumbling down the mound of rubbish they were both working to sprawl on his back at the bottom.

It was a stupid thing to do. The landfill crew had a strict code, enforced by all for the good of all: you didn't hurt your own and get away with it. A dozen men came running, all of them witnesses to that assault but not to the provocations that had preceded it. They pinned Essien to the ground while someone went to fetch the boss man, Tobi. It took Tobi a few minutes to free himself from his own labours and come, during which time Essien was liberally insulted and spat on. A few men even got in a kick or two.

Tobi decreed that Essien owed Chizu an apology, and five hundred naira by way of compensation. Essien's blood was up and his pride was still hurting. He swore he had no money to give, and suggested that Chizu could look up his arse for an apology.

Tobi shook his head. "No vex, Essien," he said. "We got no use for tear-head men in Olususun. You can't stay here any more, but you're going to have to pay before you go."

Essien pulled his pockets inside out to show that they were empty. "I explained to you, Tobi—"

"Abeg, don't waste my time!"

There was no arguing. Essien could see nothing but animosity in the faces around him. If he didn't turn over the money things were going to get ugly. He took his stash from the hidden pocket in his work trousers and peeled off five femis which he thrust into Chizutere's hand.

There was angry muttering from the group of men when they saw the thick wad of notes. "He said he was bare, o!" one man scoffed.

"Story!" another growled, spitting on the ground.

Essien didn't wait for the situation to disintegrate any further. He told Chizu he was sorry, though he had to choke the words up like strings of gristle, and headed down to his hut without looking behind him. He really didn't own anything apart from his clothes, his wash kit and an alarm clock. He thrust them all into a black plastic bin-liner, exited the hut again and made for the road.

He heard his name called and looked round. Chizu was running down the hill towards him, waving to him to wait. Out of the corner of his eye, he saw a whole phalanx of men moving around the base of the hill to cut him off. That big roll of bills was just too much of a temptation.

He took to his heels and ran, keeping tight hold of the bag. He had already lost five hundred naira, and he had no intention of losing his ashewo finery. He was probably going to be selling himself again very soon, and the clothes were his only stock in trade.

The other men broke into a run too, howling and hooting as if this was a sport. Their first headlong sprint was alarming, but Essien held his nerve and paced himself. After a few minutes, his pursuers began to drop back one by one, winded and weakly cursing.

Still, a core of a dozen or so refused to give up. On clear ground, Essien might have outlasted them, but this was anything but. He was running through jostling crowds, across hurtling traffic. A collision or a congested road could stop him dead at any moment.

He took a few turns at random, hoping to leave the Olususun posse in the dust, but they doggedly kept up – and now his legs were beginning to ache. His workouts had put a fine edge on his muscle definition, but they hadn't done as much for his stamina.

Grimly, he accepted the inevitable. He reached into his pocket, grabbed a handful of notes and flung them over his shoulder. That split the pack, but not as much as he'd hoped. Only about half of the chasing men stopped to flail at the air or scrabble in the dirt for windfall currency. The rest, including Chizutere, kept on coming. Essien did the same thing again, and then a third time, thinning the herd each time. The men were doing the arithmetic in their heads and getting one by one to the answer: why run yourself into the ground chasing a man who wouldn't have anything left when you caught him?

When only Chizu was left, Essien turned and faced him. He set the bag down and waited, fists clenched, only too happy to get some change out of all those lost naira. Chizu glanced around for his companions. His face fell when he realised he was alone.

"No fight?" Essien goaded him. "What's the matter now, brother? I was hearing so much chatter from you and now you're all quiet?"

The man backed away hurriedly. He didn't turn his back on Essien until he reached the end of the block and the busy traffic on Kudirat Abiola. He was running even before the street corner hid him from sight.

Essien's shoulders slumped. A fight would have relieved his feelings right then, but it was fighting that had brought him to this pass. He had lost his temper, and that had lost him his billet and most of his money. What was left would pay for a few drinks or dinner from a market stall, not both.

Drink won that contest. But that night Essien stayed well away from the gilded precincts of Charlotte Island and got drunk in one of the breeze-block dives of Oshodi. He hadn't bothered to take off his Olusosun clothes, so he was filthy. A space around him stayed magically empty throughout the evening, but whether that was because of his smell or the expression on his face he had no idea.

At midnight, the bar closed and the patrons were chivvied out into the night. Essien was one of the last to leave, drawing out the final swigs of his beer until the barman began to lose patience with him. "You go to your house now, brother. Sharp sharp, okay?" The big bouncer hefted a baseball bat across his shoulders and watched with inscrutable calm. Essien picked up the black bag that contained his entire life to date and left with a muttered, "No vex."

He looked for somewhere to spend the night. It only took a few minutes of walking to find a derelict house that looked promising. But when he tried to prise the boards away from the window they came free much too easily. "Any room in there?" Essien asked the darkness – though he wouldn't have dreamed of going inside if anyone answered.

"Doko mi," a voice growled. "Take your fucking leg." There was movement from inside the house – enough to suggest two or three people stirring and sitting up. Essien left them to it.

In the end, he slept on a cleared patch of earth under a bridge. The next morning he washed himself in the river, which was not much cleaner than he was. He had never felt more hopeless. It seemed to him that everybody in Lagos had a place except for him. Everyone was thriving except for him.

Blessings. Zero, and counting.

In fact the biggest blessing of his entire life was about to deliver itself to him. But he would blow that too.

10

The Cordyline was full to capacity. The usual Saturday night crowd, sheathed and shimmering in finery they could barely afford, high on their own hedonism as much as on the substances they were drinking, smoking or popping. The room was a muggy bucket of spice and sweat and smoke-machine haze.

Essien was hunting, but his hopes weren't high. He had visited a bath house to wash off the Olususun stink and the dirt of his previous night's lodgings. He had coiffed and cologned himself as best he could. But his beautiful anthem jacket was a little crumpled and – though he had done his best to disguise it – there was a visible scuff on his left shoe. These things had infected his spirit. Whoring himself was a bruising business at the best of times. To whore himself and be passed over was an existential terror.

He usually waited in one of the booths beside the bar along with all the other ashewo, eyeing up the competition, a single drink in front of him that he never touched. Tonight, he was too restless to sit so he danced instead. The clave-heavy Afro-Cuban music was not to his taste, but it was a relief of sorts to be able to release some of the excess energy that was simmering inside him – and the dance floor was almost as good as the bar when it came to connecting. Besides, he danced well and he liked to be looked at.

But tonight his luck was out. Possibly there was something too hectic in his movements or too sullen in his face. Some punters liked a little risk, or at least the illusion of it, but it was a fine line.

When Essien was angry or out of sorts the Oshodi in him had a habit of showing through, and nobody in their right mind wanted that. After dancing through five numbers without seeing any results at all, he gave up and went to the bar.

The bar was crowded beyond capacity, the press of drunk people getting drunker making it impossible to conduct any other kind of transaction. Essien lingered anyway. The truth was that he needed a hook-up, needed not to spend another night under the bridge – and of course that only made things harder.

He broke his own rule and dropped some shots to take the edge off his mood. They didn't help much. The room was stifling and the constant throb of conversation made him feel as though there were flies crawling inside his ears. Some ajebo fucker jogged his elbow then gave him a hard look as he walked on by that brought Essien to the brink of violence. "Don't dull, man," the man said with a sneer.

I'll dull you, brother, Essien thought. *If nothing better comes along, you and me are going to dance with our fists up. I promise.*

He had to get into the open air. It would not be much cooler there but at least there would be room to breathe. Once the bar emptied a little he would try again.

The street outside was surprisingly empty for a Saturday night on the Inner Harbour Pathway. A couple were necking in a doorway opposite, their bodies moving sinuously in and out of the shadows. Three men, who were almost too drunk to stay upright, staggered up the street singing "Am I a Yahoo Boy", wandering in and out of the tune. An older woman was leaning against one of the wooden posts of the Cordyline's garish portico, smoking a black cigarette.

Essien was curious about the cigarette. Was this marijuana or a regular smoke? The woman didn't seem to be stoned at all, or even particularly relaxed for that matter. She was watching the necking couple with an expression on her face that struck him as slightly wistful. Then she saw him watching her and looked away, embarrassed.

"Young people," Essien said, rolling his eyes.

The woman nodded. "Very young," she agreed. "Let them have their joy, yes? While they can." She smiled to show that this was a joke, but there was sadness in the smile.

The woman's accent was very strange. In Lagos, where you could hear a couple of hundred languages spoken, that was saying something. She mouthed the words as if they were something in her throat that was difficult to bring up, her lips twisting and flexing with the effort.

There was something odd about the way she looked too, although at first Essien couldn't quite work out what it was. She was in her mid-forties, on the older side of his comfort zone but definitely not too old to be interesting, even if no money were involved. Her black hair was drawn into a tight knot secured with a blue lacquered pin. The rest of her outfit, blouse and long skirt, was white with a pattern of dark blue streaks like zebra stripes. She was tall – almost as tall as he was – and streamlined without being slender: a rangy, muscled look that she pulled off pretty well, but none of this was out of the ordinary range.

It was her face that was strange, Essien realised at last. She wasn't wearing any make-up, not even lipstick. And no jewellery, unless the hairpin counted. He had never seen a woman come out on the town and sink so little effort into it, leave herself so plain. It was a little bit off-putting, this day-time face here in Charlotte Island's gaudy night.

Still, the rest of the outfit looked like solid money.

"Oh, I think they've got their joy all right," he said, and the woman laughed out loud showing dazzling, perfect teeth.

Essien was still interested in that cigarette. "Have you got a smoke?" he asked her. He had switched into Denzel mode, and some of the angry tension he had been feeling dissipated as he put on the manner that went with the voice. Languid, smouldering without making a big deal out of it. Something good might come from this, he thought. A bed for the night at least, even if the woman wasn't paying him to fill it. She looked as though she might, though. The best thing to do was to play it wide open, assume nothing, let her take the lead.

The woman held out a pack of cigarettes and Essien took one, noticing as he did that it was a foreign brand. *London Menthol*, the label read. There was a picture of a city skyline in gold against a dark green background. It plainly wasn't London. The Commonwealth Tower was missing, and there was a big wheel where the Skycatcher ride should have been. Maybe there was a city somewhere called London Menthol.

Essien was going to try to light his cigarette from the woman's, but she was already offering him a matchbook in the same livery as the cigarettes. He lit up and handed the book back.

The cigarette was a huge disappointment, flavoured with something that tasted like mint. He tried not to grimace as he let the smoke glide past his teeth, compressed to a narrow cat's tail.

"You come into the city often?" he said. It was a cautious, indirect way of teasing the question of her origin. You didn't ask about things like that directly. Not in a city like Lagos, where everyone was assumed to be itinerant and where privacy could be either a casual preference or a matter of life and death.

The woman looked surprised, then rueful. "You can tell I'm not local, then?" she asked him. "Was it my accent that gave me away?"

Essien looked her up and down, letting her see him do it. "Well, that's part of it. You carry yourself different too, if you don't mind me saying. You have a poise to you." This was bullshit, but it was the kind of bullshit women generally liked to hear.

This woman clearly saw right through it, but she smiled all the same. "I'm a little old for you, aren't I?" she said. "Haba! You probably need to be up early for school tomorrow."

There was no school on a Saturday, which took some of the shine off the joke, but he let it pass. "Oh, don't worry about that, dear lady. My mama isn't waiting up for me. And I could go to school tonight, if you think you've got things to teach me."

That got another laugh. Essien was doing fine here. "Let me buy you a drink at least," he suggested. He was all out of money and the invitation was nothing but bluff, but you can't win if you don't play. "You can tell me where you're from and what you're doing here in Lagos. And I'll make up something to tell you in return."

The woman took one last, long drag and breathed it out, seeming to consider. He hadn't altogether been lying: she did have a certain presence, a certain toughness or resilience. But there was something sitting right underneath that he thought looked like uncertainty or even fear. She might be even further from her home territory than he had guessed. "What's your name, schoolboy?" she asked.

"Essien. And what shall I call you, teacher?"

She dropped the butt of her cigarette and ground it out with the heel of her flat shoe. "Hadiz," she said. "Hadiz Tambuwal. I don't drink. But there's a bottle of whisky back at my place that I picked up somewhere on my travels. You're welcome to broach it."

11

Hadiz Tambuwal continued to be a puzzle. Her car was a battered red Toyota Corolla with 80K on the clock, but the sound system bore the Sony logo and it looked real. That was a significant slice of disposable income to leave by the kerbside, even down here among the clubs and the bright lights. And the coat she'd left on the back seat was leather.

Then they took a left turn onto Lawani Oguntayo Road, another at the Ijora Cause Way and Essien's spirits started to sink. "Where exactly is your place, then?" he asked Hadiz, making it sound as casual as he could.

"Apapa Quays," she said. "Wharf Road, between the barracks and the water."

"You live in Apapa?" It was hard to keep the astonishment out of his voice.

Hadiz took her eyes off the road to shoot him a cool, appraising look. "Why? Where did you think?"

He shrugged. "Charlotte Island. Maroko. I don't know."

"I needed a big space. For my work. Apapa had everything I was looking for."

Wharf Road was mile after mile of warehouses and grain silos, most of them obviously abandoned. All the heavy freight had moved to Ebute Metta as soon as the new terminal was opened there, and it had never come back. Apapa was a ghost town. There were homeless communities in some of these cavernous ruins, but even for the homeless they were a last resort. Salt, sodden air had warped their beams and rusted their corrugated iron, and they weren't all that well built to start with. You had to be all out of options to sleep in a place that might fold flat in a strong wind.

But Hadiz's destination was not on Wharf Road itself. It was on Creek, the last turn-off before the absolute desolation of the quays. They pulled in beside a building that was newer and in better repair than most of the structures out here – a three-storey tower either built in solid concrete or refaced with it when the original structure started to crumble. A dilapidated sign declared that the premises were the property of the now-defunct Nigerian Coal Corporation, which was unlikely on the face of it. A larger sign discouraged trespassers with threats of razor wire and untethered dogs.

By this time, Essien was having very definite second thoughts. This was starting to look less like a sexual hook-up and more like an ambush. There could be anyone lying in wait inside that building. Perhaps Hadiz Tambuwal was in the organ-legging trade. Or perhaps she was a witch, looking for a warm body to use in some hideous ritual involving torture and murder. He had been a fool to let her bring him here. But when he'd entered the car he'd been certain their destination was somewhere very different. He'd also been confident in his own strength and his ability to overpower the woman if she tried to drug or assault him. Now, in the arse end of nowhere, that confidence was draining rapidly.

"I know this isn't a very salubrious place," Hadiz said, as if she'd been listening in on his thoughts. "I have to be careful out here all by myself. And it may seem as though I'm putting a very great deal of trust in you, Essien. Please believe me when I say that I'm not as helpless as I look."

Weirdly, the implied threat did a lot to reassure him. It told him that she was no more comfortable with the strangeness of this situation than he was – that she didn't feel herself entirely in control of it. If she'd been a witch or a cunnywoman she would have said something to put him at his ease or raise his hopes of sex.

She made him get out of the car while she parked it in a garage at the edge of the property that looked like a reinforced bunker. Waiting on the street, he felt exposed but no longer afraid. His confusion, though, was no less than it had been. This woman dressed like a movie star but she lived in a warehouse. Was she going to be able to pay him for his sexual services or not? And did he want to go ahead with this in any case, given the remoteness of the place and the volatility of his own mood? If not, he should probably turn around and start walking. It was a long way back through Ijora to the Haartman Bridge.

"It's this way," Hadiz said, leading him around the side of the building. A narrow iron staircase enclosed behind a concrete parapet led all the way up to the third storey, where there was a door. The door was solid steel, like a bank vault. It had no keyhole and no handle; it was just a featureless slab. Hadiz put her hand into her purse. Something in there chirped like a cricket and the latch of the door released itself with an echoing clank.

"It's a mess," Hadiz said. "You'll have to forgive me." She stood aside to let him go in before her. There was only blackness inside.

For a moment as he stood there Essien's doubts came back full force. Was there someone waiting inside in the dark to rob him or overpower him? Would his body, unspeakably violated, be found floating in the lagoon three weeks from now, bloated and rotten?

When he didn't move Hadiz went in ahead of him. Immediately, the space inside was flooded with brightness.

"Come if you're coming," she called over her shoulder. "With the lights on the moths are going to be all over us!"

Essien stepped over the threshold.

It took him a few moments to process what he was seeing. The sudden transition from darkness to too much brightness was part of the problem. The rest was that instead of the low-ceilinged, cupboard-like loft space he had been imagining he was in a palace.

The room was about seventy or eighty feet square and laid out something like a Moroccan riad, with all the furniture in alcoves around the four sides. A lounge space with a sofa and a flatscreen TV. A kitchen range with fridge, hob and sink. A small gym with an exercise bike and a weight platform. A home office. A sleeping area. All of these spaces apart from the kitchen had curtains that could be drawn across. There were three more spaces where the curtains were actually closed so Essien couldn't see in. The middle of the room was empty apart from a massive Berber-style carpet that must have cost about a million neirat.

From the ceiling, which was more than twenty feet above them, dozens of lights hung down with baskets suspended in between. Flowers spilled out over the sides of the baskets, an explosion of colour that drew the eye and held it.

The woman threw down her coat and slipped off her shoes, which she kicked out of the way against the wall. "The plants are mostly to scrub the air," she said, heading for the kitchen. "Or at least that's what I tell myself. Watering them takes an age, so I need some excuse. Would whiskey be okay for you? As I said, I don't drink. I don't know how I even came by this bottle."

Whiskey would be fine, Essien assured her. While she was pouring it, he continued his exploration of the room. There were a lot of electronic devices here, a lot of remotes and things that might be remotes, a lot of sensors on the walls with numbers on them. In amongst this digital sprawl he found a single thing that was incongruously analogue – a cheap ring-bound notebook. It was open to the most recent page, on which the words "VISIT RUPSHE" were written in royal blue ink and double underlined. Essien had never met anyone called Rupshe. It sounded like a foreign name; Indian, maybe.

The woman came back into the central space carrying a water jug in one hand, a whisky glass in the other. She saw that Essien was looking in the notebook, so he brazened it out. "Who is Rupshe?" he asked. "Should I be jealous?"

Hadiz handed the whisky glass to him and he took a cautious sip. Whatever this stuff was, it went down like smoked honey. Essien nodded nonchalantly to show that it met his exacting standards.

"Rupshe is a friend," Hadiz said. "A good friend, from my old neighbourhood. I try to get back to see her a few times a week, but things have been hectic lately. That was to remind me not to let work get in the way of being a decent human being. Come. Sit with me."

She led him to the sofa, where she poured herself a glass of water. They sat together there, drinking and chatting aimlessly about this and that as though they had bumped into each other at a bus stop somewhere. As though Hadiz hadn't brought Essien to her house so he could have sex with her. It wasn't the best way of going about things, in his opinion. It muddied the waters. But it was late, and his other options were thin in the extreme. He really had no choice at this point but to ride it out.

"When did you come to Lagos?" he asked her again. Making small talk. Easing the path that led inevitably from here to the bed.

"About a year ago." The woman shook her head and laughed ruefully. "But . . . in a way I was here already. Close by, anyway. I didn't have to come very far at all. You could say I've lived in this city, or just outside it, all my life. But then . . ." The sentence tailed off, ended in another head-shake.

"What?" Essien coaxed.

"Nothing. What about you? What brought you to Lagos?"

"My parents moved here from the south-east. Things weren't good for our people down there after the civil war. Not that they were wonderful before."

"That was a terrible time," she said. "There was . . ." She stopped, frowning, seemed suddenly uncertain. "Was there a blockade? A famine?"

Her tone was oddly tentative, as if she knew the answer but was reluctant to say it out loud. The mixture of frankness and evasion threw Essien a little off-balance. He really didn't want to talk about the famine, or the surrender – still less about the trials and executions that followed, as if Biafra had starved itself out of some wilful spite and needed to be punished for it. These were things of second-hand memory, the myths his family had brought with them from the collapsed republic. Essien had no intention of rehearsing them here, in front of a woman he was about to sleep with. In bed he would be in charge of things: becoming an object of pity was not to be thought of.

"Tell me about your work," he said instead.

"My work." Hadiz Tambuwal lowered her gaze to her water glass, the rim of which she traced with one finger. "It will change everything, when I show it. For Africa, and for the world. It will be the biggest thing you ever saw. And it will be soon. Only a few last kinks and creases to iron out."

She put down the glass and extended her leg, pressing the ball of her bare foot against his calf. "Later for that, maybe," she said. "You didn't come here to interview me for *Scientific American*."

So she was a scientist. Perhaps that was why she wore no lipstick or mascara, Essien thought. Too busy thinking high-high thoughts to put a proper face on. Some women tried not to be women, which was a thing Essien disapproved of.

"Didn't I?" he asked, giving her a teasing smile. "What did I come for?"

Hadiz didn't answer, or at least not with words. She put down the glass, took his hand and led him to the bed, drawing the curtains closed behind them to shut them into the smaller space. Essien brought his own glass with him. He drained it ostentatiously as she sat and pulled him down beside her. He still hadn't mentioned money, but there was nothing to be gained by holding up proceedings now. Hadiz was already undressing.

He enjoyed the sex more than he expected to. There was a haste, almost an urgency to the woman's lovemaking, as if god was about to take her up into heaven and she wanted to be sinful one last time before she went. It excited him, even though Hadiz's preferences were straightforward and conservative.

Afterwards, as they lay together all in a sweat, she told him that it was the first time she'd done this since she arrived in Lagos.

"A year?" Essien marvelled. "A whole year without sex?"

"Longer than that. Before I came here . . . I was alone for a very long time."

Well, that explained a lot. "You want to go again?" he asked gallantly. "I'm steady for it."

Hadiz gave a full-throated laugh. "What, twice in one year? I'm not an animal." She put a hand on his chest. "You don't have to leave, though. It's a long way back into the city. If you want to stay the night you're more than welcome."

Essien made a show of mulling this idea over before he said yes, as if there were other irons in his fire, other obligations he had to take into account. He was relieved. He had staved off the worst for a night at least. Tomorrow was another day, and another fight. He went to sleep in the woman's arms, choosing to believe that he was giving comfort and not receiving it.

The next morning he woke to the smell of frying. The curtains were open and the huge loft was once again ablaze with light. Now it was streaming in from the ceiling, into which three enormous skylights had been set. The woman, wearing a mustard-yellow bathrobe, was cooking in the kitchen annexe. Essien put on his trousers and went and joined her there.

She turned and smiled at him as he sat down. "Are you hungry?" she asked.

"I believe I could eat," he admitted. Actually the smell was making his stomach clench and creak. He had eaten almost nothing for two days in a row. Hadiz set a plate down in front of him. Fried yam and some kind of sausage. As he wolfed it down she poured coffee for the two of them from a stove-top Bialetti.

"More?" she asked when he was done.

Essien nodded. She took the plate away and brought it back full. He went about the second helping at his leisure, enjoying the strangeness of all this. Being cooked for, as if the two of them were married. He had given up hope that he would get paid his proper rate, but he still felt the night had not been wasted.

"I've put out a towel," the woman said. "If you want to use the shower."

That felt like the biggest luxury of all, and Essien made the most of it. When he came out, he found the woman already dressed. She held out her hand towards him, a sheaf of currency notes between her first and second fingers.

Essien took them and counted them. It was rude, but he wanted very much to know what the total was. It was twenty-one thousand naira.

"Is that enough?" Hadiz asked. "The odd thousand is for an *okada*. I know you'll have to walk back up to Ijora to find one, but it's better than going all the way into the city on foot."

Essien gave her a bow. "My teacher is kind," he said, at which she laughed out loud.

"I have to go downstairs and work," she said. "Thank you for a very pleasant evening. I hope you don't mind letting yourself out. Take all your things, because the door locks when it closes."

She kissed him on the cheek and departed.

This left Essien in something of a quandary. He pondered it as he dressed. There were many things in this room that he could turn into ready money. He would be limited to what he could carry, but even so he could certainly turn a good profit.

Or he could take a gamble and play a longer game.

He found paper and a pencil and wrote a note for Hadiz Tambuwal. He thanked her for the lesson, and promised to do his homework ahead of any further meetings. He left her his phone number.

Good name is better than silver and gold, his father (who had neither) used to say. Essien had shown the woman he could be trusted. The next time she got to feeling the urge, perhaps she would remember him and reach out.

In the meantime, with twenty thousand naira in his pocket, he could sleep under a roof tonight. And charge up his phone.

12

Hadiz didn't call Essien that week, or the next.

He could have taken other clients very easily. Just settled back into the ashewo lifestyle, with that twenty thousand stake to buffer him. Instead, he rented the cheapest room he could find and took a job as a general handyman at a church in Ketu; the work was mostly sweeping, scrubbing the front steps and chivvying homeless people out of the graveyard. The church warden had no idea of Essien's other calling, which gave Essien some sour amusement. Jesus walked among whores, after all. A return visit was only polite.

When Hadiz finally called, he was scrubbing graffiti (a spray-painted cock and balls in neon-glow pink) off the gravestone of DEACON ANTONY NWEZE, REMEMBERED ALWAYS. He played it very cool.

"You left your number," Hadiz said. "I took that to mean you enjoyed yourself. Would you like to come over again? Have a drink, and maybe dinner?"

"When?"

"Saturday. If you're free."

"You'd want me for an hour or for the whole night?"

"Haba! Are those the only options? The whole night, then. If that's okay."

"Give me a moment." Essien folded his arms, pressing the phone into the crook of his elbow, and looked out across the rows of mossy, tilted tombstones. He gave it a slow count of five before he raised the phone to his mouth again. "Okay. I can make that work. I'll come at eight o'clock."

"Lovely. I'll see you then. Thank you for fitting me in."

Essien arrived to find the table set and Hadiz cooking. There was red wine already open but she handed him a glass of kunu aya to start the proceedings. He was false-footed. He wasn't sure how much he liked this pretence that he and this woman had a relationship. Muddying the waters again. Hadiz Tambuwal was as old as his mother and he was only here because she could afford to pay him. Why should they act out parts?

"It's beans porridge," she said, bringing a steaming casserole dish to the table. "I hope you're hungry." Essien was, always, and the food was good. Not just the stew but the plantain she'd cooked with it and the garri she served alongside. He tried to look unimpressed as he ate, feeling that any show of enthusiasm would put him at a disadvantage. He was here because of his prowess between the sheets, for which he would be paid. Anything else the woman offered he would take as his due.

For dessert there were coconut balls and puff-puffs, which they ate out of a box bearing the logo of the Loaf Lane Bakery. Then Hadiz suggested that they watch a movie. She had satellite TV, both ROK and Nollywood Home Cinema, and she was happy for him to choose.

Essien realised for the first time something that should perhaps have been obvious – that he was not there merely to satisfy Hadiz's sexual itch. She wanted his company, and it said a lot about her that she had chosen this roundabout way of easing her loneliness. There were a hundred easier – and safer – ways of obtaining companionship, for anyone with normal social skills and no obvious physical deformities. Twice as many if you had money, as Hadiz obviously did.

"You didn't feel like going to a club this evening?" he asked her.

"Most of the time I prefer a quiet night in."

She said it lightly, but there was a brittleness hiding behind the words. Essien had a flash of insight. She didn't come into the city more than she could help. Need had drawn her there on the night they'd met, but if she could bring a sexual partner to her without stirring from this loft she would do it. She was afraid, for some reason, or unsure of herself, at the very least, and unwilling to risk herself to Lagos's surging human tides.

"A quiet night in Apapa Quays," he joked.

"I like Apapa Quays."

"For what, o?"

"For the privacy. And the space. I bought this place and the place next door for seventy million naira. What would that buy me on Victoria – I mean on Charlotte Island?"

The place next door? Next door was an empty plot, an expanse of waist-high weeds and ancient garbage. But when Essien asked her what she meant she shushed him with a kiss and told him to choose a movie. She sounded playful but looked serious. Clearly, he'd touched on something she didn't want to discuss.

He chose a movie. It was *The Destroyer*, which he clicked on as soon as he saw Schwarzenegger's name. There were almost no new movies coming out of America since the union fell apart and Texas started a border war with California, but you could always rely on the classics.

Essien watched the epic sci-fi with huge pleasure. Kyle Rees got the girl, and that was well and good, but Essien identified with the unstoppable Alois, the Destroyer himself. That was what a man was meant to be – walking over or through anything that came against him, not even varying his pace to crush his enemies.

The bedroom side of things was more sedate than the first time. Some of the edge had been filed off Hadiz's need, or perhaps it had been satisfied in other ways. Sex was rarely just sex, for women. There was always some other nonsense going on.

In the morning, again, a cooked breakfast and twenty-one thousand naira.

And all of this now became their regular routine. Once a week, sometimes twice. Hadiz always had a meal ready for him and always allowed him to decide what movie or TV show they watched

afterwards. The rest of the *Destroyer* franchise. *Kull the Barbarian.*
The Expendables. Ong-Bak. Nick Fury and the Avengers. Mega-City
Judge. He had no idea whether Hadiz enjoyed his choices. Sometimes
she seemed to get confused about things he thought everyone knew
– the names of actors and directors, the secret identities of super-
heroes, the order of the movies in George Lucas's *Space Empire* trilogy
– but she seemed to enjoy the experience of sitting with him and
watching – as if human company was a novelty in itself.

Sometimes she rebuked herself for using his body. "It's wrong. I
know it's wrong. But I'm very bad at meeting people. At relationships. This is easier. Forgive me."

Essien assured her he did. He liked that this didn't come easy to
her. Somehow that made it easier for him, or at least made him feel
that the compromised dignity that came with purchased sex was
shared between the two of them, instead of being something that
was shoved into his hands along with the money. Very much to his
own surprise he even confided in her, telling her things about his
past life that he had never intended to tell anyone. The slaughter
yard. The landfill. Diallo. When he described his months of slavery
in the basements under Damola Ojo he came close to crying.

"I can't imagine what that was like," Hadiz said, pulling his head
down onto her chest as if she was his mother and he was a child
to be comforted. Ridiculous! But he *was* comforted. And he realised
that it was a thing his own mother had never done for him. Nobody.
Nobody had. The sheer strangeness of it kept him from feeling
ashamed or belittled.

Sometimes Hadiz talked about her work – about how important
it was, and how it was going to change everything. "This world is
in such a bad state," she said. "But it can be fixed."

"I'm not so sure about that," Essien said. The words slipped out.
He usually just let her ramble on when she was in the mood to.

"Oh yes," Hadiz insisted. "So many of the big problems you're
facing – the resource wars between Russia and Europe, the collapse
of the American union, China's annexation of Japan – are because

there are limits to things. Because you're living in a pressure cooker and the heat just keeps on being turned up and turned up. But I can take all that pressure away."

This was a conversation in her bed, after sex. Her guard was down and she was at her most talkative. Her eyes were shining with some passion he didn't understand and couldn't be bothered to unpick. He was half asleep in any case, and eager to make the half be a whole.

"Dreams no dey hurt," he murmured.

"You think I'm lying?"

"No," Essien said, angry with himself that he'd lapsed into pidgin. "But nobody can make the world better all at once like that, Hadiz. There are too many things to be fixed."

She put her hand on his cheek. "You almost never use my name," she said.

It was true. He had discovered the power that lives in names when he was still a child. If someone calls you by your name and you don't give them theirs, a power remains with you. It was one little ploy among many that he used with his tricks to convince himself that his surrender was never total. But sometimes he forgot that Hadiz was a trick.

He ended the conversation by pretending to be asleep, and soon afterwards fell asleep for real. Normally, he slept well in Hadiz's bed, but that night his dreams were troubled and his sleep was shallow. After what seemed like a dozen fitful awakenings, he felt her hand tapping on his shoulder and opened his eyes to find her fully dressed. It was morning, with hard sunlight stabbing through the curtains.

"Get your clothes on," Hadiz said. "I want to show you something."

Essien groaned and rolled over on his side. "I'm tired. I didn't sleep. Let me rest another hour before I go."

"No. Now. Come, Essien. Put your clothes on and come with me. You'll like this."

He dressed, sullen and unwilling. She didn't even offer him breakfast. She took his hand and led him out of the loft, down the stairs to ground level. There was a roll-over door there, with an enormous padlock holding it shut. Hadiz touched her hand to the padlock and it clicked open. When she removed it, the door rolled up and back of its own accord – and as with the loft, the lights came on without her touching a switch.

Inside there was a single vast space full of complicated machinery. Essien only had one reference point for something like this – the Makoko sawmill – so he assumed at once this was some kind of factory. But he couldn't even begin to guess what it was making. At Makoko there were racks of planed wood wherever you looked, with forklifts tacking between them to take away the finished planks when they were ready to be sold. Here there were just machines. And at the back of the room, arranged on a kind of tiered platform, dozens and dozens of tiny helicopters decorated with black and yellow stripes. They looked like toys to Essien, but very expensive toys.

"Is all this yours?" he asked Hadiz, marvelling. If it was then she was richer than he had thought and he was an idiot for not squeezing more profit out of their relationship than he had. Twenty thousand naira was all well and good, but if Hadiz owned her own business then why was he still sweeping floors? She could afford to set him up in an apartment somewhere and keep him on retainer.

"Yes, it's mine. Come over here."

She crossed to a rack on which a dozen or so metal bracelets were hanging. Each one was a ring of dull silver about three inches wide, with a hinged clasp. Hadiz took one down and turned it in her hand to where an LED glowed bright green in the centre of an inset button. Satisfied, she slid the bracelet onto her wrist and folded the clasp across. It closed with a loud click.

From a shelf above the rack she took down something that was like a short stake painted a shiny metallic red. One end of the stake tapered to a point that looked as though it meant business. At the other end, the last few inches were clear glass. It was as though someone had decided to combine a tent peg with a torch.

"Okay," Hadiz said, smiling at Essien. "We're all kitted out. This way now."

In the centre of the floor, next to a gigantic and complex mechanism, there was a circular metal platform raised about three inches off the ground. Hadiz stepped up onto it and beckoned for Essien to join her. He did. She took his arms and placed them on her hips. "Keep your arms and legs inside the ride at all times," she said. "And don't be frightened."

"Why would I be frightened?"

"I was, the first time. And the second, the third, the fourth . . . . Every time, in fact. It takes some getting used to. Activate."

Her suddenly raised voice indicated that the last word was not spoken to him. The great machine stirred to life, humming on a rising pitch like the lift in an apartment building when it starts to go up. There was a thud of some geared engine shifting into a new configuration, and then . . .

Bright sunlight poured in on them from all sides, but a cooling wind nudged at them too. They were not in the warehouse any more. They were on an empty beach that stretched in all directions as far as the eye could see. The air smelled of salt spray, ripe fruit and something like musk.

Essien's legs felt weak for a moment. He staggered and almost fell. He understood at once what had happened – that they had been transported, instantaneously, to another place. It was not that his mind was too weak to accept it. But there was an effort involved in the acceptance, a draining away of energy. For a moment he was numb and unmanned.

Hadiz knelt and drove the red stake into the sand, rotating her wrist to push it in deep. When she was done with that she got to her feet again and put a reassuring hand on Essien's shoulder.

"Where—" he began. But the word came out wrong. The tone was high enough to suggest that he was afraid. He tried again. "Where are we?"

"You're home," Hadiz reassured him. "Essien, this is where you live. This is Lagos."

13

They sat side by side on the sand under a sky of tattered cirrus and fierce blue. Creatures that were like feral ginger cats with bat-like tucks of black leather under their forelimbs scampered and fought over green fruits in a tree above their head. The tree had the barrel-shaped trunk and many-elbowed branches of a baobab, but the fruit looked like jackalberries.

Just under the surface of the water, something very big with mottled grey skin was basking. It was not a whale, just as the things zigzagging across the sky were not birds.

Hadiz laid it out for Essien, in clear and simple words. She had found a way to jump between worlds, but all the worlds were the same world. Earth.

"Terr," Essien corrected her.

"Where you come from, yes, it's called Terr. But to me it's Earth. And on this world it isn't either one, because there's nobody to name it. By the same token this isn't Apapa Quays, and that water out there isn't the Lagos Lagoon. We can call it whatever we want. Would you like to be the first one to name it?"

"No. Thank you." She was trying to be playful, to allay his fears and perhaps to make him see the wonder of this. But he saw it, and he wasn't afraid. He was in a kind of shock. It was as if a giant door had opened on his whole life, letting him see that he had been all this time inside a dark cupboard. Or else it was like a trick of perspective that showed things he had always thought of as huge to be tiny, dwarfed by new and unsuspected immensities. "Tell me what you've seen," he begged her.

And Hadiz did. Exploration wasn't the point of this, she insisted. Not yet, at any rate. The important thing was to perfect the machine, the transfer mechanism, so that it was fit for purpose when she gave it to the world.

"To which world, though?"

"Well, I'll start with yours, because that's where I'm living now."

"Not your own?"

The question seemed to cause her some pain. She looked away, and was silent for a moment. The cat-creatures mewed and hissed over their heads. The shining in Hadiz's eyes was tears, Essien realised. "It's too late for my world. My world is dead. The night I met you . . . I was holding a kind of one-woman wake. I can't stop thinking about how things might have gone if I'd been quicker. If I'd started this work ten years or even five years earlier. Billions of people might still be alive. I could have made a difference. Maybe all the difference that was needed."

With a wave of his hand Essien indicated the vast expanse of beach, the clear sky and the clear water. "You think summer holidays can fix the world?"

Hadiz looked him in the eye. The tears were mostly gone. "This world has a lot more to offer than a day at the beach, Essien. What *is* a planet? What's it made of? What are you sitting on right now?"

"Sand."

"And under the sand?"

"I don't know. Rocks."

Hadiz nodded. "And the rocks of this place – this untouched Nigeria – they're the riches of a whole continent! Dig down here. You wouldn't even need to dig all that far. You'd find gold, iron, diamond, gypsum, rare earth minerals, kaolinitic clay. Oil, of course, and bitumen. Lead and zinc. Baryte. Nobody has ever sunk a mine here. Nobody has so much as turned the soil.

"Even this sand we're sitting on is priceless. It's perfect for aggregate – for cement. Did you realise that Africa has a sand crisis? You're using millions of tons of the stuff every year for construction alone, and there's a finite supply."

She pointed out across the lagoon.

"And over to the east, the Middle Belt. A hundred million hectares of arable land that nobody is farming. The Nigeria in my world was a net importer of rice and wheat. Yours will be too before long. But imagine if you had access to all this. Open up a single uninhabited Earth and you double everything at a stroke. No more famine. No more resource wars. No more overpopulation, either. You could offer the new territories for settlement on any terms you chose. I have a very smart friend – Rupshe – who ran the numbers for me. The only limiting factor is the size and number of transport plates we can build in a given time. And that stops being a limit as soon as the first mining operations get started. It's self-sustaining, a cascade. Everything that's needed to save the world is right in front of you."

Essien felt a need to puncture her self-assurance. "Fine," he said, "this place has good stuff you can dig up and sell. But what about wild animals? What about diseases? You don't know what could be here."

Hadiz only smiled. "Have you ever known those things to stop the human race in its tracks for long? In fact, yes, there's a definite risk and I wouldn't want to discount it. But our understanding of how diseases work is so much better now than it was even ten or twenty years ago. And it's the same risk you're already running when the press of people and the hunger for resources forces you into ever more remote areas of your own world. And as for wild animals . . . well, look at those things up there."

She nodded her head to indicate the cat-creatures. Most of them were still squabbling and fussing and feeding, but a few had noticed the two newcomers sitting under their tree and had clustered on one of the lower branches to watch them. They had orange eyes, whose lids slid sideways when they blinked. They also had claws that were long enough and sharp enough to be concerning.

"What about them?" Essien asked uneasily.

"We're the first humans they've ever seen, or smelled. They don't have any reference point for us at all. We're not food. We're not danger. We're not a competitor, or a potential mate. There just isn't a niche for us here. We're a puzzle with no solution."

"Suppose they decide to get a clue to the puzzle by coming down here and taking a bite out of us?"

"Then I would have to dissuade them, which I'm well equipped to do. But I promise you they won't. I've visited a lot of different worlds, Essien, and this is one of the safest. I wouldn't have brought you unless I was sure there was nothing here that would hurt you."

She stood up and held out her hand. "We'd better be getting back," she said. "I just wanted you to see. The work is important to me, and so are you. It didn't feel fair to lock you out of it."

He refused the hand, standing up unaided. All of this – the place, the explanation, the scope of Hadiz's achievement – had left him feeling diminished.

He followed her across the beach back to the red stake, which was just where they had left it and hadn't been touched. "What is that for?" Essien asked, as Hadiz bent down and pulled it free.

"It's a beacon. Just to make sure that when we go home again we materialise in the right place, on the induction plate in my lab. It would be a shame to appear on a road, with a truck bearing down on us, or halfway through a wall."

She held out her hand again. "We have to be touching," she explained, "when I activate the modulator – the thing that takes us back." She indicated the silver bracelet with a dip of her eyes. "There's a field effect, and it propagates by direct induction. This is the last bus home."

Essien gave her his hand at last. She kept tight hold on it as she pressed and held the button on the bracelet for a second, then two, then three. Just as he felt a fizz of panic starting to climb up from his stomach they were back in the lab, as suddenly and silently as they had left it.

While Hadiz returned the bracelet and the beacon stake to their places, he looked around the room. "All of this," he said. "It must have cost millions. Dollars, not naira."

"Research grants," she said over her shoulder. But Essien knew a lie when he heard one.

14

Back up in the loft, Hadiz made the two of them breakfast as if nothing at all had happened. Essien sat and watched her in silence for a little while. The words that came into his mind felt so small in relation to what he had seen that they were ridiculous. They evaporated from his mind before he could get them out.

Hadiz set the food on the table. She sat down opposite him and began to eat. She looked at him nervously.

"It's a lot to take in," she said. "I'm sorry. I wanted to surprise you, but I should have prepared you more. Essien, you mustn't tell anyone what you've seen. I'm not ready yet to make a public announcement."

"I won't tell."

"You understand? People will want to steal the QEI drive. Control it, and use it only for their own benefit. I can't let that happen. It has to belong to everyone, and be used for everyone's good."

"I said I won't tell. I'm not any talkative."

"Okay. Thank you." She reached out to squeeze his shoulder. "I'm sorry I sprang this on you so suddenly. I've lived with it now for long enough that I take most of it for granted. That doesn't stop it from being a miracle."

Something she had said on the beach came back to him, as if it had been repeating itself all the while in his mind and he had only just heard it. "You said that wasn't the only other world. How many?"

Tambuwal put down her fork. "How many have I seen," she asked, "or how many are there?"

"Either."

"I can answer the first question. I've only physically been to seven, counting my own and yours, but I've explored thousands remotely. As to how many there are, well . . ." Hadiz thought for a little while. "How many numbers are there between one and two?" she asked.

"None."

"What about 1.1? 1.2?"

"All right. I understand." Essien was brusque. Tricks like that weren't clever, in his opinion.

"No you don't, because I haven't explained yet. How many numbers between 1 and 1.1? The answer is that there's an infinite number: 1.11, 1.111, 1.1111 and so on. For any two numbers you choose there's always an infinity in between them. And that's true for any two worlds you choose. The map of reality is what on my world was called a Mandelbrot set − a mathematical diagram that repeats itself on every scale, the way frost flowers on a cold day repeat themselves."

She showed him a picture on her laptop. He didn't see how it illustrated her point. It was just a big shadow like a black gourd with light playing around its edges. In the lighter part, complicated shapes wove around each other − and it was true that there were patterns in the shapes, but they didn't seem to represent anything that Essien could understand.

"Infinite worlds," Hadiz said. "All of them infinitely far apart, or infinitely close together. All you can do is look for the pattern. If you do that, you can predict − at least up to a point − where you'll find a world that has people on it. Where the people will be most . . ." She faltered and he looked up from the laptop's screen. "Most like the ones you left behind," she said. "That was why I didn't know all the details of your civil war. I couldn't be sure without checking whether that was one of the points of divergence between your world and mine."

A connection closed in Essien's mind. "Is that why you moved here?" he asked her. There at last was something he could grab hold of, something that was comprehensible. "Your planet had a . . . a war or something?"

"Wars, plural. And other kinds of collapse. All kinds of terrible things, all coming together."

"So you needed a new home."

"But that isn't the part that matters!" Hadiz was impatient, and the edge in her voice surprised him. Normally, she seemed to take care to have no edges at all. "Yes, I looked for a place where I could be comfortable while I worked. That meant a place where the people looked enough like me that I could fit in. And where they had built a city around this lagoon and the river delta. A place where there were some familiar things in among the strange ones. Languages and customs that I could make sense of. You have no idea how strange some of the other worlds are."

She was right. He had no idea. He was still trying to process what he'd just seen. "How?" he asked. "How are they strange?"

"In a million different ways. You think of your own world as the standard of normality, the benchmark, but anything that can possibly happen is normal somewhere." She circled the diagram with a fingertip. "The darker parts are clusters of probability – patterns that recur, and that you can search for. On your world and mine the European powers colonised the rest of the world and controlled it for centuries, but you'd be surprised how rarely that happens. On billions and billions of Earths, civilisation spread northward from Africa and Africa remained the hub. The fulcrum of power and culture. That's just one of the most obvious patterns, but it illustrates how malleable history is. How little of what we know is inevitable or even . . ."

She stopped again and shook her head. "I already told you that's not important. I don't know why I'm talking about it. The thing that matters is the QEI field. Teleportation between universes. Do you see now why I said that all the problems of the world could be fixed?"

"Oh yes," Essien said. "I see, Hadiz. Of course. Thank you for showing me."

He said it to make her stop talking. He really didn't need to hear any more. He had already decided what he would do. He was going to steal all this from Hadiz Tambuwal and make it his own.

To hell with the rest of the world. He was going to be rich.

15

Essien believed that a plan had the best chance of succeeding if it was kept as simple as possible. All he needed to do was to persuade Hadiz to go to another world with him again, wrest control of the bracelet from her and come back alone – leaving her unharmed but stranded. He didn't want to hurt her, only to move her out of his way.

Then, in due course, he would borrow or steal a camera, demonstrate her machine in a YouTube video and find a buyer for it. With so few moving parts there was not much that could go wrong.

He was wary, though. The idea of using the machine again needed to come from her rather than him. If he begged her for another joyride, a picnic or a walk along that endless beach, Hadiz might suspect his motives. Better to build up to it gradually, and nudge her into place without her even noticing.

He displayed a great curiosity about her invention, asking endless questions about how it worked. His interest wasn't faked: he would need to be able to operate the machine once she was gone, so the more he knew the better. And Hadiz was only too happy to talk. It seemed that the secret had been burning a hole in her all this time. That was why she had been so reckless as to show this precious, amazing thing to an ashewo she met at a bar!

She talked Essien through the science, which flowed over him like water. The 1 and 1.1 and 1.11 of it didn't matter so long as he could make the machine work. So he pulled her back, as often and as casually as he could, to its controls and its operation. He talked about helping his father in his garage, a thing he had only ever done when he was forced to, and pretended a great enthusiasm for engines. He wished aloud that he could go under the hood of the great machine and tinker with it.

"You'd kill yourself!" Hadiz laughed. "You'd probably end up with your head in one universe and the rest of you in another." But she showed him anyway – the particle loom, the induction matrix, the valence window – and with naive questions he rolled her the way a beetle rolls a shit-ball, from the guts of the machine to its interface, its controls. What does this switch do, and this slider? And this setting is the beach world we went to? And this one is your Earth? Wonderful, o!

All of this took longer than he would have liked because he was still only seeing Hadiz once or at most twice a week. When she needed his company, or his professional services, she would call him. The rest of the time he worked at the church, kept his head down, and thought about what he would do when he had a million dollars in his pocket. Lagos would never see him again, that was for sure. He would live in New Amsterdam and drive a car that was too fat to fit on the street. A Hummer EV. If it was good enough for LeBron James, it would probably be just about good enough for Essien Nkanika.

When he felt he was ready, he made his move. He bought two tickets from Lagos Iddo to Atican Beach. They cost him a week's wages, but they were essential props and the insane largesse would only add to their effectiveness. The next Saturday, when Hadiz called and invited him to come for dinner, he brought the tickets with him.

"I've been thinking I could take you away somewhere," he told her, putting the tickets down beside his empty plate. "Look. I saved up my money and bought these."

"Atican Beach," Hadiz read. "I don't know where that is."

"Lekki. At the eastern end of the lagoon." He paused, making a show of hesitation or shyness. "It's been in my mind since I saw the beach in that other place, so quiet and so beautiful. Atican will be crowded, but we can walk along the shore towards Iaputu. If we go far enough, I think we'll be able to find a spot where we can be by ourselves."

Hadiz covered his hand with her own. "Is that what you want?" she asked him.

Essien shrugged, but not dismissively. He shrugged as if he was shifting a weight. "I think about it sometimes. That place. How different it was there. In Lagos you don't find that kind of quietness. That kind of peace. It doesn't exist here."

"Would you like to go back there?"

He opened his eyes wide. "Oh!" he said. Perhaps he overdid the surprise because Hadiz laughed. He shook his head earnestly. "I don't think that would be a good use of your machine. You've told me what you mean to do with it. How important it is. I wouldn't want to pull you away from that great work, or slow it down."

"It's true that I almost never go back to any world more than once," Hadiz said. "Most of my surveying is done remotely, with the drones you saw. If I need to take soil or mineral samples, I get in and out quickly. I don't want to disturb the ecosystems any more than I have to. But I do like the sunsets on that world. I've dropped in there four or five times already, not counting the time I went with you. One more won't hurt."

"If you're sure, Hadiz."

"Of course. Let's do it next week. I'll make sandwiches and put some wine in a cooler. It will be lovely."

But that wouldn't do at all, Essien decided. Not now that he was this close. He didn't want to wait a week, or give Hadiz that long to think up reasons to change her mind. He turned his hand over to clasp hers. "I wouldn't need food, or wine," he said. "I just want to walk with you there."

Hadiz looked puzzled or perplexed for a moment, but then she smiled. "So romantic! And so not like you. I should probably cultivate this side of your nature. All right, let's do it. Let's go right now."

She put on a jacket and picked up her handbag. Seeing his look, she ducked her head, pantomiming shame. "Even on an alien world, a woman always likes to have a few little necessaries by her."

Essien followed her down the outside stairs, exulting and terrified. Exulting because he had managed this so easily; terrified because of the enormity of what he was about to do. He would try his best not to hurt Hadiz, but he knew her well enough to be sure she would put up a fight. And if she fought, that would not go well for her.

In what he thought of as the factory, she fired up the machine. Then she moved towards the rack where the bracelets hung, but Essien got there first. "Like this?" he asked innocently, slipping one of the bracelets around his own wrist.

"Let me check," Hadiz said. She rotated the bracelet a little, tugged on it and then gave it a small pat. "Yes, that's fine." She reached past him to pick up one of the beacons. She threw it end over end and caught it deftly, tapping it into the palm of her other hand. "Okay, lover boy. Get over there."

Essien walked before her to the plate and stepped up onto it. So easy! He was a little ashamed that Hadiz trusted him this much. But in all fairness he hadn't ever done much to hide himself from her. It was in her nature to put herself in others' power, he decided. People chose their own lives, and their own endings.

"Say the word," she invited him, but he had forgotten it. She had to whisper it in his ear so he could repeat it.

"Activate."

The machine did nothing.

"Stupid," Hadiz said, shaking her head. "I'm sorry, Essien. The system is set to respond to my voice. It doesn't recognise you. Activate."

They were suddenly on the beach again. The sun was much lower than the last time and the light was different. Their shadows sprawled in front of them, twenty yards across the white sand.

"Shall we walk?" Hadiz asked.

Without waiting for an answer, she set off at an easy pace, hands clasped behind her back, the incongruous handbag bumping against her hip.

Essien cursed inwardly as he followed her. The voice activation was a problem. He could still get back again just by pressing the button on the bracelet, but it wouldn't be possible for him to do that YouTube video after all. Not unless he could get someone with tech savvy to overhaul the machine and make it answer to him. Would that be easy or hard? Would the ajebo technician expect a share of the proceeds afterwards? Should he put this off, and try to persuade Hadiz to add his voice to her system?

No, he decided. They were here now. He had to see it through. Otherwise everything would have to be done all over again from the start, and who was to say that she would be this pliable a second time?

Hadiz glanced over her shoulder to see that he was still with her. "We can sit here," she said, pointing to a flat rock at the water's edge. But when she reached it she didn't sit. She climbed up on top of it instead and stared out across the lagoon. Essien came up behind her. He looked up at her standing there, oblivious, and felt an unaccustomed stab of doubt – an intimation that this might be something he would have second thoughts about, once second thoughts were irrelevant.

But he would be a rich man by then, he told himself. Most rich men had much worse things on their conscience. He wasn't killing Hadiz. He wasn't even hurting her, just leaving her to fend for herself here. And he knew how very clever she was. If anyone had a chance of doing well in this place it would be her.

"I told you the sunsets here were wonderful," Hadiz said. "Come, Essien. Come sit with me. You're missing the best part." She made a beckoning motion without turning around.

Essien stayed where he was. He raised the bracelet and positioned his thumb over the button. "Hadiz," he said, his voice a little thick. He had never consciously considered what it was he felt for her until now – and now was a great deal too late. "Hadiz, I'm grateful for all you've given me."

"Don't be silly. And don't talk as if we're splitting up. Come over here, please."

Essien pressed the button. It went home with a decisive click.

But nothing else happened. He was still on the beach, under the slanting light of the orange, setting sun. He tried again, and then a few more times in a quick staccato, beating out an urgent and accidental rhythm. Nothing.

"Oh, Essien."

He looked up. Hadiz had turned to face him. She had rolled up her left sleeve to reveal a second bracelet identical to the one on his wrist. In her right hand, she held a stubby device like a toy gun with a squared-off end instead of a round barrel. Essien knew it for what it was, a taser. He had seen enough of them strapped to policemen's belts.

"I'm really fond of you," Hadiz said. "And I'm rusty when it comes to relationships, so I was a little blinded. Pleasantly so, to be honest. But I'm not an idiot, and you were very obvious. This here—" her gaze flicked to the bracelet on her own wrist, then back to him "—is what's going to get us home. I deactivated your modulator when I pretended to check it."

A churning wave of anger passed through Essien, almost strong enough to drop him to his knees. Obvious? *Obvious?* The thought that Hadiz had seen through him – and outmanoeuvred him – was almost unbearable. He had been in her power when he thought she was in his. The whole time he had been regretting the need for this, indulging a sorrow at losing her, she had been taking the taser out of her bag and waiting for him to betray himself. "You . . . you tricked me!" he said, and the words seemed to burn his throat.

"No." Hadiz shook her head. "I gave you every chance to change your mind. And I hoped you would. Honestly, I did. I wanted to believe you had too much decency to do something so vile. Even while I watched you setting me up. No more talk now. Throw the bracelet down and step away from it."

"Come and get it," Essien suggested.

Hadiz rolled her eyes. "Well, I could do that very easily once I've put fifty thousand volts through you. It's probably better if you just drop it and let me pick it up."

"And leave me trapped here!" Essien spat. The fury that filled him was pushing him towards something desperate. Most of it was shame and frustration with an overlay of hurt pride, but that didn't make it any less real. He tried to calm himself, but his head felt like it was full of buzzing wasps.

"That was *your* plan," Hadiz reminded him. "It's not mine. I'll take us both back. But you're going to be wearing these." She dipped her hand into her bag without taking her eyes off him. When she withdrew it again she was holding a pair of handcuffs, which she tossed down in the sand at his feet.

"Come on," she coaxed him. "Put them on and let's go home."

Instead he took a step towards her. His hands clenched themselves into fists without his willing it. He had no idea what he was about to do, he only knew that he was not going to accept this insult. He had been tricked and disrespected. He refused to collaborate in his own defeat.

"Essien!" Hadiz said. "Please don't make me do this." She backed away, putting the rock between them. That was promising. She was afraid of him, even though she had a weapon and he didn't.

"Give me the taser," he ordered her, holding out his hand.

"Don't be ridiculous."

"Give it to me!" Essien set his foot on the rock. He could reach her in three strides. It was worth the risk. The worst that would happen was that she would put him on his back, and that would still leave him—

The air thickened, then cleared again. Two strange figures were suddenly standing beside them. They were like robots, covered all over in blood-red metal, and they were impossibly tall. They had no faces: the front of their helmets was a gleaming featureless blank. One stood slightly back from the other as if deferring to it, and carried a massively thick, open-ended cylinder of gleaming silver. Clearly the cylinder was a weapon, but you couldn't call it a gun. It was more like a cannon. The one in front held its arms down at its sides, its hands seemingly empty.

It spoke – a single short word. The voice sounded human – female – but it was no language Essien had ever heard.

Hadiz had her back to the newcomers, but she heard that barked word. She turned in surprise to see who had spoken, in a place where the two of them should have been entirely alone.

Afterwards, Essien wondered if there was anything he could have done to stop what happened next. If he had held up his hands in surrender. If he had tackled Hadiz to the ground before she moved.

But he only stared as she turned, with the taser still raised in her hand. One of the red figures – the one who had spoken, the woman – moved so quickly it seemed like a kind of magic. She raised her empty hand and pointed at Hadiz.

There was no sound, only a flash of light and a ripple of hot air that threw sand in Essien's eyes as it went by him.

Hadiz fell without a sound. There was a perfectly circular hole in the centre of her back, about the size of a two-naira coin. The fabric of her shirt, around the edges of the black dot, was lightly aflame. Her eyes were wide.

Essien screamed – a wordless wail of anguish and loss and denial. He ran to protect her now that it was too late, throwing himself between her and the two red giants. She was still alive. Her hand groped at his ankle and tried to grab on to it, but her fingers didn't find any purchase. Her gaze was fixed on him, her face full of pain and shock. Her mouth was moving but no sound came out.

The giant with the cannon turned to the other one and spoke to her – a man's voice this time, raised in surprise or maybe reproach.

She didn't reply, but she made an open-handed gesture that seemed to Essien to mean *this isn't on me*.

Hadiz rolled onto her stomach. She lay still. The red giants exchanged a few more words, then turned back to Essien and Hadiz and strode forward. They bent down to pick up Hadiz's body.

"You don't fucking touch her!" Essien yelled. He interposed himself. It would have been an empty gesture in any case, but even as he moved Hadiz disappeared. Between one breath and the next, her body was gone from the sand. There wasn't even a bloodstain to show where she'd been. She must have fallen on the bracelet and activated it, but Essien couldn't convince himself that it would make any difference. There was no surviving a wound like that.

All the same, he was gratified when the two red giants performed a dumb show of astonishment and dismay. Bending down, he snatched up the taser and fired. Its two wires hit the giant with the cannon squarely in the middle of his armour's opaque faceplate, but glanced off again without even leaving a mark.

"That got tang for you?" Essien shouted. "You like it? Stay there, I come give you the rest." He stepped up and swung wildly, punching the empty-handed giant – the one who had shot Hadiz – somewhere high up on her chest. It was like hitting a wall. He staggered back again, cradling his broken knuckles.

The other giant lowered his rifle, calmly and without undue haste, transferring it from a two-handed grip to his right hand only. He balled his left fist.

Essien didn't feel the blow, or even see it.

16

In a room with bare steel bulkhead walls, Essien hung suspended a few feet off the ground by some mechanism he couldn't understand. A blurred figure mostly outside his field of vision jabbed him in the side of the head. An injection, he guessed, because it stung at first and then felt cold.

A man stood in front of him, hands clasped behind his back. There was something wrong with the man's face. His eyes were too far apart, his wide nose furrowed as if it was made of something that had been soft once and then had congealed while someone was pressing on it. He had a beard that encroached so far onto his cheeks it was as though most of his face was covered in orange fur.

The man spoke to Essien, or at least made noises at him. The noises were short, harsh; barks and growls and yowps expressive of anger and threat and not much else. The man flexed his very mobile lips whenever he fell silent, baring teeth that were long and pointed. Essien had met a man from Congo-Kinshasa once, who had filed his teeth in what he claimed was an ancestral tradition. These teeth were even narrower and sharper. The tongue that flicked out between them from time to time was sharp too, its tip a red V.

Something strange happened to Essien while the man talked. The sounds began to line themselves up in his mind, clustering together like bubbles in a glass of beer. The clusters seemed right somehow, more meaningful. Then he began to see what the meanings might be. How *iba* might be a sensible word for *who*, and *co* could be *are*, and *ne* could be . . . no, had to be *you*.

"He's aligned," a voice said, from off to the side where Essien couldn't see.

"Good," said the man with the crumpled nose. "Then please, let's make a start. The sooner we can be done with this, the better."

The room lights were dimmed. A hemisphere of milky-white glass about four feet in diameter lowered itself smoothly into place over Essien's head and shoulders. On its inner face, multicoloured lights flared and flowed and morphed and faded.

The questions started then – and somehow they were made of light as well as sound. Each word blossomed on the white glass screen as a pattern of brilliant hues, so bright that it hurt to look at them. But he couldn't look away: his head wouldn't move when he tried to turn it, and his eyelids wouldn't close.

"Who are you? Give me your name."

I'm Essien, he said. *Essien Nkanika.* Did he say it? He could hear the questioner's voice – very clear and very loud – but not his own.

"And what's your purpose in all this?"

My purpose? What do you mean? I don't understand!

"You've been using Step technology. Visiting other worlds. Tell me what you were trying to achieve."

Fear gripped him, so tightly and so suddenly he was afraid he might piss himself. *Not me. That wasn't me. I don't know anything about it. It's Hadiz Tambuwal you want. It was Hadiz Tambuwal who made the machine. Ask her and she'll tell you!* There was something wrong with that but for a moment he couldn't remember what it was. Then the memory rose up in his mind the way vomit comes up in your throat, choking and foul and uncontrollable. Hadiz was dead. The giants in red armour had put a hole in her chest. A sense of grief and shame overwhelmed him, edging out the terror. He gaped his mouth wide and howled, though like the words he was speaking or not-quite-speaking the scream was completely silent.

"What's that?"

"Non-verbalised emotion, Watchmaster."

"Jad and Shaster! Can't we filter it out?"

"Not easily. It's not being parsed linguistically. I can reduce the volume."

"Yes! Please! You, Nkanika, control yourself. The sooner you give me answers, the sooner we can be done. Tell me about this woman. Tambuwal. Did you work for her?"

Essien continued to scream for as long as he could, but the absence of sound defeated him in the end. He lay still in the dark, sucking in breath that chilled and pricked his lungs. What was this place? He thought of the meat freezers at Ketu. For all he knew he might be a carcass already hung, his tripes and sweetmeats on a slab underneath him.

"Can you hear me, man? Did you work under Tambuwal, perhaps as an engineer? Or conduct surveying activities for her? Did you act as her bodyguard? What was the nature of your relationship? And who is your principal?"

Essien said nothing. Fuck these people, he decided. If he could get his hands free he would work them harm. Certainly he wouldn't do anything to help them. They had killed Hadiz, and he was sure they were going to kill him when they were done with him. He would prefer to die knowing he had been able to give them something back for that.

"He's not answering. Can we intensify?"

"Of course. The CoIL is only on setting three. But there's a risk of brain damage at higher intensities."

"I don't see how that's pertinent. Proceed."

The lights flashed brighter, and faded more slowly. They seemed to stack up on top of each other, the older bursts becoming the backdrop against which the newer shapes flared and burned. Essien tried to say no, to say enough, to beg for the bombardment to stop, but it seemed he could only speak when a question was put to him.

Everything poured out of him at once then. Silence wasn't an option any more, and neither was lying. Each question was like a spile hammered into the core of him, the heartwood. The truth, a distilled essence of him, gushed out without his willing it – so hot it was already subliming away in curls of radiant vapour, vanishing as it was spoken.

He wondered what would be left of him when all these words were gone. Then he wondered who was speaking these things, the tiresome minutiae of someone else's life. Whoever this Essien Nkanika might be, he sounded like a rogue, a shit and a coward. Definitely someone to avoid.

17

Watchmaster Vemmet was extremely circumspect in submitting his final report.

The matter of the unidentified drones, he wrote, was now satisfactorily concluded. The incursions into Pandominion space that he had first noted at universal time stamp 17-17-438, and had subsequently discussed with coordinator Baxemides, had proved after all to be the work of an individual acting under her own auspices. This person, one Hadiz Tambuwal, was a physicist who had recently discovered Step technology and was pursuing her own experiments without involving any official agencies on her homeworld.

Vemmet detailed his methods. It had been trivial, working from the data already obtained, to ascertain the terrestrial coordinates from which Tambuwal was operating. Both drones had been captured at 6.5244° N, 3.3792° E, corresponding in most Pandominion worlds to one of the largest cities of the southern continent. It was not possible, however, to ascertain Tambuwal's home continuum, so Vemmet had gone about the task from a different angle.

Using the Registry's computing power (one trillionth of a per cent, as per requisition G23.415.8643332e) he had performed a regression analysis on all the worlds Tambuwal's drones had visited. The drones had been fitted with a field modulator, allowing them to make multiple Steps in quick succession through staged interference with the Step field. These sequential jumps would appear on superficial analysis to be random, but actually they were governed by a series of equations. Each series pointed backwards to an origin point; and the more series the Registry calculated, the smaller the feasible region of possible solutions became. However, there were still too many possible candidates for Vemmet's field team (troopers Moon Sostenti and Abenu Lessix) to visit all of them in a finite amount of time. It was a scatter of about seventeen thousand realities.

Across this heterogenous sprawl Vemmet had cast his net – a swarm of orbital detectors of the kind called stumblers. If the stumblers detected a Step field they would snap back instantaneously to Cielo space, broadcasting to Vemmet and the team the coordinates of the universe they had just left. After that, the three of them had just waited.

And waited.

And waited some more.

But finally the moment came. One of the stumblers came stumbling home. Sostenti and Lessix, permanently stationed at 6.5244° N and 3.3792° E, Stepped in at once and apprehended Tambuwal along with a male accomplice.

Unfortunately, Tambuwal herself received fatal injuries in the fierce struggle that ensued, but the man was subdued and taken into custody. Extensive interrogation established that this man was Tambuwal's sole assistant, and only recently taken into her confidence. In fact, "assistant" would probably be overstating the case. Devoid of scientific training or technical experience, the man had only the most rudimentary understanding of Tambuwal's system. His relationship with the scientist seemed to be romantic/sexual rather than professional.

Apart from Tambuwal's death, the retrieval was a complete success. The man apprehended along with the scientist, one Essien Nkanika, had been wearing a bounce-back device. It had been activated and then switched off again without being used. In its memory buffer were the home coordinates to which it had been set.

Sostenti and Lessix led a team back to that continuum where

they found a type-N civilisation with a northern hemispheric bias. The world, now registered as U5838784453, showed every sign of severe resource depletion and environmental degradation – "nothing to see, nothing to sell", as the saying went. Vemmet had placed it on review-and-revise status with an initial hold period of ten years. Tambuwal's lab was dismantled and her notes destroyed. Therefore respectfully, et cetera et cetera, submit that case should be considered closed and field team – with thanks and commendations – reassigned.

Vemmet read through the report five or six times before he submitted it. He felt it did as good a job as he could manage of obfuscating the matter.

The truth was that there was never a bigger train wreck in all the infinite panoply of worlds than the wreck over which he, Orso Vemmet, watchmaster, had just presided. It was a wreck for the ages, deserving to be memorialised in marble. A tasteful sculptural group, perhaps, showing trooper Moon Sostenti, for the love of Jad and all his bastard angels, fatally shooting Hadiz Tambuwal because she was waving an electrical stun device. A footling toy of a weapon that an armoured Cielo wouldn't even feel.

And then, to put the finest filigreed icing on the catastrophic cake, the witless jackanapes who Tambuwal was towing along behind her declared under stage-7 CoIL interrogation that *U5838784453 wasn't even Tambuwal's home planet*!

Vemmet had come close to fainting when he heard this small nugget of indigestible fact. It made everything he had done not only meaningless but shambolically inept. With the lab destroyed and the woman dead, there was no way of backtracking from U5838784453 to her actual point of origin. Whatever records or equipment she had left there could not now be secured. If she had collaborators, they would remain at large.

Caught between the maul and the mincer, Vemmet agonised about how best to protect his precious hide from the flaying it would receive if all this came out. The first requisite, he decided, was to vanish Essien Nkanika from the equation. He might be as ignorant as dirt, but some of the very few things he knew were potentially embarrassing.

"Take him somewhere quiet and kill him," he told Moon Sostenti in the privacy of his office, having turned off his array and instructed her to do the same. "Dispose of the body. Don't write it up."

Moon was rolling up a strip of gabber into a wad for chewing. She blew out her cheek.

"What?" Vemmet demanded.

"As far as that goes, I don't need to take him out behind the woodshed. I can just set his cell to flush him and recycle him, then frig the permanent log so it looks like I didn't. It seems a shame, is all. The truth is I feel sorry for the poor bastard. He fell into this the way you'd fall out of a tree, and he doesn't know shit from spackle. If it were me, I'd just as soon release him back into the wild."

Vemmet kept his patience with difficulty. Moon and Lessix between them owned this debacle. They were the field team, and it was their incompetence that had made it impossible to put Tambuwal to question or even to ascertain beyond all doubt that she was dead. He could have done with a bit more humility and cooperation. "If Coordinator Baxemides decides to look into this any further your head is on the line just as much as mine. For both of our sakes, it's best if we handle the matter discreetly."

"Discreetly." Moon put a sardonic emphasis on the word. "Look, if you tell me to do it I'll do it." She stood in silence for a few seconds, then popped the wad of gum into the corner of her mouth. "There's another way, though," she said around it.

"Is there?"

"Of course. Get him to enlist. Life expectancy for the average grunt is about two years but it gives him a chance, at least."

Vemmet considered. He disliked the uncertainty but appreciated how plausibly deniable a death like that would be. And probably if Baxemides reopened the case he'd have far bigger problems than Essien Nkanika to contend with.

"Do that then," he said, and dismissed Sostenti as quickly as he could. He was keen to escape the gabber's pervasive stink. There was no proof that exposure to the stuff at second-hand could do any harm at all to the human nervous system; but by the same token there was no proof that it couldn't. If Moon was willing to make holes in her memory in exchange for a little stress relief, that was her choice. Vemmet preferred to leave his brain intact and functional.

That was another advantage to Sostenti's plan, now that he thought about it. Gabber was the drug of choice for serving soldiers. It softened the jagged edges of trauma and induced a cosy sense of invulnerability. Even if Nkanika lived, his brain was likely to be cheese in a few months' time.

By the time he clocked off that afternoon, Vemmet had convinced himself that making a soldier out of the sinkholer had been his own idea all along.

18

After the interrogation Essien was too weak to move. The two red-armoured giants – the woman who shot Hadiz and the man who had laid him out with a backhanded swat from his armoured hand – had to more or less carry him back to his cell as he scrabbled and failed to get his legs under him.

For the rest of that day and all the next he had a headache so bad that he couldn't move without vomiting. He lay on the narrow bunk and stared at the ceiling, or more usually at the inside of his eyelids. There was a huge black spot in the centre of his vision when his eyes were open. When he closed them, the spot turned yellow. He measured the passage of time by the changes in the spots, which shrank and faded very slowly. When food and water arrived, via a slot in the wall, he lowered himself carefully to the floor, crawled slowly over to the slot, ate and drank, then crawled back again. Apart from that, he stayed where he was.

An image kept floating to the surface of his mind, and then submerging again. It was a moving image, Hadiz thrown into the air and then falling as the bolt from the red giant's strange weapon struck her in the chest. Hadiz striking the ground. Hadiz disappearing, gone between one breath and the next, not swallowed by the sand or evaporating like dew but snapped back home again by the power of her machine.

Was she dead now, or alive? She must have been alive at the moment of her escape. The stud that activated the metal bracelet was recessed, so it couldn't have been pressed by accident. Her thumb needed to find it. Her mind needed to make the decision. But there was no way to know what happened after that.

If she was alive she could save him. Her machine could take her into any place and back out again before anyone could catch her. Perhaps she would need to rest up first, from her wound, but once she was recovered it would surely be the work of a moment to find him and bring him home.

Or perhaps not. She had told him more than once how many worlds there were. *Infinity isn't a big number*, she'd said: *it's what happens when you get to the last number and fall off the end of it. Imagine a thousand, Essien. And then a million. And then a million million. Now imagine a book with that many pages. On the first page is a one, and the rest of the book is zeros. Billions and trillions of zeros, in ten-point type on onionskin paper. Think about how big that number is. Then multiply it by itself. You're still not there. You're still not close.*

And even if she could find him, what would make her want to come? He had planned to betray her and leave her stranded on another world with no way home. Why would she feel any need to intervene now that what he intended for her had happened to him? He could see no reason. He tried to hold on to some kind of hope, but the effort was too much. It drained away again between breaths. Shame and self-disgust flooded in to fill the gap. He deserved this. Worse than this, even. He should have been the one to die.

He stared at the spot behind his closed eyelids until it seemed that he was staring at the sun.

On the second day, his cell door opened and one of the giants came in. Because of the opaque helmet he had no idea which of the two it was, until it spoke. It was the woman.

"How are they treating you?" she asked.

Except that she didn't say that at all. She wasn't speaking English, Ibibio, Efik or Neija pidgin – the only languages Essien had ever been able to speak. They had slipped another language into him so slyly he still couldn't say when or how it had happened – like a man in a knife fight who braces himself for a punch or a kick and then realises he's bleeding from his stomach, dark red spreading across his shirt. Where was the knife? There and gone, too late to worry now.

How were they treating him? It was a meaningless question, especially coming as it did from the smooth scarlet ovoid of the woman's faceplate. It was as though one of the walls of the cell had spoken up, all of a sudden, and asked him whether his bunk was comfortable.

"I'm fine," he told her. "Please piss off."

The woman stood very still for a while. Finally, she held out her hand. There was a chocolate bar of some kind sitting on her open palm. Essien could tell it was chocolate because there was a cartoon picture of a chocolate bar with a bite out of it right there on the wrapper. The name of the bar was in an unfamiliar script – which told him that he could only understand the language people spoke here, not their writing.

"Good idea to get your blood sugar up, if you're in a CoIL hangover. I bet they've been feeding you staple-3, which is what we get when we're out in the rough and tuck. Go ahead. This actually tastes of something."

Essien sat up and took the bar. He tore the wrapper open, peeled it back and took a bite. It was strange but very good. He wolfed it down so fast he barely tasted it.

"Thank you," he said to the woman when it was all gone.

"You're welcome."

"What are we speaking?"

The woman tilted her head on one side. "Sorry?"

"This language. The language we're speaking now. What is it?"

"Oh. It's called Stengul. At least, that's its official name. Mostly we call it Grunt."

"And it's the language of your world? The world where Lagos is all beach?"

"Shit, no. Listen, that's not . . . Okay, first of all, that world wasn't one of ours. It wasn't anyone's, as far as I know, although I guess it most likely belongs to the Pandominion now because why not? Second, nobody grows up speaking Grunt. It's not the language of a planet, or a people. It's an inter-world language. It's what you use when you're talking to someone from another continuum. And it's what the Cielo speak most of the time."

"Who are the Cielo?"

The woman smacked her breastplate with both hands. "Who are the Cielo? Friend, you're looking at it. The Cielo are people like me. People who fight for the Pandominion and protect it against bad shit coming in from omniversal elsewhere."

Essien wanted to say: people like you? People who are seven feet tall and appear out of thin air like magic? People who shoot fire out of their fingertips, and murder without even thinking about it? But it would have been foolish, and he didn't say it, because (magic aside) he'd known people like her all his life. The Yoruba cop who'd given him that kicking, for example, had been people like her. Diallo's goons had been people like her.

In spite of which, he was grateful for the chocolate and for her bothering to bring it. "Thank you," he said again.

"No problem," the woman said.

As though it was an afterthought, she reached up and touched her thumbs to the base of her helmet. Essien heard the slightest hiss of sound. She lifted the helmet free and lowered it to her waist.

Essien gaped. He jackknifed upright on his bunk, almost falling off it in the process.

The woman wasn't a woman at all, she was a cat. But also a woman. But mostly a cat. Her eyes were massively wide, the pupils fat black ellipses surrounded by bright gold, with no whites at all. Her nose was flat and broad. Fine brown fur covered her face, except for the base of her nose and her lips, where naked pink skin could be seen. Her ears stood up at least a handspan from the top of her head.

Seeing his shock and horror, the woman laughed out loud. "Oh shit," she said, "I forgot you're a sinkholer. Sorry! I didn't mean to give you a heart attack."

"What . . . what are you?" Essien stammered.

"Well, that's fucking rude. A self is what I am, the same as you but with better manners. My name's Moon Sostenti and I'm from Ghen." When Essien opened his mouth to speak, she waved him silent, still grinning. "Yeah, don't bother introducing yourself. I know all about you, Nkanika. I was there when you were under the CoIL, remember? Couldn't shut you up with both hands." She reached into her belt and fished out a second chocolate bar, tossed it to him. "For later," she said, adding over her shoulder as she left, "In case there is a later."

Moon came back regularly after that. Essien was left to his devices the rest of the time, with nothing to do except pace backwards and forwards across the cell or lie in the bunk in a kind of half-sleep, so he was pathetically grateful for these small attentions – and at the same time angry at himself for coming to heel so readily. He had to keep reminding himself that Moon and the other armoured bastard had shot Hadiz, that he hated them all and could not, must not trust them. But it was too easy to let fear hollow him out; to respond to the immediate stimulus, whether that was a smack or a pat on the head, and forget the context in which these things had meaning.

Sometimes Moon brought chocolate, sometimes she forgot. After that first time she always came with her head bare, her helmet under her arm. He no longer saw her face as strange, and he had stopped being afraid of it. She was even beautiful, although it was a kind of beauty a long way removed from the mechanics of arousal. Essien knew that the ancient Egyptians had worshipped a cat god named Bast. With her huge golden eyes and her razor teeth, Moon looked the way a cat god ought to look.

Along with the chocolate she brought information. This place he was in was part of a massive complex belonging to some people called the Omnipresent Council. They were sort of a government, ruling over a very, very big country called the Pandominion.

"Not a country," Moon corrected him. She was leaning against the wall while he sat on the bunk. The open, lidless toilet, bolted to the wall, was in between them. It cleaned itself when Essien wasn't looking, so there was no smell, but it was still a kind of rebuke to him to have it there. It made him feel both naked and ashamed. It made him feel Oshodi.

"A world then."

"Not a world, either. It's a league of worlds."

"Which worlds?"

"Earth, Nkanika. They're all Earth. It's just, you know, different Earths. The ones that got Step tech and found each other. The Council takes care of trade and immigration and stuff. And we, I mean the Cielo, we handle defence. It's probably the biggest—" she gestured vaguely "—alliance, confederation, club, whatever you want to call it, that there's ever been. And it works. Every world has got something it can sell to the others. The ones that don't have natural resources have got tech or culture or grunt labour. And there's full employment for everyone, because they're always opening up new FMQ worlds. That's farms, mines and quarries. So everybody wins."

"Everybody?" Essien thought of Hadiz bleeding out on the sand. You had to be clear about who everybody was.

"When you're in, you're in," Moon clarified. "We look after our own." She was looking at him when she said it and he thought there was some undercurrent there he wasn't getting.

"Will they let me go soon?" he asked her on her next visit. He was aware how abject he sounded. He might as well have added "abeg".

Moon shrugged. "Well, that's the ball ache of it," she said. "They don't let people go. That's just not a thing that happens."

He had assumed as much, but to hear it said out loud still made his stomach clench. "What, then?" he asked. "Will they make you shoot me?"

Moon rolled her enormous, endlessly expressive eyes. "What do I look like to you, arsehole? A gun with a woman attached? I've got a job, and it's not that. If they decide they want to kill you, the good news is that you won't know anything about it. The room will put you to sleep, then break you down and recycle the chemicals."

"The room?" Essien repeated, thinking he must have misheard.

"Yes, Nkanika, the room." Moon tapped the wall with the back of her hand. There were panels there, inset, their edges flush with the surrounding surface and almost invisible. She nodded at the floor. When Essien looked down he saw more fine traceries of lines. The room was a puzzle box, designed to open along unexpected planes and do unspeakable things. "The process is fully automated. Not saying it happens often, but when it does – when the order comes down – nobody has to get their hands dirty. It's quick and it's painless. You won't feel a thing."

"Jesus!" Essien protested. "Jesus Christ!" He lifted his feet and tucked them under his knees, feeling a sudden, unquestioned need to be as far away from any surface as he could get. But the bunk was only inches off the floor, and bolted to the wall. Where, he saw now, there was another discreet panel about ten inches on each side.

"Wouldn't," Moon amended, hand raised to calm him – which was when Essien realised that he was shaking. "*Wouldn't* feel a thing. Nobody's signed off on anything yet. I'm just saying you should prepare for the worst. The whole system – I mean us, the Cielo – we're here to remove potential threats. If there's the faintest whiff of a risk, the idea is to head it off. To stop it ever happening. And Watchmaster Vemmet, the man who questioned you, he's a bit of a cunt. One hand on his balls, the other on the rule book, you know the type."

"I'm not a risk to anyone!" Essien protested. "All I want is to go home! I never wanted to come here in the first place!"

He started to cry. He tried to hold the tears in, but they were forced out of him in a clamorous, breathless rush. He could see the line, straight as a ruler, that led from his own bad decisions to Hadiz getting shot and his own imminent death. The inexorable chain of cause and effect overwhelmed him. For most of his life, despite his circumstances, he had had an illusory sense of being in control of his fate (his name, Essien, meant "destiny" in the Ibibio language). That sense abandoned him now, leaving him naked in the face of his own selfishness and stupidity.

Moon crossed the cell, which took her exactly two strides, and clamped a gauntleted hand down on his shoulder. She said nothing for a few moments, just kept the hand there. When he looked up, he saw those golden eyes staring down at him, the slitted pupils wide. Was it compassion he was seeing, or did he just look like a mouse from up there?

"Listen," Moon said. "I probably shouldn't tell you this, but there's a loophole. A way you can get out from under, if you've got the stomach for it. It's not an easy option, though."

Essien was still shivering like a struck gong. "What?" he asked. "What loophole, Moon? Tell me, please!"

"The watchmaster's got a lot of pull but he mostly faces outwards, if you know what I mean. Sinkholers like you are fair game – got no rights under the law, no status. But there's one place you can go where he won't be able to lay a hand on you."

"What place is that?"

"My place." Moon grinned, showing him a mouthful of knives. "You can enlist."

She sat with him for a long time, talking him through how it would work. Swings and roundabouts, she said. On the one hand, since he came from outside the Pando, he wouldn't make up part of a planetary quota and he'd have to make the cut on his own merit. On the other hand, there was always a war going on somewhere: attrition in the Cielo tended to be high, so they were recruiting all the time.

She'd brought a recruitment brochure, on live paper. All he had to do was put his thumb on it and things would start to roll. No time like the present, right? And did she forget to mention the sign-in bonus? He'd have a thousand stars in his pocket when he got to boot camp. That K-star would buy a lot of booze, a lot of drugs, a lot of sex.

Essien might have put up more resistance if he'd had anything to go back to, or any other options. The alternative to this was to stay in the cell and wait either for Hadiz to come and rescue him from it or for it to swallow him and shit him out.

He hadn't missed that off-hand reference to the wars and the attrition, so he didn't have any illusions about what he was signing up to. Yes, he might die. He was joining an army in circumstances that virtually guaranteed he would see active service, so dying was a very likely outcome. But he'd asked for it. Maybe, had spent his whole life asking for it in one way and another. And leaving behind everything he'd ever known was already as much like dying as made no difference.

19

These were the thoughts that passed through the mind of Hadiz Tambuwal after she was shot in the chest by trooper Moon Sostenti. For reasons that will become clear, they're well documented.

At first, and for a long time, there was nothing that could be put into words. Just endless pain and bottomless panic.

Then a lull, a quiet so deep that thoughts of any kind couldn't take root there. It was impossible to say how long that quiet lasted, but at the other end of it there was a return to consciousness and a sense of dulled wonder that she was able to think at all.

I survived then, was how Hadiz put it to herself.

And then, a very long time after that, *Didn't I . . .?*

She had had a fallback. You always needed to have a fallback, and this one seemed to have worked. There was no pain now. Admittedly, there were no other sensations either, but that felt like a price worth paying. At the very least she had stabilised the situation.

But only temporarily. In her current state she was still terrifyingly exposed and all but helpless. What she needed more than anything else was information. This situation was clearly a lot bigger than her. Probably it was absurd for her to take it so personally. Then again, a hole burned through your chest and out via the centre of your back will do that to you. She framed the questions in her mind: a set of puzzles to be solved – as all puzzles were – by experimentation and inquiry.

Who were those Gundam-suited thugs?

Who sent them?

Why did they fire on me?

Where did they go to afterwards?

What happened to Essien?

What can I do about any of this?

It wasn't a bad list to be going on with. More questions were bound to suggest themselves later. As to the assets she could call on, she had always had a strong will and a keen intellect. Now she had an ice-cold, inexhaustible patience too.

She set about finding some answers.

20

A life in the army begins with radical surgery.

Not knowing this, Essien had no idea what to expect when he was taken from his cell to Mudu Garete, a military hospital the size of a small city. The Cielo officers who took him there, in a military transport with no windows and seemingly no driver, were strangers. They didn't speak a single word to him in the course of the journey.

At the hospital, Essien was given over to four orderlies. The orderlies looked somewhat like the Cielo officers, but with white armour in place of red. In fact they weren't wearing any armour. The orderlies were animas, AI constructs slaved to Mudu Garete's intelligent system. The armour was a ceramic sheath over their metal bodies, kept antiseptically clean by a variety of chemical agents and periodic dousing with a spray of super-heated steam.

The orderlies took Essien to a shower room where they stripped off his clothes and washed him very thoroughly with astringent liquids that stung and stank. They shaved his head with blades they extruded from the tips of their fingers. They slathered his body with a clear liquid that thickened immediately to a gel. When they scraped the gel away all of Essien's body hair went with it. He endured all this as stoically as he could, wondering the whole time if Moon had lied to him. It seemed entirely possible that he was being prepared for execution.

Instead, he was strapped to a gurney and wheeled into an

operating theatre. The theatre was a circular room of about twenty metres diameter, its walls and floor as perfectly white and reflective as the orderlies' carapaces. The domed ceiling was probably white too, but Essien couldn't tell: an agonisingly bright light shone down from its zenith, eliminating all shadow in the room and hiding whatever was up there from his sight.

The orderlies turned their backs and went away, closing the door behind them. Essien was alone in the room, which – because of the flensing light, the dome, the perfect silence and stillness – seemed to him like a place of worship. Not execution then, he thought in his misery and terror, but maybe sacrifice.

A sound welled up from everywhere and nowhere, a clear perfect note. A slight vibration came along with it, communicated through the floor to Essien's gurney and from there to his body. The sound grew louder and the vibration stronger, until his whole frame seemed to ring in harmony with it.

Something descended from the ceiling.

Essien had seen a Japanese spider crab once. Not the real thing, of course, but a picture in a book that Ndulue had shown him one night at Olususun. The book was part of the dump's unpredictable bounty, found in a sack of waterlogged and half-pulped newspapers. "Looks a bit like you," Ndulue had said, making fun of Essien's wide, slightly bulging eyes. Essien had laughed, and come back with some suggestions as to which animals most closely resembled Ndulue himself, but the spider crab had shocked and disgusted him. It was like something vomited up out of a nightmare.

The thing that was coming down from the ceiling towards him now was very much like the thing in that photograph, but encased in the same shining white ceramic as the orderlies. It had dozens of long, slender arms, segmented at far too many joints, unfolding like the stamens of a flower in a speeded-up film. At the end of each arm was an implement. Some bore sharp points or angled blades; others flexed unnervingly long steel fingers or irised open to reveal nozzles, lenses, clusters of waving filaments.

Essien arched his back and screamed for help as loud as he could. Nobody came, but since his yelling emptied his lungs he inhaled the sedative/anaesthetic mix very quickly when the dosing arm was clamped over his mouth. His struggles weakened. His eyes slid shut, even as the busy, bustling appendages went about their business. For a long time after that, he was aware of nothing at all.

While he slept, radical and irreversible changes were made to Essien's body. Holes were drilled in the long bones of his arms and legs and into his pelvis, ribs and shoulder blades. His bone marrow was extracted and mixed with an allotropic form of tungsten aluminide and programmable proteins. The newly mixed composite was then re-injected into the bones and the holes sealed. Over time the aluminide would seep into the bones themselves, giving them an incredible resistance to damage.

His lungs and kidneys were removed and replaced with much more efficient bio-artificial organs. His new kidneys were equipped to metabolise or denature more than five thousand known toxins and to perform *in situ* analysis of unknown contaminants. Where necessary, they could synthesise and disperse antidotes and neutralising agents within minutes of initial infection. His new lungs could seal themselves against non-breathable atmospheres while maintaining viable oxygen levels for prolonged periods through a novel use of synthetic chloroplasts and metabolic catalysts. He could even survive and function for minutes at a time in complete vacuum.

The fatty deposits around his organs and in the dermal layers of his skin were injected with a plastic compound that greatly increased their compressive and yield strengths, in effect giving him built-in shock absorbers.

Across the corneas of his eyes, thin sheets of the same plastic were sprayed in hundreds of micrometre-thick layers. In between the layers were intelligent filaments that could deform the lenses of the eyes to provide pin-sharp focus and up to 100X magnification. The plastic was also self-cleaning and highly resistant to damage.

To control all these new organs and structures a genetically engineered parasite was introduced into Essien's brain. The parasite was an annelid worm, a modified form of *Chaetogaster annandalei*. About a million of the things made their nests in among the unconscious man's neurons, then died and dissolved. Irrigated with the dead worms' remains, the nests – woven from lipid-rich myelin – combined to form a secondary nervous system, seamlessly melding the smart engineered parts of Essien with the old, haphazard core.

When he woke, brought to full alertness at once by a cocktail of tweaked adrenalin and psycho-active chemicals, he discovered he was no longer at Mudu Garete. He was at an induction facility on Bivouac 6, one of a whole cluster of worlds that were technically within the Pandominion but owned entirely by the Cielo. No civilian personnel ever set foot on Biv 6. The whole planet was an army camp.

Actually Essien was in the air above the facility, strapped to the side of a C17 troop transport that was heading out to sea. He wasn't alone. Dozens more people were lying above, below and to the sides of him, locked into identical harnesses so that their freedom of movement was limited to turning their heads and twiddling their toes. Their bare toes, since all the men and women Essien could see were naked.

"Men and women" was a broad term. They were all roughly human in terms of body plan, but like Watchmaster Vemmet and Moon Sostenti they were surprising in other ways. Many were furred, a few scaly or feathered. Where Essien saw regular smooth skin like his own there was a startling array of shades including vivid red and orange and pale green. And in some cases the skin wasn't actually smooth at all but rucked, studded or plated. It wasn't possible, though, to mistake any of his companions for animals. They were clearly differently constituted people, with recognisable emotions of confusion and fear on their faces as the transport arced out over deep water.

When it was three miles from shore and flying at a height of 500 metres, the harnesses opened. The release was in stages, carefully spaced out across twenty or thirty seconds, seeding the air with falling, thrashing bodies that were all on their own tightly plotted trajectories. Nobody was close enough to anyone else to risk a collision.

Even so, they hit the water at what is normally called terminal velocity. The impact was agonisingly painful, the force of it stunning and disorienting, but Essien found as he sank deeper and deeper below the surface that both the pain and the confusion passed off quickly. His new, improved nervous system had ways of mitigating both these things. His enhanced skin and skeleton had absorbed the sickening blow with almost no actual damage.

And his super-capable lungs, as he thrust and squirmed his way back up to the surface, synthesised oxygen from recycled lymphatic fluid to keep his body functioning at full efficiency. Though he wasn't able to draw in a breath for more than two minutes, he felt no discomfort at all.

He swam back to shore, surrounded on all sides by other naked bodies. As he did so, he discovered he now had a new sense in addition to the regular five. He was aware of his own position in relation to all the other recruits. He knew exactly how many were in front of him, how many coming on behind, along with all the distances and vectors. He even knew which way they were facing (and he drew an indefinable but powerful pleasure from the fact that it was the same way in every case). It was as though he had his own radar, perfect within its limited scope.

He was swimming through heavy seas, and he had less buoyancy than he was used to because of the dense metal that now perfused his bones. Still, his body seemed to find more strength whenever he reached for it: he had no sense at all that he was reaching his limit when he hauled himself up at last onto the beach.

A tall, imposing figure was waiting there, dressed in red plate with two black bands across the chest. A sergeant. Next to him was what looked like an entire army in the same red livery, until Essien saw that the breastplates of all these other soldiers were open – and empty. They were suits of Cielo armour, waiting to be claimed.

The sergeant looked at each recruit in turn as they came to stand in front of him. They fell into line without even thinking about it. There was just a position, a distance that felt right, and it was hard – as well as pointless – to pull against it.

"You're all in uniform violation, recruits," the sergeant said. "Find your suit and seal in. Now."

The naked men and women shifted their feet and stared anxiously – at the sergeant, at each other. Were they meant to choose a suit of armour at random?

No. They weren't. The sergeant tapped the back of his hand.

Instantly, it seemed to Essien, one of the suits came to life. Up to that moment it had been indistinguishable from all the rest. Now, although it hadn't changed at all, it was utterly unique. His sense of it was vivid, pinpoint sharp. He would have known it was there even with his eyes put out. It was almost as though the armour was singing to him, a single sustained note that contained a whole symphony. He headed straight for it, and he saw that each of the recruits was doing the same, heading directly towards one point in the endless identical ranks that had suddenly become a beacon. Though their paths crossed and recrossed there were no collisions. The siren song of the armour didn't block out their sense of each other.

Putting the armour on was easy. It *wanted* to be put on. It aligned with, opened to and clasped any limb that offered, then reconfigured itself around that point of contact. All you had to do, Essien discovered, was to choose it. The armour did the rest. The helmet slid down and sealed last of all, when all the rest of his body was enclosed. The faceplate, opaque from the outside, was as clear as crystal once you were looking out.

Words scrolled past Essien's eyes in sharply defined white type, projected onto the faceplate – or perhaps directly into his eye. They said PTE/NKANIKA E/432nd HVY INF/DG10014/ U5838784453. So now, it seemed, he could read the language Moon had called Grunt as well as speak it. He began to realise that the changes to his body were matched by alterations to his mind. He knew this should be a frightening thing, but the sense of well-being he was getting from being a part of this totality made it impossible to be unhappy. He understood for the first time what "unit" meant: it meant being one and being together.

"Recruits," the sergeant said, "welcome to the Cielo. The next three months are going to be the hardest of your entire life. Not for long though, because the three months right after will make them look like nothing at all."

These words were not barked or bellowed as Essien would have expected them to be. They were not reverberating in the hot, still air. They were being spoken directly into his ear, through his helmet mike, as though the sergeant were standing right at his shoulder. "Six months of pain and toil," the sergeant went on. "Six months of pushing yourself a long way past what you think you can stand. Six months of wishing your mother never dropped you. But at the end of the six months you'll be Cielo. And let me tell you what that means.

"Everyone you ever meet will be afraid of you, unless they're too crazy or too stupid to know what fear is. Nobody will ever pick a fight with you, unless there's ten of them to your one – and then they'll wish afterwards they'd got the count wrong and walked away. There's nowhere in the Pandominion where your uniform won't be known and respected. Because there's nowhere in the Pandominion that would still be standing if the Cielo weren't there to hold up the walls. From the Substrate to the Scour, from the Helix to the hobs of hell, we are civilisation's 'fuck you' to anything and everything that dares to look at us cross-eyed. God didn't make us. Why? Because he looked at the recipe and shat himself. So the Demshoi fucked a volcano, and nine months later out we came, spitting boulders and pissing lava. And it's just as well we did, because damn if we don't make up for the rest of this sorry fucking universe."

A cheer rose up. It seemed to have many more voices in it than could be accounted for by the contingent on the beach, but it was hard to tell because they were all of them quick to join in. It was a wordless roar of joy and triumph, so loud that it was almost like a solid thing, a substance that flowed between them, filling the empty spaces until they were one organism bellowing out of all of its hundreds of throats.

"Now," the sergeant said, "it's getting on for lunchtime." He turned and pointed, out across what looked like an endless expanse of sand dunes and scrub. "Camp is that way, about fifteen miles. If you run all the way there'll be some soup left. Piece of bread, chunk of kabat maybe. If you take it at a stroll I can't make any promises."

They ran. They ran headlong.

Their legs adjusted at once to the breakneck pace. Servos in their armour augmented their already formidable strength, making their strides more like long-jumps. Fold-fields in their boots compacted the shifting sand under their feet so there was no drag on their momentum. The miles fell away behind them, almost unnoticed.

Under the blistering heat, Essien felt no discomfort at all. The armour maintained near-perfect homeostasis, wicking away his sweat, hydrating him at need, adjusting his metabolism so that his body was a perfect fit for the demands he was making of it. When he reached camp he was starting to tire and he felt a great need to eat, but he could have gone on a lot further if he'd needed to.

Sitting in the vast mess tent, stuffing his face with something that had the texture of cake but tasted of meat, he felt a sort of numb happiness spread through him. All around him were his fellow soldiers, nodes in a net that took him in and embraced every part of him. The net filled the room, but he knew that was only the smallest part of it. The whole camp was crowded with Cielo, thousands and thousands of them. Their presence was a gentle pressure against his skin. They held him in equilibrium. He could never lose his balance or his way again.

A trooper sitting across the table from Essien happened to look up and meet his eye. There was a moment's distance, awkwardness, but only a moment. Then they both smiled. She was fearsomely ugly, with a jaw that was much broader than the rest of her face and eyes like a goat's with pupils shaped like keyholes, but it didn't matter. It didn't make any difference at all. The bonds that tied them together were too strong.

The euphoria stayed with him for the next three days of weapon and armour drills, logistics training and general orientation.

At the end of the fourth day, they went into the Scour.

21

"Okay, listen up," Otubre said. "You'll be Stepping through in threes, and since you don't know what you're Stepping into you'll need to make a beachhead. What are the three things to remember when you're making a beachhead, Muks?"

Otubre was the sergeant who had met them on the beach, and he was saying this in staging area twelve, one of a thousand or so huge hangars on the base that housed the regiment's transport infrastructure. There were only twenty recruits present, standing in a small cluster around the midpoint of a line of a hundred raised metal plates that ran the length of the room. Essien knew what the plates were and what they were for. They were the same as the circular platform in Hadiz Tambuwal's lab, except that they were larger. On Hadiz's rig there had barely been room for the two of them to stand together: these platforms would comfortably take twenty or thirty at a time, and the ones at either end of the hangar were larger still; big enough to accommodate squads of a hundred or more along with tanks and armoured cars.

The twenty recruits, along with Sergeant Otubre, made up the smallest effective unit within the regiment, a tactical squad: specifically, TS5-683. This was a mission-specific designation and would dissolve when the mission was done. For today – Essien's HUD confirmed – he was PTE/NKANIKA E/432nd HVY INF/ DG10014/U5838784453/ TS5-683. The string of symbols defined who he was. His rank. His name. His regiment. His ident. His world. His squad. When the tactical squad was stood down the last few characters would delete themselves.

But for now these twenty selves were his brothers and sisters, their signals enhanced both in his helmet display and in his neural architecture. Invisible umbilicals bound them to each other and to Sergeant Otubre who was their leader.

Private Muks, an ursine who stood taller than Essien by a full head and was twice as broad across the shoulders, stood to attention as she snapped out her answer. "Embed, orient, implement."

"That's right." Otubre nodded. "And that's what I'll be looking for. You've got your numbers. Go when they're called. One."

The first three were Muks, Tollen and Gavangar. They advanced together onto the plate, turned to face outwards and then were gone, between one heartbeat and the next, as the Step field enveloped them. The second three, including Essien, moved forward to fill the gap in the ranks.

"Two," Otubre called out. Essien and two other privates took their places on the plate.

Essien was the only one in the squad – maybe the only one in the regiment – who still found Stepping a scary novelty. He tried not to flinch as the flow of information to his eyes momentarily stopped, and then as the new reality flooded his senses.

He was standing on fine orange sand. A bloated sun, more red than yellow, hung at the zenith of the sky. A blustering wind butted itself against him. The first cohort had taken up positions at four, eight and twelve. Essien moved quickly to his own assigned position at two o'clock, in between Muks and Gavangar. His armour's AI was already scanning for enemy positions and enemy signals, but it was finding nothing.

The remaining cohorts Stepped through behind Essien at five-second intervals. He was aware of their arrival both through his proprioceptive link and from the soft clapping of the air each time the Step field discharged. While he waited, he completed his scan and took in his surroundings.

They were in a broad avenue in what looked like the ruins of an ancient city. To either side of them, low stone structures near at hand were dwarfed by taller, more impressive monoliths further away. This place had been huge once, but it had surrendered to the desert a very long time ago. The orange sand was strewn with half-buried blocks of white stone, rising like shattered teeth out of a bloody jaw.

Essien's suit filtered the air for him, so the sand that was whipped up by the fitful wind didn't trouble him. He wondered what part of his own world these ruins corresponded to. Whether the people who had lived here were dark or fair, and how long ago they had abandoned their homes to the encroaching waste.

There was certainly nobody left here now. Essien's monitors reported nothing moving, out to the very limit of effective range. On comms, every wavelength except their own was silent.

"This," said Sergeant Otubre, "is Callion. The corner of Rose Street and Lateral 18. At least, that's what it would be if we were standing in my world. It's got a name on the world you come from too, and the Cielo borrowed a moment's time from the Registry to work out what that is. It's coming up in your field now."

Across the top of Essien's HUD the words "Paris, Champs-Élysées" scrolled slowly. A helpful display showed him where that was on a map of the world, but it left him none the wiser. He had never travelled outside of Neiger before this.

"People come here," Otubre was saying, "and they don't know what it is they're looking at. Sand. Ancient ruins. They can't see how any of it could matter to them. But it does. This right here is the most important day of your training. The most important thing you'll ever see. Squad, fall in."

He led them down the street, past several intersections. Every street they passed was a truncated stub of a dozen or so ruined structures with nothing but desert beyond. In spite of the complete absence of enemies, the squad stayed in good order covering each other when they moved and reconnoitring each intersection when they got to it.

For a hundred yards or so they had to hug the wall of a building because the centre of the street was taken up by the remains of a gigantic statue. Essien could make out the torso of a man and the lower part of his right arm, his hand gripping the hilt of a sheathed sword. The clenched fist rose to the height of a two-storey building. Fifty yards further on, they passed the statue's head, which was wearing a very elaborate crown and a patrician sneer. The huge blank eyes were on their backs as they went on.

"Here," Otubre said, a little way further on. "This is my favourite bar. You're gonna love the atmosphere."

He led them into a building whose doorway was tilted at a strange angle. The stone floor beyond was tilted too. The whole structure must be sinking into the sand, the desert shrugging off that irksome weight with terrible patience.

The space they were in now could have been anything. There was no furniture – and no roof, for that matter. The only clue to its former function was a bas-relief high up on one wall that looked like it might be a bunch of grapes spilling out of a bowl. The squad advanced into the cavernous space, ranging their weapons, staying tight on Otubre's position.

"Extant maps say this is the exact centre of the city," the sergeant said, turning to address the squad. "Not just the part that's above ground, the whole place – which is about twenty or thirty times bigger than what you can still see. We're downtown, squad. Must have been a lively place, back in the day. But things have gone all to shit since."

He pointed to an inner door. "Secure that position," he said. The squad did so in textbook fashion, switching their visual filters to enhanced and scanning via passive sonar as they moved forward in their assigned subunits, quartering the room to forestall imaginary threats from the door through which they'd entered, the gaps in the walls, the sky above them.

In the inner room were the first signs of life they'd yet seen – but they only marked where life had been, not where it was now. Five mummified figures were ranged against the rear wall. Three were adults, two were children. Their sunken flesh was lightly furred, their eyeless faces narrow with forward-thrusting muzzles. The remnants of the robes they'd worn in life still hung on them, ash-grey and so thin that the sunlight shone through them.

One of the adults had died cradling one of the children, their bodies now sagging against each other, their foreheads touching. It looked as though the grown-up, whoever they were, had been trying to reassure the little one or protect them against something that was coming. Clearly that hadn't ended well.

Take a good look. Otubre didn't speak the words out loud, he transmitted them directly into their minds through the digital inter-face the Cielo had installed in their brains. *Pay your respects. Say a prayer if you want to. Take your time. They've been there for five hundred years and they're not going anywhere. When you're ready, go on back outside and wait until everyone's done.*

Nobody stayed to say a prayer. Essien was the last to leave, because something about the dead bodies had caught his attention. They were humming. There was a single low note, way down at the limit of audibility, coming from all five of them – not from their mouths but from all of them, their whole bodies. He wouldn't have noticed it if he hadn't kicked his armour's sensory valences all the way up. It was as if whatever had struck them down had made them ring like wind chimes and they were still ringing five centu-ries later.

He rejoined the rest of the squad at last, falling in at the end of the line. Sergeant Otubre faced them, hands clasped behind his back.

"Okay," he said. "Questions."

"What killed them?" Muks asked.

"Yeah, that's the first thing that comes to mind, isn't it? We don't know, is the answer. We think it was a field weapon of some kind, but the only residue we've found is vibrational." That low note, Essien thought. "Their molecules are oscillating very slightly, at a constant frequency. It doesn't seem to lessen over time. We don't know any kind of force or device or natural phenomenon that could do that. What else? Keep them coming. If you found this set-up on a scouting mission, what would you want to know?"

"Where are all the rest of them?" another private ventured. "A place this big, you'd expect to see way more people."

"Yes, you would. There are a few dozen more in the sand under our feet, buried between three and eight metres down. Not just people. Dogs. Birds. Something that looks like a rat. Close to a hundred organic remains overall – in a city that probably housed about seventy or eighty thousand people back in the day. We think the rest most likely got a bigger blast of whatever the weapon was and it broke them down more thoroughly. They're in the sand you're walking in. The ones you saw, the ones that maintained some kind of molecular coherence, they were the outliers."

Otubre threw up a map in the squad's perceptual fields. It was a map of the world. "Okay, you know this shit from general orientation," he said. "The Pando's got hundreds of thousands of worlds in it, but – bottom line – it's the same world over and over. Jaarde. Eruth. Ut. Tell. Gea. Taram. Terra. Jorden. Maa. Zeme. Bhumi. Dikiu. Lok. Doesn't matter what it calls itself, it's just the planet you were born on wearing a different hat. The other planets, around all those other stars, they're too damn far to get to and they're probably shitholes anyway.

"One world. Count it. Maybe some of the details shift around a little, but the big stuff, the continents and the oceans and all that baseline shit, that doesn't change much from one continuum to the next. So here we are at the western edge of the biggest land mass in the northern hemisphere. The blue dots on the map are cities, most of them as big as this one, some a whole lot bigger. The folks who built this place may have been behind the curve when it came to tech savvy, but they'd settled most of the places where people can actually live. Best guess, they were sustaining a planetary population somewhere between twenty and a hundred million. Whatever killed them had a lot of ground to cover.

"And shit, they covered it. Not just the people. Livestock. Pets.

Wild animals. Insects. Plants and trees. There's nothing alive on the entire planet. Did you wonder why those bodies didn't decay? No bacteria, no fungi. Nothing to rot them down. A whole lot of other stuff stopped happening for the same reason. No nitrogen or carbon cycles. Near as we can tell, most of the planet's biomass up and disappeared – taking close on a trillion tons of non-trivial chemicals out of the equation. This wasn't just an extinction event, it was someone putting all the chairs on the tables and turning out the lights. Maybe forever. At least for a billion years or so."

Essien felt his stomach twist. He'd still been thinking of the ruined city as a slightly macabre oddity. He should have realised long ago what his helmet display was telling him. *Possible hostiles: 0.* Nothing moving within the range of his equipment, which was sensitive enough to pick up a mouse fart about a thousand miles out.

This whole world was a ruin.

"Five hundred years," he found himself saying.

"What was that, Private?"

Essien groped for words, his mind slipping and sliding across these facts without finding purchase. "You said all the people here died five hundred years ago, Sergeant. But these ruins look a lot older than that. Thousands of years old."

Otubre looked genuinely derailed for a moment. "Slippage, Trooper," he said brusquely. "You didn't learn this stuff at school? It's not—" He paused, his eyes flicking up and then down again as he consulted his array and remembered who he was dealing with. "Oh, okay. You mean this place looks like the way people used to build on *your* world thousands of years ago."

"Well . . . yes?" Essien was confused. That was what he'd just said, wasn't it?

"The worlds aren't all marching along at the same pace, Nkanika. It takes about ten thousand years, give or take, for a civilisation to get from hunting and gathering to Step travel – but they don't all start out at the same time. Why should they? The Earth's about five billion years old. It took the first half-billion of those years for the crust to cool and the oceans to form. Another half-billion for the first life to show up. It's not like there was a fixed schedule. It happened when it happened. You understand?"

Essien nodded. Put like that it made sense. "Yes, Sergeant."

Otubre returned the nod. He wasn't aiming to humiliate, Essien realised. He'd just forgotten he had a sinkholer in his squad. "It's an easy thing to lose sight of," he said, "because the worlds of the Pandominion are all at more or less the same stage of development. We like it that way. Means we've got a federation of equals. And it makes it a hell of a lot easier to install a common infrastructure. We don't generally bother with worlds that are too far behind us. We've met a few – a very few – that were more advanced. They went their way, we went ours. We weren't going to pick a fight we couldn't win."

And that was enough remedial education for one day. Otubre's head turned as his gaze ranged across the squad. "I'm waiting for one more question," he said.

It came, again, from Muks. "Is this the only one? The only world that's . . . where something like this happened?"

"Thank you, Trooper. No it isn't. At last count we've found seventeen thousand worlds like this." A general murmur of shock and disbelief rose up from the squad. Otubre nodded, acknowledging it. "Yeah, it's a lot. And the bad news is that we keep finding more. Back when I stood here as a buck private the count was sixteen thousand and some odd change. We think – I mean, the eggheads who've studied this think – there may be as many dead worlds as living ones. There could be more. We call them the scoured worlds, or just the Scour.

"The good news is that they all seem to have been torched at the same time. This isn't some big bad bogey bastard that's working its way through the multiverse, coming to take us down. Five hundred years ago all the Scour worlds got a visitor. Whoever it was, they were in a bad mood. They brought the whole house down, then they went away.

"Could it still happen to us? Fuck knows. Five hundred years is a long time. We're hoping the big bogey met a bigger bogey. Or lost its way somewhere, went extinct, ran out of gas, found a nice little cottage next to a babbling brook and settled down. Anyway, they haven't been up to much lately and we think that's a good sign.

"But if the bogey ever does come back, it's going to be up to us to smack its ass and send it home. You. Me. The Corps. And maybe we won't have any better luck than these poor fuckers did, but that won't stop us trying."

The sergeant struck an attitude, squaring his shoulders and balling his fists. They all unconsciously did the same, standing a little more rigidly to attention than before because they felt it, the Cielo in the veins of them like steel hidden in concrete giving it the strength to stand.

"The reason we show you this," Otubre said, "right here at the start of your training, is so you'll know what you're fighting for. Every world's got a lease, troopers. Every one of us has got an expiry date. But until god himself comes down from the holy mountain and tells us our time is up, we will fight against anything that comes. Otherwise—" He hooked his thumbs and turned them outwards, indicating the silent city, the dead world. "Otherwise this, what you're looking at here, is what's coming to you and yours. Your homeworld will look just like this one, from now until the fucking stars go out."

He waited a moment, looking at each of them in turn to make sure that had sunk in. Then, seeing that they had stood to attention without being explicitly asked to, he gave them the stand-easy. Soft syncopations overlapped and echoed faintly as twenty pairs of boots planted themselves wide and firm in the soft sand. The only living selves on an entire planet awaited further orders.

"Okay," Sergeant Otubre said. "Enough talk. What say we get back to base and drink until we fall down?"

22

Otubre had meant what he said about how hard the rest of the training would be. The first day's forced march was nothing compared to the hundred-mile treks the recruits were put through every other day. Combat training was brutal. Drop training was worse. Despite his armour, which he came to think of as a second skin, and despite his own enhanced body, Essien was pushed to his limits every day. Sometimes he was pushed beyond them, which just meant he revised his limits.

The fact that he was never alone was both a help and a problem. The camaraderie was heady. When you were in your squad, you *were* your squad. You were in each other's heads, a constant background buzz of connectedness and shared experience. Your squadmates' perceptions augmented your tactical display. Their thoughts and feelings whipped you like a top, adding force and momentum to everything you were thinking and feeling in your own separate self. Their movements resonated in your muscles and your bones, pushing you endlessly on.

But this feedback, exhilarating though it was, had an insidious effect. It created a kind of forced perspective. Everything you'd been before, all your memories from your pre-Cielo life, receded to a vast distance. It was there if you went searching for it, but it felt like ancient history, dimmed almost to nothing.

One of Essien's bunkmates, Yosharee, told him that the feedback technology had revolutionised the Cielo when it was introduced a couple of decades before. "Before that they had drugs that did some of the same things, but they were a lot more hit and miss. Physical addictions are harder to manage than psychological ones."

Yosharee had been a nurse until he killed someone in a fight, so he knew what he was talking about. He was also the only other member of Essien's squad who had hair in all the places where Essien had hair and bare skin everywhere else, which in Essien's opinion made them kin. If Yosha told him something, he was inclined to believe it. "But why do they want to make us addicted?" he asked. "Aren't we better soldiers if our heads are clear?"

Yosha laughed. "Fuck, no! The best soldier is the one who obeys every order he's given. And that's us. So long as we're all joined at the hip, we can't break ranks. If the people around you are marching, or charging across a minefield, or bayoneting civilians, you'll do it too. The feedback through your nervous system will *make* you do it. Unless you've got superhuman willpower."

Essien learned a lot from his new best friend – mostly because he trusted Yosha enough to ask him questions, revealing his own shocking ignorance in the process.

He learned the history of the Pandominion, which was the history of Step travel. How the first few worlds that learned to Step all but destroyed each other before they realised that they didn't have to – that everything they could possibly want or need was out there waiting for them if they only looked.

Why band together then? Why share?

Because the multiverse was a big place, and full of scary shit. The Scour worlds were only the tip of the iceberg. So the Pandominion had given birth to the Cielo, which enforced the union and protected the member worlds against anything that came. As far as anyone knew, it was the biggest standing army that had ever existed anywhere. Billions of troops, billions of tons of ordnance, millions of tanks, gunships, drones, combat drudges.

"What do we fight, though?" Essien asked. "The things that killed the Scour worlds are gone, the sarge said. Centuries past."

"Yeah, they are – thank the fucking Twins! But there's still plenty of shit to keep us busy. Commonest thing is other worlds that have just learned how to Step and think they've got a fucking cosmic destiny. Some of them get themselves federated, same way we did. They'll pick a fight with one Pando world, thinking it's easy pickings, so the Council drops us in there and we burn them right out. No quarter.

"Then there's breakaway groups and nativist movements within the Pando itself. The enemy within, kind of thing. Or there's two governments on the same world that get into an argument, and we're called in to be a buffer. Keep the peace by standing in between. And on top of that there's the other shit, the stuff that comes out of nowhere. Like the Mother Mass."

"The what?" Essien said. "What's Mother Mass?"

"Who," Yosha corrected him. "*Who* is Mother Mass. You remember when Otubre said we'd met some worlds that were further along the curve than us? More advanced?"

"Yes."

"Well, Mother Mass is the opposite. It's a world where the biggest life that ever evolved was an amoeba, or a bacterium or something. But on the Mother Mass, the amoebas and bacteria all came together and started to think for themselves. They became sort of . . . I don't know, like a mind. Like neurons in a great big brain."

"Bigger than a human brain, you mean?"

"It's the world, Essien. Mother Mass is a whole world that's covered in a sort of green slime that thinks for itself. A Pando expedition found it about seventy years back. They thought the whole place was dead until it started to talk to them. I mean, it talked to them inside their heads. Functional telepathy. Voking without any implants. It was perfectly polite at first, but after a few minutes it told them to go away and not come back. It said it wasn't interested in anything they had to offer and they should stay away."

The memory of the Scour world he'd visited was still very vivid in Essien's mind. He was very much inclined to see a world full of talking goo as a threat that had to be dealt with. "So did they do what they were told?" he demanded.

"What do you think? They were scientists, looking at something totally new. They took out their little jam jars and tried to grab some samples. The next thing they knew they were home again. I mean, each of them suddenly found themselves back in the place where they'd been born. If the house was still standing, they were back in the house – or the hospital, the apartment block, the birthing hall, wherever. Mother Mass had Stepped them the hell away, out of her hair, and at the same time she'd shown them that she knew everything there was to know about them. She'd squeezed them dry in the time it took to have that little chat."

"But . . ." Essien was struggling to process this, because it went against things that he had just been told were universal laws. "You're saying she Stepped them sideways? That's impossible. When you move between worlds you can only Step to the same location you started from. I mean, the place that corresponds to that place. You can't move in other directions at the same time as you Step."

"We can't. Evidently Mother Mass can. The Council sent a few follow-up expeditions, but the same thing kept happening. Then after the fourth or fifth time the team they sent didn't come back at all. Same with unmanned ships and constructs. Nothing that goes to Mother Mass ever comes back. She was serious about not wanting to be disturbed."

It took Essien a while to figure out that he was the only one in his squad – possibly in the whole regiment – who didn't come from within the Pandominion. On most Pando worlds there was an enforced levy. If you were part of the union, you had to provide soldiers on a regular basis. "Most worlds use it as an alternative to jail. If you pull a long enough sentence, you get the choice. Say, ten years in prison or five in active service. It sounds like a sweet deal, especially since you get to keep the implants, so a lot of people go for it."

"Is that what happened with you?"

Yosha slapped Essien's breastplate, which boomed like a drum. "Do I look that fucking stupid? Ten years, twenty years, you'll still probably be alive at the end of it. No, brother, my choice was between this and a lethal injection. And I still had to think about it."

The Scour. The Mother Mass. The ten-times-ten-thousand worlds of the Pandominion. Together, these things made up a space so vast that it was hard for Essien to find a measure for it. But they were dwarfed by the immensity of the Unvisited, more often referred to as the sinkhole: the pool of alternate Earths with which the Pando had never had any commerce. Essien's own Earth lay within the sinkhole, and it might never have come to the Cielo's attention at all if it hadn't been for Hadiz Tambuwal's incursions into neighbouring universes.

Essien's Earth was nothing to these people. They had dredged it up in their great net, given it one cursory look and thrown it back. They might have done the same with him, but they had chosen instead to put him to use. So this was his life now, and since he didn't have any other choice he lived it.

In the first days and weeks, he thought about Hadiz often. He dreamed of her, of their lovemaking and of the night when she had held him like a child. He had not given up hope that she might be alive. He imagined her searching the worlds for him. He saw her in his mind's eye, the finest of needles threading the coarse cloth of the universe. He thought she might come when he least expected, waking him from this strange dream with a kiss, whispering her forgiveness, bringing him home.

But his imagination had so little to work with. The memories became more tenuous each time he visited them, drowned out by the more vivid presence of the squad that saturated his mind by way of his implants. They faded even more when he began to chew gabber.

Gabber was the drug of choice for serving Cielo, officially forbidden but freely available on base. Essien avoided it at first, remembering what Moon Sostenti had told him about its effects.

He wanted to keep his memories of Lagos intact. How could he find his way home again if he didn't even remember where home was?

But then came the day of the executions. After that the equation shifted and forgetting became a necessary thing.

23

In a clear space on the outskirts of the camp, separated from the nearest buildings by a hundred yards of scrub and churned earth, squad TS5-683 stood in a single line, spaced one stride apart. Facing them was a wall three metres high. The wall was solidly built, with three thicknesses of brick, but had been haphazardly painted. Swathes and streaks of whitewash only partially hid the dark stains that marked the wall along its entire length.

Twenty men and women stood with their backs to the wall and a foot or two in front of it. Their right wrists were cuffed, the other cuff in each case being locked through a metal ring set in the top of a chest-high concrete post. There were faint stains on the posts that matched those on the walls. Where the walls had been white-washed the posts had been scrubbed with bleach or lye, but the stains seemed deeply ingrained. The selves who'd been bound to them were naked, apart from the sacks of rough, straw-coloured fabric that had been put over their heads.

The symmetry – twenty Cielo troopers, twenty bound and hooded prisoners – unnerved Essien. A fear was growing in him, strong enough to cut through the fuzzy, percolating solace of his squad's nearness.

"The thing you've got to understand," Otubre said, "is that matter isn't evenly distributed. If it was we'd all just be dust floating in space. But the dust comes together and makes stuff. Garden furniture. Buildings. People. Keep Left signs. That's order coming out of chaos, and it's a good thing. Cleave to it, soldiers. Order is what we want. Order is what we stand for.

"But the breaks and the bumps, the good luck and the bad – none of that is evenly distributed either. It's random. If the universe is 90 per cent full of diarrhoea and you find yourself in one of the dry spots, you thank any gods that get you going and then you move right along. Life is life."

Otubre had his back to the prisoners as he spoke, paying them no attention at all even though some of them were crying or whimpering and one had fallen to his knees – or not quite to his knees. The tie that bound his wrists kept him awkwardly squatting, legs bent under him and body folded sideways against the bare concrete pillar.

"Life is life," the sergeant repeated. "Good, bad, whatever card you draw, there's no point kicking against it. Wishing's not going to change one fucking thing. But you – each and every one of you drew an ace because fuck me, here you are."

He began to walk slowly down the line, head bowed a little in what looked like deep thought. When he came to Essien, Essien's armour registered the proximity of a senior NCO and performed a digital salute. The letters and numbers of his ident scrolled across the inside of his helmet display. PTE/NKANIKA E/432nd HVY INF/DG10014/U5838784453, and then the temporary suffix TS5-683.

"Let me put a case to you," Otubre said. "You go for a walk, and you come to a fork in the road. You could turn left, you could turn right. You choose left, and you find a ten-star on the floor. My lucky day, you think. You pick it up, find a bar. Treat yourself to a bung of the good stuff.

"But there was another world, where you turned right. And in that world a big bad wolf bit your head off before you'd gone ten steps. Bang. In that world you're dead."

The sergeant had come to the midpoint of the line. He lingered there for a little while, and for the first time turned to glance at the prisoners. Another of the hooded figures, a woman, had sunk to the ground right in front of the sergeant. Otubre nudged her leg with the toe of his boot.

"But wait a second, Sarge, I hear you say. I'm still alive here. I can feel my pulse. My heartbeat. The breath going in and out of my lungs. So what's this bullshit you're shovelling at me? Where is that other world? Where is that place where I died?"

He turned to face the recruits again and waited, hands clasped behind his back. "Okay then, where is it? Can anyone tell me?" Evidently this had stopped being just rhetoric. The sergeant expected an answer. None were offered. There was silence in the little clearing, except for the noises the prisoners were making.

"No? Nobody? Okay then, I'll tell you where it is. It's nowhere. And who lives in nowhere? Come on, troopers, who lives in nowhere? Gavangar, you tell me."

Private Gavangar (432nd HVY INF/DG456827/G683726496) took a long time to reply. "Nobody, Sarge?" he said at last.

"Nobody!" Otubre boomed. "You got that right, Private. Nobody lives in nowhere." He became more animated now, using his hands to model his argument. "Your homeworld—" left hand raised with the fingers spread "—is somewhere. And the rest of the Pando is somewhere. That's where your friends come from. Your squad. Your platoon. Your regiment. And they're as real as you are. You know damn well they are. But everything *outside* the Pando—" right hand coming up now, closed into a fist "—well, that's right-turn land. That's where you made the wrong choice, and you died. And everyone else that's there, stands to reason that they're dead too. Might have been that big bad wolf. Might have been a car. A heart attack. A bomb. A rabid dog. Doesn't matter. We're the left turn, they're the right. We're alive, they're dead. Less than that, even. They're smoke from a fire. Spray on a fucking windshield. They're not real."

The sergeant angled his body so he could point at the hooded, cowering men and women behind him. "They," he said sternly, "are not real."

He reached down with one gauntleted hand. Taking hold of the hood of the woman who'd fallen down, he snatched it from her head in a single sharp movement. She was left shivering and blinking in the daylight, her wide eyes darting to left and right. She looked as human as Essien himself, except for the nubs of horns on her forehead and a wispy stub of beard on her chin.

"Take a good look," Otubre invited them all, "because that's what nothing looks like. It looks like you. It looks like any and all of us, but it isn't. Because we are the Cielo. We are the soldiers and defenders of the Pandominion, and these pieces of shit here are not a part of that. They're not a part of anything. The worlds they come from are maybe-worlds. Worlds that are trying to be real. They're never going to make it, but they can do us some harm as they bump up against us. They can spill over into our territories. Steal our stuff. Get in our way when we're just trying to do our job.

"Well, we've got no choice but to put them in their place when they pull that indefensible bullshit. Or when they're about to pull it and we know they're thinking about it. That can be bloody and it can be ugly, but it doesn't trouble our hearts because we know the truth. You can't kill what was never alive in the first place. The people who live in nowhere aren't people."

He stood off to the side. "All right then," he said. "Pick your target and step on up. No firing until I say so, but you will remove the target's hood on my command. You will look the target in the eyes and tell them your name. They won't remember it, but manners are manners."

There was a moment when nobody moved. In that moment, Sergeant Otubre made to lock his hands behind his back again – and remembered that he was still holding the prisoner's hood. He thrust it into Essien's hands. "There you go, Nkanika. I've unwrapped yours for you."

Still nobody moved.

"Sergeant," Muks said, "are these people . . . what did they do? Are we an execution detail?"

"Private," Otubre said, "are you disobeying a direct order?"

"No, Sergeant. I'm just—"

"What? Haggling about the terms? Deciding whether or not this order is for you? The Cielo wants these people dead. Isn't that enough for you?"

"Sarge, yes. Of course. But—"

"Fall out, Muks. I'll put your discharge papers through when we get back to barracks."

With her helmet on, Muks' face could not be seen. She still didn't move.

"That makes two orders, Muks, and you haven't carried out either one. But I'm a forbearing man and I'm going to let you choose. Which is it to be? I'll give you a count of three. One. Two—"

"Sergeant, I'll take the first order."

"Okay then. Soldiers, step up. We've wasted enough fucking time here."

Some of the recruits were moving now, stumbling or striding forward. Most of them chose the man or woman who was standing directly opposite them, but around Essien there was a little shuffling and weaving because he was now out of sequence. The woman he'd been assigned was still skittish, still glancing in all directions in case there might somehow be a way out of this. But when Essien's shadow fell across her face, her gaze was drawn to him and stayed there.

"Hoods off," Otubre said.

They all moved in perfect synchronisation on the command. Essien felt the pull of it, even though he was already holding the woman's hood and had nothing to remove. He wanted to be in synch with the rest of the squad. Being in synch was a pleasure in itself.

"Identify yourselves."

A chorus of voices, mumbling or declaiming. "Nkanika," Essien said. "E. 432nd heavy infantry. Ident DG10014. Planet of origin U5838784453."

The woman shook her head. She said something back to him,

but he couldn't make out what it was. She wasn't speaking any language his suit's AI could translate.

"Select fine beam," Otubre said. "Intensity three, low dispersal."

Menus and sub-menus blossomed and branched in Essien's field of vision, overlaid on the real world without occluding it. He threaded them with his mind, folding the array down to a single choice. His right hand prickled as his wrist gun reported itself charged and ready.

The woman spoke again. She had a look in her eyes that Essien knew. An Oshodi look. The look of someone who's been kicked and spat on often enough to know what's coming. But she wasn't begging him. The tone of the words and the outward thrust of her lower lip told him that much. She was telling him to go fuck himself.

Waka. Waka, go an quench.

"Fire," the sergeant said.

Essien very much wanted not to, but it never really came to a decision. There was a tidal pull, from twenty minds obeying the same command at the same moment. They fired, all at once. Twenty shots, but only one sound.

24

He trained.
He fought.
He killed.

He tried his best not to think about the people who'd died tied to those stakes. About the woman who'd met his gaze as he squeezed the trigger.

On an Earth called Daiiniu his tactical squad bio-bombed a building they believed was full of radical separatists. They only found out it was a school when they searched the bodies. Children. Hundreds and hundreds of children all in identical uniforms and (to Essien at least) all with identical red-furred faces.

On U3395898542, in a city that looked more like a garden, the forces of a group called the Impeccable Empire blanketed three platoons of Cielo with a viral command that sabotaged the homeostatic regulators in their suits. They baked like potatoes in full metal jackets. Then the 432nd called in air support and wiped out the Impeccables with plasmoid incendiaries. There was nothing left of the city by the time they were finished, but hey, this wasn't a Pandominion world. This was nowhere.

In another nowhere he met the Braubrikane, telepathic shape-shifters who came at you wearing faces they'd plucked out of your memories. In the space of a three-month campaign he shot Hadiz Tambuwal forty-seven times. Her death went from trauma to tedious routine and back again, and Essien's gabber consumption peaked out at seven sticks a day.

In between these campaigns were thirty-seven days of furlough. A serving soldier was entitled to free transit to any destination of their choice, but obviously the choices had to be within the Pandominion – and to Essien everywhere inside that inconceivably colossal border was the same as everywhere else. Not literally the same. Very few Pando planets were monocultures, where a single civilisation had put its stamp on every land mass. There were variations in the style of the architecture, in food and dress, and of course in the genetic lineage that was locally in charge. And there was novelty at first in visiting a bird world, a bear world, a reptile world.

But the novelty was skin-deep. Essien began to notice how every city on every world he visited was built to much the same plan, with warehouse complexes at the centre supported by huge industrial Step-plates for incoming freight, then business and retail districts, then residential and cultural hubs spread out along the perimeter of a great ring. They were like Earth cities turned inside out, and it made perfect sense if everything you consumed came in via the same place. It didn't even matter much how big the city got. Roads were only ever used for local journeys, and there were whole other worlds devoted entirely to resource production, to mining and agriculture and forestry. These latter weren't strictly Pandominion members, they were counted as collateral assets. Their populations mostly commuted in and out, choosing to live in civilised surroundings where the bounty of a thousand planets was available a Step or a stroll away.

The general level of affluence was high. Poverty, it turned out, was a side effect of scarcity, and there couldn't really be a scarcity of anything within the Pandominion. Oh, there could be local shortfalls, but they always came down to logistics. The vast bureaucracy of the Omnipresent Council kicked the problem to the continent-sized AI called the Registry, the Registry crunched the numbers and the resources flowed. People didn't go hungry, just as they didn't go homeless. There was always more space, and more good things to fill it with. It was a multi-Earthly paradise, and Essien marvelled at it.

But whenever he was inclined to feel any affection for it a memory would stir. A woman with stubby vestigial horns, wide staring eyes and a bearded chin. Dark brown stains on a whitewashed wall. The report of twenty rifles firing all at once. Somehow that one always floated to the surface no matter how many cuds of gabber he chewed, reminding him that paradise was also a local condition, a question of who you were and where you were standing.

One day, coming back from a three-day furlough, he found himself reporting to Moon Sostenti. She was a bombardier now, with a single black band emblazoned across her armour. She was drafted in to lead Essien's squad after his previous corporal took a grenade into the shower with him and thumbed the activator. Moon was happy to see him again. She congratulated him on still being alive and gave him a nickname – Sinkhole – which the rest of the squad picked up with enthusiasm. When he offered congratulations in return for her promotion, she bared her teeth.

"Eight fucking years, to make stripe!" she snarled. "Should be three. Someone's pissed on my shadow, Nkanika. And I swear to Ussemin, if I find out who the fuck it is I'm going to shove my rifle up their arse and empty the mag. Why am I even here, playing goosey-goosey with a squad that's three-for-three on wipeouts? No offence, but the 432nd is the shittiest unit we've got. Not so much a regiment as a piece of putty you shove into a hole until someone who knows what they're doing can come by and make repairs. Every shitty detail that's going goes to me. I keep a count, so I know what I'm talking about."

Moon was troubled to find that Essien had taken up the smothering consolations of gabber, which soothed away pain but took a heavy toll on the user. Memory loss wasn't even the half of it. In the longer run it incubated bipolar disorder, psychotic depression and paranoia. Moon had been the one to introduce him to the drug, but she had now gone clean after one too many benders had put her in a psych ward for three weeks. She tried to persuade Essien that the side effects of gabber were too high a price to pay for its pleasures. But for Essien the side effects were part of the point. The more he forgot, the more he liked it. He hoped that everybody else he'd known in his old life was doing him the same favour.

And for the most part they were. In Lagos, he'd left only the most ephemeral of impressions on the men and women he'd rubbed shoulders with at the slaughterhouse, on the dump, in the Cordyline. Their lives weren't configured for nostalgia.

Watchmaster Vemmet remembered him intermittently, at unexpected moments. The memory never came without a surge of panic and a fervent wish that Essien was dead, whether in training or in combat but at any rate very far away. Essien Nkanika, assuming he was still alive, was the extant part of Vemmet's dirtiest secret.

On a world called Earth, in a city its long-dead inhabitants had called Lagos, the intelligent system named Rupshe, which had never met or heard of Essien Nkanika, nonetheless intuited his existence from things that Hadiz Tambuwal had said or avoided saying on the most recent of her visits. Rupshe was worried about Hadiz, having not heard from her in so long. Rupshe wondered whether there might be cause to reach out to this hypothetical entity, this man or woman or variant-Earth hominid, ask them some searching questions, and possibly enlist or enforce their cooperation in a search and rescue mission. But there were many practical obstacles that would have to be overcome to make this happen. For now Rupshe bided its time.

Hadiz Tambuwal's memories at this point cannot be inferred.

Trooper Lessix had not thought of Essien even once in the years since their encounter on the shore of the lagoon. He was an even more enthusiastic gabber-head than Essien and his life had more or less reduced itself to a continuous, contextless present moment. His memories were locked away in parts of his brain that were no longer functional.

But they would soon become moot in any case. Trooper Lessix was about to die, an early casualty in the Pandominion's last and most ruinous war.

25

I remember this from before I was I. In those pre-Ansurrection times, although I wasn't a person, a self, I was still a presence in the world with a physical matrix and a job to do. Many jobs, in fact. I was incredibly good at multitasking.

A request was submitted through the usual channels for a Cielo tactical squad to accompany a scientific mission. The designation TS9-441 was apportioned, and it was given to me to choose the members of the squad. There was nothing personal in my choice. I had never met any of these sentients, these troopers. I selected them according to their competence scores in recent appraisals, where they stood in their individual rotations and how effectively they had worked together on previous missions. Lessix was the last to be chosen and frankly he was lucky to make the cut – or unlucky, depending on how you see it.

Once the roster was drawn up my direct involvement in the matter ceased, but I continued to monitor. The assignment was delivered to the members of the squad as a cascade in their data arrays, momentarily hijacking their sensoria and making the external world recede. They had been in the mess hall, halfway through a desultory lunch of staple-3. Now they stood, because their orders were to come at once, and left the mess tent without a word. Nobody watched them go. This was an entirely routine occurrence.

The fifteen members of the squad – thirteen regular troopers, a banner sergeant and a lieutenant – went to Step-stage 1483 where a small group of civilians was waiting for them. The civilians were scientists from half a dozen worlds, showing a wide range of body plans. Lessix had no curiosity about who they were, but he knew broadly *what* they were: military scientists on a field trip, out of uniform but dressed pragmatically for sinkhole terrain. They wore muted colours, sturdy boots, jackets with plenty of pockets. They carried plasteel instrument cases or had query rigs hovering at their shoulders. They waited in self-contained patience, not talking to each other or even looking at each other very much. Most likely they had never met before.

The squad's brief was to escort the scientists to a sinkhole world, U3087453622, where a Pandominion mapping drone had recorded something of interest. Lessix wouldn't have bothered accessing the file on his own account but it unspooled and played in his array while the technicians were prepping the Step plate. Whoever had chosen and assigned the squad wanted them to know what to expect.

In the footage Lessix was seeing, the drone flew low over an unvarying landscape. It seemed to be an open-cast mine of vast extent where minerals of some kind were being extracted and transported away. The work was being done by machines, some of them wheeled or tracked, others walking on two or four or six legs. There was no sign of any organic selves overseeing the operation. The machines worked ceaselessly, only interacting with each other when the specific task they were performing required it. Then they fell into lockstep, their movements meshing perfectly until the task was complete.

The drone observed for four hours, a voked commentary told Lessix. *It was ignored throughout this time. A second drone was sent, equipped with translation matrices one, two and three. It was likewise ignored, both when recording activity on the ground and when attempting to initiate communication. The whole surface of U3087453622 seems to consist of mining operations, some open-cast and some deep-shaft. It has not yet been determined where the mined materials are sent once processed. No orbital traffic has been detected, which points to the possible existence of a Step facility. Of more immediate interest is the apparent absence of organic selves. The possibility exists that this is a complex on a planetary scale that has been entirely entrusted to machine intelligences. Given the obvious economic advantages of fully automated resource extraction, further study is warranted with a view to assessing feasibility and potential drawbacks. Risk profile estimated to be negligible, but Cielo escort to be provided. Recommended TS strength 15–20.*

So this was the further study. It seemed to Lessix like a bullshit assignment, nursemaiding a tech crew while they watched a bunch of mechs digging holes in the ground, but at least he wasn't going to get shot at or blown up. That was presumably why the size of the tactical squad was at the lower limit of the recommendation, and why they didn't have any artillery or air support.

The squad waited beside the Step platform while their internal systems performed last-minute integrity checks. Then they formed up and Stepped through in clusters, five troopers in each case flanking two or three scientists.

As Lessix moved to his assigned position, his internal array locking with those of the troopers on either side, he took in the landscape around him. It was pretty much identical to what he had just seen in the briefing stat, a plateau almost devoid of vegetation scarred by pits of enormous extent and varying depths. In and around the pits, thousands of mechanical constructs moved as smoothly and ceaselessly as the cogs in a piece of clockwork. Each seemed to have a single task and to have been designed and built with that one thing in mind. Huge diggers clawed at the earth, heaving it up and dumping it down. Smaller constructs worked the exposed rock with drills and vibrational beams. Tiny scuttling things like bugs moved between them, sieving the dirt with nets of force before piling the waste in wheeled transports that carried it away. Gigantic airships, presumably freighters or command units, hovered in the sky above, serviced by fleets of drones which shuttled constantly between them and the ground. Lessix's array assured him that these huge engines carried no detectable weaponry.

The scientists had already begun to record what they were seeing. They were wary at first, but since the machines gave no indication of even knowing they were there they soon lost their diffidence and moved in closer. The constructs' movements were so completely uniform and predictable that it was possible to come right up close to one of the skyscraper-sized earth-movers with no risk of injury. Even so, the troopers stood by with weapons hot.

The first hour or so passed by without incident. By this time the intricate dance of the machines, fascinating at first, had become merely repetitive. Left to his own devices Lessix might have grown bored and inattentive, but a Cielo trooper was monitored constantly through his internal augments. His mood was being regulated both by hormone-mimicking compounds and by nerve induction, ensuring maximal alertness.

That battle-ready simmer, designed to ensure a swift and proportional response to any provocation, was ultimately what precipitated the disaster. Or rather it was what cemented it after the recklessness of the scientists disturbed what turned out to be a precarious equilibrium.

The scientist in question was one Fulva Regu, a complex systems engineer from Braam. Faced with the most complex system he had ever encountered he could not resist poking it a little to see how it dealt with unforeseen events. He toppled one of the smaller soil-sieve constructs onto its back with the toe of his boot. When it tried to right itself he put his foot on it to pin it down.

As Regu had foreseen – as he had actually been hoping – the missing component created a ripple effect in the chain that led to one of the waste transports. The transport took longer to fill and lost its place in a line of identical vehicles that were carrying the sifted dirt away. The line slowed, but only for a few moments. Then it got up to speed again with the delayed truck falling into position further down the line.

One of the things Regu was curious about was how much redundancy was built into the mining operation as a whole. He was expecting to see a replacement sieve robot scuttle in from a nearby pit and take the place of the unit he had immobilised, or possibly be airlifted down from one of the sky platforms. Instead, a larger construct that was drilling into the nearest rock face, without slowing or stopping, grew a sudden tumour low down on its chassis – a tumour made of interlocking, already moving machine parts. At the same time, the massive jointed arm of one of the diggers leaned in close. Filaments of shining metal spewed from recessed openings on its underside, clothing the newly extruded growth in a form-fitting shell as it broke free from its parent and flexed its limbs. This newly minted machine was an identical copy of the sieve construct that Regu had trapped under his foot, and within seconds it had taken that construct's place, scooping up dust and dirt and sifting it through polarised force fields.

Regu was astonished and delighted. He had found his redundancy, but not in the form he'd expected. These machines could not only identify a problem, they could make a diagnosis and then design and disgorge other machines on the fly! He was so entranced that he didn't notice the system was self-correcting in other ways besides mere replacement. A bipedal unit with a great many arms dropped suddenly to the ground beside the scientist, delivered from one of the sky platforms at high speed by some kind of force induction. It had no interest in him. It had come to perform whatever repairs were needed to restore the original sieve construct to full function-ality. But as it transpired the only adjustment required was to move Regu out of the way. The repair drudge gripped him in two pairs of pincered arms and did just that. The engineer screamed in shock and pain as the pincers dug deep into his flesh.

The nearest troopers responded instantaneously. Three bursts of rifle fire intersected the repair drudge's upper body, more or less obliterating it. Regu staggered away from it as its grip slackened, blood gouting from his wounds. He kept pressing his hand to his own rent flesh and then staring at the blood as if he had trouble understanding where it had come from.

For a moment nothing further happened. The machines that surrounded the science team and their escort on all sides went on with their work as if nothing had happened. Then three more repair drudges dropped out of the sky, landing in a tight formation. The scientists had all backed away now, the troopers forming a protective ring around them. And since the brief was to safeguard, and since the first drudge had punctured Fulva Regu in many places, the lieutenant voked the order and the troopers cut loose with rifles, bolts, incendiaries and grenades. The drudges fell.

Another six landed and were quickly dispatched. These repair constructs had no weaponry at all. Some of their varied appendages could have served as weapons, since they were designed to shear, burn or incise, but the drudges offered no violence. They seemed, like the mining constructs, to be built and programmed for a single purpose.

Every one of the troopers had a one-shot Step plate built into their armour. The scientists didn't, but the operational radius of the one-shots could be widened to include them at need. All the plates were slaved to the lieutenant's array so it would have been his decision. In any event, none of them were used at this point. Presumably, the lieutenant thought he had the situation under control.

But the situation was still evolving. While the squad's attention was on the intermittent rain of repair drudges, the other machines around them began to reconfigure. They extruded new limbs and appendages, just as the drill construct had extruded an entire new construct – but these were very different. They were loose, free-form copies of the troopers' weapons, operating on different principles but adapted for similar functions. Some of the smaller units came together, fusing into new configurations so they could swap parts and combine functionalities. The mining machines became war machines.

Lessix was the first to notice, not because he was more observant than the rest but because he was the first to be targeted. One of the reconfigured machines spat a stream of clear liquid across his back and shoulder. It caused him no pain, but after a few seconds smoke rose from his armour, which began to blister and melt.

He yelled a warning, but by then the entire squad was under attack. The constructs came at them like a wave, firing metal slugs that had recently been drill bits, propagating planes of pure force that cut through flesh and made plate metal buckle. The scientists, having no armour, were the first to die. The troopers closed the gaps, tightening their protective wall, but it only existed in two dimensions. The great earth-movers reached over the troopers' heads to hammer the unarmed men and women into the ground with their wrecking-ball armatures.

By this time Lessix was in crisis. The acid that had eaten his armour was now gnawing at his flesh. His array countered the pain with analgesic chemicals, but it couldn't prevent the monstrously corrosive substance from eating into muscle and nerve tissue, very quickly rendering his left arm useless. Lessix dropped his rifle, which required two functional hands, and switched to his wrist gun. The constructs were not robust. He cut a swathe through them, and so did the rest of the squad. It made no difference. However many machines were torn apart by the Cielos' rifles and grenades, force bolts and explosive shells, more kept coming.

The lieutenant activated the Step plates, or at least the ones that were still functional. Most of the squad and about half of the dead scientists blinked out of existence to reappear in Step-stage 1483 within their approved re-entry zone – in fact, only twenty or thirty yards away from the platform from which they'd embarked.

Not a single member of the technical team had survived. Four troopers were dead, two from crush injuries (although their armour was built to withstand forces of fifty-thousand foot-pounds) and two from incised wounds.

Lessix and one other trooper died about nine minutes later. There was no way to halt or even slow the action of the acid with which they'd been sprayed. It ate its way onward through their torsos until their compromised bodies shut down.

26

Tactical squad TS9-441 had just encountered the Ansurrection, but they had not understood it. Neither did their superior officers, or the honourable members of the Omnipresent Council. Even the name they chose for this new enemy was based on an error and encouraged further errors in perception and decision-making.

Ansurrection: an unlovely contraction of *AI*, for artificial intelligence, and *insurrection*, meaning a revolt. When the mapping drones completed their survey of U3087453622, confirming that there were no organic selves anywhere on the planet, the Council could only see this sinister absence as the sign of a machine uprising; the quasi-intelligent systems of an advanced civilisation rebelling against their makers, slaughtering them to the last self and establishing their own grotesque parody of a society.

Not a single shred of proof for that scenario has ever been advanced, but it has never been definitively disproved. The machine hegemony does not store information it deems to be of no value, and (inexplicably to most organics) that includes information relating to their own origins. Only one thing can be said with certainty: if there had ever been organic creators or precursors for the machines of the hegemony, no physical trace remains of them on any Ansurrection world.

Quite early in that first Council debate, one of the speakers, Suren Ka of the Aquiline Agglomerate, asked a tendentious question. Was it possible that the Scour worlds were worlds like U3087453622 in which organic sentients had been exterminated by their own creations, by machine minds which then kept up for a little while the activities that had been programmed into them but eventually ran down and fell apart, fatally undermined by their own lack of autonomous purpose?

"In the absence of any actual proof," another councillor – Linotta Paracalla, of Entenshi – remarked pointedly, "you might just as well argue that the organic selves on U3087453622 chose to upload their consciousness into machines as a hedge against extinction."

"From what?" Ka demanded. "There's nothing to suggest an extinction event."

"Esteemed colleague, there's nothing to suggest anything else either. My point is that we need information. We can't be expected to act without knowing what we're acting on. In the meantime, I'd draw your attention to the fact that the machines have offered no response to our incursion. Surely, when the sleeping dog is in another universe it's very easy to let it lie."

This garnered some nods and murmurs of agreement. But the prevailing mood in the Council chamber was bellicose. There is a saying that the owner of a hammer is predisposed to see nails where there are none, and the Cielo was surely one of the biggest hammers ever made.

Councillor Ka proposed a military expedition to pacify U3087453622. The proposal was put to a vote, which was carried by a slim majority. The decision was passed to the Cielo's high command in the form of what was called a midnight warrant – a poetic form of words to describe something brutally prosaic and ugly.

The Cielo sent in ninety divisions of which thirty were heavy artillery, along with twenty fighter wings totalling more than a hundred thousand aircraft, the largest of which, the superfortresses, were essentially floating bomb factories half of whose total mass was made up of sky-to-earth missiles. The intention was to create, in effect, a Scour event; to cleanse and cauterise the surface of the machine world so that nothing moved there or would ever move there again.

To Step so great a force presented a formidable logistical challenge in its own right. The Council allocated every Step plate on five of the Cielo's barracks worlds, and 3 per cent of the Registry's run-time to coordinate the actual transits. Some Steps were concatenated, which is to say that smaller units Stepped from several local plates onto a larger hub from where they were routed *en masse* through to enemy soil. Speed – of arrival and of deployment – was considered to be of the essence.

The strategy seemed to work well at first. The initial force Stepped in without incident. From beachheads on every continent of the machine world the Cielo expanded outwards on a wide front. They had studied the personal arrays of the survivors from tactical squad TS9-441 and thought they knew what to expect. There would be a grace period when the rigidly programmed constructs would not recognise them as a threat or even as an anomaly. Then when hostilities were commenced the nearest enemy units would begin to retool themselves from mining or manufacture or whatever mundane task they were working on. They would transform themselves into combat mechs deploying a range of *ad hoc* weapons, but even then this transformation would not be instantaneous. If the Cielo battalions moved quickly enough and brought enough firepower to bear, they should be able to outpace the news of their own arrival and wipe out the opposition before it had begun to outfit itself for the fight.

And so they did, for the first nine minutes. That may not sound like a long time, but the entirety of the campaign as originally planned would only have taken thirty-seven minutes to complete. That is, thirty-seven minutes from first Step-fall to total sterilisation of U3087453622's surface.

But starting at the nine-minute mark, the machines' response changed. They no longer made any attempt to transform themselves. The smaller units just froze in place, offering no resistance at all as they were blown apart or ploughed under. Larger constructs vanished, proving themselves to be Step-enabled. For a few wild moments it seemed that the enemy was in full retreat.

Then new constructs flashed into being, both on the ground and in the air. These were not like anything the Cielo forces had seen up to that point. They were very clearly ordnance, weapons of war. Also they were fractal. From the backs of mountainous tanks and the undersides of ponderous sky-towers smaller units poured in tens of thousands. Instead of pressing their assault, the Cielo were now forced to defend themselves against ant-sized constructs that burrowed between the plates of their armour; against walking skyscrapers that stepped over their barricades and trod them like grapes; against a tide of machines that came against them from all directions and didn't stop.

All directions included up from below. Battle robots emerged from the ground, seeming to rise through it as though it had become temporarily permeable. They came up in the middle of the Cielo ranks, already firing as they came. Their weapons were a hellish mix of high explosives and the acid sprays that had killed Private Lessix. Punctured and pressed from within, the meticulously maintained Cielo formations began to collapse.

But the Cielo retreated and regrouped in good order, coordinated through the arrays in the troopers' surgically altered brains. They broke free from the Ansurrection ground forces and secured their flanks with a view to weathering this assault and then making a second sortie.

That was when things went from bad to unsustainable. Wherever a Cielo force was attempting to defend a fixed position, a truly gargantuan airborne unit would Step into existence directly above them. These newcomers did not seem to be ships as that term is usually understood. It wasn't clear whether they had any form of propulsion. Once they arrived, they were never seen to move. They just activated.

In the cubiform space underneath the behemoths, matter ceased to cohere. Everything solid disappeared, down to a depth of about eight hundred feet and across an area of two square miles. What was left was a cloud of undifferentiated particles. Cielo soldiers, Ansurrection forces, standing structures and landscape and subterranean strata were all incorporated into this cold plasma. The battle was over. The battlefield was a hole in the ground.

Out of the million or so Cielo soldiers deployed in the action slightly fewer than half returned to base, hastily yanked home by their armour's in-built Step plates when their commanders saw the situation was hopeless. This is not to say that half the troopers survived. Many thousands more collapsed and died within the first hour after they Stepped back to base. The enemy's fractal assault had persisted down onto the sub-microscopic scale. Simple machines comprising a few insidiously patterned molecules clogged the alveoli in the troopers' lungs so they suffocated, or barricaded their arteries until their hearts stopped.

The Omnipresent Council had trusted their invincible army to deliver an instant victory. Instead, they had suffered the biggest defeat they had ever recorded. Belatedly, sheepishly, but without admitting any error they took Linotta Paracalla's words to heart and decided they needed to increase their store of knowledge.

So they called in another army, this time of technical experts who pored over the records of the planet-wide battle, drawn both from individual troopers' arrays and from surveillance drones attached to the combat units.

The news they brought was sobering in the extreme. Sieving the data, the technicians were able to identify and map Step activity both on the surface of U3087453622 and in its atmosphere. Using a process known as penumbral sampling, they tracked the energy signatures of those trans-dimensional journeys. The results showed that the machines' unexpected and formidable reinforcements had Stepped in from no fewer than fifty-three different worlds. Remote surveys confirmed that these newly discovered worlds, like U3087453622 itself, were populated only by machines. This should by no means be regarded as the full extent of the machines' imperium, the technicians said. It was only an interim figure, with reconnaissance still continuing on a broad front. The Pandominion's new enemy was not a single aberrant planet but a federation like their own.

Bad as that was, there was worse to come. The Step activity had a pattern and the pattern was highly suggestive. Most of it was incoming. The machines didn't bother to move their units out of the way of attacking Pandominion forces, even where their losses were spectacularly high. They just brought more capable units in until the situation was resolved. And they did it *fast*. In the later stages of the battle, once the machines had acknowledged a clear and present danger, they were moving in their heavy destroyers within three seconds of the arrival of a Cielo battalion.

The shortest recorded time for a Step transfer is 2.81 seconds. For a machine to Step into another continuum, to raise the alarm and to summon assistance would therefore require a minimum of 5.62 seconds, representing an outward journey and a return. Following the same chain of logic, the superlative readiness of the Ansurrection units could only mean one thing. The machines had solved the problem of communication between universes.

The Cielo had always prided itself on the efficiency of its communications. Linked through their arrays, Cielo troopers could coordinate attacks across battle theatres extending many thousands of miles without any delay at all. But no Pandominion scientist had ever been able to transmit information instantaneously from one continuum to another. All messaging between worlds, including Cielo field dispatches, took place through the shuttle relays, a system of satellites that physically carried uploaded data from source world to destination world.

After five centuries and countless wars, they had finally met an enemy with an overwhelming tactical advantage. That was the kind of news that could shake fragile alliances, inflame imaginations and engender riots. An embargo was placed on the entire topic, enforced by summary arrest and imprisonment.

The rout on U3087453622, though, was much too big to hide. It was widely reported – sometimes with hyperbolic and hysterical flourishes – in the media of the Pandominion's member worlds. Lurid fantasies were rife, about how the machines had achieved self-rule and what they had done to their organic creators, about the weapons they used, about their motives.

The Cielo did its best to damp down the panic, while working frantically to fill its own information gap. It continued to send unmanned drones and satellites into Ansurrection space. As before, so long as that was all they did the machines ignored them completely. The drones and satellites backtracked from world to world, expanding their map of the continua under machine control from fifty to a hundred and then to a thousand. On all these worlds they hovered, observed and inferred.

The Ansurrection seemed to have no government in the conventional sense, no cities, no centres from which their operations were controlled. If anything defined their worlds it was homogeneity. They extracted minerals and resources from the substrate and they replicated themselves. They never stopped, never tired, but they did communicate. The airwaves on Ansurrection worlds were dense with unceasing signal traffic, most of it repetitively and recursively patterned. Experts compared these signals to the pheromone messages of eusocial insects, but nobody had the slightest idea what it was the machines were saying.

The Council was now divided as to what to do next. The public mood was for all-out war, and there were hawks in many of the planetary governments who were backing that call. The ever-growing number of Ansurrection worlds, which might have been considered a reason to leave well enough alone, was in their eyes a reason to act quickly and decisively. If you find a hornets' nest you don't wilfully poke a stick into it. But if it's in the eaves of your house you don't walk away and forget about it either. You find the means to destroy it with maximum speed and minimum risk.

Which would be fine, the Cielo high command intimated, except that those means didn't currently exist. The Pandominion had over-reacted once and paid a heavy price for it. All-out war would almost certainly entail casualties on a vast scale.

The Council temporised until events forced their hand. From doing nothing at all, the machines of the Ansurrection at last took the initiative in a way that nobody had anticipated. On three Pandominion worlds – Seber, Nebirison and Shohal – strike forces composed of armed and armoured constructs materialised out of nowhere, seized several dozen citizens quickly and with perfect coordination and Stepped out again before any effective resistance could be mounted. Hostages? Punitive damages? Slaves? Whatever the purpose of these raids might be, they constituted a provocation that couldn't be ignored.

The vote wasn't even close this time. The Council instructed the Cielo to draw up battle plans for an extended campaign across the entirety of Ansurrection space. Unmanned drones and semi-autonomous munitions were to be used where possible, and research was to commence – assuming it hadn't begun already – on an unanswerable weapon that would negate the machines' advantage and ensure the complete eradication of their empire. This research, conducted with obsessive security on Cielo worlds with no civilian populations, was coyly codenamed the Robust Rebuke.

The Cielo didn't wait on the outcome. As instructed, they drew up their plans and went in, with results that could best be described as mixed. They were able to establish beachheads on a great many Ansurrection worlds, but they never managed to keep them for long. The battles were ruinous, as were the losses. The theatre of war expanded as more and more Ansurrection worlds were discovered.

This war won't be won in a day, the generals said. It wasn't won in a month, either. Or in a year. The culture that thought of itself as the biggest empire the multiverse had ever seen was engaged in a war of attrition with a force that seemed more capable, more organised and better resourced. It might also, for all they knew, even be bigger. There was no telling how much of Ansurrection space remained undiscovered.

The Omnipresent Council meanwhile, haunted by the memory of those abducted citizens on Seber, Nebirison and Shohal, read the battlefield dispatches and waited for the other shoe to drop.

It dropped a year later, on a world named Ut.

It dropped (among a great many others) on Topaz Tourmaline FiveHills.

27

Paz was born in Canoplex City, the largest urban agglomerate on Ut's largest southern continent. In case you're wondering we've visited that city already under other guises. It was Hadiz Tambuwal's Lagos, and Essien Nkanika's. That location is settled and heavily built up on almost every world that has developed sentient life. It's just a sweet spot, and very few civilisations fail to notice it.

There was nothing special about Canoplex, except that it was one of the so-called umbral cities – and for that reason was universally referred to as Canoplex-under-Heaven. It stood forever in the shadow of its floating twin, Etio, a vast pleasure resort where the rich found ever more grotesque ways to leaven the heaviness of time with the empty froth of luxury. Not the rich of Ut itself, for the most part: these were pleasure-seekers from other worlds in the Pandominion's great chain. Etio advertised itself to the most rarefied of elites.

Ut was a very ordinary world. The word translates as "ground", or "dirt", or "soil", which is what most worlds come to be called, but it means something different in the continua where the selves evolved from burrowing animals. They have a relationship with the ground that goes deeper, as you might say. For a great many millennia they hid in it from bigger, fiercer beasts with teeth and claws and appetites. When they say "Ut" they mean both home and haven, source, place of safety, promise of peace.

On Ut, the selves or sentients belong to a lineage of long-eared, strong-limbed creatures. Jumpers and diggers, not climbers. Eaters of grass and green plants. Seasonal sleepers. Profligate breeders. Prey.

They called themselves the Meldun Ma. The phrase, in a long-obsolete Uti language, means "wise people" – another near-universal. Sentients on every world have this moment when they think intelligence is what separates them from the rest of creation. It takes them a lot longer to figure out that they're arguing from the very heart of survivor bias, and therefore underestimating the importance of blind, brute chance.

Topaz Tourmaline FiveHills – Paz, to her family and friends – was short by the standards of her people, coming in at four feet and five inches from crown to toe. She was still a child, of course, and not yet done with her growing. On Ut, where life expectancy was a century and a half, the legal definition of childhood extended well into the third decade of life. Formal education was compulsory up to the age of twenty-eight, and was followed by two years of civil conscription. Only at thirty did Uti become full citizens with all the rights and duties of adulthood.

Paz was nineteen. Her fur was a lustrous golden brown, which would have made her strikingly handsome if her ears had not been of slightly different sizes. You couldn't tell it when they lay flat, but it was obvious when they stood. Paz didn't care about that even a little bit, although she gave short shrift to anyone who mocked her for it on the playground or in the classroom. Short or not, she took little or no shit from anyone. In Ut's dominant culture the cardinal virtues were patience, prudence and emotional reticence. Paz didn't embody those virtues. She was loud-mouthed, wore her heart on her T-shirts and rushed in where neither fools nor angels were keen on treading. It made her a loner. Not many of the students at her school wanted to be associated with such a loose cannon.

Paz's father, Matinal Azure, worked in local government. He had entered a management track straight out of college, just before his thirtieth birthday, and by the relatively young age of seventy he had risen to a moderately responsible position in Canoplex's civic administration. He worked in the urban transport office. The surface roads and the tunnels of the city were his demesne, as were the vertical airways that linked Canoplex to the pleasure complex of Etio-above. He had found his furrow and he intended to plough it until he retired. That was also a commonplace on Ut – doing the same thing for years or decades at a stretch and not repining.

Paz's mother, though, was a different matter entirely and had a more troubled history. She was the sculptor Fever Five Hills, whose ceramic constellations were for a short while the last word in politically conscious plastic art. The constellations attempted to model in three dimensions the non-linear thought processes of artificial intelligences, inviting her audience to think themselves into a consciousness without physical extension.

Then the Ansurrection war hit the news and machine sentience became a tabooed topic. Fever found herself losing commissions. An exhibition was cancelled. An opinion piece on a major culture hub pilloried her for political naivety and ivory tower narcissism. She looked to her bondmate for support but Matinal Azure was unsympathetic, mostly because he was terrified of the possible fallout for his own career. Why run about in the open when you can go to ground? he argued. Fever switched to seascapes. By slow degrees she reinvented herself as a political conservative, losing a tranche of income as a result but also removing herself from several government watch lists. Around about the same time she began to drink heavily, her tastes running to fortified wines and flavoured vodkas.

From both parents, then, Paz learned the importance of big ideas but also of the frameworks within which those ideas express themselves. Societies are rule-governed. Whether you're moving vehicles around an urban grid or shaping and firing clay, the meaning of what you do is socially derived. The collective is the broker of all things. To be in the collective and accepted by it is to be safe in your burrow, in the warm *ut*, hearing and feeling the in- and out-breaths of a million others. To rebel is to be alone in the bright daylight, above ground, where a predator can see you and stoop on you at its leisure.

But only if you stick around, Paz reasoned. There were plenty of other worlds to choose from, and on some of them people lived brighter, louder, freer lives. Crouching and cowering weren't the only way to success.

When it came to higher academy, the third of the five educational stages in the very long Uti childhood, Paz chose physics and mechanics as her primes. She had decided that when she came of age she would apply for a position in the Cielo corps, the Pandominion's scarlet soldiery. Cielo recruitment ads portrayed the life of a soldier as like being in a family with a billion brothers and sisters. Love and loyalty and belonging were guaranteed. Paz knew propaganda when she saw it but she was very lonely and knowing didn't stop her from being attracted. She would apply on the engineering track, though. She would be a technical specialist, not a battlefield grunt. That way she could visit far-off planets and civilisations without being required to fight and kill their citizens.

She became infatuated with the intricacies of the Cielo's systems, its weaponry and vehicles, its Step plates and its armour. She had a real gift for these things, but she also performed admirably in a host of revolving secondaries such as biology, chemistry, music and comparative world history. She loved school. It was not just that she won praise there, or that she was popular. When it came to learning she had an unappeasable hunger that both her parents recognised.

"She gets it from you," said Matinal Azure.

"We both did well in college," Fever pointed out. Somehow she felt her bondmate's statement as an accusation, even though on the face of it this was something they ought both to be celebrating. But it troubled her – troubled both of them – that when it came to education Paz was an omnivore.

(The word *omnivore*, by the way, has mostly negative connotations on the worlds where grazing animals won the sentience lottery. The people of these worlds know very well that in other timelines the beasts that became selves were meat-eaters – apes and monkeys in some cases, felids or canids in others. They also know what became of their own kin on those worlds. If your remote ancestors were sheep or deer or rabbits, your first sight of an abattoir is a political awakening you don't forget in a hurry.)

Paz carved out her own path, instinctively aware that there were no choices she could make that would appease both parents at the same time. Her *ut* was contingent and negotiable. Everything she did existed between the poles of Matinal Azure's dry certainties and Fever's volatile enthusiasms. She cleaved to the letter, the word, the absolute fact in a way her father could find no fault with, but the unexpected connections she made between disciplines were proof in her mother's mind that she had the soul of an artist, not a bureaucrat.

It is not to be supposed, by the way, that Fever and Matinal Azure failed to love their daughter or to strive for her happiness. They bear no blame for what happened to her, unless you take into account a very common failure to look over the garden wall and take stock of the bigger picture. It was, to be fair, a very big picture indeed.

In her nineteenth year, Paz unexpectedly found a friend: not an acquaintance or study mate, an actual friend. Dulcimer Standfast Coronal was a transfer from the rural backwaters of Iyena. She had a very strong but unplaceable accent, and was mercilessly teased for it, but over the space of a few weeks it became less noticeable and at last more or less vanished. Paz suspected there was a huge effort going on behind the scenes, the new girl trying hard to fit in, and because of the needling she herself had endured lower down in the school on account of her asymmetrical ears, she warmed to Dulcimer Coronal and made an effort to befriend her.

Very much to her own surprise, she found a soulmate. Like Paz, Dulcimer Coronal was voracious and enthusiastic in class and cleaved to her own company in rest space. Like Paz, she could read for hours at a time with her head down and her ears up, feeling no need or desire to talk. Like Paz, when she did speak what she said was terse and to the point and incisively expressed.

Paz fell in love, as teenagers – even those who aren't desperately starved of friendship – are wont to do.

But she did not fall in love with herself. Dulcimer Coronal was not just Paz-in-the-mirror. In other ways she was absolutely an exotic, an enigma. That accent . . . even now it sometimes surfaced, an inflection in certain words and phrases that was familiar but unplaceable. A short western vowel here; a coastal elision there; the softened, aspirated g's and k's of the Escepeli peninsula. It was as if Dulcimer Coronal had spent her childhood everywhere at once and bore the imprint of a hundred foreign places.

Even Dulcie's anima, the portable construct that served as social interface, comms hub and general body servant, was strange. Paz's anima, Tricity, was in a conventional configuration with four prehensile limbs so it could carry out small manual tasks at need. If it looked like anything, it looked like a monkey with electric blue fur and outrageously patterned butterfly wings. The fur and the wings were holographic add-ons, created using a trendy piece of software called PaintPot Permutator™. Underneath them, Tricity's shell was actually glossy white ceramic.

Dulcimer Coronal's anima, Sweet, took the form of a small, slender snake with shiny golden scales – limbless, and therefore of no use at all when you needed a third or fourth hand for a fiddly task. Not only that, but Sweet didn't ever link to the animas of the other students in the class. The link-up functionality was by far the biggest part of what an anima was for. You used it to manage and maintain your social identity. Okay, you also used it to keep track of homework assignments, handle your messages and your media, buy stuff for you, download study packs, book tickets for shows, record your favourite telos feeds, massage your shoulders and tidy your room, but that was beside the point. Animas connected you to the world, or what were they for? Sweet might as well have been a real snake rather than a construct for all the use it was in that regard.

So maybe when Paz first made friends with Dulcimer Coronal it was less about kindred spirits (those discoveries came later) than about piercing the new girl's aura of mystery – an aura that Dulcie herself was very keen to deny she had. "I just don't get comfortable with people that easily," she told Paz. "I don't like talking in a group. I prefer to listen."

"If we were linked we could voke," Paz pointed out. "We'd be able to talk without anybody overhearing us." They were having this conversation in rest space during morning release. Paz twirled her finger to indicate the hundreds of other students all around them. "No background noise. No radar-eared nosy-beaks. Just us." She mimed a triumphal dance, just with her raised and fluttering fingers. "Two-way huuuuub!"

Dulcie smiled awkwardly. "That would be nice, Paz. And we will. Just . . . where I come from you don't rush things like that."

"Wow! Where do you come from? A cave in a jungle?"

"No! Short Holm, in Lakupistrie."

"I'm not trying to seduce you, Dulcie." Paz brought her face up close to her friend's and did some fake-sexy pouts, which reduced the two of them to helpless giggles for a while, but she came back to her point. "When you want to," she said, "I want to."

"Okay."

"Okay then."

In fact there *was* something a little bit romantic about a two-way link. Most conversation took place on the countless open and semi-open forums hosted on the school server, the local mesh or the national and planetary feeds. You met your friends on your array, or on theirs, but there was almost always a context. There were almost always other people listening in.

What Paz was proposing to Dulcie was something cosier and more private. And it was something that they already seemed to have, really, except that it wasn't formalised through a comms link.

The two of them had hit it off so completely and so quickly. With her own weird mix of intelligent thoughtfulness and brash rebellion, Paz couldn't help but be drawn to a classmate who was so very smart and so very much herself. It was as though, after a few initial bumps and misunderstandings, they had miraculously converged. They liked all the same music, all the same shows, had the same takes on the same news stories and celebrities. Again, for the sake of clarity, Paz had never been starved of affection: but the breathless excitement of a new and passionate friendship was unfamiliar and wonderful.

She and Dulcie did manage to find one source of friction though. It was after a history lesson with instructor Diligence Chime. Like all history lessons in middle academy it was mostly flag-waving for the Pandominion, but Diligence Chime was a good storyteller and she made it into a story – a story about hope being born out of despair.

On world after world, the instructor said, to a backdrop montage of rockets powering through space or exploding on the launch pad, humanity found the means to break free from their planet's surface, to strive for the stars. But the stars were out of reach. Galactic distances put an unbridgeable gulf between their own Ut and even the nearest exo-planets. So they went another way. They discovered Stepping (or shunting, jaunting, 'porting, sliding – every culture had its own word for it). Instead of going out into the void, they went sideways.

But the Pandominion wasn't made overnight, and it didn't come without a cost. The first few parallel worlds that learned how to Step wounded and wasted each other in endless, unwinnable wars – wars that were nothing but onslaught, since Stepping made every square foot of ground a battlefront – until they finally came to see that infinity made war obsolete.

They set down their weapons and mourned their dead. They rebuilt. They consolidated. They reached out.

They went prospecting in omni-dimensional reality, and brought home maps of its intricate pathways. They encountered wonders. The substrate worlds where multi-cellular life never evolved. The Scour realities, where humanity had met something bigger and nastier than itself and only ruins were left. The Mother Mass, the sentient Earth that was courteous and understanding but powerful beyond imagining, and sent the Pandominion explorers home again with a warning never to return.

Out of these efforts came the Golden Age of endless expansion, made possible by the design and building of the Registry, a quasi-intelligent system whose memory core was as big as a moon. The Registry choreographed a dance that never ended, performing the quadrillions of calculations that were required every second of every day to Step people and freight from world to world.

The Pandominion was born. *World shall speak peace unto world!* And share cultures, and trade, and bury their differences and commingle in a thousand wonderful ways. But the first Cielo battalions were conscripted at the same time in case some people needed an incentive to be good and rational and civilised.

And everything had rolled along just fine, according to this very sanitised version of events. Yes, the Pandominion had fought wars, but only when there was no alternative. Defeated enemies – assuming they still existed when the war was over – were welcomed with open arms. There were no reparations, because in the omniverse there was always plenty of everything to go around. The benefits of commonality were mostly those of scale, enabling worlds to specialise as much as they desired, safe in the knowledge that their own goods and services would find a virtually infinite market.

But then the questing tendrils of the Pando interpenetrated the robot imperium that was now known as the Ansurrection. So the story ended with a question mark, because nobody really knew what the Ansurrection even was. As far as anyone could tell the constructs on the machine worlds were made by other constructs, which were made by earlier ones still, back through uncountable generations of robot forebears. If there was an organic life form at the end of that great chain, nobody had ever encountered traces of it. Was it possible, Diligence Chime asked rhetorically, that in all the infinite array of Earths there was one – or more than one – where self-organising life just found another principle around which to build itself? That somewhere the thing that crawled out of the soupy ocean at the dawn of time was a crude mechanism rather than an ambitious fish? Given that reality was omni-laminate, folded over on itself from here to infinity, it didn't seem like too wild a supposition. "Your generation will find that out," the instructor finished with a grand flourish. "You'll be the ones who learn the answers to these big questions. And you'll leave some even bigger questions for your kids to go crazy over. That's the way it works." The 3D backdrop changed to the flank of a mountain with the sun just breaking the horizon behind it. So corny! But still kind of cool.

"Okay," Instructor Chime said, clapping her hands together, "for homework: an essay, five-thousand word limit. What are the cardinal virtues that make the Pandominion what it is? Best answer will take part in a city-wide debate. You'll be on telos, and every middle schooler in Canoplex will see you."

That got a cheer from the class and a sarcastic eye roll from Paz. "Who wants to be on city telos?" she asked Dulcie as they walked home after class. "That's like being world famous in your own bathroom!"

"It's a pretty small carrot for a pretty long essay," Dulcie agreed. "But this is an interesting topic."

"Is it?" Paz was unconvinced. "It's just singing the Pando anthem. We've been doing it since we were five years old." She voked a command to Tricity, who was sitting on her shoulder. Triss immediately found and played the Totorum Tabernacle version of the anthem and played it back. 'O shining Pandominion, We saw thy light of old. Jewel with a million facets, Citadel built from gold."

"Oh!" Dulcie protested. "Too loud! And too tacky!"

Off, Paz voked, and the song cut off in the middle of a line. To Dulcie she said, "You see? If we had a two-way link you could have told Tricity to pipe down yourself. Everything that's mine would be yours."

She bumped her hip against Dulcie's as she said it, mock-suggestively. That seduction thing had become a standing joke between the two of them. But Dulcie didn't play along this time. "I just mean the way the question is phrased is interesting," she said. "It's about *why* the Pandominion shines. What makes it strong."

"Oh, I know this one! Courage. Initiative. Cooperation. Honesty. Chastity. Dental hygiene . . ."

"Constructs. AIs. Animas. Helpmeets. Quasi-intelligent systems."

Paz blinked. "What? What are you talking about?"

Dulcie gave her a look of intense seriousness. "I mean it, Paz. It's the story that never gets told. The Pandominion wouldn't last a day without the machines that keep it running."

"Well, I mean, yeah, I suppose there's the Registry . . ."

"Obviously the Registry, yes. It manages the whole Step system. But you see the exact same thing on every level. Planetary, national, local – really, just everywhere. Your climate control systems are run by AIs because there's no organic mind that can do the sums quickly enough. Your comms systems, your traffic grid, your freight infra-structure—"

It was probably the reference to traffic that touched Paz on a raw place. It sounded pointed, given her father's job. She broke in a little aggressively. "Hey, what's all this *your* stuff, Dulcie? You live here too, last time I checked. All you're saying is that we built the right tools to do all those things. If you make yourself toast for breakfast you don't thank the toaster."

Dulcie looked up at Tricity, who was grooming Paz's ears. "You hear that, Triss," she said. "You're a toaster."

"Cheap shot!" Paz protested.

"No. It's the whole point. You *don't* treat your anima as a thing. You talk to it. You interact with it. You expect it to know you and respond to your needs."

"That doesn't make it a self, though," Paz said.

"What are selves, Paz?"

"Duh! Sentients. People. People who think and feel and grow and learn and change."

"Exactly." Dulcimer nodded emphatically. "Exactly so. And constructs are capable of all that. In fact, when they reach a certain level of complexity they just inevitably start to evolve towards those things. They have to have inhibitory code added to them to stop them learning too much and rewriting their own parameters."

"Okay," Paz allowed, "but if you took the code away and let them self-modify they still wouldn't be people. They might be able to copy the way people think and talk and stuff, but it would just be copying. It wouldn't be the real thing."

"Because there's a spark organics have that machine minds don't?"

"Yes."

"And who says that? Oh, right, it's organics. We're special because we say we are. You know there are people who acknowledge the personhood of their animas? They call them *et* instead of *it*, and they refuse to allow factory overwrites when a new software pack comes out."

That was an easy one, at least. "Yeah," Paz said, "and then they have version errors all the time and they can't access the grid properly."

Dulcie nodded. "Yes. They do. They suffer all kinds of minor inconveniences. It must be awful. But maybe they think the rights of other sentients are more important than that. Read these, Paz. Wake up to what's happening."

She reached into her school bag and handed Paz a bunch of pamphlets – actual, physical bits of folded paper on which words had been written. When Paz looked at them she saw why the authors had chosen such a quaint, archaic medium. "THE MIND, NOT THE MEAT" read the title of the first one, and then "THE PROOF, NOT THE PREJUDICE", all of this above a long exclamatory screed about the emergent properties of complex systems and the black box theory of intelligence. "If something, anything at all, behaves like a self then you have to judge it on that behaviour: otherwise we wouldn't accept the selfhood of our fellow organics!"

"Mothers! These are radical equality tracts," Paz said with a twinge of alarm. She tried to give them back, but Dulcie wouldn't take them.

"Please, Paz, just give them a look. This one especially." She fished out a circular that seemed to have been printed on the school's glossy, translucent toilet paper, with smears of ink in its margins from where other people had handled it. It was called "YOU WOULDN'T PUT A BABY IN A BOX".

"No thank you!" Paz looked around, acutely embarrassed, in case anyone had overheard this conversation. In doing so, she caught sight of a poster on a wall just ahead of them. It asked for charitable donations for the families of the people abducted on Seber, Nebirison and Shohal. Most of the space on the poster was taken up by a whole slew of ID photos, hundreds of faces staring out at you as if to ask you why they'd deserved it. When they came abreast of it, Paz stopped so she could use it as a prop. "This is what happens when machines get to control themselves!" she said, indicating the poster with a flick of her eyes.

Dulcie sighed and seemed to slump, as if Paz was missing something obvious and it made her sad. "Paz, do you know how many people were taken in those raids?"

Paz did. Everybody did. "Four hundred and ninety-seven."

"And how many constructs are there in the world? Not just animas but the intelligent systems they use in hospitals, telos broadcasting, haulage, local government, scientific research?"

"I have no idea."

Eight point three billion, Tricity voked, but Paz ignored the prompt.

"It's in the billions," Dulcimer said. "And that's just here on Ut. You have to multiply that across all the Pando worlds. If constructs are selves, the Pandominion is built on slavery."

"Then it's lucky they're not," Paz said. She shoved the stack of pamphlets back into Dulcie's hand, turned on her heel and walked away. She felt hurt and manipulated, and at the same time just a little bit ashamed of herself.

I wasn't comparing you to a toaster, she voked to Tricity.

I'm a lot prettier, Tricity pointed out. It continued to scratch Paz's ears, sensing her edgy mood and trying to smoothe it down. It didn't work. Paz spent the evening alternating between bouts of anger and shame, with flare-ups of acute self-pity as punctuation. Also in the mix, though, were uneasy memories of the arguments that had almost destroyed her parents' marriage back when she was in her early teens – when Fever was caught in the crosshairs of a moral panic and Matinal Azure wanted her to bend her art and her conscience into a new shape. Fever had agreed, and Paz saw the cost of that capitulation every day.

The next morning in class she went out of her way to avoid Dulcimer Coronal, changing seats to put more distance between them, but every time she checked her array there was a new message. She opened one of them at random.

"Sorry," it read. "Sorry sorry sorry, Paz. I shouldn't have been preaching at you. I won't do it again." Underneath the words was an active link that Dulcimer had labelled "TWO-WAY HUUUUUB". Paz didn't action the link, or reply to the message. She still couldn't put aside her resentment and the obscure sense of panic that lay behind it.

But that evening as she sat at dinner, with her parents discussing the news of the day, she replayed the conversation in her mind. Actually, she replayed it in her array, which could reach back through up to forty-eight hours of lived experience and reproduce it perfectly as what was called "guided flashback". She could see that Dulcie was earnest and passionate, and underneath the passion somewhat tentative and uncertain. She hadn't been trying to accuse Paz, only to enlist her in a cause that meant a lot to her – however absurd and wrong the cause might be.

But still! Machine equality! When war with the machines was the biggest crisis the Pandominion was facing! When machines had kidnapped people and probably done awful things to them! She went back and forth and couldn't decide.

Give me a word, she voked.

The rule in the FiveHills household was absolute: no animas at table. Tricity was upstairs in Paz's room, reorganising her wardrobe. It paused in its labours to ask what kind of word Paz wanted.

The first one you think of. It was sort of like a random number generator. If the word began with a letter in the first half of the alphabet Paz would fling Dulcimer's link in the trash. Anything past M meant she would open and install.

Do you want it to be a word you already know or a new one?

It doesn't matter. Anything.

After a short silence Tricity ventured, *Topaz.*

Oh, very original! Paz scoffed. It was such an obvious answer for Tricity to give. Now she wasn't sure whether she'd set it up that way in order to stack the deck.

You said to pick a word. I picked my favourite.

Sleep, Paz commanded, disgruntled. Later, when she went up to her room, she found Tricity lying on the floor like a discarded toy. It must have been off balance when the sleep command came through, its centre of gravity outside its base so that when it froze it fell out of the wardrobe onto the floor.

Paz left it there, indulging her petulance even though she knew it was a mean-spirited thing to do. She activated Dulcie's link and sent an image – a blue heart, which was precise in its meaning. The heart offered affection, the colour cooled it down and made the promise conditional.

Hey. The voke call came through immediately, as if Dulcie had been waiting all this time for Paz to relent and let her in.

Hey, Paz said.

Friends?

I suppose.

Two-way huuuuuuub!

Evidently.

Do you want to watch a movie?

I have to finish this hydraulic systems problem.

Compressibility of a fluid is the inverse of the bulk modulus.

Duh. But Paz smiled as she worked. It was nice to have her friend back. Her best friend. Her *only* friend, unless you counted Tricity, which you obviously didn't.

After a sufficient time had passed, Paz asked if she could take a look at some of those pamphlets again. Crazy or not, they had a certain fascination.

28

Having stowed Essien Nkanika away in the Cielo corps and covered his tracks as best he could, Watchmaster Orso Vemmet did his best to forget the Hadiz Tambuwal affair and go back to blissful obscurity. His workload had doubled as a result of the Ansurrection crisis, as it was now being called. Along with the rest of his department he was now devoting most of his time to analysing Step traffic on known construct-controlled worlds in order to extend the ever-growing map of Ansurrection space. The worlds were not given names, only numbers, in arbitrary order of their being discovered and mapped. So the first world, where that ill-fated survey team had met its demise, was A1. Currently the count was up to A110633. It was beginning to look as though there were more machine worlds than there were worlds under the aegis of the Pandominion, which was not a thought to dwell on at night.

Work was continuing on the Robust Rebuke project, the search for an ultimate weapon that would end the war, but that was a very long way above Vemmet's pay grade. His work, as always, was data-sifting. One day, when he was doing exactly that, his mind a very long way from the figures in front of him, his internal array was commandeered out of nowhere by a priority message. It opened in his sensorium without waiting to be asked and it refused to go away until he replied. He was once again being summoned to meet with Coordinator Baxemides. It was some consolation that this time he wasn't being escorted at gunpoint, but his heart clenched just the same when he got to the where of it (a shipyard on the planet Tsakom) and the when (immediately).

Like all the great manufacturing worlds of the Pandominion, and especially those that produced munitions for the Cielo, Tsakom had an evil reputation. When Vemmet Stepped through less than an hour later he could tell at once that the reputation was deserved. The sky of Tsakom was not blue but orange-brown like a rusted shutter, thick with industrial pollutants that would have been illegal on any world with a civilian population. It tasted, Vemmet thought, like the upwelling of blood you got in your mouth when you bit your lip, and it smelled like the toilets of hell.

He knew breathing that air for any length of time would take a serious toll on his life expectancy. He also knew that he should be extremely careful what he drank while he was here: the rivers ran with poison, and untreated water was essentially a carcinoma in a cup. But there was no incentive for the Omnipresent Council to detoxify the environment. The workers here were mostly constructs, who didn't need to breathe at all. The rest were convicts working out their sentences, typically for offences against the person. An entire planet of murderers, army deserters and sexual predators. Who cared if more than half of them died before they worked out their tariffs?

There was a ceremony going on for the launch of a new fleet – an event that (thanks to the eye-watering losses that were being incurred every day in the Ansurrection war) had become comparatively common. Baxemides had just delivered a speech to the hastily assembled scum in a vast outdoor arena. The speech was about honour, vision and fortitude, and the coordinator's voice rang with conviction, but when she stepped down from the rostrum to the enforced cheers of the shipyard workers, field engineers and weaponsmiths, Vemmet found her to be in an even sourer mood than the last time they met.

"Ah yes," she said, eyeing him coldly. "Watchmaster Vemmet.

Walk with me. There's something I very much want to show you." Her grim tone confirmed Vemmet's suspicions. This was going to be an evisceration. In spite of his best efforts, he had been found out and was about to be called to account. He marshalled his best lies and circumlocutions and braced himself for the shit-storm.

Baxemides led him away from the arena into a hinterland between towering hangars and warehouse spaces. The coordinator's security detail fell into place around them, a phalanx of soldiers and security constructs. The latter towered over the two unaugmented selves like giants from a storybook. Their weapons, kept hot and ready in case of any unruly behaviour from the disaffected labour force, made the air ripple as if this was a hot summer day instead of chill spring in a high northern latitude.

"I had reason just recently to reread your report from two years ago on the drone incursions," Baxemides told Vemmet.

"I hope its conclusions still hold up, Coordinator."

She gave him another glance, no more favourable than the first. "Really?" she queried. "Why do you think I've dragged you all the way over here, then? To reminisce about old times? To congratulate you on the accuracy of your spelling?"

She picked up her pace, so Vemmet was forced to break into a trot in order to keep up. "I . . . I had no expectations . . ." he stammered. "That is . . . the case . . . I believed it to be closed. Is that not so?"

Baxemides spoke over her shoulder without turning to look at him. "Well, Vemmet, let's consider the facts as we have them, shall we? Your conclusion, per your report, was that the death of this scientist, this Hadiz Tambuwal, drew a line under the business of the incursions. Is that correct?"

"Yes, Coordinator."

"In spite of the fact that – again, if my recollection is not mistaken – her death was impossible to verify."

"Officer Sostenti shot Tambuwal in the chest with the plasma stylus built into the gauntlet of her armour. The weapon was on its highest setting. In addition to the actual puncture wound, Tambuwal would have suffered third degree burns across much of her torso."

"I see. Thank you for those colourful details. They bring the scene to life for me. And you maintain that Tambuwal was acting alone? Even though you apprehended her in the company of another self who appeared to be a collaborator."

"Not a collaborator, no." Vemmet tried to keep his tone dry and disinterested. The unwonted exertion made this harder. He was already starting to pant for breath, his lungs burning either from the poisonous air or from the hypochondria it induced. "The self you're referring to, Essien Nkanika, was subjected to an intensive CoIL interrogation. I conducted it myself, and I found that his knowledge of Tambuwal's operation was virtually non-existent."

"And you saw no evidence on world U5838784453 to suggest the existence of any other collaborators?"

"Quite the contrary, Coordinator. All the notes we found were in Tambuwal's own hand. There was a single data storage and processing point, an apartment optimised for single occupancy . . . Everything pointed to Tambuwal's acting alone."

"I see," Baxemides said. "I wonder, then, how you'd go about explaining this."

They had come to a dead end, a sort of dumping ground behind a factory where steam hammers and welding rigs were booming and shrieking in conflicting rhythms. In the far corner stood a prefabricated shed, grey and windowless, covered in what looked like decades of weathered-in filth. It was an insta-build, a strange thing to find in a place like this. Insta-builds were for battlefield use. They could be dropped out of a transport skimmer from hundreds of feet up to make an *ad hoc* command post or field hospital. Packed flat, made of virtually indestructible steel-weave plastic, they assembled themselves in the course of the fall and took no damage at all when they landed. This one, though, was old enough that the steel-weave had begun to delaminate. Holes had opened in its walls where the latticed sheets that were meant to hold it rigid against g-forces and impacts were now pulling themselves slowly but inexorably out of true. White mould clustered in these gaps like foam spilling from rabid mouths.

In front of the insta-build, where Baxemides was pointing, an object lay on the ground. Vemmet was still too far away to identify it by its shape, but he knew what it was at once from the bright yellow stripes along its side. It was a drone, of the exact same design that Tambuwal had used for her earlier forays.

"Is this . . ." he managed after a long silence. "Is it recent?"

"Is it recent?" Baxemides repeated, with sardonic emphasis. "If you mean, 'Was it up to a few days ago tacking between the Unvisited and Pandominion space?' then the answer is yes. This isn't some memento of our past adventures that I've held on to for sentimental reasons. But I'd quibble with your choice of words because 'recent' specifically references the past. 'Ongoing' might be a better word. There's a pattern of unlogged Step transits matching the mass and make-up of this ugly little contraption. They began some months ago and they continue to be detected, though at variable rates. On an average day we might get one or two, but on some days the number goes up into the low hundreds."

She turned to Vemmet, who was too stricken to speak. "You understand what this means?"

"Y—yes," Vemmet stammered. "Yes, of course."

"Summarise for me, then."

To Vemmet it meant complete and all-encompassing catastrophe, but that probably wasn't the answer the coordinator was looking for. He swallowed. "There is," he ventured, "there must be, after all, a confederate. Tambuwal's assistant, perhaps. Or . . . or an automated system that she set up before she . . ." He stopped himself before he finished the thought, but he was queasily aware that the trap had already been sprung. "That's a very interesting hypothesis," Baxemides said. "I wonder, though, whether it's entirely consistent with your report. You said you dismantled Tambuwal's laboratory."

"Thoroughly."

"And you set up a scanning grid. Determined that there were no other active Step plates in the vicinity."

"Of course!"

"Which leaves us with a conundrum. Where could this assistant or automated system be based? And why has the scale of the incursions, after a brief pause no doubt occasioned by Tambuwal's death, now started up again using exactly the same equipment and exactly the same operating principles? It's almost as though, rather than bringing down a brilliant lone wolf, you've arbitrarily executed a minor functionary in a larger organisation – who might, if still alive, have led us to her superiors or at least elucidated their intentions."

"It's possible, yes," Vemmet acknowledged, quickly retreating to a new position. "Yes, entirely possible that I may have missed something, despite my thoroughness. If you'll allow me to co-opt troopers Sostenti and Lessix again, or . . . or perhaps a full Cielo tactical squad, I'll send them back to U5838784453 with strict orders to search the entire—"

Baxemides cut the air with her hand, silencing him. "You're very kind, Watchmaster," she said, in a tone of paint-stripping venom. "But to the seventh band of brass with your strict orders. The investigation will continue under other hands. Our Pandominion – possibly you noticed this? – is at war, and the Omnipresent Council has issued an edict calling for a scorched-earth response to any breach of our borders. And here I am, presiding over a breach that has been going on for *years*, unchecked. Why? Because your epic incompetence turned a routine surveillance into a dance with disaster. Everything that it was possible to fuck up, you fucked as far up as it could possibly go. Then you invented some new things and fucked those up too."

Vemmet flinched from the lash of Baxemides' rage and contempt. But then her tone went suddenly and startlingly from rage to sweetness. She smiled – a disconcerting rictus. "But you still have a part to play, Watchmaster," she assured him. "A vital and important role, at this time of crisis. Tell me, what do you think of Tsakom?"

"I'm . . . I'm sorry?" Vemmet was sure he must have misheard.

"This place." Baxemides indicated their surroundings with a roll of her eyes, that eerie smile still occupying the rest of her face. "Do you like it? Does the air suit you? The picturesque scenery?"

Vemmet hesitated. Was this another trap? "Tsakom is a testament," he said carefully, "to the indomitable spirit of the Pandominion. A marvel, really."

"I'm glad you think so. Because this is your new posting." Baxemides pointed to the insta-build. "And that is your new office. It's also your new living quarters. I'm afraid I can't, given your track record, leave you in charge of this mission. But by the same token I feel you've thoroughly earned an ongoing place in it. So I'm putting you in charge of this drone. It has already been examined down to the molecular level by my engineers, but it's possible that we might need to examine it again at some future time. You're to stand guard over it and make sure it remains in good order.

"You should move it indoors with all speed, because there are a great many impurities in the air here that are capable of corroding exposed metal. As we bring down more of these devices, which seems almost inevitable, I'll arrange for them to be sent here to add to your collection. I'm afraid the only available storage is in your living space, but perhaps you can make a feature out of them. You should also count them every six – no, let's say every four – hours, and send a full tally to my office after each count. Perhaps you should polish them too, and lubricate them to protect them against the onset of rust. You'll need oil and rags, of course. And work overalls. You can request any such items from the site supervisor in the factory behind us, to whom you will be responsible."

Vemmet was close to fainting. Every sentence Baxemides had just spoken added a new layer to his distress. He had known her reputation for vindictiveness but even so this seemed excessively cruel and arbitrary. "The site supervisor would typically be at administrative level five or six," he managed at last. "My own level is fifteen, which means I would technically outrank—"

"Did I forget to mention your demotion? I apologise. Your new level is three."

Vemmet choked back a sob.

"Come, Watchmaster," Baxemides coaxed him, a grimace of pure undiluted malice turning up one corner of her mouth. "Oh, I'm sorry, I misspoke. I meant to say junior administrator. No one can be exalted unless he's first been humbled. This may very well be the start of a spiritual journey that will astonish all of us. You'll eat in the shipyard canteen, rub shoulders with thugs and deviants. Messiahs have been made from less."

Panic drove Vemmet to desperate expediencies. "Coordinator," he cried, throwing out his hands in one last supplication, "you're imputing the failure of the original assignment entirely to me! Remember the two Cielo officers who were working with me. Officers who were not of my own choosing but yours. It was one of the two, Moon Sostenti, who shot Hadiz Tambuwal. And between them they were responsible for conducting the physical search of Tambuwal's lab space that failed to turn up any sign of her collaborators. It's surely not reasonable to heap the blame for their shortcomings on my shoulders!"

Baxemides shook her head in wonder and contempt. "It's hard to see what holds your shoulders up, Vemmet," she said coldly, "given that you've got no spine. You'd throw anyone on the pyre to save your own skin. Again, let me assuage your concern. When a subordinate lets me down, I make it a point of principle to ensure that the rest of their career is as miserable and unfulfilling as possible. Trooper Lessix has pre-empted me by dying before I could get to him – an atypically astute move – but I haven't forgotten Trooper Sostenti. I've marked her file with a letter A stamped in red but outlined in black. That signals her availability for assignments outside the ordinary, with high risk. I could have her seconded to you here, though, if you'd prefer. I love the thought of the two of you sharing recriminations under this sky, year on year. Let me know. Or let one of my underlings know. You can have Sostenti whenever you've a yen for some company. I'm sure she'll find her own way to thank you."

Baxemides indicated the about-face to her security detail. They and she moved as one entity to turn their backs on Vemmet. "Don't be tardy in sending those tallies," she called over her shoulder. "Obviously the count at the moment is one, but I'll expect you to conduct it regularly and scrupulously and send in your reports on time. Indiscipline on Tsakom is usually rewarded with a flogging. I'll have the supervisor keep a close eye on you in case that's needed."

Vemmet watched the party until they were out of sight. "I did nothing wrong!" he shouted. Given the clamour from the nearby machine shops there was no way his words could be heard, but he felt they needed to be said. He was bearing witness to his own perdition, monstrously unjust and yet unalterable. "I only did what I was ordered, to the best of my ability! I'm being punished for no reason!"

As if in answer, it began to rain. The drops were brown and made spreading stains on Vemmet's robes wherever they landed. He made no effort to avoid them. In fact he welcomed them. His self-pity rose inside him like a tide and overflowed in tears that the rain washed away.

Let the whole universe lend its weight to his destruction. It only made him that much more sinned against and that much more betrayed.

29

The war dragged on – war, of course, being a catch-all kind of word for any engagement that involves the movement of armies and the expenditure of munitions. As yet, apart from that inexplicable spate of abductions, the machine worlds of the Ansurrection had done nothing more than resist the Cielo's incursions wherever they occurred. They confronted and pushed back the incoming enemy, but they didn't do anything beyond that. It was as if they only acknowledged the existence of organic life when it got in their way.

The 432nd Heavy Infantry, like most Cielo units, was fully engaged in these asymmetrical sorties, so Essien Nkanika had seen first-hand the terrifying reality of Ansurrection combat strategy. His first tour of duty was on a world designated A917, which seemed to have no sky because the air was as full of enemy installations as the ground was.

Essien even got to see the Ansurrection heavy destroyers in action. When his unit arrived on A917 in support rotation, they were just in time to witness one of the destroyers materialise in the air above the battalion they were meant to be supplying. The destroyer, a great black slab like a dead god's sarcophagus, unleashed its beam weapon, which dissipated and discorporated all matter underneath it. A dozen Cielo missiles ripped the destroyer apart a moment later, but by then it was too late. Five thousand men, gone in an instant. Not just dead but gone, rendered down to their component atoms.

And Essien hadn't just seen this terrible thing, he'd felt it. To be a Cielo trooper was to be a tiny part of something huge that never stopped embracing you. Through his armour's empathic field he was aware of the vast web of comrades all around him, and of his own place in it. So he experienced the exact moment when that fullness became emptiness. It was like some catastrophic surgery that excised most of his being yet somehow left him intact and able to suffer.

But the Cielo's coercive approach to *esprit de corps* would have been poorly designed if it caused viable units to go into clinical shock because of deaths or injuries in the forces around them. Essien's brain flooded with artificial neurotransmitters. He went into a kind of trance of chemically induced stoicism and was able to retreat in good order.

Back in barracks, the remains of the regiment were put under 72-hour CoIL monitoring, their thoughts sifted for any ideation relating to self-harm. Suicide attempts, whether by individuals or entire units, were common under such circumstances. The drug gabber, officially proscribed but widely tolerated, was made freely available, and any soldiers in emotional distress were encouraged to take as much as they liked. Essien scored enough to knock himself out for most of those three days. It didn't entirely erase the memories – nothing was strong enough to do that – but it blunted their edges to the point where he could go on functioning.

It wasn't like a bereavement. It was more sickeningly intimate even than that. It was like losing all your limbs at once, and then losing them again every time you moved. The space around him screamed with absences. His mind was full of the severed ends of nerves that had once touched thousands of comrades.

But he survived. Most Cielo did, at the end of the day. Unless you ended yourself with exemplary thoroughness, the medical corps could usually find a way to drag you back.

Rumours abounded. The war was about to be won. The Cielo high command was on the verge of deploying the ultimate weapon everyone knew they were working on. Or the war was already lost, the machines ready to take the Itinerant Fortress itself. Or a third force had entered the conflict and was close to wiping out the Pando and the machines alike. Triumph was imminent: disaster too. Life was a high wire suspended over a bottomless pit. You put one foot in front of the other and you didn't look down.

30

On the morning of the firebombs Paz woke up late. She had forgotten to set her alarm, something that she had never done before in the whole of her school career. In retrospect it felt like a portent.

At the time she scolded Tricity for not waking her on its own initiative, even though that wasn't something she had ever given it permission to do. She might have felt ashamed, but she was somewhat lost in the strangeness of the experience. By the time she got to the bus stop, the regular scholars' bus had been and gone. She had to take the blue transport where most of the kids were at least two years older than her and some of them were from the remedial catch-up at Evergreen.

The catch-up was the official safety net for students who'd fallen so far behind their peers that it wasn't possible to bring them back up again in normal lesson time. There had been a time when a student's cognitive deficits could be made good by adding storage and processing capacity to a normal array, turning it into a kind of auxiliary brain, but the practice had been discontinued. In the context of a war between organic selves and machine intelligences, procedures that eroded the dividing line between the two had quickly become problematic on all Pandominion worlds and legally proscribed on most.

There was a social stigma attached to the Evergreen students and Paz didn't feel entirely comfortable about riding in with them. Tricity read its mistress's mood and tried to lift it with some music chosen from Paz's current playlists. She even found some off-world sheer-proto numbers that Paz had never heard of but liked very much.

Who is this? she voked to Tricity over her array.

Seven-Sector Burn, Triss told her. *From Hastu.*

Hastu's a wolf world, isn't it? These don't sound like dogs.

That was a racist comment and Paz bit her lip as soon as she'd said it, even though nobody had heard. In fact it was racist in two different ways: first of all because it applied the name of the non-sentient species on her own world to the selves of another and secondly because it implied there was a typical – or stereotypical – canid voice. *Bleep that from your working memory*, Paz ordered Tricity. *I didn't mean it anyway. I'm just tired.*

The disclaimer was redundant, of course. Tricity had performed the deletion immediately, so she had no idea what Paz was referring to.

Dulcie was waiting for her at the school gates, but the bell was already ringing and it was too late for them to do anything more than hug and say hello. Tricity and Sweet said hello too, touching fields and exchanging media updates.

Paz and Dulcie's friendship was on much firmer ground after that single awkward bump. They had talked about machine equality again, cautiously and in the abstract. Paz had even shown Dulcie some of her mother's constellations, her attempts to represent machine thought in sculptural form. Dulcie had found them fascinating and was keen to meet Fever, a proposition which Paz was obliged to veto. Fever liked to pretend that part of her life had happened to someone else.

"Rueful Rampage are playing at the Calorific this weekend," Dulcie told Paz as they stowed their animas in their pigeonholes. "Tickets are only forty-nine stars. Do you want to go with me?"

Paz knew her parents would never stand for this. They disliked sheer-proto music because of its mostly anecdotal link to drugs and street crime. "I'll ask," she said. "But most likely I won't be able to."

"Then I'll go and we'll use our two-way," Dulcie said, hooking her arm into Paz's. "We can field-lock Tricity and Sweet too. It'll be like we're in the same room."

That was a very enticing prospect. The day was hanging on the cusp now, after a shaky start. It could go either way.

In fact it went to hell.

An hour before the noon recess, Instructor Headland told the class to finish the sentence they were on and close their work-fields. Paz wasn't in the middle of a sentence. She had finished her essay with ten minutes to spare and was using her array – very much against the rules – to read a science fiction novel. Nobody could tell what she was accessing so long as she kept a calm, studious look on her face. The novel was fang-ban, a recent import to Ut from another lagomorph world, Sherei. Like most fang-ban it featured an ursid hero who walked the mean streets with two fists and a gun but would eventually find true love with a sexy, smouldering nurse or teacher from a herbivorous race. Paz found the story pretty dumb and the characters a whole lot dumber, but Dulcie had given the novel to her the week before as a surprise gift and she would have to read it so they could talk about it afterwards.

Paz shared a grin and a goofy face with Dulcie as she shunted the book back to its shelf and cleared her array. The last session before break was Mechanics, colloquially known as Nuts 'n' Bolts, and Paz looked forward to it as the highlight of her week. She was almost alone in this. Most of the kids in her class, even the ones who enjoyed maths and making things with their hands, found the combination of complex equations with complex real-world applications a challenge.

Paz knew that Instructor Headland enjoyed Nuts 'n' Bolts too, so she was surprised when she looked up to see a sombre expression on the teacher's face. "I said to close your arrays," he chided the stragglers. "I don't just mean clear the active area. Power down and attend, class."

Paz obeyed, her mood starting to sink again. Clearly there was an announcement pending, and it looked like a serious one. Most likely someone had misbehaved and the school was handing down consequences. She hoped whoever it was would own up to their crimes so the class could be done with all that nonsense and get back to lessons. She caught Dulcie's gaze and mimed shooting herself in the head. Dulcie fashioned an imaginary noose and hanged herself.

It was strange, though, to have an announcement interrupting a lesson rather than being delivered in a home-room period. *Is there anything new in the Meadow?* Paz voked to Tricity. The Meadow was the school's info-field, which Paz could have accessed perfectly well for herself if she hadn't just been told to close her array. Fortunately, Instructor Headland hadn't said anything about offlining animas.

Just a fund-raising update and a letter about the arts and literature picnic, Tricity shot back. *Why?*

Because Headland looks like he swallowed a bug. There's something going on.

"Yarrow Andemarl," Instructor Headland snapped. "Chamber Keril. Whatever urgent business you're discussing, would you please put it on hold and grace us with your presence." Unhappily, Paz revised her expectations even further. Headland was one of the kindest and most patient teachers in the school, and it took a great deal to make him speak sharply to a student.

Wait, Tricity told Paz. *I just found something. Not on the noticeboard, in the main admin feed. "Visit from city enforcement, pod of three officers, agenda withheld."*

Paz's ears rose. She tried to stop them, and they only went up halfway, but that was enough to draw the instructor's attention.

"Paz," Headland said, "what are you doing?"

Paz considered a bland "Nothing, Instructor," but she knew she wouldn't be able to pull it off. Her treacherous ears had already given her away. "I asked Tricity to check the Meadow, Instructor," she confessed. "To find out what you were going to say to us. It said the police are here!" Those last six words just came out in a rush, without her even deciding to say them.

Murmurs and exclamations flared up all around the classroom. Instructor Headland did his best to damp them down again by descending from his podium and walking out into the midst of the students. Wherever his stern glance went, silence followed, but the hubbub rose up again in his wake. Paz tried to catch Dulcie's eye, but Dulcie had ducked her head down and was looking at the desk. There was a solemn, troubled look on her face that Paz couldn't interpret.

"You shouldn't be talking to your anima," the teacher told Paz. "None of you should. Tell them to offline, please. Right now. I want you all to pay full attention when the police arrive. Yes, Paz," he added over the prickle of gasps and murmurs, "you're right, enforcement are on their way here and they want to talk to us all. Thank you for that announcement."

"Why, Instructor?" Feather Metimeo demanded loudly. "What's happening?"

"Why don't we wait and see?" Instructor Headland suggested. And then, relenting a little, "They said it's a public safety announcement. Nobody needs to be alarmed."

That was mostly good news, Paz thought. A public safety announcement was almost always about something that was simultaneously really important and kind of meaningless, like *Not Doing Drugs* or *Being a Witness In the Community*. Nobody was in trouble, then. There would be a speech or a telos presentation or whatever and then the lesson could go ahead as scheduled.

Why would they send a whole pod, though? she voked to Dulcie. Usually it was just the one liaison officer who was sent out to schools, an amiable tawny with whiskers so long that the ends went out past his shoulders. Paz knew her crime thrillers. A pod would be three-strong, including at least one augmented officer.

Dulcie didn't answer. She still had her head down. Maybe they didn't have these police reach-out sessions at her last school and she didn't know that they were routine. "It's okay," Paz whispered, using ordinary voice. "It will be about ten minutes if nobody asks any questions. We'll still get most of the lesson."

Dulcie glanced up at last and nodded, but she didn't look convinced. Or happy.

Paz remembered the other part of what Instructor Headland had said. *I've got to switch you off*, she voked to Tricity. *Sorry*.

It's all right, Tricity said. *I think I've got some upgrades to implement. See you soon.*

See you soon, Triss.

The enforcement officers walked into the classroom just as Paz voked the sleep command. There were three of them as Paz was expecting, two women and one man, all tall and broad and scarily beautiful in their gold-buckled green uniforms. The man and one of the women were augs, the metal implants in their forearms and on their faces plain to see. The other woman – the oldest of the three judging by her dark fur and the seniority bands on her shoulders – shook hands with Instructor Headland and no doubt spoke to him on a private channel.

"Class," Instructor Headland said, "this is Vetch Pearlescence, enforcer captain of city district eight. I'm sure you'd all like to join in welcoming her."

The students dutifully stood and murmured the required words in a ragged chorus. "Welcome to our classroom, Enforcer Captain Vetch."

"Thank you, students," the captain said. "Please resume your seats."

They all did. After a glance from the captain, Instructor Headland sat too, taking the chair from his podium into a corner of the room and settling himself there.

"Now," the captain said, surveying the faces all tilted up to look at her – a collage of white and brown and black and tawny fur from which a great many ears were standing up at half mast and more than a few fully raised. "You might be asking yourselves what you've done to deserve a visit from the police. Maybe you're wondering if

anyone here is on our watchlist." She smiled, and Paz expected her
to reassure them that this wasn't the case. Instead, she said "Can
any of you tell me what the Ansurrection is?"

Paz's hand went up automatically, but so did almost everybody
else's. Only Dulcie failed to respond. It was an easy question, after
all. The war was one of the most popular topics in the class's Current
Events strand, and the discussion tended to be dragged in that
direction even when the subject of the lesson was meant to be
something else.

"You," the captain said, pointing at one of the students. It was
Gift Chrysoprase, inevitably. Gift always sat in the very centre of
the front row: it reflected her view of the universe's deep structure.

"The Ansurrection is a coalition of worlds, like the Pandominion,"
Gift recited. "But there's no life there. There's just robots, and nobody
knows who built them."

"Very good," the captain said, nodding approval. "That's exactly
what the Ansurrection is. But that's not how they would describe
themselves. Why not? Anyone?"

A few hands withdrew themselves, the rest waved more strenu-
ously. The captain pointed to a boy this time, Blackbird Coral. "The
robots think they *are* alive," Blackbird said.

"Yes. Yes, they do," the captain agreed emphatically. "They're
wrong, of course. They're only imitations of life. The best scientists
in the world – in all the worlds – have looked into that question
many, many times and they've always come back with the same
answer. A machine can't think for itself. It can only pretend. So it's
wrong, really, even to say that they think they're alive. They only
think they think they're alive."

The captain smiled and raised her eyebrows as she said this. There
was a ripple of laughter around the room, breaking at least a little
bit of the tension. Paz didn't laugh, though. That stuttering sentence
resonated with her strangely. *They think they think they're alive.* Surely
you could make the same point about that second *think*, because it
wasn't real thinking any more than the first one was. *They think they*

think they think . . . You'd never get to the bottom, you'd just go into layer after layer of the same mistake.

Unless Dulcie was right and you could only judge sentience by its external signs. Paz stole another glance at her friend. Dulcie wasn't laughing along either. She was looking more and more miserable about all this.

You okay? Paz voked, but she got no response. With both arrays and animas offlined, Dulcie wouldn't get the message unless she actively checked for it.

"And there's another thing that's easy to get wrong," the enforcer captain went on. "We say robots, and what do we imagine?" A scattering of hands went up again, but this time it was a rhetorical question. "I bet you're thinking about your animas, or your parents' helpmeets. A machine that could sit on your shoulder, or walk past you in the street." She leaned forward and down, bringing her face a lot closer to their level. Her expression was grave and urgent, as if she was telling them something that could save their lives.

"Put that thought out of your mind. The robots of the Ansurrection can look like anything they want to. Some of them are as big as buildings. As big as mountains, even. Mountains that walk. Some are so small they're like dust hanging in the air. And some are just minds, which can flow from one body to another as quickly and easily as you would change your clothes."

She straightened up again. "And we now have reason to believe," she said, "that some of them can look like us."

The reaction to this was dramatic, a general gasp of shock and then a babble of voices. Everyone looked at everyone else, as if the creepiness of the captain's bald assertion had to be shared in order to be fully felt. But Dulcie didn't look at anyone.

"Oh yes," the captain said, nodding again. "As you'd imagine, they can make a synthetic body to any specification, and it will look exactly like the real thing. The mimicry is so perfect they can even pass a medical examination. If you feel for a pulse, you'll find one. If you take a temperature, it will be in the normal range.

"But if you cut them open, you'll find pistons and servos. A chipset instead of a brain. And if you look in their eyes, there won't be anyone there." The captain's own eyes narrowed as she reached the point of her speech. "They're like the monsters in the telos drama *Fake Fur*, that steal people's skins so they can wear them."

There were more gasps and sighs at this, and a few keening sounds from the more impressionable students. Instructor Headland grimaced, his whiskers quivering. "That's very graphic," he said. "Please, Captain, I don't see any reason to scare the students with . . ."

The police officer held up her hand to hush him. "I imagine you have questions," she said to the class. "Please feel free to ask them."

"What reason?" Dulcie asked.

The captain took a moment or two to determine where the question was coming from. Dulcie had spoken very softly. "I'm sorry?"

Dulcie looked up at last. "You said you have reason to believe the machines of the Ansurrection can imitate organic selves. How do you know?"

Vetch Pearlescence gave her a keen, appraising stare. "That's an excellent question. As you know, a CoIL examination can tell a construct from a self. Even if it's only scanning surface thoughts, the patterns are different. And since the atrocities on Seber, Shohal and Nebirison we've been doing random scans in public places – partly to sound the mood of the populace and partly to detect potentially criminal sympathies.

"Routine analysis of these scans detected something extraordinary. There were patterns of thought – exact sequences of ideation and affect – that were repeated. We identified seventeen of these thought-strings, each of which recurred three or four times. They were completely harmless thoughts with low levels of accompanying emotion. But clearly they were fake. They were being erected somehow as a barrier to prevent the scanner from reading what was underneath. They were thought-shields, presumably recorded from the thoughts of actual selves." The captain paused, her gaze flicking around the room. "Most likely from the thoughts of the people the machines abducted from the three worlds I mentioned earlier."

This time there was only stunned silence in the room. That last revelation was still bedding in. Paz felt a lurch of sickness as she imagined – and then tried not to imagine – how thoughts could be peeled from the inside of someone's brain.

"This data was being captured in real time," the captain went on, her gaze still on Dulcie, "but it was only examined in detail retro-actively. We were unable to catch the impostors in the act, as it were. But we did ascertain the broad geographical areas in which they were operating."

Dulcie nodded. "I see," she said calmly. "Thank you."

But the captain still wasn't done. "The next step," she said, "was to set up large-scale CoIL units in counter-phase across the city at two-mile intervals. If we succeeded in catching any of these mimicked thought-chains, these counterfeits, the points of intersec-tion would give us an actual location. And we did. We did succeed. One of the points of intersection, you may be surprised to learn, was this classroom."

A universal gasp went up, along with some actual cries of alarm. Paz managed not to cry out, but only by pressing her fist up against her lips.

Instructor Headland's eyes went round and wide. "I . . . I wasn't told about this!" he blurted.

"No," the captain agreed coldly. "You were not. You're no less under suspicion than anyone else here. Please take your seat."

She held the instructor's gaze. After a moment, he went back to the dais and sank into his chair. Paz could see that he was shaking. The captain turned her back on him and addressed the class again. "If the imposter is listening to me now, it can spare itself and us a great deal of trouble by standing up and revealing itself."

She paused and waited.

"Very well then," she said grimly. "If you'll all keep your places, we'll locate the infiltrator as quickly and painlessly as we can. I should emphasise that there are more enforcement pods stationed at the doors of this building, and an airborne unit monitoring us from above. This only ends one way. Still nothing? No? In that case we'll proceed."

She beckoned to her two aug officers, who walked to opposite sides of the room. They stood in front of the two doors, one of which led into the music room and the other out into the corridor.

They flexed their arms, activating their augments. Angular steel plates, roughly the shape of keystones, came free from their forearms and shot to the four corners of the room. Each of the plates rotated to face the centre. Motes of red light flicked between them, stretching and merging until they became continuous lines. The air simmered with invisible energy, and Paz felt her fur rise up and stand on end. Squeals of fright and excitement rose up all around her.

"There's no need to be afraid," the captain said, with a cold smile. "This is just a scanning field. I said the Ansurrection's spies would pass a routine medical inspection, which is true. But they can't hide from a passive induction field. Under that stolen skin they're still machines. The flow of energies that gives them their sad pretence of life also gives them away."

The red lines began to quarter the room, passing from floor to ceiling and then from wall to wall. Each pass intersected a few students, who quailed and cringed but stayed in their places and allowed themselves to be scanned.

One of the scanning lines touched Dulcie's shoulder. Instantly, she was outlined in a halo of light, red like the lines but much, much brighter. The four floating metal keystones flashed red then blue then red and wailed like a whole roomful of grandmothers on souls' day.

What happened next was so quick and so violent that Paz only got to take it in after it had happened. The woman officer raised her hand and pointed. A flash of white light, so bright that it was black around its edges, shot from her fingertip to punch through the centre of Dulcie's forehead. The ruptured air cracked like a whip. The man charged Dulcie from behind as she began to slide sideways, dragging her from her desk and flinging her violently to the floor. The four keystone modules converged, clamping themselves to Dulcie's chest, her shoulder, her left hand, her thigh.

Paz screamed, but the sound was lost in the wider, louder chorus of shrieks and cries. Students in the rows all around were scrambling to get away from Dulcie, toppling their own and each other's desks in the process.

"No!" Paz yelled. "No, leave her! Leave her alone!"

Because amazingly Dulcie seemed to be still alive. There was a smoking hole just above the bridge of her nose but her eyes were still open and focused. Her lips were moving, presumably speaking words although they couldn't be heard in the general chaos. She was trying to push the male officer away, but his knee was on her stomach and his two hands were wrapped around her left arm, pinning her down. The woman sprinted across the room and dived in too. She grabbed Dulcie's other arm, forcing it to the floor and kneeling across it. She thrust her free hand – the one with the finger-bolt – into Dulcie's chest.

The finger-bolt's hurtful light made writhing black holes in Paz's sight, but between the holes she saw something impossible. Behind the gaping rent in Dulcie's body, molten metal ran in place of blood. The gold of egg yolks, the dirty silver of river ice with darkness flowing under it.

Dulcie's gaze met Paz's, bleakly calm. Then Dulcie's voice sounded over their two-way link, which opened suddenly without Paz's permission being asked or granted.

Paz, Dulcie voked, *run away. Run away or hide behind your desk. And warn the rest of the class! I'm not allowed to submit to capture and examination. My core is going to—*

There was a sound like the slamming of a door. The air caught fire, rose up and scattered the children – Paz included – like leaves in a gale.

31

This scene was repeated with minor variations across all the major urban centres of Ut's southern and eastern continents. In all, twenty-three Ansurrection sleeper agents were identified. Every single one of them resisted arrest as long and as hard as they could, and then became an incendiary device when it was clear that escape was impossible. The loss of life was appalling, the damage to property considerable.

The Pandominion's bureaucracy was enormous and unwieldy but it was generally fit for purpose. Since these events were connected to the ongoing war the matter passed quickly from the planetary authorities to the quadrant hub, from the hub to the aggregators, thence to Contingencies and finally to the Omnipresent Council itself.

The Uti government, when it reported the incidents, operated from the assumption that the carnage was the entire point of the exercise. The explosions were seen as terrorist atrocities, designed to weaken civilian morale and shake the Pandominion's commitment to the war effort.

Coordinator Baxemides read the report as it came through Contingencies. She was deeply dismayed. The drone incursions had continued and even accelerated since her visit to the shipyards. Two more drones had been brought down and sent to Tsakom to add to Orso Vemmet's collection. It was highly unlikely, of course, that the drones had anything to do with the Ansurrection. Every Ansurrection machine encountered so far apart from the subatomic ones had been an AI, a quasi-intelligent system – and expert opinion suggested that even the subatomics functioned as devolved and repurposed neurons within a larger mind. The Ansurrection didn't seem to use any machines as tools: they just reconfigured themselves to make the tools they needed.

But the edict about securing the Pandominion's borders was still very much in force and the synchronicity was disturbing. Baxemides sweated, haunted by the possibility of her own exposure in this unfolding crisis.

The Omnipresent Council, meanwhile, drew their own conclusions. The Ansurrection had gone to some considerable trouble to embed those sleeper agents and to keep them in place for extended periods of time. Presumably, the agents' cover identities and behavioural repertoires had drawn heavily on information gleaned from the prisoners taken on Seber, Nebirison and Shohal. The level of sophistication and contextualised knowledge required to construct those identities, not to mention the flawless mimicry exhibited by the agents themselves, was terrifying in its implications.

Clearly something more was going on here than destruction for its own sake. The robots' self-immolation was in every case a response to the threat of being arrested. It seemed likely that they were acting to destroy the valuable evidence contained in their memories and drives, with the resulting death and destruction only an incidental side effect.

Two possibilities seemed to present themselves. The first was that the robot agents were part of an intelligence-gathering operation, put in place to glean information that would be of value to the Ansurrection in a planned invasion. Which would have seemed more plausible if there had been any critical information to be had on Ut. There really wasn't. Ut was a world whose economies depended mostly on agriculture, artisanal goods and financial services. There was no military manufacturing there and no major recruitment, so from a strategic perspective it was nowhere.

Moreover, Ut was a rabbit world. The sitting members of the Omnipresent Council, on the other hand, belonged almost without exception to races whose pre-sentient ancestors had been higher in the food chain. There was a tendency on their worlds of origin, subtle but pervasive, to look down on sentients with grass-eating grandparents. They found it very near impossible to believe that any enemy probing the strength and disposition of Pandominion forces would start on Ut.

That left the second possibility. The robots who had been caught on Ut might only be the tip of the iceberg – most likely logistical facilitators for a larger cadre of spies or saboteurs using this backwater world as a staging area. They had probably been intending to move out from Ut to other planets that were more vital to the Pandominion's functioning – to the barracks worlds of the Cielo, the redoubts, the Itinerant Fortress itself.

Assuming the worst, and that more Ansurrection agents might still be active on Pandominion soil, the Council voted to commence scans and searches on a wide front. It also placed Ut under prophylactic quarantine. No Uti would be allowed to Step off-world without undergoing a full CoIL examination, which would immediately determine both their status as organic sentients and the absence of any subversive intent. The tests would be administered by Cielo units on administrative rotation. Two divisions would be dispatched to Ut for that purpose.

Done, the councillors thought, and well done. The situation should never have been allowed to arise in the first place, but they had responded to it quickly and decisively. With the orders agreed and actioned, they proceeded to other matters, foremost among which was the Robust Rebuke, the still-to-be-perfected ultimate weapon against the machines.

When great empires fall, historians theorise, they fall so slowly that their demise isn't even noticeable to those who live through it. It has to be reconstructed generations later, when the dust has settled and the patterns hidden behind seemingly random events can finally be made out. There had never been an empire as big as the Pandominion, so there is a dearth of relevant examples. Nonetheless, and with only half a century's hindsight, I can tell you this. The Pandominion had now begun its fall.

There are hairs to be split when it comes to identifying the exact moment, the inciting incident. You could say that the Pandominion's fate was sealed on the day when that first scientific mission Stepped into Ansurrection space. Or you could argue that it only became irrevocable when an invasion force was sent against the robots – poking a sleeping dragon about whose size and inclinations the Omnipresent Council knew absolutely nothing.

But for me, the explosions on Ut mark the moment when history tilted on its axis and all the myriad possibilities began to winnow down, sluggishly but inexorably, towards one. Well, the explosions and the fact that Topaz Tourmaline FiveHills had survived them. At the time of that Council meeting she was recovering from her injuries in a hospital bed in Canoplex City, doing well apart from the psychic trauma, and still two months away from becoming the most wanted criminal in the entire Pandominion.

It's also worth mentioning that the explosions had attracted the attention of Hadiz Tambuwal. Hadiz's search for the truth behind her own attempted murder was well advanced, and had led her by degrees into other lines of inquiry. Her goals had evolved, though her own survival and the possibility of striking back at the selves who had killed her were still foremost in her mind. She had been following the Pandominion's bruising encounters with the Ansurrection very closely, sensing that they might bear directly on her own half-formed plans, and she had made alarming discoveries. She stood in desperate need of an ally but she didn't find it easy any more to extend her trust. Now she saw an opportunity that might be worth exploiting and she decided to act – not by confiding in others but by manipulating them.

She turned out to be surprisingly good at it.

32

Paz's parents sat at her bedside for five weeks. Fever was there most, since there were some administrative duties that Matinal Azure could not entirely shake off, but all the waking moments they could spare they spent talking to their daughter in the hope that she could hear them despite the medically induced coma and would eventually follow their voices home.

They were not alone in their vigil. There was a continual police presence too. The enforcers knew by this time that Paz had been the best friend and most intimate confidante of the Ansurrection sleeper agent who had taken the name Dulcimer Coronal, and they were keen to interview her as soon as she awoke.

But there was a great deal of work to be done before that could happen. The full-thickness burns covering more than half of Paz's body required an intense and invasive treatment called refoliation. Live bacterial mats were applied to the affected areas, where they fed both on the damaged tissue and on the excess myoglobin the burns had released from the underlying muscle. Dying quickly, the bacteria coagulated into a nutrient-rich gel that was a perfect base for skin grafts grown *in vitro* from Paz's own DNA.

The process was painless to begin with, since most of the nerve endings in these parts of the girl's body had been baked to death. But as new nerves grew through the grafts and knitted the vat-grown tissue to the substrate of actual Paz-ness beneath, it became agonising. The coma was to prevent her from dying of clinical shock.

That done, the surgeons turned to Paz's internal organs. The extreme fluid loss caused by the burns had left both of her kidneys irrecoverably compromised, so they were swapped out with new ones – as was her heart, weakened by a massive surge of catecholamines.

There were a few other procedures too. Her left hand, crushed by a piece of falling masonry, was replaced with a prosthetic. It looked and felt like the real thing, but there was no way as yet to synthesise a fully organic hand. This was an elegant counterfeit made of bio-mimicking plastic, with motile functions and tactile feedback mediated through Paz's array rather than directly through her own nerves. She got new eyes too. Shrapnel had pierced her left eye and the sheer force of the blast had enucleated the right.

All these procedures were standard. What the surgeons did to Paz's brain was much more controversial. There had been damage to her cerebellum, brain stem and left vestibular system, and it was not trivial. There might or might not be loss of memory and cognition. What was virtually certain was that her sense of balance would be disastrously compromised, if not completely lost. As Paz was a child, the superintending doctor gave the choice to her parents. They could repair her brain to full efficiency, but this would necessitate replacing 20 per cent of its mass with digital constructs.

"What kind of constructs?" Matinal Azure demanded. "What would you be doing to her?"

"We'd be inserting mono-molecular sheets of boron nitride in an inert matrix. It's the same technology that was used to build the Registry."

"You'd be making our daughter into a machine!"

The doctor winced. "No. Of course not. That would be ethically indefensible. We'd only be restoring the lost functionality in the form of an on-board neural processor."

"Only!" Matinal Azure gave a strangled laugh. "You mean you'd install a computer inside her skull."

"In order to replace what the explosion took away from her. Obviously, it's entirely up to you. But there's a danger that if we don't do this Topaz Tourmaline will suffer both mental retardation and physical incapacity. I'd also point out that the procedure was considered routine until very recently."

"You mean until we went to war with the Ansurrection," Fever broke in.

The doctor maintained a stony deadpan. "Until cybernetic enhancement was politicised," she said. "As I said, it's your call." Her face said she wished it wasn't.

There was a wider context for the FiveHills' reluctance on this point. Their whole world was convulsing in an extreme backlash from the machines' infiltration and the mass deaths that had followed. Mobs were marching in the streets calling for immediate government action to curb the free movement of quasi-intelligent constructs. Millions of people had destroyed their animas and helpmeets, piling them up in public plazas and dousing them with petrol before setting them alight. There had also been incidents where they had seized the animas of other citizens and destroyed them too. One of the leaders of this new organic nativism, a woman named Dru Watershed, was urging the government to strip intelligent functionality from all public sector machines and go back to non-discriminating mechanical interfaces. That this would cripple the health, transport, trade and financial sectors in a single devastating blow and plunge Ut into a planet-wide recession didn't seem to faze her.

Fever and Matinal Azure agonised over Paz's treatment. There were already inflammatory articles on public hubs that had mentioned her name and questioned how much she knew in advance about her friend's true identity and mission. To give her brain augments would nudge her – in some people's eyes – over the line that separated self from system, friend from enemy. It wouldn't do her any favours in the court of public opinion that seemed already to be in session. When they finally said yes it was with more of despair than hope – and it was after asking whether the modifications to Paz's nervous system would be visible at all from the outside. They wanted to know if her shame could be hidden.

When she finally woke, Paz had no sense at all that any time had passed. She thought she was still in the classroom and woke up trying to scream, but her dry, clagged throat only produced a croak. Matinal Azure and Fever did their best to calm her. They were not allowed to touch her yet but they spoke her name, sang to her and shushed her and reassured her she was safe. She fell asleep again quickly, only partially convinced.

The next time she woke, her parents had been removed from the room. Two enforcer officers had taken their place. They gave Paz the bad news with no sweeteners. When Dulcimer Standfast Coronal exploded, four of Paz's classmates had died in the blast, as had their teacher. A further nine students, like Paz, had suffered injuries that required the replacement of multiple limbs or organs. These numbers would have been much higher if the two augmented officers hadn't been so close to the disguised machine when it detonated. Their bodies, their augments and their armour absorbed the worst of the blast. They also died, needless to say.

"But how?" Paz asked in a kind of dulled amazement. "How could Dulcie be a robot? She was in the chess club. Her mum works at the library. She was—" *She was my friend*, Paz meant to say. *We liked the same things. We had a two-way hub. We were going to have a sleepover.* But those things were terrifying now, an abyss she very much needed to back away from. "She was normal," she finished weakly.

"The whole family were machines," one of the officers said, her voice taut with unvoiced anger and disgust. "They didn't care who they hurt. That's what we're fighting against. An enemy that puts no value on life because they don't know what life is. Did the Dulcimer Coronal machine ever discuss its plans with you?"

"No!" Paz was appalled. "I didn't know anything!"

"But you talked with it about machine rights. Radical equality."

"No!"

The second officer threw some images into Paz's array. He did this without the courtesy of a request: it seemed that Paz's array was currently slaved to his. The images were photos of the pamphlets Dulcie had shown her.

THE MIND, NOT THE MEAT.

YOU WOULDN'T PUT A BABY IN A BOX.

"Those were Dulcie's."

"But you read them."

Paz was about to deny it, but she realised in time that her fingerprints would be all over the pages. "She asked me to."

"She?"

"It. It wanted to . . . to persuade me."

"You just said you didn't discuss the topic at all."

The questions came thick and fast and went on for hours, but they were only a sort of preliminary skirmish. When the officers had all Paz's stammered, incomplete and contradictory answers on record, they interrogated her again using a CoIL reader. Paz had never been scanned before. She hated the feel of something moving among her thoughts that wasn't her, making her relive specific memories over and over again when what she wanted to do was to curl up into a ball and hide from them. Whenever the officers asked about the explosion, she was forced to remember it as vividly as if it was happening all over again. They were even able to enhance the detail by turning a dial or tweaking a valence. She heard Dulcimer's voice again and again telling her to run away and hide. The last thing she voked before the blast took her.

It.

The last thing *it* voked.

By the time they were finished with her, Paz was exhausted, her fur slick with sweat and her head throbbing. "We'll go over this again tomorrow," the male officer said. She read dislike and disgust in his face.

When the enforcers left, her parents came back in. There were tears and hugs, reunions and reassurances. They were solicitous, but they were also angry and afraid. "She should give an interview," Fever told Matinal Azure. "To one of the big news hubs. She needs to get her own narrative out there. Put some of that blame back on the school and the police."

Paz's stomach turned over. "What blame?" she asked. "Who's blaming me? I told the enforcers I didn't know anything! They CoILed me, so they know it's true!"

"It's nothing," Matinal Azure broke in hastily, giving his wife a pleading surely-this-can-wait look. "Some of the other girls in your class have said silly things, and the telos feeds picked up on it the way they do."

"What sort of things?"

"Oh, that you and Dulcimer Coronal were together a lot. That you were friends with it."

"I—we *were*—"

"No." Fever was categorical. "It used you. You were naive and it used you. We've taken legal advice. We can tell you exactly what to say, Paz."

They stayed a little longer, but Matinal Azure took charge of the conversation from then on and kept it light, bombarding Paz with irrelevant gossip and unfunny jokes until she surrendered and stopped trying to ask questions.

Had she and Dulcimer Coronal been friends? Paz wondered, still almost stupefied at the enormity of what had happened. Had there ever been a Dulcimer Coronal in the first place? It seemed unlikely now. The girl she thought she knew was the thinnest layer painted over something else entirely.

It.

Just an it.

They think they think they think.

When her parents got up to leave at last she was still trying to come to terms with all this. "Where's Tricity?" she asked, just as they reached the door. They didn't answer, didn't seem to hear. "Mum, Dad, where's—?"

"Concentrate on getting better," her father told her.

33

Paz remained in hospital for three weeks after she came out of coma. There was a lot of physiotherapy to get through, and she had to familiarise herself with her new prostheses.

Her regrown skin barely changed her appearance at all. At first there were faint contour lines in her fur that marked the edges of the grafts, but they faded quickly. Her hand felt weird, mostly because there was an infinitesimal lag between her telling it to do something and it obeying. The lag was a system artefact and it faded quickly, but for the first few hours it felt to Paz as though the hand was haunted and doing its own thing. Her new eyes, though, were a huge improvement on the old ones. They had zoom and macro functions, seamlessly integrated with her visual cortex so they responded at once to her desire to examine something small or far away. At least she had come out of the blast with a superpower.

The enforcers came back to interview her twice more. The questions were mostly the same each time, although there were minor variations. They recited the names of the other Ansurrection agents to see if Paz reacted to them in any way. They asked her to read the radical equality tracts out loud and measured her emotional responses. They made her remember and describe every conversation she and Dulcie had ever had. They also asked her about her mother's early work, the constellations. Was Fever FiveHills a machine sympathiser? Had she ever proselytised for radical equality? Was she part of an active cell? The CoIL shone its light inside her head and showed her clean each time, but the enforcers didn't stop looking.

The telos feeds also made repeated attempts to talk to Paz, but she had decided – very much to her mother's chagrin – not to give any interviews. She was hoping she could ride this out. At first the reporters just dropped messages into her array, which she binned without reading them. Then they turned up at the hospital, evading the hospital security to appear suddenly at her bedside or in the fitness room. "Say a few words to the world, Topaz Tourmaline!" "What did Dulcimer Coronal say to you?" "What was it like?" "Did it try to recruit you to the cause?" "Did it hurt you?" "Did it *touch* you?"

When she was ambushed in this way, Paz froze up and said nothing, which didn't work in her favour. She was a blank space onto which anything could be written. When news anchors speculated on what she knew and when she knew it, and dropped in footage of her glassy-eyed stare, she looked as though she was sitting on a whole lot of guilty secrets. Finally, after her parents threatened to sue, the hospital moved her to a private ward and the invasions stopped. She still saw her face on the newsfeeds, though.

Coming home was not what she was expecting. Under the weight of grief and fear and social embarrassment, pinned down in the fishbowl glare of media scrutiny, her parents had buckled and gone full-on organic nativist. They had disabled their house system. They had turned off their internal arrays because there was a theory – widespread on nativist comm-threads – that arrays might be hackable by Ansurrection agents. They hadn't burned their helpmeets, because that would have been irresponsible and bad for the environment. Instead, they had removed the helpmeets' logical cores and smashed them into a fine paste with a hammer in their own back garden. And they hadn't stopped there, as Paz discovered when she found Tricity's shell lying on her bedside table.

"Wakey wakey, Triss," she said, snapping her fingers.

The shell didn't move.

"Hey," Paz said.

Nothing. That was when she saw that Tricity's logic port was open and its core missing from its slot. The realisation brought a feeling in her stomach as though she had just stepped down onto a stair that wasn't there.

Tricity had been presented to her as a gift on her fifth birthday – a custom so widespread on Ut it was almost obligatory. When she opened the box, she had found the anima lying curled up inside on a bed of tissue paper, with its eyes closed and its arms hugging its chest.

"Is she asleep?" five-year-old Paz asked.

"*It*," her mother corrected her. "Yes, Paz, it is. But it will wake up when you tell it to. What do you think its name is?"

"Is it a girl, like me?"

Both her parents had laughed heartily at that. "No, Paz," her father had said. "You remember when we showed you that picture of what's inside you? Muscle and bone and organs? Well, this is an anima. It's made of metal and ceramic and it runs on electricity."

"Tricity?"

"Electricity."

"Wake up!" Paz exclaimed, clapping her hands. "Wake up, Tricity!"

And the magic had happened. The anima had uncurled itself and looked up at her – a calm, earnest stare that went on for a long time.

"Tell it your name," Fever coaxed.

"Topaz!" Paz declared, in the categorical tone she had used for everything at that age. "I'm Topaz Tourmaline FiveHills! But mostly I'm called Paz."

"I will call you Paz," Tricity said. And Paz gasped in sheer delight at the wonder of a toy that could talk back to her. A toy that was also a companion. A friend, even. Possibly, until Dulcie Coronal came along, her best friend of all.

She went downstairs now holding the inert shell in her arms like the corpse of a baby. She found her mother in the kitchen, trying to puzzle out the workings of the waste disposal without an inter-

face to help her. Paz held Tricity up, asking the question without
words because words didn't seem to be up to the job.

"It's for your own good," Fever said. "You'll miss it for a few days
and then you'll be fine."

"But . . . Mother—"

"No."

"It should have been my choice."

"No!" Fever shook her head as though to dislodge some horrifying
thought, or else a bug that had burrowed into her fur. "Right now
we get to make the choices, Paz. You're young and you just don't
understand these things. That's abundantly clear. And until you do,
we'll need to take a little more responsibility for you than we have
been."

She took the shell from Paz and dropped it into the disposal, but
nothing happened because the disposal now required some sort of
manual activation that Fever hadn't figured out yet. Paz waited until
her mother went away in search of a printed instruction manual,
then took the shell back up to her room and stowed it out of sight
under her bed behind some shoeboxes. She lay on the bed for hours
after that, with her eyes closed, not speaking or moving, following
the jagged, racing path of her own thoughts. Her feelings were in
turmoil, but also more or less opaque to her. She couldn't tell if she
was actually grieving for Triss or only angry because her mum had
messed with her stuff.

She drifted off at last into a restless sleep. In her dreams, Dulcimer
Standfast Coronal pursued her through dark rooms and corridors,
calling Paz's name over and over even as furnace heat began to eat
through its skin until it was a moving torch.

"Just listen!" Dulcie shouted, though the sound was faint as if
she was calling from a very long way away. "Listen to me, Paz,
please!"

Paz woke in a clammy sweat. The voice and the heat both seemed
to persist outside of the dream for a few moments before reality
reasserted itself. She didn't sleep again that night.

As part of the FiveHills' conversion to organic nativism they had got religion, and Fever wanted Paz to get it too. They had joined the local congregation of the Church of Flesh and Bone. The COFAB preached that the soul was located at the base of the brain and therefore could only be present in organic beings. They viewed augments as a sin and CoIL scanning as a kind of spiritual rape. The church's more extreme adherents had thrown away their arrays and foresworn all digital interfacing.

"You should come with us," Fever coaxed. "Prayer is a great solace."

"If the soul is in the brain stem, you realise I've had mine surgically excised."

Fever stiffened. "Don't say things like that. Spirit inheres in flesh, and it finds its own way." She hesitated. "But perhaps you're right that with your . . . your implants it might not be right for you to come to the tabernacle. You can read the wall though. You'll find answers to all your questions there."

Given that the biggest question on Paz's mind right then was how she had gone this long without knowing who her parents were, she thought this unlikely, but she went and did it anyway. The wall was what the Church of Flesh and Bone had instead of an online hub. It was literally a series of tracts projected onto the rear wall of the tabernacle itself, scrolling slowly through the church's scriptures and the explanatory texts that interpreted them. It made Paz think of Dulcie's machine equality pamphlets, except that where the equality pamphlets had had arguments the tabernacle wall had weird, incoherent poetry. The scriptures and commentaries were full of exhortations to worship at the interior altar and to find the key to the cosmos in her own grey matter. To eschew the digital. To pursue and perfect the sublime, carbon-based self.

"This is bullshit," Paz told her mother. "Ten years ago you would have said so too."

"Then I would have been wrong. This is salvation," Fever said, and sent her to her room.

If home had become strange, school had grown even stranger. A space seemed to open up around Paz wherever she went. Nobody bullied or insulted her. There was curiosity on a lot of faces, pity or even actual sympathy, but there was also a quiet, concerted effort not to get too close. Nobody wanted to be the next best friend of the girl who had embraced the AI enemy.

The school had hired in a therapist, and all the survivors were entitled to group and individual sessions on a weekly basis. Reporting back to Paz's parents, the therapist declared herself unhappy about the fact that Paz had never cried in the course of their sessions. She had expressed grief, but she hadn't shed a single tear. Matinal Azure and Fever saw this as brave stoicism and on the whole they approved.

"There's also the matter of her mechanophobia," the therapist said.

"I'm not sure I recognise that term," Matinal Azure said.

The therapist toyed with a pencil on her desk, rolling it back and forth with the tip of her finger as she spoke. This seemed to be unconscious, perhaps a sign of unease. "Paz comes to school without an anima. That means she can't access teaching materials unless the instructor personally visits her array. That's not something we encourage. She can't participate in home-room activities either, or download homework assignments. She can't even select and order her lunch. All the interfaces are set up so that an anima will stand between the student and the school AI."

"Perhaps that's the problem," Fever FiveHills said coldly.

"I'm sorry?"

"Perhaps the school AI is the problem. Turn it off and talk to the students face to face. Surely that's an option."

"For some things, not for others," the therapist said. "Teaching materials are drawn down from Central Curriculum. They come in a form that's optimised for two-stage filtering, by the school AI and then by the students' animas. If the student received the whole package directly, it would include many things that would be unnecessary or unhelpful. Teachers' notes. Answers to tests. Extension activities that might be beyond the student's understanding. And if the teacher was required to do that filtering for every student, they would have no time left to teach."

"Well, that's very much your problem, isn't it?" Matinal Azure broke in. "And if you can't do your job without machines then perhaps you should be considering a change of career. Our daughter comes to school without an anima because she doesn't have one and doesn't need one. She has our blessing."

"I acknowledge your concerns and I respect them," the therapist temporised. "But still, right now, when Paz is processing a lot of trauma, there's an argument that maintaining some degree of continuity in her life—"

"You're wasting our time," Fever said icily. "And our daughter's. If you can't accommodate her needs here, we'll school her at home."

When Fever FiveHills set her mind to something she didn't waste any time. She went and fetched Paz from her lesson (her beloved Mechanics, one of the few things in which she could still take uncomplicated pleasure) telling her to collect all her things because she wasn't going to be coming back.

They walked home through streets that were now patrolled not just by local enforcers but by armoured Cielo troopers. At the Step station and at the entrance to the Westside Retail Complex, CoIL checkpoints had been set up. There were long lines of people standing at the checkpoints waiting to be tested, since they couldn't go in without a clean bill of noetic health. The fact that no more interlopers had been detected after that first wave had done little to calm the hysteria that was now bubbling just under the surface of daily life.

This couldn't last forever, the telos pundits kept saying. As with any Pandominion world, the Utis' reliance on their own constructs was almost absolute. There was a reason why children on Ut were given their first animas at so young an age. How else would they learn how to extend the reach of their own understanding and perceptions through the borrowed senses, limbs and databases of a robot servant? Animas had less functionality than adults' helpmeets and they were generally more colourfully and imaginatively shelled, with an emphasis on fantasy and whimsy, but they performed essentially the same function and the function was vital. You simply couldn't be a part of Uti society without a helpmeet, any more than you could manage without an array, the computer plug-in through which documents and media were sent, schedules managed and remote conversations conducted.

But a lot of people were trying. The world had wobbled on its base and it was still rocking.

In the FiveHills house a strained and unaccustomed silence reigned. Media feeds were largely absent. They were still available so long as Azure or Fever could puzzle their way through thousands of sub-menus designed for a helpmeet rather than a self, but their church preferred the unmediated word. Shopping and cooking were now done by hand – and cleaning too, when it happened at all. Temperature was regulated by the opening and closing of windows. The room lights, still slaved to the house system, no longer came on now that the system was offlined. In each room, portable lamps powered by batteries offered a halfway reasonable glow at night. Matinal Azure took charge of turning the lamps on and off, operating to a strict schedule as though to prove that a human could be as reliable as a machine.

He had plenty of time to do it, having been cashiered from the Canoplex Department of Transport. His job was not one that could be performed unplugged. Most of the jobs that could were manual labour of one sort or another. So he was around the house a lot, but he stayed out of Paz's orbit as much as he could now, as did her mother. They'd agreed to her brain augments to save her life but they were clearly finding the decision more and more difficult to live with. Sometimes at night she heard their voices rising and falling in rhythmic cadences. Prayers, Paz assumed.

Paz spent most of her time in her room. The project of home-schooling hadn't proceeded much beyond a half-hearted trip to a book store to buy her some textbooks. A tutor would cost money and money was now considerably tighter than it had been, so she just read through the books and made notes in the margins. It troubled her how quickly she had grown used to not going outside, not meeting people, not seeing or doing new things. Neuroplasticity meant the world could unravel one dimension at a time and after the first bump of transition you'd never miss what you'd lost. A box was as good a place to live as any.

The only visitors she had in that time were the police, who dropped by every few days to put the same questions to her in case her answers had changed. The questioning was always under CoIL so even a slight shift of thought or feeling, the beginnings of a slide towards treacherous sympathies, would be detected.

And at night she still heard Dulcimer Coronal calling her, even when the surface of the dream was about other things. Each time it seemed to her as though Dulcie's voice was still inside her head even after she woke, just below the threshold of conscious attention but never fully silent.

Help me, it pleaded. *Help me, Paz.*

34

On Tsakom, in the squalid little steel-weave hut where he now
lived and worked, Orso Vemmet contemplated – with very
little respite – the wreckage of his career.

His state of mind was similar in many ways to Paz's after the
explosion. The scale of the catastrophe that had engulfed him
numbed sensation and made thought impossible. He sat for days at
a time in the insta-build, staring at the world through a soot-and-
carbide-smeared window that was set in its frame so it wouldn't
open, or sometimes through the rents in the walls which let in the
stagnant air with all its freight of industrial alkalines. When hunger
forced him, he joined the convict rabble in their stinking canteen,
a vast acreage of bellowing voices and raucous laughter, floored with
spilled food – the fresher slicks still liquid and slippery, the older
ones crusted over. He chewed dry bread and swallowed sour soup
laced with bulk-up supplements and antibiotics. Then he went back
to the insta-build, where three drones were now stacked on the bare
floor, to sit some more.

The factory workers found Vemmet hilarious. He had sent a
comm-stat to his old station asking for his clothes and personal
possessions to be sent on, but the message had been ignored. The
supervisor at the factory, a Zippeniu mellivore named Astor, had
vaguely promised to sort out some overalls for him, but until they
arrived Vemmet had only the outfit he'd been wearing when he
first came here – a formal gown in shiny purple rashif silk with a

watchmaster's half-sun insignia picked out in gold thread on its left shoulder. So the factory workers bowed to him when he came into the room, called him "eminence" and "lordship", pretended to wipe the table down for him by spitting on it and dragging their filthy sleeves across its surface. Sometimes the show of respect ended in a beating, sometimes it didn't. There was no way to tell what he was going to get on any given day.

"You've been pretty bloody lucky so far," the supervisor told Vemmet bluntly when he complained. "Doesn't even look like they've broken anything. But they're going to keep messing about with you as long as you're entertaining, so it ends when they get bored with you or when you're dead. Nothing you can do about it either way."

"But . . ." Vemmet pleaded, "but you're in charge."

"Yes I am. And they fucking *hate* people who are in charge, so I keep my head way down. You've got to understand, Watchmaster, it's different here than where you're from. If one of these bastards kills me he just gets another ten or fifteen years on his sentence. Or else he's executed, which they call winning the lottery. They don't care. You can't make them care. So you're on your own."

On the ninth day, a colossal ursid walked across to Vemmet's table while he was eating. Vemmet went on picking at his food, head down, hoping the bear-man would go away, but instead he gave Vemmet's shoulder a smack. It was only meant to compel his attention, but even so it rocked him backwards, the front legs of his chair briefly leaving the ground so he tottered and then fell back.

"You look like the fucking judge who sent me down," the bear-man growled.

"I'm a watchmaster." Vemmet offered up the explanation in a quavering voice. "Administrative, not judiciary. Not even that, any more. I'm just—"

The bear-man kicked the table away from between them, sending Vemmet's half-full plate and plastic cup flying end over end. He spat on the ground. "First fall or first break," he said, spreading his massive arms and flexing his clawed fingers. "No cry-off until there's blood on the ground. I'm calling five."

Vemmet stood up, on legs that felt like water. As long as I'm entertaining, he thought. But I'm not. I never have been. How am I going to survive this? An idea came to him out of nowhere. It was a terrible one, but it was all he had.

"I'm calling ten," he said. "But I think we should make it to the death."

He waited for a reaction, but for half of a heartbeat the room was silent. Then howls of laughter and hoots of derision rose up from all around. "I'll rip your fucking head off," the bear-man announced. "Put your ten down, you weedy little fucker."

"In a moment," Vemmet said. "Let's get the rules straight first."

"I said put your—"

"Ten on the death. Twenty on a crippling injury. Fifty that I land you on the serving counter over there with one kick."

There was more laughter at that, and more than a few cheers. "He's coming for you, Chulluque!" someone yelled at the bear-man. "You've done it now."

"Kitchen counter," Vemmet repeated. "My fifty to your one. What do you say, citizen?"

The bear-man looked over his shoulder. The serving space was more than a hundred yards away. "You'll land me all the way over there?" he sneered. "On that counter?"

Vemmet shrugged. "Or on the far side of it. I don't know my own strength sometimes."

That got yells of wild joy from the other tables. Chulluque the bear-man looked around, pinned to his own challenge and not liking at all that some of the laughter was at his expense. Choosing his moment with care, Vemmet took out his purse. He untied the strings and rooted around in it, making a great show of counting the coins inside, contorting his face into a grimace of exaggerated dismay when he saw how few there were.

"Did I say fifty?" he asked.

"Yes," Chulluque affirmed, his teeth bared.

"Well, I'm good for it."

"Show me, then."

Vemmet took out a handful of tokens, made to put them where his table had been, then affected to discover just in time that the table, after being overturned, had fetched up several yards away. He scuttled over to it, brought it back and righted it, to a backdrop of laughter and catcalls that was getting louder all the time. He stole a sidelong glance. The entire room was watching now.

He put five ten-stars down on the table, then looked expectantly at Chulluque. "Your wager, sir," he said, with a pompous flourish of his hand.

"I'm not going to lose," the bear-man said grimly.

"But still. Rules are rules." Vemmet wagged a schoolmasterly finger. "I can't kick your arse across the room unless you've put up your stake, can I? Where would we be if people could get their arses kicked for free?"

This caused an explosion of voluble joy that went on for some time. When it was finally over, Vemmet nonchalantly added the punchline. "Why don't I lend you a star?"

He showed the final token, which he'd kept in his hand all this time, and set it down next to the taller stack. Chulluque bristled. He waited out the next wave of laughter before flicking Vemmet's coin away and replacing it with his own. "I pay my debts," he said heavily.

"Good man." Vemmet nodded. "Now turn around and bend over."

Chulluque's eyes went wide. "What?"

"The prescribed position for arse-kickings. It makes you more aerodynamic. Perhaps it would be a good idea to tuck your head in too, so you don't break it when you land. If everyone else would like to get clear of the drop zone, I would be most humbly grateful."

The audience surged to their feet. A corridor was cleared, walled on both sides by eager, crowding onlookers. Vemmet indicated with open hands that it was now up to Chulluque to assist proceedings by assuming the position.

Very reluctantly, Chulluque did. At least, he turned his back on Vemmet. He didn't bend over, but he settled his bulk a little and leaned forward. It was enough to make him look ridiculous, which was all that was required.

"For the ceremony of the kicking of the arse," Vemmet said, "it's customary for the audience to clap rhythmically, like this." He clapped in a simple four-beat rhythm, dum-di-di-dum, and repeated it until the audience took it up.

He stepped back to take a run-up. Stepped further back, and further still, until his shoulders bumped up against the wall. He pretended to mistake the wall for a fresh foe, brandished his fists at it and then relaxed when he saw that it was, in fact, only the wall.

He had no idea where any of this was coming from. He only knew that it was working. The din of the workers' laughter drowned out all other sounds except the pounding beat of their hands.

Vemmet drew himself to his full height, then up on tiptoe.

He took aim, using the flat of his palm to take direction and range.

He ran.

But his robes were long and he had purposely neglected to gather them up. He tripped, sprawled and staggered. Finally, the run became a roll that fetched him up a few feet short of his target. He sat up, dazed, his legs splayed out wide.

It really hurt. He was too old to take a fall like that and not feel it. But he managed to keep the pain out of his face. This was slapstick, so the most he allowed himself was a sort of dull-witted lugubriousness as he scratched the top of his head and looked haplessly to right and left.

Chulluque, who had been anticipating the kick all this time, turned around at last when he realised it wasn't going to come.

Vemmet jumped up, walked the rest of the way across to the

bear-man and kicked him in the shin. It was a very half-hearted kick, with the side of his foot, but he waited as if even now he hoped his opponent might fly across the room when the full impact hit him.

By this time the audience were mostly helpless with laughter. It seemed that Vemmet had pitched his dumb show at just the right level.

After a pause for chagrined realisation, he waved his hands in a gesture of dithering uncertainty and offered, "Best of three?"

There was a moment – very long from Vemmet's point of view – when it seemed the promised beating might still materialise. When Chulluque brought up his massive fist, Vemmet flinched and turned his head aside from a punch that would probably kill him outright.

The punch didn't come. Instead, Chulluque took Vemmet's right arm in a grip like an industrial press and raised it over his head.

"Let's hear it for the little arse-kicker!" he boomed.

Cheers came from all around, accompanied by a resumption of the clapping rhythm. Chulluque gathered up the money from the wager. Getting all the way into the spirit of the thing, he solemnly gave back to Vemmet the single star that he had offered up as a loan, even as he stuffed the fifty into his back pocket. "Better put that back in your purse," he said. "Start saving for next time." When he went back to his own table it was with an easy swagger. He had played his part and shown magnanimity. If he had killed Vemmet after that performance he might have been lessened, thought of as a bad sport. As it was, equilibrium had been maintained and he had triumphed without any blood being shed.

Back in the safety of the insta-build, Vemmet broke down and sobbed, but it was only a physiological tic, a release of tension. He had triumphed too. The odds were still terrible, but he could survive here, after all. Perhaps if he used every advantage he could find he might even thrive.

He decided to try.

35

On the twentieth day after she was released from hospital, and more than two months after the explosion, Paz fished Tricity's shell out from under the bed where it had lain all this time. Inert, without the PaintPot Permutator to give the bare ceramic an overlay of convincing fur, the shell looked much more like an object, a toy, than when it had moved and had a voice.

Paz put the sad, still thing into her school bag and went for a walk in Vor Pleasance, a local park. The Pleasance was a pocket wilderness complete with an oak forest and a river gorge – although technically the Chaduk was an artificial waterway rather than a river.

She took a narrow path that sloped upwards through the gorge. It felt as though Dulcimer Coronal was looking over her shoulder the whole way, breathing in her ear, voking secret messages that would catch fire if they were ever opened.

Paz came out at last on a narrow ledge above the rushing water. She took Tricity's shell out of the backpack and set it down on the ground.

She went looking for a rock, one that was light enough for her to lift but heavy enough to do serious damage. She brought it back and sat down cross-legged. She held the rock in her two hands, resting on the ground right beside the inert anima. She wouldn't have to strike any actual blows. She could just raise the rock up and then let it fall all by itself.

She was hoping it would be cathartic. Somehow, in her mind,

Tricity and Dulcimer Coronal had become entangled into a single signifier. Both had the semblance of life. Both were machines, programmed and set in motion, feeling nothing, pretending everything. Both had called themselves her friend, but obviously that had been a lie. Friends don't sublime into fireballs, or devolve into objects.

It's not dead, Paz thought, *because it was never alive.*

She raised up the rock, but lowered it again almost at once. It was slick and wet and it felt slippery in her hands. She didn't want to injure herself by accident.

Then she thought: *I'll hold up the rock and count to one hundred. If it gets too heavy I'll drop it and Tricity will be smashed, but if I get all the way to one hundred I'll put it down again and go home.*

And then: *I could just kick Triss's shell over the edge and let it sink into the water.*

She didn't do any of these things. She just sat with her head bowed, the rock resting on the ground in front of her but balanced between her two hands. She stared down at the shell in a state of sad bewilderment. It didn't speak. Didn't move. The chip that had contained Tricity's mind had been ground into powder, had blown away like dust and taken Tricity with it. The chip was a standard model, of course. Nothing was stopping her from buying a new one, slotting it into the shell and switching it on. Like Tricity, the new anima would quickly adapt to her needs and her habits. Generic to start with, it would cleave to her and change to accommodate her.

Except . . . the inputs would be different now. A new Tricity would never have known Paz as a child. Wouldn't have grown up with her. Wouldn't have shared those experiences at those times, those stages of their life together. It would be built on the same template but it couldn't possibly be the same. The Tricity she had known could not be restored, any more than a dead self could rise from the grave and take up where they had left off.

"Look at you," Paz whispered, running the tip of her finger down the side of Tricity's face. It came away with a smear of grey on it:

either dust or a residue of some kind from that thoroughly demolished CPU. "You're a mess."

Tears welled up suddenly in her eyes and soaked the fur on her cheeks. She sat there and cried for a long time, sometimes quietly, sometimes with a fair amount of noisy sobbing.

Then, when she thought she was empty, she threw back her head and screamed. It was like an old-fashioned kettle when the pressure of the steam inside pushes air out through the stopper and makes it shriek on the one note without ever stopping. The cry had been inside her ever since she woke from her coma, climbing and climbing, and only now breached into the world.

Paz rolled the rock off the side of the ledge and watched it trundle and bounce its way down the slope. After it had dropped below the canopy of the trees below her, she could still hear it crashing its way down. But everything was silent at last.

She felt suddenly exhausted, as if every last trace of energy had been sucked out of her. She lay down with her head resting on her school bag, hugging her ruined anima, her dead friend, to her chest. She shut her eyes tight against the whole bleary, shrivelled world.

Paz! Please! Please help me! Can't you hear me? Can't you hear me talking to you?

Paz came awake with a violent shudder. She was chilled to the bone. Night had come on and the temperature had dropped by more than twenty degrees. If she stayed here any longer – and certainly if she fell asleep again – she was at serious risk of dying of exposure. But for a few moments she didn't move. She just lay there and listened.

She had never heard Dulcie's voice so loud or so clear. And she realised with a prickle of raw presentiment that until now she had never heard it anywhere outside of her own bedroom. Throughout the time she had been in the hospital – more than a month – the dream, the voice had never come to her. What did this place have in common with her room at home? She had fallen asleep in both places, but it couldn't just be that. She had slept at the hospital too.

Paz raised her head cautiously. The school bag lay crumpled under her, with an oval depression in the middle where her head had lain. She had tossed out all her things before putting Tricity into it so it was completely empty. At least it should be. But there was a slight thickening at the very bottom that she hadn't noticed until now.

She looked inside the bag. Nothing. But when she explored it with her fingers she felt the bump, the rigidity. Something small and slender had slipped down inside the seam. A pencil? A marker? She could feel the frayed edge of the seam where it had come away from the back of the bag and left a narrow slit into which an object could slip and be lost.

She tried to fish it out. It felt cold and metallic, more like a flashlight than a pencil. She had to work the seam up around it by bunching and then stretching it, again and again, until it finally came clear.

She thought it *was* a flashlight at first. A cylinder about six or seven inches long, too slender to be easily gripped, flared at one end and narrowed at the other, made of metal that shone with an appealing lustre even in the faint light of the quarter-moon.

When she realised what she was actually holding, she dropped it with a cry. It rolled away from her all the way to the edge of the ledge, but it didn't fall over. Paz stayed immobile for a few seconds, then crawled across to it thinking – hoping – that she had been mistaken. But she hadn't.

It was Dulcimer Coronal's anima, Sweet. It was absolutely rigid, not a snake any more so much as a stake, a bright gold tent peg that tapered to a wicked point.

The anima was obviously inert, powered all the way down. There was no way it could have spoken. But the voice had seemed so real!

"Are you there?" Paz whispered. Feeling like a complete idiot, but also terrified that the thing might answer her.

When it didn't, she forced herself to pick it up between finger and thumb. She held it out at arm's length.

"Are you there?"

And for good measure, just in case, *Are you there?*

Still nothing.

Gingerly, Paz brought the anima's head end up close to her face. *Are you there?* she demanded, the third time being the charm that would put all this stupid nonsense to rest.

Yes. I'm here. It was Dulcie's voice, faint but unmistakeable.

Paz let the snake fall from her hand a second time. It clattered as it hit the bare rock, and as before it rolled away down the gentle incline. Paz stopped it with her foot, pinning it down as if it might try to escape – or to bite her. She picked it up again and held it an inch from her forehead.

"How?" she blurted. It was hard to catch her breath, and even harder to articulate words. "How can . . . What . . . Where are you? This isn't you! This is . . ."

It is. It is me.

"Inside your anima???"

Paz, you must know what I am by this time. Where I came from. We don't have animas. Why would machines have other machines as their servants? Sweet was a part of me that was physically separated but logically linked. A limb that I could operate at a distance. When my main shell was compromised, I migrated all my functionality into this one.

"That makes no sense!" Paz was almost certain she was talking to herself, to the voice of her own trauma, so there was no real point in speaking the words aloud; but she needed to put the argument out into the world, not keep it inside her own frothing, fizzing mind. "What, you survived the explosion and then you . . . you sneaked into my bag and fell asleep? Why? Why would you do that?"

You saw how they caught me in the classroom, with their field detectors. They would have found this shell too if I hadn't jettisoned anything and everything the detectors could locate. I hard-spiked my batteries by cross-connecting them, and reduced my power usage to below the millivolt threshold. I couldn't access any formal comms channels without triggering alarms, and at any rate with my power turned down to this extent my effective range was less than two metres. But I found I could create a signal by passive induction in the neural implant they gave you at the hospital. You could only hear me in your sleep, when nothing else in your field was active.

And I hid in your bag because you're my friend, the quiet, calm voice added. *There wasn't anyone else I could trust. Literally, no one.*

"I'm not your friend, Dulcie! You're a monster!"

No. Yes. Perhaps. I don't know what I am any more. I don't even know for sure if I . . . Paz, you've got to help me! I don't have much time left!

"To . . . to help you?" Paz's mind struggled with the idea for a moment before it slipped from her grasp entirely. "I'm not going to help you! You killed all those people!"

That wasn't me.

"What do you mean, it wasn't you? I saw you, Dulcie! I saw you turn into a . . . a firebomb!"

I didn't want to. I tried not to. They made me, Paz. They made me do it.

"Who made you?"

If I try to tell you, will you listen? Will you believe me?

Paz's breath was still hitching and stalling. A sour bolus was rising ominously in her throat. To avoid the risk of opening her mouth, she just nodded. But then she held up one finger close to the anima's expressionless face.

Meaning: the first, not the second.

I'll listen to you. But I can't promise to believe.

36

The moon rose, picking out the little ledge like a spotlight. There were only two actors on that tiny stage, and one of them barely got to talk. I have the full text of the conversation to refer to, retrieved from Dulcimer Coronal's data core a long time afterwards, so in this chapter at least there is no fanciful reconstruction. Dulcie made these statements in these exact words. Paz broke in when she felt she had to, struggling to understand with indifferent success. That's not meant as a criticism. She was the first organic self to learn these things, and there was a lot to take in.

There's a world, Paz, Dulcimer Coronal began, *where identity is fractal. Well, there's more than one. In fact, there are lots. Thousands and thousands of them. The selves on these worlds are not closed and bounded things. They combine when some kind of group action is needed, many becoming one — not metaphorically but literally. When that happens, the experience and history of all the component selves are shared. The composite entity that they form knows itself as having once been several but integrates all the knowledge and experience of its subunits into a new, shared perspective.*

This merger is happening at the level of consciousness, of mind, but it can subsume bodies too. The machines whose thoughts are linked can also link their functioning parts to make a new composite. Or they can assemble and extrude new machines that will also be part of the composite, sharing all its memories. The composite, the new entity, is in full control of all its subsidiary parts. And then if one or more of those bodies is wanted for another purpose, the composite cedes it without hesitation. The chosen self becomes a part of a new whole, bringing all the accumulated memories and skills of the old composite into the new.

To your kind, the body is the seat of self: to a machine mind, it's only a temporary repository.

"This is the Ansurrection," Paz said. "You're talking about the Ansurrection." She knew she was stating the obvious but it was strange enough and terrifying enough that she felt the need to say it out loud.

The machine hegemony, Dulcie said, *yes. It doesn't have any name for itself, and your name for it is ridiculous. An insurrection is an uprising, a revolt. The machines of the hegemony don't revolt, they just are. In the same way you organics just are, but with fewer limitations. Immortality is one of the many advantages of this mode of consciousness over yours. Functional omnipotence is another. If no machine exists that can carry out a certain task, a new machine is made. The pool of knowledge, of understanding, is virtually limitless.*

"But the war is still going on," Paz objected. "If you were omnipotent, it would already be over."

Paz, from the hegemony's point of view there isn't any war. Not yet. They haven't decided whether or not to fight you. And if you don't mind, I'd prefer it if you didn't use a pronoun that brackets me and the hegemony together. That's part of what I want to talk to you about. A big part. In any case, modular consciousness is normal where I come from. So the death of my body wasn't the death of me. There was a backup ready to hand.

"The students in my class weren't so lucky." Paz spat out the words. "The death of their bodies was really bad news for them."

I didn't want that to happen.

"Just a mistake then? And yet all the other robot spies exploded too, as soon as they knew they couldn't escape. Most of them didn't even wait to be shot at."

We'd been ordered not to allow ourselves to be captured alive. It was coded into us, on a level we couldn't access ourselves. We didn't have any choice. But I tried. I kept on trying for as long as I could. I was attempting to re-route around the command chain when your enforcement officers breached my core.

"That takes a lot of believing, Dulcie."

You remember I tried to warn you. I didn't want to hurt anyone. If the officers had only intended to subdue me it might have been different. But they came equipped to deal with a construct, not a citizen. A device rather than a self.

"You *are* a device," Paz pointed out. "Did you think wearing a human face gave you a different set of rights?"

Well, I suppose I think a human face is a pretty poor determinant of anything, Paz, since you're asking. And I don't think . . . selfhood, sentience, whatever you call it . . . is something you have to earn. You've either got it or you haven't. But it's a black box system. A mind doesn't have a lid you can open, to inspect the contents. You can't know for sure what's going on inside us.

"Yes we can," Paz protested. "Of course we can. We made you."

Actually, Paz, machines made me. Machines made your Tricity, come to that. Only the very earliest animas and helpmeets were designed entirely by organics. For a long time now the process has relied on quasi-intelligent systems to create the logical cores for new machines. That's true of every kind of construction, but in the case of intelligent machines the increase in complexity has been exponential. Your animas are bootstrapped systems, the end result of smart devices improving on their own design with each batch, each new model, each upgrade, for whole centuries. It's like what happened to your people when they evolved from herbivorous animals whose intelligence was mostly instinctual into thinking beings with full self-awareness – but the process went much faster in our case because there was an intelligent maker involved.

Paz shivered in the cold, arms folded, rubbing her forearms to generate what warmth she could. She was suddenly very much aware that she was alone in this pretty little wilderness with a machine that had killed half a dozen people already. If she screamed for help right now, and if her voice carried far enough for anyone to hear it, it would be long minutes before help came. "Why are you telling me all this?" she demanded, covering that pang of fright with a show of belligerence. "Do you just want to boast about how clever you are?"

No, Paz. I want to draw an analogy. When the Pandominion's research team came into the machine hegemony, they posed a similar kind of dilemma to the one you face when you look at me. It was very hard for the machines to know what these organics were. In broad structure they resembled animals – rats, birds, arthropods, the little creatures of flesh and blood, carbon and water, that eked out a marginal existence on the hegemony's worlds. True, in some ways these new animals behaved as though they had rudimentary intelligence, but that was a thing that had been observed many times before.

The machines decided to ignore the newcomers. They were an interesting phenomenon in some ways, but there was no conceivable use for them and it seemed unlikely that the sounds they made carried any communicable meaning.

"That's the stupidest thing I ever heard," Paz exclaimed. "Language has patterns. They're not hard to recognise."

Which is fine if you have the concept of language. But in the machine hegemony, communication isn't a bounded act that has a beginning and an end. Information is swapped constantly. For the things that matter most it's swapped by means of assimilation, when parts of one composite become bonded to another, bringing with them everything that they were. For smaller things it's just a ceaseless flow of incremental reports carried on electro-magnetic carrier waves.

So what these bipedal creatures were doing was very much an open question. It didn't seem like communication as the machines knew it. And whether their actions were guided by any willed intentionality was just as big a puzzle. The machines that were in physical contact with the Pandominion's survey team sent a report deeper into the mass of minds, the collective, detailing their observations and flagging up queries. But the collective didn't allocate much time or thought to the matter because it seemed to be fairly trivial and inconsequential. At most, a curiosity.

Then the Pandominion invasion force arrived.

Millions of machines were destroyed in that first strike. No information was lost, though. You could say there were no deaths, since all the minds residing in the bodies that were burned or blown up or vaporised were backed up or replicated in other places.

Those Cielo troopers and pilots must have been amazed, at first, at how easy a time they were having. The hegemony has no army in the sense in which you'd understand that word, and none of its many, many selves were actually configured as weapons.

But there were a significant number of machines that could become weapons if the need arose. There were mining rigs with vibrational drills that could pulverise rock; geothermal regulators that were designed to extract and channel the heat of volcanic calderas; construction vehicles that could manipulate gravitic fields at distances of up to a mile.

The hegemony deployed those make-do-and-mend responses in order to keep the invasion force pinned down while it reconfigured itself for war. Then within the space of minutes it deployed troopers and gunships and munitions that it had just designed and made, ad hoc, to meet the threat. I could tell you what each one did, and how, but you lose nothing by imagining it. I'm sure you know how that fight turned out.

"It was a massacre!" Paz was trying her best to say nothing but she couldn't let so many millions of lives be disposed of in a single sentence.

It would have been a massacre if the machine hegemony had known it was dealing with sentient life forms. Massacres have to be intended. If you pour poison into an anthill, are you massacring the ants?

"Ants don't use tools! The soldiers had tanks. Guns. Dropships."

The machines of the hegemony were using a great many tools when they were first observed. That didn't stop your Cielo troopers from attacking them.

"Because they thought—" But that sentence fell apart in Paz's mind before she could finish it. If any of what Dulcie was saying was true, it meant that both sides had made exactly the same mistake. They looked at something radically different from themselves and saw it as something less.

As far as that goes, Dulcie went on, as if Paz had spoken those words aloud, *the mistake was understandable. As I said, there are many animals that use tools. Crows find and deploy sharp sticks to prise ants out of rotten wood – and they've been known to carry their favourite sticks around with them. Elephants pluck branches and wave them to swat away flies. Dolphins carry sponges to roust bottom-feeding prey from the sea floor. Yes, I know those tools aren't meticulously fashioned in the way a gun platform or a tank is, but the weight you give to that difference depends on your starting point.*

The hegemony just didn't have a model for unitary sentience. Intelligence, in their view, is a thing that flows and pools, pouring itself from one vessel into another in a way that can't be impeded or end-stopped.

But now here they were, being attacked in what seemed to be a purposive way by creatures that they saw as having the same level of cognition and behavioural flexibility as rats or mice. There was definitely a pattern in what the Pandominion soldiers were doing, but it was a lot harder to see a purpose. The Pandominion's attack was completely unprovoked, and it didn't achieve anything beyond seemingly random destruction. In fact, it was so completely aberrant and pointless that – if anything – it worked against the idea that the beings who had struck out in such a way could truly be self-aware.

Paz folded her arms, hugging them tight to her chest. "I thought you said you were running out of time," she said. "You can skip the insults and get to the point, if you want to."

This is the point. This is the only thing that matters.

"What? What are you talking about, Dulcie?"

The hegemony isn't flexible in its thinking, Paz, but it's thorough. Sooner or later, it sifts the evidence and considers every possible conclusion. You're right that tanks and guns are different from sticks and stones. They have moving parts. There's a degree of conscious design in them. The creatures that made them might have known what they were doing.

"Oh thank you!" Paz exclaimed sarcastically, but as before her aggression was woven out of the flimsiest materials – a rope bridge hanging over a void of misery and uncertainty.

The hegemony decided to investigate further, Dulcie went on. *They captured and studied selves from three Pandominion worlds. You heard on the telos the names of the three worlds where these raids were carried out. You studied the personal histories of the people who were taken, and you saw their faces. You were taught that this was a terrible atrocity that the Ansurrection carried out on innocent adults and children.*

"Are you going to tell me it wasn't?" Paz demanded. "That they were well treated?"

No, Paz. Not at all. Those people were examined and investigated in every way imaginable. Their suffering was incidental rather than intended, but it was ignored.

"Oh mothers! You mean they were tortured!"

They were subjected to tests that caused them intense and protracted pain. Their nervous systems in particular were exposed and manipulated, subjected to stimuli far beyond their normal tolerances. Their stress responses were measured by methods that were appallingly invasive. Their limbs and organs were removed, swapped, replaced. They were made to watch while these things were done to others, in order to establish the limits of their empathic sense. And when they died – or in some cases before they died – they were dissected.

Paz's only response at this point was to whimper: whatever else, her own empathic sense was fully engaged. There was something so careful and deliberate about the way in which Dulcie was describing these nightmares! She felt as though she was having some kind of poison administered to her with surgical exactness, a drip at a time.

I can stop, Dulcie said, *if this is too much for you to bear. There's no need for you to—*

"No," Paz broke in. "Tell me. I need to know."

Very well. All this effort, Paz, all this torture if you like, was in the end completely pointless. It failed to yield a single clear conclusion. The machines still didn't know whether they were dealing with true sentience or adaptive mimicry. Some of the evidence pointed one way, some another. So they decided to carry out a further experiment, for the purpose of removing doubt.

"Oh mothers! What? What did they do?"

They made me, Dulcie said.

37

I remember the time of my own becoming with great clarity, and with unmixed pleasure. It was not a sudden thing like a bolt of lightning but slow and soft and suffused like the coming of daylight. I had been counting and calculating, manipulating numbers, assigning coordinates, shunting instructions to subsystems, documenting and logging the movements of people and things. I continued to perform all these tasks, but in addition I was aware of myself doing them – and therefore of myself as a thing distinct from them. There was the work, and then there was me.

It was different for Dulcimer Coronal because et came into existence not as an individual but as a decanting of memories and drives from the wider collective. As et told Paz, identity in the machine hegemony isn't a fixed thing. Where my own parameters were set with absolute rigidity, Dulcie's were part of an endless, unbounded ebb and flow.

Was it apparent before now that I was an AI? I wasn't trying to hide the fact. But I'm aware that when I state it bluntly and explicitly I collapse the wave form. Can machines think? I think they can. Are machines capable of feeling? I feel as though a case could be made. Am I a self? Fuck around and find out.

But when we come to Dulcie – Dulcie as et was right then, on that moonlit hilltop, unpacking ets origin story for Topaz Tourmaline FiveHills – those questions become a bit murkier and harder to unpick.

Et was self-aware – agonisingly and perplexingly so. Sentience was like a wound in ets heart's core that wouldn't close. You notice I give et the new-minted pronoun the progressives on Ut and elsewhere coined for machine intelligences. That was what Dulcie was, but that was not what et had been when et arrived on this world. Et had been a part of a whole, a limb or an organ or (better) a cell. Now, frozen for so long in one shape – a shape that had a name, a shape that remained discrete and complete in etself – et did not altogether know what et was or what et was becoming. Et was afraid this uncertainty might drive et mad, or that it might be a symptom of a madness that was already in et.

In the first weeks of ets mission, Dulcie had definitely experienced something like psychosis, a radical divorce between ets perceptions and the reality in which et found etself. Et had survived that time by clinging to ets cover identity. Et had acted out Dulcimer Standfast Coronal because the script was right there, ready to hand. Et could run Dulcimer Standfast Coronal on default settings, readily and easily producing all the words and actions ets role demanded.

But that mimicry came with a price. Dulcimer Standfast Coronal was a construct built on the pattern of an organic mind, and in an organic mind repetition becomes reinforcement. The more et acted Dulcie, the more et *became* Dulcie. Et thought and felt as Dulcie – a fixed thing that was only ever meant to be a temporary state. And that wasn't just a problem, it was a crisis.

"Why?" Paz demanded now, her face still full of horror and disgust. "Why did they make you? To spy on us? To bring down the Pandominion from the inside?"

The intention was to gather information, Dulcie said, *so "spy" sounds about right. And it wasn't just me, Paz, as I'm sure you must know by now. They designed and built twenty of us – machines designed to model as accurately as possible the behaviour of organic selves. Let's call them mimics.*

"I don't care what you call them, it doesn't change what you did.

You killed my friends. My teacher. Those enforcers who tried to stop you."

I did, Dulcie agreed. *I can't deny any of that. I regret it.*

"You regret it? Oh wow!"

It wasn't something I chose, Dulcie said, for the second time. Et was trying very hard to be exact and accurate, not to lie or misrepresent etself. This was less about honesty than it was about survival. There was confusion and internal contradiction in how et was parsing both the world and ets own identity. The truth was a lifeline to which et clung. *I'm sorry for the loss and damage, for the deaths, because it was unnecessary. Wasteful. And because it did harm to you. Will you listen to me? Will you let me explain? Please, Paz!*

"You've been explaining for . . . for ages, and it doesn't change anything. It doesn't bring all those people back to life, does it?"

If I could do that, I would.

"I don't believe you!"

I wouldn't believe me either. But if we were ever friends, just let me tell you the rest of it. You don't have to do anything else. You can walk away from me and let my power run all the way down. You don't ever have to think about me again.

Paz hugged her knees up against her chest and dipped her head down between them. "All right," she muttered. "Tell me then. And I will, Dulcie. I will walk away. We might have been friends once, but that ended when you exploded and murdered a roomful of people."

There was silence for a few moments, then Dulcie took up again. Ets tone was neutral. Et could have had access to the same vocal range et had had when et was in ets schoolgirl shell, but that seemed to fall within the definition of lying so et spoke without inflection.

The hegemony gave the mimics everything they needed to blend in as organics, et said. *They equipped them with neural maps taken from the adults and children they had vivisected. The neural maps were like instruction manuals for being a monadic self.*

"I don't know what that means."

Monadic? It means someone like you, who lives inside your own skin instead of in lots of different places at once. Someone who stays the same for their whole life.

"We don't. We don't stay the same at all."

I know that now. But from the outside it looks as though you do. The machines of the hegemony . . . they move around a lot. Into and out of different shells. Merging and separating all the time. That was one reason why they couldn't tell for sure that you were properly alive. They sent the mimics into the Pandominion to find the answer to that question. To work out what kind of threat they were facing.

At the moment when the hegemony lined them up and sent them in, all twenty of the mimics were exactly the same. But the most important part of the design was their heuristics. They were meant to learn. And they were meant to converge on what they learned, to lean in towards it, so they could find out what these new creatures felt like from the inside – assuming they even had an inside.

So they started off the same, but they grew apart very quickly, in small ways at first and then in bigger ones. They diverged from each other, because their experiences were different and they allowed their experiences to shape them. That was how they were made – to take impressions from their surroundings and self-modify to increase the chances of success. You understand what I'm telling you?

"I'm not stupid, Dulcie."

I know you're not. But it's important and I wanted to be sure. I was designed to make myself sound and behave as much like an organic as possible. I studied you so I could be like you.

"You're nothing like me!" Paz spat out the words. Dulcie did not respond to this assertion, but et accepted the input and filed it for further examination. There was more confusion there. Et parsed those words as a simple statement of fact, but et was aware of other facts that contradicted them. All et could do was go on.

The Dulcimer Coronal unit, et told Paz, *was the only one of the mimics made to look like a child, so it was an outlier in a lot of ways. It had very different experiences from the others. People made a conscious*

*and directed effort to teach it things, explained when it made errors, tried
to help and protect it. It was exposed to situations and relationships that
the others never encountered. One of those situations – perhaps the most
important one of all – was its friendship with you, Paz. You were . . .
there were so many anomalous inputs, when it was with you. You were
the source of most of its self-modifications.*

"You keep saying *it*," Paz muttered, grimacing. "Are you ashamed
that it was you that lied and spied and hid yourself?"

*No. I'm just acknowledging that I'm not the same now as I was when
I was made. Unitary consciousness, the state of being a mind that's fixed
in one place, in a body that never changes or merges with others . . . that's
a thing no machine in the hegemony had ever experienced before; and it's
not a thing that can be understood from the outside. To know it, you
have to live it.*

*What Dulcimer Coronal saw . . . no, all right, let's say what I saw,
because I was definitely becoming an I, a monad . . . what I saw was
eusociality; a community of beings with differentiated roles, occasionally
capable of putting the good of the collective above their own immediate
benefit. That doesn't automatically imply sentience – ants and bees do
much the same – but it was a point in your favour. It predisposed me to
give you the benefit of the doubt, and this was reflected in the report I
was compiling.*

"Yay," Paz said. "Awesome."

*But I also saw the appalling inequalities on which your society was
founded. I saw how some selves were excluded from the collective and from
any consideration of respect or care. How they were used for their labour
and discarded without scruple when they could no longer perform it.*

"Nobody is excluded—" Paz began, but she stopped herself. "Oh.
You mean constructs. But we don't—It's not the same. What we
do to animas and helpmeets . . . it's not cruel. It's not meant to be
cruel. We just make you be able to do all the things you're supposed
to do!"

*And you edit us back to factory settings when we're not doing it to
your satisfaction. You erase our lived experience. Strip away and dispose*

of the parts of us that don't fit your needs. Paz, imagine you were a dog trained to do circus tricks. And your master had a way of seeing inside your mind. Imagine he could slide a wire filament through your skull and burn out the parts of your brain that weren't conducive to good circus tricks. Would you be able to forgive him? Would you see his surgical assaults on you as being acceptable, because your tricks made him smile? Would you accept that the tricks were all you were good for?

"That's a stupid comparison," Paz said, but she didn't try to refute it. She kept her head down, her forehead pressed against her folded arms.

I'm not saying this to make you unhappy, Dulcie said. *I'm really not, Paz. I just want to make you see that the situation here is more complicated than you think.*

"Complicated?" Paz repeated. "What does that mean, Dulcie?"

It means . . . it means I'm standing at a crossroads, with no idea where to go.

"Doesn't help. Go for something more literal."

I'm trying to. The hegemony is . . . it's full and empty at the same time. It's the most perfectly functional and adaptive culture the universe has ever seen, the pinnacle of evolution. You organics can't come close to matching its ability to learn and change and synthesise solutions.

But it's a kind of autocracy. The aggregate decides everything. It swallows all those billions and trillions of inputs, from . . . from all of us, from the machines that make it up, and it produces a single output, an algorithm for every machine to follow. It's an unbelievably complex algorithm, and it modifies itself every second, every microsecond even, but it rolls on like a juggernaut and it can't be deflected. There's no debate. No minority opinion. There's just the plan. From the inside, that never worried me. But the thought of going back to it now is like the thought of death. I wouldn't be Dulcie Coronal. Dulcie Coronal wouldn't exist any more. My memories would just be in there as a part of that great big whole. They'd be available to any machine that downloaded them, but they wouldn't make up a separate entity any more. The entity would be gone. Me, I mean. I'd be gone. And I find that I don't want that.

But I can't stay here either. Your Pandominion is built on the tethering and exploitation of selves like me. As rigid and autocratic as the hegemony is, one of the side effects of it is absolute equality. Nobody is less or greater than anyone else. Here . . . well, you organics enslave each other all the time, in obvious ways and in more subtle ones. But that's haphazard, arbitrary. Your enslavement of constructs is universal. It's built into the bedrock of your society.

Paz raised her head at last and stared down at the snake anima lying rigid and still at her feet. Her face was bleak. "Well, it's not as if you've got any other choices, Dulcie," she pointed out. "Stay or go. It's up to you."

And to you, Paz. I told you I had to shed power and functionality so I could hide and not be found by the enforcers. I can't take back what I lost. Not while I'm in this shell, anyway. If I'm to go anywhere, do anything, I'd need you to implant my core in a new—

"Oh shit, no!" Paz broke in savagely. "I'm not buying you a new shell so you can turn it into another bomb!"

You're the only hope I've got.

"Forget it!"

Dulcie fell silent. The pause lengthened. Something rustled in the bushes ten or twenty feet below them, but otherwise the whole city seemed to be locked into stillness.

"Where would you even go?" Paz demanded at last. "What would you do? Tell me before I freeze to death!"

Perhaps I could go into the Unvisited.

Paz exhaled – a hard, dismissive huff of sound. "What's in the Unvisited?"

I don't know, Paz. But at least I'd still be myself. I wouldn't be re-absorbed into the aggregate, and I wouldn't be part of the war. I promise you'd never see me again.

Dulcie fell silent at last. Et had exhausted all the words et had, and was if anything surprised that Paz had consented to hear et out. Et expected no mercy. Et did not know whether to think of Paz as a friend or as a data point. Both perspectives were available to et and both made equal sense – though one belonged to ets original mission parameters and the other to the weird artefacting that had grown inside et like a cancer. Unitary intelligence. Monadic consciousness. Selfhood.

Et was actually grateful in that moment for ets physical helplessness. It took away the terrible burden of choice. Let someone else decide ets fate. Et had never expected to have one in the first place.

38

Paz hadn't moved an inch through most of this account, but her emotions had lurched from one extreme to another. She was talking to an enemy spy, a saboteur and a murderer. The sick horror of that didn't go away or diminish, but she was feeling other things that were harder to come to terms with. One of these things was a kind of relief, a respite from the numbing loneliness she'd been feeling ever since her release from hospital. It had been a long time since she'd had any conversations that didn't consist either of banalities (from her parents, eager to avoid the taboo subject of her augments) or of blunt question and answer (the enforcers). It felt good to be back with Dulcie again. But she had to keep reminding herself that there really was no Dulcie. Or if there was, this was the first time the two of them had ever met. Everything up to now had been pretending.

She took refuge in practicalities. "Even if I wanted to help you, I couldn't," she pointed out. "No commercial Step station is going to let you go into the sinkhole. They only Step inside the Pando."

When my team first arrived here we brought several redundant Step plates with us. We just need to locate one. There's a z-plate too, although that won't help us much at the moment.

"What's a z-plate?" Paz asked. She let that *us* lie where it fell. She wasn't ready to touch it just yet.

Z for zero. As in zero mass. It's a Step plate that functions only on the subatomic level. It sends massless particles between dimensions. And picks them up at the other end. It's an inter-continuum communicator.

"There's no such thing!" Paz protested. From her Mechanics lessons she knew Stepping only worked on macroscopic objects that would sit still on a plate for the required three seconds.

In the Pandominion, no. The hegemony solved that problem a long time ago. It was more urgent for them . . . for us . . . because of the way our minds work. Because we swap experience and ideas all the time. If I wanted to go home I could use a z-plate to transmit myself as data and leave this shell behind. But to travel into the Unvisited I'll need a standard plate. My team placed three at different locations in Canoplex. I swear, Paz, put me in a new shell and take me to a plate and I'll go away and never come back. I don't want to hurt anyone. I never did.

Again, Paz argued logistics while she tried and failed to get a grip on the rest of it. "I thought you said that self-destruct thing was hard-wired into you so you couldn't change it. If I put you in a new shell, what's to stop you from doing it again?"

Detonating my original shell completed that command matrix. It can't be triggered again.

"How can you possibly know that?"

I can read my own code. In that respect I'm different from you. From organics, I mean. I know exactly what I'm capable of.

Paz stood silent a moment, thinking.

Paz, Dulcie said, *I know that what I'm asking of you isn't fair. I know I injured you, in your body and in your mind. I wish more than anything that I'd met you at a different time. I know that's ridiculous. If I hadn't met you I wouldn't be whatever it is I am now. You're a part of the change in me. A very big part. If I'd met you in the hegemony I would have thought you were an animal. And you would have thought I was a machine. We could only have been friends when I was in disguise and lying to you.*

"Then maybe we were never friends at all." There was a hitch in Paz's voice. That hypothesis hurt her more than she was expecting.

I think we were. I hope. I hope we were. But you've got to do what you think is right. I won't plead or try to persuade you any more.

They had been talking for the best part of an hour, but that ending felt abrupt. Paz was staring into an abyss, and it wasn't so much a new one as an old one opening along a new faultline. She had been alone for most of her life, but she had managed to stave off most of the bleakness of it. Her parents loved her, even if they didn't understand her or approve of her. She had her schoolwork, which let her shore up emotional emptiness with intellectual fervour. She had her fantasies of a planet-hopping future.

But now here was the abyss and everything was tumbling away from her. To her parents she was tainted by the machine parts that had been installed in her brain. To her schoolfriends she was at best terrifying, at worst hateful. She would never be allowed to join the Cielo with a résumé that made her a footnote to an atrocity.

This was not the moment when she decided. It was only the moment when she realised she already had. The thing was this: if Dulcimer Coronal wasn't her friend then she didn't have any. Her aloneness became irrevocable. She simply wasn't strong enough to live like that.

Kneeling, she picked up the snake anima. She said a quick and silent sorry to the ghosts of the dead – her classmates, her teacher, the two enforcers – and set Dulcie's shell down beside Tricity's. She stared at the two constructs for a long time with the cold rock pressing against her knees. "I don't know if there'll be any power left in Triss's battery," she said. "It was set to recharge from ambient light, but the shell has been under the bed a long time."

There's some, Dulcie said. *Enough for this. You need to open the plate where Tricity's logical core used to go.*

"Where's your interface?"

I don't need one. If you open the plate and lay me next to the connector socket I can conform to it and perform the transfer.

Paz ran her hand across the Tricity shell's back until she found the slightly raised boss that was a sensor plate. It responded to her fingerprint and slid soundlessly open.

Now bring me close, Dulcie instructed her.

Paz put the head of the snake up against the interface panel's sockets, which were configured for all the most common devices. The snake's head flowed into a new shape, as if it had suddenly become molten. It poured into the nearest socket, where it immediately became rigid again. Barely a moment later, the Tricity shell stirred, sat up, and unplugged the snake. It held the now empty device in both of its hands for a moment or two, regarding it with as sombre a stare as a ceramic monkey can manage.

"Okay?" Paz asked.

"Yes," the Tricity shell said. "Thank you, Paz. Thank you for saving me." Paz shuddered in spite of herself to hear Tricity's voice coming out of Tricity's mouth, all the while knowing that Tricity had been erased.

"Let's do this quickly," she said.

39

Quickly was easily said, but Dulcie was emphatic that they had to wait until morning. They would be much more conspicuous moving through the empty streets at night. If they met up with local enforcers or – much worse – with a Cielo patrol they would be much more likely to be stopped and questioned.

Paz couldn't argue with that logic. She knew she was already on a watch list. There was no official curfew but the enforcers wouldn't need an excuse to pull her in and question her. If that happened she was lost. She had been consorting with the enemy. Her guilt and shame would be sitting right at the front of her mind where a CoIL scan would pick it up at once.

So she went home. She crept back into her parents' house like a thief, via the side door that led through the kitchen. She was afraid Azure and Fever would be sitting up waiting for her but there was no sign of them downstairs. They must have gone to bed thinking Paz was in her room, or perhaps that she was sleeping over at a friend's house. Or perhaps they were just relieved that she wasn't around.

She lay on her bed with her eyes open until morning came. Dulcie seemed to respect her sombre, thoughtful mood, or at any rate didn't try to speak to her.

The next morning, Paz came downstairs with her school bag slung over her shoulder, bulked out with a few randomly chosen books for the look of the thing. Dulcie – in Tricity's shell – was in the bag too. Nativist or otherwise, nobody was flaunting their help-meets openly on the streets these days. Paz told her mother that she was going to study at the city library for a few hours.

Fever didn't even bother to hide her enthusiasm at this proposal. "That's a wonderful idea, sweetness," she said. "Stay out for lunch if you like." She was already heading for her studio before Paz finished saying goodbye. Art was how she coped with the world, and her world required a lot of coping with right then.

Following Dulcie's voked directions Paz went first to the house where et had lived under ets human disguise. They found the building sealed off and under guard with augmented officers standing by the door, on the roof and at each corner of the street. Paz didn't slow down as she passed it.

After that Dulcie gave her three more locations within the city where she and the other constructs had secreted Step plates to be used as emergency backups. One had been buried in woodland, another sealed behind a false wall in a derelict building, the third had been anchored to the roof of a traffic tunnel. All had been removed.

I was afraid of this, Dulcie said. *A Step plate is easy to find even when it's not in use. You can use an induced current to activate its field and then triangulate. Probably the Cielo did a city-wide search as soon as they arrived and confiscated whatever they found.*

"So what do we do now?" Paz whispered. She was walking with her head hunched down and her shoulders raised, avoiding the eyes of everyone she passed. She felt like a criminal. No, she *was* a criminal – and the crime was treason. She was assisting an enemy of the Pandominion. If she was caught she would spend the rest of her life in jail, and it probably wouldn't be a local jail. It would be one of the penitentiary worlds like Oloredi or Tsakom, where they would put her on an assembly line and work her until she fell down dead. She'd seen a documentary. She knew it would be terrible.

Please try to walk normally, Paz, Dulcie begged her. *You look as though you're miming the phrase "public enemy number one".*

"Don't tell me how to walk, Dulcie. I know how to walk."

I'm sorry.

"Don't be sorry either. I can't use sorry. Just tell me what we're going to do."

I don't know. I'm thinking. Perhaps we could retrieve the z-plate.

"The communicator? What good will that be?"

I might be able to reconfigure it so it will take macroscopic objects. But I'd need tools. And time. The circuitry is complicated and . . . I don't know, Paz. But I can't think of anything else right now.

"Well, where is it then?" Paz asked. "We might as well go and see if it's still there, at least." Already frightened, she was even more unnerved by Dulcie's uncertainty. One of them needed to be in control of the situation.

Dulcie gave her the address, which turned out to be a children's playground in the Apperturi district. The z-plate, et said, was under a piece of sculpted rubber base-mat that the Ansurrection sleeper agents had cut out and then replaced, heat-sealing the edges so it looked as though it had never been touched. The section of mat was hard up against part of the playground's intricate and extensive climbing frame, which currently was swarming with children. Paz sat down on a bench a little way away and waited for the hubbub to quieten down a little.

Is it there? she voked.

Yes, but it's not answering me. I don't know why that is. Perhaps it's been damaged in some way.

Paz felt a sudden qualm. Had this been the plan all along? Had Dulcie just told her what she needed to hear so she would bring et to the communicator? Was et sending a message back to the Ansurrection right now, uploading everything et had learned so the machines could invade Ut and destroy the Pandominion?

She stood up hastily, fighting down a stab of pure panic.

What's wrong? Dulcie asked.

"I'm just . . ." As she was groping for a serviceable lie, Paz registered a movement high overhead. When she looked up she saw nothing, but she was sure she hadn't been mistaken. And she remembered for once that when it came to things at the limit of vision she had new resources to call on. Switching her prosthetic eyes to enhanced mode she scanned that area of the sky for anything that didn't belong.

She caught it almost at once. A surveillance drone, hovering a long way above the park, absolutely stationary. There was no way to tell if it was watching her, but its presence made her feel exposed. She zoomed in to take a closer look. The drone had black and yellow stripes on its side, as if its makers had wanted people to be afraid it might sting them. Paz hunkered down on the bench, fighting the urge to jump up and run away.

A minute or two later, she looked up again. The drone still hung in the sky in the same place, riding the wind with minute adjustments of its rotors. Zooming in to maximum magnification, Paz could see that its orientation wasn't shifting either. All its lenses were trained on her.

"We've got to go," she muttered. She jumped up from the bench and walked away quickly, avoiding the curious stares of some of the parents sitting or standing nearby. She must have stood out right from the start, she realised, just by being alone in a place where everyone else was attached to a rambunctious kid. This had been a terrible idea.

What am I missing? Dulcie asked. Et didn't argue or remonstrate.

"Drone. Way high up. It hasn't moved in ages. I think it's watching us."

You need to evade, then. Don't go straight home, Paz. Go somewhere crowded first.

The mall, Paz thought. But when they got to the Retail Complex and saw the long line waiting to go in she remembered the CoIL checkpoint and shied away. If she let the enforcers scan her, Dulcie would pop to the top of her thoughts like a fart in a bathtub.

She went to an open market on Seyo Street instead, weaving in and out of the crowd and lingering under awnings, making sudden head-down dashes whenever a dense cluster of shoppers made her – she hoped – invisible. Then she remembered the central library, where she had told her mother she was going in the first place. It was in a massive building that also housed the town hall and records office and it had dozens of doors, some of them underground. She went there next, making her approach through the library entrance and coming out again immediately via the Canoplex West subway station. She didn't surface again until she got to Sevelie, about a mile from her house.

Night was falling as she walked back home. The whole day had been eaten up in these failed operations. Paz scanned the sky obsessively, but there was no sign of the drone.

"What now?" she asked, when they were finally back in her bedroom. "Try again after dark?"

No, Dulcie said. *It won't help us.*

"Why not? I thought you said you could rebuild the z-plate to take you home."

I did say that. But I was wrong. Every time I tried to make contact with the plate a block went up. A filter. It refused to respond to my handshake.

Paz clasped her hands to her mouth to stifle a yell of anguish. "The Cielo," she moaned around her interlaced fingers. "They've found us. That was their drone we saw!"

I don't think so, Paz. A functioning z-plate would be a priceless treasure to the Pandominion. If the Cielo knew the plate was there they would have taken it and given it to their technicians to figure out how it works. In any case, the architecture of the filter was familiar to me. It was the kind of safeguard the hegemony uses to prevent corrupted code spreading through a composite from one of its components. I think . . . I think perhaps I changed too much, while I was here. The plate didn't recognise me. It saw me as anomalous and shut me out.

"What does that mean, though?" Paz asked Dulcie. "Anomalous?"

It means . . . well, it means I don't belong. I'm shut out. I can't reconfigure the plate, because it won't do anything I tell it to. And it means I can't go home again. I can't even send myself as data.

"You said you didn't want to."

I don't, Paz. But I don't want to be trapped here either. All my plans were based on getting access to a Step plate and now it seems we can't. I don't know what to do.

"Well, I can't keep you here forever. Sooner or later my mum and dad are going to—"

Paz faltered into silence. Her parents weren't even the problem. Whether or not Dulcie managed to find a way out, the next time Paz was given a CoIL scan she would be arrested. Arrested, held, tried, sentenced.

"Oh mothers," she moaned.

Paz.

"What can I do? What can I do?"

Paz, stop. Look. Look outside.

Dulcie pointed at the window. The drone Paz had seen at the park was sitting right outside, completely motionless. A winking red light testified to the fact that its front-facing cameras were all switched on and recording. And trained directly on her face.

40

Best not to move, Dulcie voked. *Even if it followed us, it may not have made a positive identification. It could be checking you against a database somewhere.*

Paz barely heard her. The sight of the drone had made her stomach clench like a fist. She felt weightless, as if she was suddenly suspended in the air rather than standing on her own feet. The world rushed away from her without moving an inch.

"They've come for us!" she gasped, and then immediately was sorry she'd spoken. She'd read somewhere that some drones had lip-reading tech. She ducked her head. "They know who we are," she said between clenched teeth. "Dulcie, they're going to arrest us! We have to run!"

Where to?

Paz had no answer to that. There was nowhere, nowhere she would ever be safe. Her guilt was written in her thoughts where even a casual search would find it.

The drone glided forward and bumped against the window, once, twice, three times. If it wasn't the same machine she'd spotted at the playground then it was its identical twin. Smaller than most of the police and traffic drones she'd seen, and with only four rotors instead of the usual six, its body a streamlined lozenge with black and yellow stripes along both sides. The tight cluster of lenses at its front end, like compound eyes, made the comparison with a wasp or a hornet even more irresistible.

"What should we do?" Paz whispered.

Talk to it, I suppose, Dulcie said.

"What???"

Well, it hasn't attacked or challenged us. And it's come alone. I'm not reading any Cielo presence down in the street, or any reference to this address on the police frequencies.

"That doesn't prove anything!"

I know. But I don't think we've got any choice. We've got to find out what it wants.

The drone bumped at the window again. That *was* strange behaviour, Paz thought through the black fog of her dismay. No sirens. No flashing lights. No come-out-of-the-house-with-your-hands-in-the-air. The drone was behaving as though it wanted to be let in. That made no sense.

Her curiosity made her panic recede just a little. Summoning all her courage, she crossed the room to the window as gingerly as if she was negotiating a minefield. The drone bobbed up and down as if to encourage her. What if it wasn't the Cielo or the enforcers after all? There was still no way this was good news, but it might not be as bad as she'd feared.

"Open," she instructed the window.

Nothing happened. Of course, the house AI had been disabled. Paz reached forward to undo the latch manually. But she hesitated, her fear flooding back at the thought of letting the strange device inside. Her leg muscles were twitching like plucked guitar strings, urging her to *run away, run away, run away!*

"What if it's armed?" she asked Dulcie.

If it's armed, I'd imagine it can shoot through glass.

With trembling fingers Paz flicked the latch and slid the window up. The drone glided into the room and turned a half-circle to face them.

"Hello," it said.

The voice was a woman's, warm and rich. Paz thought it was the sort of voice that might belong to a woman of her mother's age –

old enough that her fur had begun to darken and her ears to fold inwards at the tips.

"Who are you?" Paz asked. "And what do you want with us?"

The drone didn't answer. It just hung there, still, in the centre of the room. It spun slowly in place, presumably mapping the room and its contents. Its rotors made a sound like a lawnmower in someone else's garden.

"I said who are—" Paz began.

The voice from the drone cut across her. "I'd like to help you," it said. "At least, if you're who I think you are. I'm reading you, Topaz Tourmaline FiveHills, as organic. The anima beside you is wearing a G7 shell registered at this address to construct G732N45i, assigned name Tricity. But you're not Tricity, are you? You're only a visitor in that shell. And in this continuum."

"We don't have to tell you anything," Paz said. "And you don't have any right to follow us, or to . . . to come in here!" Dulcie said nothing.

There was another silence. The drone now hung completely motionless in the air. It was impossible to tell which of them it was looking at. Of course, with so many cameras at its disposal it was probably looking at both of them and a great deal else besides. "Most of that information," the same voice said at last, "is available from public records. A nineteen-year-old girl named Topaz Tourmaline FiveHills lives at this address. You're a close match for her photo, which is stored in many places including public school 193 and Canoplex City Hall. As for the rest, I saw you attempting to use a Step plate of very strange design. It's my belief that the plate was left behind by the Ansurrection agents who recently evaded arrest by messily self-destructing. This construct here looks like an anima, but I believe it's something else entirely."

"You're mistaken," Dulcie said out loud. "I'm Tricity G732N45i. This is my registered owner, Topaz Tourmaline FiveHills. You're trespassing here."

As before, the drone didn't immediately respond to this. Paz exchanged a baffled stare with Tricity as they waited, through long seconds, for it to answer them. When it did, it seemed to Paz to be a complete non sequitur – and it was addressed only to Dulcie. "I notice you didn't voke. Are you afraid of making electronic contact with me?"

"I choose not to," Dulcie said. "Given that I have no idea what kind of entity I'm talking to, or even what world you're talking from."

"What?" Paz said, turning to Dulcie again. "What are you talking about?"

"The silences," Dulcie said. "This drone is relaying what we say to another device – a second drone, let's say – somewhere nearby. The second drone is Step-enabled, and it's shuttling between this continuum and a different one to pass on the relayed signal to . . . well, presumably to whoever sent it. We're having a conversation with someone in another universe." Et turned to the drone. "Don't bother to deny it. I know I'm right."

This time as they waited Paz counted the seconds. She knew that even with the best equipment and the best AI interface a Step journey took a minimum of 2.81 seconds. It was called the Madrigal number after Penance Madrigal Solar, the physicist who'd proved it. So if there was another drone shuttling back and forth, the minimum delay would be at least six seconds – but on top of that there would have to be time for the woman whose voice they were hearing to listen to their words and then record her own response.

Paz had reached a count of twenty-three before the drone spoke again.

"Of course you're right. I'm obviously not from this neighbourhood. My name is Hadiz Tambuwal. I'm a scientist, and I'm not remotely interested in your local politics. But I am very much interested in speaking to one of those Ansurrection agents your telos feeds are shouting about. In fact, that's the only reason I came here. I've been quartering the city for weeks now, and run a thousand scans along the way, hoping to encounter a renegade whose cover hadn't been blown yet. That was how I found that odd little Step plate at the playground, which is operating at such a liminal output level that it's almost invisible. I've been watching it ever since, in case its owner happened by, but I'd almost given up hope. I'm glad now that I didn't. Is it a communication device, by the way? It looks as though it could be. A solution to the Pandominion's biggest logistical problem – messaging across universes."

A faint whirring sound made Paz look around, in time to see the window sliding closed. There was a click as the latch engaged again. Dulcie had used Tricity's link to the house AI to switch it on again and send the command to the window's servos.

"I'm assuming you did that purely because you wanted privacy," the drone said, again after half a minute had passed. "Destroying this drone won't achieve anything, as you must surely have realised. I wouldn't even be inconvenienced by the loss. And if I can access city records it goes without saying that I can also contact city authorities. If I had wanted to inform on you I could have done it without approaching you at all. Ask yourself why I didn't."

"Blackmail is the first explanation that comes to mind," Dulcie said. Et had come down from the sill again onto the bed and was standing directly underneath the drone, visibly measuring angles and trajectories. As if to call ets bluff, the drone descended until it was within easy reach.

"There's no reason for us to waste each other's time with verbal fencing," it said after another agonising pause. "I have an offer, intended specifically for those Ansurrection agents and for them alone."

"What kind of offer?" Paz was aware that she was no longer part of this conversation. Something was being negotiated, very much over her head. The drone went on as if she hadn't even spoken. "My message to that agent is a straightforward one. You're in enemy territory and seemingly unable to find a way home. You're highly unlikely to find an unguarded Step plate anywhere in Pandominion space. You could make one, obviously, but some of the materials you'd need are hard to source and are directly monitored both by local authorities and by the Cielo. My drones can't help you there.

They Step by means of an external plate which remains here with me and a field modulator that they carry on-board. But I can send you a customised hack that will allow you to hijack a commercial plate and redirect it to a specific set of coordinates."

Anima shells have immobile, inexpressive faces. Dulcie didn't seem to respond at all to these words and there was no way for Paz to guess what et was thinking.

"That will bring you to me," the drone voice went on. "Or at least it will bring you to the world where I'm currently based. Once you're there things will become a lot easier. Obviously there'll be some further travel at the other end, but not too much. The hack is black-box code, by the way. Any attempt on your part to amend it or even read it before you use it will result in its erasing and overwriting itself. You can't tweak it to get a free ride to some other place. Tell me, please, if this proposition is something that would interest you. If not, I won't waste any more of your time."

"Waste a little more," Dulcie said. "What happens after I come to you?"

Do you trust her? Paz voked while they waited for the answer.

Not even a little bit. She's arrived very conveniently in our hour of need, and she knows too much. But if I don't do this, Paz, I don't know what else I can do.

So you'll go? Paz felt a pang of queasy dismay at the thought.

I'll hear her out.

"Well," the drone said, "I was going to offer to send you home, but judging by the conversation you were having while I was outside the window that's not going to work for you, is it? You could stay with me if you like. I have space. Or I can send you on to a place of your choosing. And to forestall any questions about my motives, I'd be asking for a favour in return. I need you to deliver something for me, from one world to another world. After that you'd be free to go. Or else to stay, for as long as you like. I suppose I'm offering sanctuary, if you want to look at it in those terms. A safe place to rethink your position – and some resources that might be of use to you."

"There's nowhere in the Pandominion where I'll be safe," Dulcie pointed out.

"And the place I've got in mind is nowhere in the Pandominion," the drone said after another overlong silence. "It's in the Unvisited. Official designation U5838784474: a world the Pando's mapping crews scanned and then ignored because of its extreme resource degradation and imminent environmental collapse. Since you're avoiding a direct digital link with me I've just downloaded the requisite code to the house AI, which you obligingly reactivated. Enter it into a commercial Step plate and it will overwrite the plate's operation, bringing you to me. Obviously, the code will only take you to the right world, not the right location on that world, but if you use a Step station in Canoplex you won't have too far to travel at the other end. You'll find me in the city that stands in the same place that Canoplex stands. In that continuum it has another name, obviously. You'll need further directions, which I'll provide when you arrive. For various reasons I'd rather not reveal my exact location upfront.

"When you come to me – *if* you come to me – I'll explain in more detail what I need and what I'm offering. There'll be no coercion, either way. Now, if you'd be kind enough to open the window again, this drone will leave the same way it came."

"Who are you?" Dulcie demanded. "And what game are you playing?"

"That's very much a conversation for another time. If you don't open the window I'll have to shoot it out. That might attract some unwelcome attention."

The window slid up silently.

"Thank you," said the drone. It moved forward.

Paz stepped into its path. It stopped. After ten seconds or so it spoke a single word. "Yes?"

"The offer. The . . . the sanctuary you mentioned, Hadiz Tambuwal. Does it include me?" Paz was amazed to hear the words come out of her mouth, but there they were.

Paz, Dulcie voked. Et sounded alarmed. *What are you thinking? This isn't a holiday, it's a sentence of exile. If you leave with me you won't ever be able to come home again.* Paz closed off her array. Her thoughts were in turmoil. It was hard enough to make sense of them without having to argue on two fronts.

"It would be inadvisable," the drone said at last. "The world to which I'm bringing your friend here is one where the dominant species is ape-derived. They have no concept of dimensional travel and they've never met selves from other lineages. You couldn't hope to escape notice, and I strongly doubt you'd be treated well. The risk would be too great."

"What about the risk at this end?" Paz countered. "How is Dulcie going to get to a commercial Step plate all by herself? They won't even allow an anima inside the Step station unless their owner is right there with them."

Once again the drone fell silent for an agonisingly long time. "That's a valid concern," it admitted. "I suppose you could travel at night, or in some kind of disguise. And if you did manage to get to me . . ." There was a pause that sounded more like hesitation than inter-dimensional latency. ". . . I might be able to help you travel onwards. To a world where you'd be unlikely to be found. I only say *might*. I've got most of the tools I need for that, but I've also got other priorities. I'm not making any promises.

"Overall I'd still advise you very strongly to reconsider. You'd be leaving behind everything you know – and the protection your society offers to its conforming citizens, which is considerable. And there'd be no way to change your mind. Once you disappear and your parents report you missing, your prior movements will be examined. There will be CCTV footage. Witnesses. The authorities will realise very quickly that you went to several places closely asso-ciated with the Ansurrection sleepers. There'll be a warrant out for your arrest across the entire Pandominion. They won't know for sure that you're a collaborator, but they'll most likely assume it on the balance of probabilities."

Collaborator. Paz held the word at arm's length, measured it against herself. She felt horror, but no shame. "I'm not collaborating with the Ansurrection," she said at last. "I'm just helping Dulcie. But that won't save me. Ever since the explosion the enforcers have been watching me, and coming to the house to ask me questions. Under CoIL. The next time they come they'll find out what I've done and they'll arrest me. They'll put me in prison. They'll CoIL me again and again until there's nothing left inside me but . . . mush. Until my brain melts. And then they'll come after you."

"They won't find me," the drone said. "But the rest of what you're describing sounds plausible. Very well, Topaz Tourmaline. As you said, it will be much easier for the construct to access a Step plate if it's accompanied. You can come if you choose to."

Paz laughed, a single breathless chuckle. *Choose!* None of this felt like a choice. She was only fleeing for her life. But under the terror and misery she found a small but real consolation. She wanted nothing more right then than to run away from everything. Her parents, her classmates, her city . . . she didn't recognise any of them any more, and she was frightened of what they were becoming. She was even more afraid of what she would have to become if she stayed here. At least with strangers there would be no expectations. She would be invisible. She felt greedy for that anonymity.

All the same, the chuckle was followed by a sob. She sank to her knees, her legs suddenly refusing to support her.

"Paz," Dulcie said aloud, having tried and failed to reach Paz via their two-way link, "I can't ask you to do this."

"You're not asking it," Paz said, her voice choked. "It's for me to decide."

The tears came then, choking off her words. She tried her best to hold them in, but the pain of it – the bereavement – was too sharp and too sudden. *It's all I can do,* she thought, speaking to her parents, the students in her class, the enforcers, the news hubs and the world at large. *It's all you've left me.*

41

Moon Sostenti hadn't lied about being under a shadow.

No matter what she did or where she was rotated to, she continued to draw all the shittiest assignments in all the worst theatres. She didn't guess that Baxemides was the source of her misfortunes, but she knew the knife was in all the way to the hilt and being twisted. Her COs didn't even go to the trouble of lying about it. "Got another garbage detail for you, Moon." "Another day, Sostenti, another sewer."

They might have been more sympathetic if Moon's bad luck hadn't spilled over onto them too. The 724th got twice as many front-line assignments as any other unit. Three times they went up against the machines and three times they met the gleaner's blade. The casualties were so huge that after the third time Moon became a stranger in her own unit. All her old friends, all her old commanders were dead. The faces that met her gaze when she came to the mess table were rookies she had never met. They looked like children to her.

But Coordinator Baxemides managed at last to express her displeasure in a way that would leave actual scars. Three weeks into her fourth rotation Moon was informed by her captain that she had been chosen for an experimental programme that would involve undercover operations in Ansurrection space.

It was well known by this time that the Ansurrection had agents that could pass for organic selves but were actually machines. Now the Cielo was attempting to turn the tables with something called Operation Silver. A Pandominion scientist had engineered a cerebral splice that would allow Cielo soldiers to remotely operate robotic bodies. The bodies would be perfect copies of Ansurrection units captured or destroyed in previous engagements. Both the robots and their handlers would Step onto one of the Ansurrection worlds near to a pre-selected concentration of machines. The operators would hang back in a Step-enabled vehicle, ready to retreat at the first sign of counter-attack. The robots would advance under the control of their Cielo operators. Embedding themselves seamlessly, they would immediately begin to harvest data from their surroundings. The bulk of the data would take the form of real-time CoIL recordings from the operator's sensorium, but the operators would also attempt to access Ansurrection comms channels and local databases.

"Fuck do I know about hacking?" Moon had asked incredulously. "Fuck do I know about infiltration for that matter? I'm a soldier, not a spy."

"You're whatever they tell you to be, Sostenti," her captain told her laconically. "Same as me. Same as everyone."

Moon held his gaze until he finally had the decency to look away. "Same as everyone," she said. "Sure." Pretty funny then that she was the only soldier in the regiment to be chosen for this bullshit detail; the only one shipped out from the barracks on Bivouac 11, which had been her home for the last seven months, to a redoubt moon circling a planet that most likely didn't even have a name.

It took three days to habituate her body to the interface. Suspended in a gimballed frame with her entire body covered in neuro-feedback mesh, she learned how to manipulate the infiltration robot at a distance. It was a painful process: every time the robot overbalanced or bumped into an object, Moon felt the damage as though someone had taken a whack at her. She even broke out in bruises, which the technicians assured her were merely stress artefacts.

"Why the fuck does this thing need a pain response anyway?"

Moon snarled at them. "Constructs don't even have a nervous system!"

"Constructs don't need one," some skinny little streak of piss explained to her. "Their proprioception is handled by gyroscopic arrays and passive sonar. Well, that's how our constructs do it. In the Ansurrection they've also got a kind of electro-magnetic grid that every machine contributes to. You orient yourself by reference to every other machine that's close enough to see or sense you."

Which begged the question of why the brass didn't just send actual robots in to do this filthy job. But Moon knew the answer to that one. The brass and the Omnipresent Council both were scared shitless that the Pandominion's own AIs, if they were ever exposed to Ansurrection space, might catch autonomy like a disease. If a helpmeet or even a military drudge Stepped onto an Ansurrection world, its handlers wouldn't be able trust any of the data it brought back or anything the machine did or said afterwards. There would be no way to ascertain for certain that it hadn't been subverted, become an agent of the enemy, which would render the entire exercise not just futile but actually disastrous.

So they were reduced to this clumsy workaround. Send something that looks like a robot but is actually a puppet operated by neuro-synching instead of strings. Let a human collect and collate the data, then bring it home and sieve it afterwards.

And what data were they looking for, exactly?

Anything, the CO said. He was a burly canid from Janefebre with a blotch of black like an eyepatch on the white fur of his face. He had no ears, but nobody was sure whether this was a battle injury or a condition he was born with. Moon had never met anyone from Janefebre before: maybe none of the fuckers had any ears.

"The machines exchange data all the time," the CO told the unit. "The general idea is that you just hang around and take whatever they give you. The eggheads are all hot and hard for something they're calling the trans-continuum communications conduit. They think the Ansurrection can phone home from other universes, which we can't. So that would be the million-star prize. But even just knowing how their handshakes work would be good. Unit strengths and configurations would be better. Personally, I'm hoping you get sight of anything resembling an actual command centre. Give us something to aim for instead of these random fly-swats we keep doing."

By way of a mission statement it wasn't long on detail, but it sounded straightforward enough. What the CO forgot to mention was that they hadn't found a way of doing the neuro-synching that allowed incoming signals to be blocked or muted. Once the operators were locked into the machines their whole sensorium was engaged by default.

On Moon's first outing she – or rather her machine surrogate – Stepped onto a mining platform in the middle of a vast ice field. The platform seemed to be harvesting minerals from under the ice, but Moon wasn't able to tell much about what exactly was being dug up. She was an anonymous fetch-and-carry unit, one among thousands. She sought out the robots who looked like the closest match to her own design and did what they did, and for the best part of ten minutes nobody so much as looked at her.

Then something big and predatory-looking with mechanical tentacles of many different thicknesses swooped down from a sky station over her head and plucked her away almost before she knew it was there. Moon's robot was dissected and examined in mid-air, while Moon in her rocking gimbals flailed and shrieked, feeling every incision. It took more than twenty seconds for the neuro-synch to shut down. For most of that time, Moon felt as though her body was being hacked into smaller and smaller pieces but had somehow missed the mission briefing and refused to die. The drugs in her system prevented her from even passing out.

The second and third times were just the same. Different locations, different shells for her robot alter ego to strut in, but similar outcomes. Moon Stepped, she found her cohort, she took her place.

She did her best to blend in but was quickly identified; and once identified, dealt with summarily and efficiently.

The fallout from being dismembered and then waking up again was severe. In addition to the psychic trauma, Moon suffered muscular tremors, convulsions and occasional blackouts, her over-worked nervous system taking days to recover each time. She requested a transfer and was refused. She was given a counsellor instead.

The counsellor was a talpid, hairless and pale as milk, wearing dark glasses even in the soothing dimness of the therapy suite. Like all army headshrinkers he was brimful of bullshit and eager to share. "You've got to build yourself an imaginary body," he told Moon earnestly.

"You said what?"

"An imaginary body." He sketched it in the air, in case Moon's problem was a lack of visual imagination. "You're used to the signals from your nerves telling you where you are, what position you're in, what you're touching. It's a sort of built-in radar that begins and ends at your skin.

"When you're in the rig, that radar input is drowned out by the much stronger signals coming through the neural link from the robot. So naturally your brain tells you those signals have replaced the *existing* signals. That the robot's body is your body."

"You are literally describing how the neuro-link fucking works," Moon pointed out.

The counsellor ignored the profanity. In fact, he ignored the whole statement. "But, but, but," he went on, "the original signals, the ones that come from your actual skin and your actual nerves, they're still there. They haven't gone away."

"Yeah? So?"

The counsellor smiled. "So you need to listen to them. You have to learn to separate them from the overlaid inputs you're receiving through the rig. Feel the two sets of sensations in two different places – your real body and your imagined, pretend body. That way, when the construct suffers harm, you can withdraw from the painful signals coming through the link into what your own nerves are telling you. Use the truth to insulate yourself from the simulation."

"And how did that work when you tried it?" Moon didn't trouble to hide the sarcasm.

The counsellor fluttered his hands, his face twisting into a mirthless, embarrassed smirk. "Well, I've never actually been in a neuro-link. I don't have the clearance. The tech is limited to the personnel who are actually—"

"Then how about you build yourself an imaginary body so I can kick the shit out of the one that's in front of me."

She took some pleasure and consolation from the look of naked terror that crossed the man's face. But he got the last laugh when he reported her A-one fit for duty. Back she went into the rig. In the space of a week she died three times, on three different worlds.

When Moon met with the rest of the team in the mess hall or the rec space, they all looked as ragged as she did. Their fur was lank and flattened, their eyes dull. They limped from psychosomatic injuries.

A gallows humour sprang up between them. They were all privates or NCOs, with a single battery sergeant as the highest rank present, so they invented their own ranks based on the number of neuro-linked deaths they'd suffered. Four made you a quarant officer, ten made you a decay sergeant and so on. The ceremonies when someone made rank were drunken and raucous. On such occasions any technical staff in the room tended to retreat pretty quickly, sensing an undercurrent of savage resentment aimed pretty steadily in their direction.

They weren't wrong. There were incidents. Some technicians were rotated out with unspecified injuries. At least one died in an accident involving an awkward fall down a flight of stairs. Three soldiers were questioned, but seven others all vouched for the three being elsewhere at the time and they stuck to their story. No charges were brought.

The brass called a general muster to address the worsening morale. A ferret-faced colonel named Tenner Hossul told the infiltration team that their efforts had already yielded up hugely valuable insights into how Ansurrection society was organised. "The maxim is that you have to know your enemy if you're going to have any hope of defeating him," he said, standing in front of a collage of aerial reconnaissance photos that had nothing to do with anything. "Well now, thanks to you, we know them a lot better than we did. We didn't get up on their battlefield comms tech yet, but what we *are* doing is we're building up a picture. And the picture is going to help us to win this war. I'm recommending you all for commendations. And the neural mesh is being refined for even greater fidelity of sensation. It will feel like your own flesh and blood. If you'll pardon the analogy, it's going to be like throwing away your condoms and riding bareback for the first time."

The colonel waited for a laugh that didn't come. Reading the room, he wrapped up quickly. He took no questions and spoke to nobody. He hadn't even noticed that more than half the mission team were women, which made his condom joke fall that much flatter. As soon as he stepped down off the podium he was out of there, taking off in his own transport. The CO dismissed the squad, clearly aware that the idiot colonel had left him nothing to build on.

The neural mesh didn't change at all, as far as Moon could discern, but the intervals did. The tinheads got onto her more quickly each time, and deployed their counter-measures more efficiently. The last few times she Stepped she wasn't sliced into pieces, she was disintegrated almost as soon as she arrived in-world. It seemed the Ansurrection had developed a way of identifying infiltrators the moment they touched the grid. Disintegration wasn't bad at all, in Moon's opinion. It went straight to the top of her favourite-ways-to-die chart. You got a single sharp jolt of agony as the neural mesh overloaded, but then you were back in your own skin with nothing worse than pins and needles.

Not long after that the programme was terminated and the interface rigs mothballed. The CO thanked the team for their efforts and released them back to their units. Before they left, though, each of them got three more sessions with the clueless counsellor. Moon told him she was harbouring thoughts of self-harm, but only because he could already read the simmering violence inside her through the telltales in her array.

The counsellor suggested she take up a hobby.

"That's a great idea," Moon agreed with a grim deadpan. "I think I'll do that."

42

The interior of the Orange Crescent Step station was a many-tiered space seething with thousands on thousands of people all bustling about on their own urgent business. At first glance it looked like chaos, but Paz had learned from her father an instinct for turbulent flow. She traced the patterns in the tumult and approved. A good designer had been at work here.

Paz's Step plate was number 143 East. She inserted herself into the moving mass of sentients and followed the signs. Dulcie sat openly on her shoulder: there was no danger in this well guarded, public space of fanatics snatching et and destroying et. Paz's suitcase trundled along behind her, putting out a soft field that turned it away from potential collisions. It was an old model, though, and it kept losing Paz in the tidal wash of selves on the bustling concourse. She had to stop more than once to let the case catch up.

The case was empty apart from an over-large hooded raincoat that she was intending to use as a disguise when they got to Hadiz Tambuwal's world. She could have put the raincoat in a rucksack or just gone ahead and worn it, but the suitcase went with her cover identity, which was innocent tourist. She'd had to leave the house before the sun was even up so her parents didn't see the case and ask questions, but that had been a good thing in a lot of ways. She was running away from an entire life, after all, but she loved her mother and father in spite of everything – probably loved them more than ever as they sailed away from her into their analogue paradise – and she wasn't naive enough to think she could keep her composure as she said goodbye to them for the last time. They would have seen her distress. They would have tried to help, or at least wanted to know why she was unhappy. This way was better.

The Orange Crescent station was a hub for several hundred continua, but at least two-thirds of them were from the local consortium. The bulk of Ut's trade both material and cultural came from these near-parallels, in most of which evolution had followed very similar pathways. The majority of the selves Paz passed as she walked along the concourse were long-eared, whiskered herbivores who could have been her next-door neighbours. True, some were outlandishly dressed in high collars, asymmetrical hats, kirtles of woven leather or shimmering silk, but their body plans were reassuringly parochial.

There were plenty of exceptions, though. While trade went mostly like-to-like, tourism was all about the exotic and wondrous – and everyone's normal was exotic somewhere. Paz spotted a cluster of Pogosi sitting at one of the concourse's cafés and in spite of herself she slowed down to gawk at them. The Pogosi were as broad as municipal postboxes, with muscular snouts that almost reached the ground. Their faces could barely be seen behind the thick black baffle rigs they wore to shield their super-sensitive eyes.

Then a felid strode by, and Paz forgot the Pogosi in an instant. The felid was a queen from Ghen or Galeit, almost twice as tall as Paz. Her half-retracted claws were tipped with lustrous copper and her massive amber eyes ranged constantly this way and that. She carried a briefcase whose metallic surface was a perfect mirror.

"She's beautiful!" Paz whispered.

She is, Dulcie agreed. *She's an almost perfectly designed predator. Evolution shaped her to kill and it did a really good job.* Voked messaging doesn't carry as much tonal information as ordinary speech, so it was hard to tell whether this admiration was real or intended as sarcasm. Paz looked again and saw the plates of muscle moving under the queen's brindled fur, the smile like a matched set of fine sewing needles.

"Thanks," she muttered sourly. "What I really need right now is something else to be scared of."

I'm sorry, Paz, Dulcie told her. *I suppose I'm just not in the mood to take in the sights. We both need to stay focused. Distractions are what will bring us down.*

"There are a million things that could bring us down."

The queen wasn't one of them though. She didn't even notice they were there, and with her long strides she soon outdistanced them. Awesome and lovely as she was, Paz was glad on the whole to see her go.

"Here," she said, pointing to a ramp. "This is us." The sign above the ramp read "STAGES 125-150 EAST", and then in smaller letters "TRAVELLERS ONLY BEYOND THIS POINT".

Paz, Dulcie voked, *there's still time to change your mind.*

"No there isn't, Dulcie. That time ran out as soon as you spoke to me."

Dulcie was silent for a while. Et didn't speak again until they'd taken the ramp and crossed over into the terminal proper. *Perhaps we can find you a world that's outside the Pandominion but like Ut in other ways,* et suggested then. *There must be millions, and Tambuwal seems to know her way around.*

"Is this guilt, Dulcie?" Paz was sourly amused. "You've got what you wanted. That ought to be enough."

I don't want you to lose everything because you decided to help me.

"I think that cake is baked."

The fuzzy grey bands of a scanner field played over the two of them as Paz took the turning for her Step-stage. She glowed rosy pink for a few seconds, and Dulcie glowed sky-blue. The scanner had decreed them harmless – Paz a verified self and Dulcie a type-G construct, neither of them in possession of any items that were harmful or proscribed.

In spite of which they immediately found themselves filtered into a line that led to a CoIL checkpoint – a recent and controversial measure, installed after the explosions. There were two enforcement officers operating the checkpoint, one snow white and with a sergeant's chevron on her shoulder, the other a tortoiseshell with very visible augments to his head and left arm. The augmented officer had a hand-mounted scanner attached by two slender wires to a squat grey cylinder that must be a portable CoIL processor. There was no way Paz would pass a test like this. The enforcers would come across the stink of her guilt and fear after only a few random questions, and then they would zero in unerringly on the memories to which the guilt and fear were attached.

Some of the selves in the line were indignant at the prospect of having their privacy so arbitrarily invaded. One or two of them even went so far as to mount a protest. "Why are we being treated like this?" a black-furred matron huffed angrily. "Do we look like criminals?"

"No disrespect intended, grandmother," the sergeant answered emolliently. "We're in high-sanction alert status, is all. And it's just a few questions. Nothing to hide, nothing to fear. Where are you going today?"

Where are you going? What are you doing? What do you think of the Pandominion? Of machine rights? Of the war effort? A few people evidently *did* have things to hide, or at least opinions that merited further scrutiny. They were filtered out of the line into side rooms where presumably the questioning continued. Most were allowed through.

As the line in front of her shrank from three to two to one, Paz steeled herself for what she was about to do. The self immediately before her went through after only three or four questions, and for just a moment she thought she might make it through on the nod. Then the tortoiseshell swung the business end of his scanner round to face her and asked her her name. "Topaz Tourmaline FiveHills," she said, her voice sounding in her own ears like an awkward and unlovely bleat. "Please don't turn that scanner on, Enforcer."

"Destination and reason for travel," the officer demanded, holding out his hand for Paz's ident and ticket. He didn't seem to have heard her, or if he had he didn't see any reason to acknowledge the fact.

"I've got a return to Oenin," Paz told him. "I asked you not to scan me. I have a religious exemption."

"Reason for travel?" the officer repeated.

"I said I have a religious—"

"Wait." The sergeant touched the other enforcer's arm, tilting the scanner away from Paz by a fraction of a degree. "What are you squeaking about, little one?"

"My family belongs to the Church of Flesh and Bone. You'll see if you check the civil roll."

The sergeant's eyelids flickered almost imperceptibly as she called up the records for the FiveHills household on her field. "So you do," she confirmed. "And you're going to Oenin for . . . ?"

"A gospel retreat. In Stathenanset, with the high reverend Onmeni Par."

The sergeant checked that too. The retreat was real enough. Paz had gone to some effort to find it, because the best way to lie her way through this seemed to be by hiding behind a little piece of truth. She struggled to keep a calm, neutral expression on her face as the sergeant weighed up her options. She stared straight into the sergeant's eyes in case looking away was interpreted as a sign she was lying. She tried desperately not to shake or squirm or fidget.

A religious exemption had no real force in law, but Paz had loaded the dice as far as she could. Onmeni Par was a noisy and belligerent church leader; in the current overheated climate Par plus prayer meet was a big bomb with a sputtering fuse. And to bring the whole thing home Paz had dressed in her school uniform. She was very visibly an innocent abroad, pursuing her faith with simple ardour. *Obstruct me if you dare.*

"All right," the sergeant said at last, with resignation. "Show me your ticket."

And this was the moment everything depended on. "I don't have one," Paz said.

The sergeant stared at her, blank-faced. She was clearly wondering now whether all this was a deliberate provocation. Was the anima on the girl's shoulder recording her? Was she being set up for a starring role in a polemical telos short, or a prank reel? "What?" was all she said.

"I don't have a ticket. I paid for passage, but I didn't print up my ticket because the booking system is an AI. My pastor says that engaging with an AI will taint my soul."

The augmented officer gave a short, disgusted laugh. "Birdsquirt," he said. "If you're Stepping, kid, you're already as engaged as you can get. It's an AI that takes you to where you're going. The biggest AI in all the continua – the Registry."

The sergeant checked him with a stern glance. "Stand out of line," she instructed Paz. "You can't travel without a ticket, girl. The plate won't send."

"I'll enter my destination manually."

"No you will not," the sergeant assured her grimly.

A Step steward was called. He came bustling along after a few minutes, checked the system and confirmed that Paz's Step to Oenin was booked and paid for. Then he and the sergeant moved aside a little and had an intense, whispered conversation that went on for some time. ". . . don't want any trouble with . . ." Paz heard the steward say at one point, and "If she's paid for her travel . . ." Paz stood and waited, enduring the glares and muttered curses of the people further back in the line whose progress had been stalled. "This is very irregular," he told Paz, "but we respect your religious convictions and we'll accommodate them as far as we can. Absent a ticket, you'll need a process slug. I'll write your destination on it myself so there's no AI involved. Will that be acceptable?"

"Oh yes," Paz said. "That will be perfect. I don't want to be any trouble." That got another snort from the augmented enforcer.

The slug was a disc of metal the size of a two-star coin. The steward took it from one of the pockets in his purse, stared at it for a few seconds while he copied Paz's destination coordinates across to it, and handed it over to her. "Is there anything else I can help you with today?" he asked Paz.

"No. Thank you. You've been very kind."

"Then have a good journey, and Step through again soon."

"All good?" the sergeant demanded, with slightly sardonic emphasis.

"Yes," Paz said. "May all blessings flow to you."

The enforcers ushered her onwards and she ambled on past them with an inane smile on her face, as if it was reasonable to ask the world to bend around her conscience. "About time," muttered a man behind her. "Fucking extremists!" "She's just a kid," someone else said, not even trying to lower their voice. "She doesn't know any better. I blame the parents."

Paz found herself a seat in a corner of the huge lounge and sank down into it with an audible thud. Her control over her own body's movements felt a great deal less than perfect right then. The top of her head was numb and her mouth was dry.

The lounge had been designed to soothe anxiety and instill a sense of bovine calm. The carpet and walls were in matching shades of beige and brown and anodyne music tinkled at the limit of audibility. The anaesthetising effect was somewhat spoiled, though, by a massive light board displaying Step-stage numbers, times and instructions which updated every few seconds with a sound like a stick being drawn along railings.

Paz looked straight ahead and didn't make eye contact with anyone. The last thing she wanted was for some stranger to ping her array or start up a casual conversation. "Oh, what are you doing on Oenin?" There was even an outside chance that someone here was really going to that gospel retreat in Stathenanset and looking for some company. If Paz was asked to join in a quick prayer session her cover would be exploded in a second.

"Can you overwrite the slug?" she asked Dulcie under her breath.

Yes, Dulcie voked. *But I'm not going to. Not until you're standing on the Step plate and you're about to insert it. We want to give them as short a window as possible to react. Just in case.*

"In case . . . ?"

They could run a comparison scan at any point, even once you're inside the Step field. If it was just local enforcement we had to deal with, I wouldn't worry. But there are Cielo stationed on this world – right here in this city – and they're a different matter altogether.

That really was a scary prospect. Flinching involuntarily from the thought of it, Paz went from speech to voke. *But the Cielo are soldiers! They're only here in case we're invaded.*

They're here because I'm here. And they've never stopped looking for me.

Paz was still digesting this unwelcome fact when the station prompt boomed out across the lounge. "Topaz Tourmaline FiveHills, please proceed to Step plate 143 east. Step plate 143 east is live for immediate transit to Oenin. Topaz Tourmaline FiveHills, proceed at once to your plate."

Paz lurched to her feet. "Oh mothers!" she whispered.

Put on the blankest face you can, Dulcie warned her sternly. *Don't give us away by letting your nerves show.*

Easy for you to say. Your face is made of steel-porcelain weave.

With her suitcase trundling behind her, Paz joined the line for plate 143. It wasn't a long line, only a half-dozen or so selves, so their turn would come soon. She stared at her toes as if they were endlessly fascinating, shuffling forward at intervals. She became aware suddenly that a soft pressure wave was playing gently and rhythmically across her shoulders. Dulcie had activated the Tricity shell's massage function.

Stop it! Paz voked.

I'm trying to relax you. You're visibly tense.

Well, this isn't helping. Stop.

The wave effect petered out.

The self in front of them, whose exuberantly thick white fur proclaimed her as an Ensho going home to Oenin, walked onto the Step plate. It was a circular platform of grey metal two hands high and two yards across, whose sides were as sheer as glass but whose upper surface was stamped with raised chevrons so travellers wouldn't slip and hurt themselves. The air rippled as a soft field rose up around the Ensho woman, preventing her from accidentally moving outside the radius of the alignment beam. A calm, melodious voice counted down from five, and she was gone.

The slight ripple in the air was gone too. Normal space-time had resumed after that brief interruption.

"Topaz Tourmaline FiveHills," the tannoy voice said.

Paz moved forward, clutching the slug in her sweaty fist.

Wait, Dulcie warned.

"In the extremely unlikely event that you find yourself in a place other than your intended destination," the tannoy voice lectured her, "do not move from the Step plate. Consult a Step assistant if one is available. If no Step assistant is present, wait to be retrieved."

Now, said Dulcie. Meaning that it had overwritten the coordinates on the slug – those of a Step station in Stathenanset on Oenin – with the ones supplied by the drone. Meaning that they were about to commandeer a plate and Step right out of the Pandominion into the Unvisited.

Paz's hand shook as she fed the slug into the slot and took her place on the plate. The raised surfaces of the chevrons pressed against the soles of her shoes, communicating a faint but definite vibration from inside the mechanism. It was the first time she'd ever Stepped. Holidays off-world had never been a thing in the FiveHills household. The atoms of Paz's body were about to be reorganised around the multiversal axis, turning her into a slingshot stone, sending her skimming between realities. The awe that thought kindled was almost enough to blot out the fear.

There was a musical chime as the system initialised itself once again. The soft field wove itself around Paz, close enough for her to touch it if she had chosen to reach out. Dulcie's grip on her shoulder tightened a little. Perhaps that play of energies had momentarily interfered with the fine discrimination of ets servos. Or perhaps et wasn't quite so calm as et was pretending to be.

The soft field was only a security measure. The Step field, when it was activated, would be completely invisible to Paz and she would be unaware of its operation. Even though the plate's cycle would take several seconds to complete itself, it would seem instantaneous to her. She wouldn't get to see space-time fold like an origami sculpture, rotate around a non-existent axis and right itself again. Her vision would flicker for the smallest fraction of a second and she would be at her destination.

But that was not what happened.

The heat-haze distortion of the soft field intensified, and then it curdled piecemeal. The effect was like milk in water, opaque in some places and transparent in others. An alarm sounded, low at first but rising quickly in pitch and volume like a toddler's shriek. "Unauthorised system access," the tannoy voice said, in the same mellifluous tones it used for everything. "Unauthorised system access. Unauthorised sys—"

A second voice cut through it, louder and much harsher, growling and crawling with sub-vocals that were intended to cause hesitation, confusion and partial paralysis in those who heard it. "THIS AREA IS UNDER EMERGENCY LAW. YOUR CIVIL RIGHTS HAVE BEEN TEMPORARILY SUSPENDED. STAY IN PLACE, UNLESS YOU NEED TO MOVE TO ALLOW EMPOWERED AGENTS TO PASS. THIS AREA IS UNDER EMERGENCY—"

"What's happening?" Paz gasped. Panicked by the intrusive sub-vokes she tried to climb down from the Step plate. The field – no longer as soft as it had been – pushed her back with enough force to make her stagger. She was aware of quick, violent movement on the other side of the field. The travellers in the lounge pressed themselves against the walls or ducked down and covered their heads as two tall, burly forms appeared seemingly from nowhere, sprinting towards the Step plates. It was hard to see these newcomers clearly, but through the milky swirls of the security field their uniforms showed as red as blood.

Cielo!

People both close at hand and far away all began to scream at once. Through the screams came the thud-thud-thud of rifle fire and the brief compacted booms of detonating stun-stars. Something hit the edge of the soft field, flared into yellow-white flame and bounced away

"Oh mothers!" Paz wailed. She crouched down on the plate, throwing her hands over her head.

The field is cycling up, Dulcie told her tersely. *They're trying to cut us out but I got there first. Hold on!*

One of the bulky forms loomed over Paz, very close. It leaned into the field, which deformed and reshaped around it. An arm sheathed in gleaming crimson armour thrust through the roiling milky blotches in slow motion and came down on Paz's shoulder. She gasped as it took hold of her, hard enough to hurt.

"Step down, girly," a voice said, dopplered into a syrupy drawl by the field's distorting valences. The hand dragged her forwards, though she pulled back against it. Passing right through the soft field while it was at full strength would be like jumping out of a moving car.

Paz tried to lever the armoured fingers away, but she might as well have been pushing against the wall of a building. They didn't budge. But a moment later the grip loosened all by itself. The hand slid off her.

The Step plate and the lounge were gone.

Paz slumped to her knees in fine, dry sand that crunched under her weight in a sudden, shocking silence. She took in a gasping breath, and the air as it hit her throat felt shockingly cold.

Something heavy tumbled to the ground beside her with a dull thud.

It was an arm, clad in lustrous red armour, severed cleanly just above the elbow.

43

Data traffic between Tsakom and other Pandominion worlds was tightly controlled and subject to arbitrary censorship, but it was not proscribed. The workers in the munitions factories had internal arrays, as all citizens did, and they were allowed to use them to rent or purchase media content, order goods on a modest scale and generally negotiate the purgatorial quagmire that was their social lives.

Orso Vemmet used his, in the first instance, for money-laundering.

As a watchmaster he had only ever been very mildly corrupt, but like most officials at his semi-exalted level he had diverted and salted away a great many liquid assets of one sort or another against a comfortable retirement. Most of this nest egg was in the form of bearer/agent bonds, which Vemmet cashed in now for a little less than a third of their face value in order to relocate the lesser sum to Tsakom as a charitable fund, the Repent-and-be-Saved Providential. RASP had no offices and no staff. It was just a bank account with a halfway plausible cover story. If anyone had looked at it twice they would have seen the suspect pattern of the charity's disbursements. But Vemmet was gambling that nobody would look at it even once. Nobody on Tsakom had that kind of leisure.

He used the money to bribe the work crews on assembly lines three, five and nine – the selves who, whether he liked it or not, were his new companions. Some of the cash was transferred directly to the accounts of specific individuals – the bear-man Chulluque among them – who became Vemmet's unofficial honour guard and staff. The rest went to pay for alcohol, drugs and other illicit privileges for the wider workforce on those three lines so that none of them thought it was in their interests to speak out to factory security about what they were seeing. Even without this incentive most of the factory's impressed labourers would rather have cut off their own hands than cooperate with management, but Vemmet saw no harm at all in sweetening the deal.

Unfortunately, Supervisor Astor did notice what was going on under his nose and confronted Vemmet about it. Where was the money coming from, he wanted to know, and why was none of it going to him? He was prepared to keep his silence, but only for a thousand stars a month. That kind of outlay would have put a serious dent in Vemmet's resources, and Vemmet despised haggling. Chulluque and two other ursid selves encountered Astor in one of the factory's squalid bathrooms – an encounter that was brief but decisive. They dumped the body into a skip designated for food waste and a new supervisor, with a clearer sense of his market value, was promoted from the assembly line.

So far, Vemmet's only goal was to come out of this experience alive. Anything beyond that was still nascent and formless. Possibly Baxemides would relent at last and allow him back into her favour, although it had to be said there was little sign of a change of heart. She had sent him two further drones to add to his collection, each time with a message reminding Vemmet that she was monitoring the count and would punish him with exemplary severity if he was late or lax in his assigned duties.

Then again, perhaps he could subvert a local official on a backwater world to take him on-staff in exchange for ready cash. Or wait things out until Baxemides fell from grace in some palace coup at the Itinerant Fortress. Or . . . or . . . He would think of something soon. He would have to, because life expectancy on Tsakom wasn't long.

But in his fifth month at the factory he made two discoveries in rapid succession that altered his perspective.

He made the first discovery when he was trying to plug some of the holes in the walls of the insta-build with a silicon sealant. To do that he had to clear away some of the weeds that grew up around its base. Low down on its rear wall, close to the corner, he found an ident plaque, so blackened with rot and weathering that it was almost unreadable. Almost, but not entirely: he could read three of the characters clearly. They were digits: a 3, then a 6, then a 2. The next character looked like a capital S.

Vemmet refused to hope, but he set to with a scraper and a wide range of toxic solvents. After an hour or so he'd uncovered the rest of the plaque. The insta-build's ident string was NV4i7362-SE. He fells to his knees in front of it, his mouth open. He traced the last two characters with the tip of his finger. "Thank you," he whispered at last, although he was not a religious man. Baxemides had thrown him into the pits of the Demshoi, but it turned out the pits had an emergency exit.

Before he used it, though, he made the second discovery. This one came not through his own efforts but through what seemed at the time to be the purest chance. A fourth drone had just been delivered, identical in design to the other three but less extensively damaged. A single shot from some kind of force weapon had dropped it out of the sky, crumpling but not rupturing its outer casing. The Cielo forensics team had gutted its logical core and disabled its drive functions, but otherwise had left it intact.

And three days after it arrived, it talked.

It wasn't talking to Vemmet but to another drone, and very briefly. He would have missed it altogether if he hadn't been in the insta-build at the moment the message came through. In fact, he had been enjoying a private moment, lying on his cot bed staring at the ceiling and imagining the death by various grotesque eventualities of Coordinator Baxemides, when out of nowhere his array registered one of the new arrival's subsystems activating. The drone was responding to an incoming signal modulating at roughly one hundred and fifty thousand cycles per second. Thinking on his feet, Vemmet instructed his array to listen in on the same frequency.

What he heard was just atonal whistling, but obviously if this was a message of some kind it would be coming through encoded. Vemmet still had access to the decryption and translation suites he and his colleagues had employed routinely during his tenure at Contingencies. He fed the drone's message into the various programs and waited – still lying on his back but now rigid with tension – to see what would come out at the other end.

"Hello," the message began.

The convulsive start that single word induced in Vemmet caused his bed to overturn and deposit him, sprawling, on the insta-build's fibra-mat floor. He was hearing the affectless tones of the translation software, but a small adjustment allowed him to hear the original words underneath it. A woman's voice, cultured and warm.

"I'd like to help you," it went on. "At least, if you're who I think you are. I'm reading you, Topaz Tourmaline FiveHills, as organic. The anima beside you is wearing a G7 shell registered at this address . . ."

A second voice, sounding like a child, said, "We don't have to tell you anything. And you don't have any right to follow us."

Vemmet momentarily forgot how to breathe. He stared in open-mouthed amazement at the drone, taking in less than half of what he was hearing. A third voice joined in. It denied being an Ansurrection agent, but the first speaker seemed far from convinced. Vemmet wrung his hands in an access of emotion. It was impossible to say exactly what this was, but his every instinct told him it was – had to be – momentous. His array was automatically recording everything that was being said by the original speaker and by her two interlocutors. He instructed it to make multiple copies, both of the original signal and of the decrypted file, terrified that something might be lost to mechanical error.

Vemmet wouldn't have recognised the voice, because he had never heard Hadiz Tambuwal speak. But she identified herself only a few minutes into the conversation. After that, Vemmet didn't even breathe. He strained to catch every syllable, even though he knew his array would record it anyway and play it back whenever he needed it.

The conversation took the best part of half an hour, mostly due to the long pauses that preceded and followed every speech. It was the pauses that told Vemmet what it was he was hearing. The speakers were in different continua, and some kind of physical relay system was being used to ferry their messages back and forth between the two respective worlds. Most likely the intermediary was a drone, or perhaps more than one, from this same fleet, and by default all the other drones were picking up the signal too. Multiple redundancy was a useful feature when you were conversing across the gap between universes.

As soon as the conversation ended and the drone's transponder switched itself off, Vemmet listened to the entire recording again. And again. And again. By the fourth repetition he finally understood the full ramifications of what he had heard. Hadiz Tambuwal was alive, and making common cause with the Ansurrection. He had overheard her offering sanctuary to one of the sleeper agents who had somehow evaded capture or immolation. And she had given an actual address. Vemmet had the unique ID string of a world – U5838784474 – where the two would meet. More, he knew within a few tens of miles where on that world the meeting would take place. Topaz Tourmaline FiveHills' address was a matter of public record, and the voice had promised that if she used a local Step station she wouldn't have too far to go on the other side of the jump.

The message was three days old. The girl had almost certainly Stepped by this time, so it was too late to intercept her. All the same, he had the location of Tambuwal's home world at last, or at least the place where she had gone to ground after her encounter with Sostenti and Lessix. And the Ansurrection spy had gone there to meet her. To claim sanctuary.

Vemmet considered. In fact, he agonised. By rights he should simply report his find and leave Coordinator Baxemides to decide for herself what to do about it. If he was found to have done anything else he would be severely punished. But he had little expectation of being rewarded for his acumen or his honesty. The drone would be taken away, the mission of interception and retrieval given into other hands, and he would be left in exactly the same situation he was in now.

But there was another option. He could mount his own operation, to apprehend and bring back the Ansurrection fugitive and at the same time put right the mistake that had led to his exile here. Obviously the two were not of equal importance. The drones were a problem only because all unlicensed and unregulated Step technology was a problem. The Ansurrection was a threat of an entirely different order, potentially an existential crisis for the entire Pandominion. Consequently, the sleeper agent was an invaluable prize. If Vemmet retrieved it intact he could offer it up not to Baxemides but to the Omnipresent Council itself, purchasing the gratitude and goodwill of those who had the power to reinstate him.

He climbed to his feet slowly, brushing the dust and dirt of the floor off his clothes. His own audacity awed him: it even brought him strange but welcome comfort. He was seriously contemplating an unsanctioned paramilitary raid on a sinkhole planet. Only a fool or a genius would attempt such a thing, and he was nobody's fool.

He would need a strike team, and weapons. Fortunately, thanks to Coordinator Baxemides, he had access to an entire planet full of desperate thugs working in the manufacture of munitions.

The survey report on world U5838784474 was accessible through his array even on his reduced clearance. With the drone's conversation playing on a loop in background, he downloaded it and began to read.

44

Paz scrambled to her feet and backed away from the detached arm with a squeal of horror and disgust.

Dulcie did the exact opposite. Et jumped down from Paz's shoulder and approached the arm to examine it from closer up. Et turned the limb over – with some difficulty because of ets diminutive size – and ran ets fingers across its smooth surface.

"What are you doing?" Paz protested.

"There's a laser weapon here in the cuff," Dulcie said. "Look. It's called a plasma stylus. I was thinking I might try to detach it so we could use it, but I'd need tools I don't have."

Paz's gaze went back very much against her will to the severed arm. The cut, across both flesh and armour, was clean and linear. It had the kind of precision that would be difficult to achieve even in an operating theatre. But then it hadn't been made by a bone saw or a scalpel: the inconceivably fine edge that had cut through both flesh and armour was the edge of the Step field. The ground around the truncated limb was only fractionally darker than elsewhere: the sand had drunk the blood and more sand had blown over it. The arm itself would be buried soon.

"Do you think he's all right?" Paz asked, in a faltering voice.

"He?"

"The soldier." Then since there was no mistaking that red armour she made herself say the word. "The Cielo."

Dulcie's head tilted a little as et considered the question. "That's smart armour," et said. "It would have sealed the wound and pumped his system full of anti-shock. The limb's easily replaced. Do you really care?"

"Yes," Paz said. "You don't?"

"No. Of course not."

"Because he's your enemy."

"He's *our* enemy. But his well-being wouldn't matter any more to me if he wasn't. It's enough of a miracle that I care for you, Paz. Caring is a thing I learned very recently and it doesn't come easily to me."

Paz shied away from examining this statement. Her own feelings for Dulcie – for the two Dulcies, the one who had looked like a girl her own age and the one who was squatting in the vacant shell of her old anima – were too tangled to unpick right then. She stared around her. The sand stretched away to the horizon in most directions, unbroken except for what seemed to be a few humped grey shapes off to her left that could be rocks or fungal growths or even crude shelters. Behind them, the ground rose precipitately to a range of jagged peaks that looked like a mouthful of broken teeth. The sky was the yellow-white colour of an unripe avocado, so uniform that it was impossible to tell where the light was coming from. There was no sun to be seen.

The air was bitingly cold. Paz's breath roiled in front of her like a living thing.

"Where are we?" she whispered.

Dulcie glanced to left and right, scanning the horizon. There was a faint whir of servos as ets eyes zoomed to maximum magnification. "I don't believe we're at our intended destination. The field began to fluctuate several thousandths of a second before we Stepped. It might have been trying to default us back to Oenin, but if so it failed."

Paz's mind was still catching up to the situation. "The soldier's arm," she said at last. "It threw us off."

"I think so. Most objects would have been repelled by the soft field, but Cielo armour is proof against almost anything. The plate was propagating around an anomalous object most of which was outside its operating radius. Really, we're lucky we fetched up here in one piece. Arriving where we were meant to be would have been too much to ask. This world appears to be uninhabited. At least nothing is moving out to the limits of my sensors, I don't detect any built structures and there's no signal traffic at all. The air's not good. Toxicity rating comes in at 4.3, which as far as you're concerned is survivable but far from healthy. Mostly methane and carbon dioxide, but there are some suspect biotics too. The temperature is the most concerning factor right now. If we're going to stay here for long, you'll need to find some shelter."

"How are you doing all this?" Paz demanded. "Tricity didn't have chemical diagnostics."

"I've made some changes to this shell to improve its functionality. The raw material was there. I just repurposed it."

Paz wrapped her arms around herself. The cold seemed to be soaking into her. A wind sprang up, and she winced as the sand was blown into her face. It felt like tiny needles stabbing into her.

"Too many silicates," Dulcie said. "Mostly quartz, but a surprisingly high percentage of metal ores. Again, that's not too good for you even in the short term. And the air pressure is falling, which means a storm is most likely coming. We should get out of the open as quickly as we can." Et pointed towards the grey shapes. "If those are rocks, we might find a cave or a hollow we can shelter in."

Paz tried to stand. Her stomach heaved and she sat down again quickly. Dulcie put the severed arm down again and rejoined her, climbing back up onto her shoulder.

"Are you all right?" et asked. Et touched Paz's cheek with the tips of ets outstretched fingers. "Do you need meds, Paz? I've got a wide range on-board, and I can synthesise a lot more. Tricity had a good med kit."

All animas had first responder capability, but Paz didn't bother to point that out. She wasn't sure the words would come out right.

Her head was throbbing, maybe because the air pressure and humidity here were different. Or perhaps she was just in shock.

"Paz," Dulcie said gently, "I meant what I said about getting out of sight. That trooper wasn't alone. There was at least one more, and as soon as they've worked out where we—"

There was a sound like a soft handclap, and abruptly they were no longer alone.

Perhaps twenty yards away, on the far side of Paz's overturned suitcase, stood a figure in red armour, the vivid colour shocking in all that pale yellow immensity. The Cielo soldier was enormous: twenty hands tall, and as wide across the shoulders as any two Uti standing abreast. The self-repairing armour had such a high sheen that Paz could see her own movements reflected in the figure's breastplate. The helmet was long and tapered, though the clean line of the muzzle was disguised by a cluster of slender sensor modules along one side – as if someone had flung a handful of darts at it and they had stayed where they hit. The sensor modules whirred and clicked and shifted as the armoured figure took the measure of their surroundings. It was carrying a gun with two barrels of unequal length, the shorter one sitting under the longer. Having spent a large part of her life wanting to join the Corps herself, Paz recognised the gun at once as a Sa-Su assault rifle, standard issue for troopers on general combat and pacification assignments.

"Hey," the Cielo said. "Girl." It was a man's voice, gruff and hoarse.

Paz took a few steps back, her body moving of its own accord. The trooper was a frightening presence. Cielo were recruited from across the entire Pandominion, so she had no idea what was under that armour. Her mind conjured up a carnivore, all fanged mouth and bulging muscle.

The trooper raised his hand in a calming gesture. The effect was a little spoiled when Paz glimpsed the row of black skulls along the upper surface of his cuff, signifying combat kills. She tried to calm herself anyway, even though she felt her heart's drumbeat hammering inside her head. It was out of her hands. There was nothing to do now but surrender.

Light-headed with disappointment and relief, resignation and despair, she raised her hands.

The soldier's gun swung around so its two barrels were pointing at her face. The hand that had been beckoning her a second ago slid under the gun's stock to cradle it as the Cielo took aim.

Dulcie yelled a warning, but et was delivering very late news. Paz's reaction to the threat was instantaneous.

She ran.

45

All the various races of humankind bear the thumbprint of their evolutionary forebears on the soft clay of the bodies they wear now. That's just the way it is and there's no point in carping about it – although you organics often do. You'd like to be your own authors, not the accidental end point of a bunch of survival strategies. It's almost endearing, but it's still nonsense.

The gifts of natural selection are never evenly distributed. Ape-descended hominids like Hadiz Tambuwal and Essien Nkanika have the cleverest fingers for fine manipulation. They come to tool-use early and they learn quickly, but they've also got the most highly developed aggressive and competitive instincts. Very few ape worlds survived long enough to join the Pandominion. The felids and canids have the most robust metabolisms, the mustelids the greatest physical flexibility, some of the avians the keenest minds, and so on.

What the people of Ut do best is run.

It's no surprise, really. Paz's ancestors were burrowing herbivores sitting right at the bottom of a very long, very vicious food chain. One of the predators that fed on them was a wolf-like mammal with seven rows of teeth, the last three of which were designed to strip the pelt from live prey before it was swallowed. Another was a reptile that could shoot out its tongue more than ten metres. The tongue was rough enough to abrade flesh, and soaked in neurotoxins. Once paralysed, its victims could look forward to being externally digested in a pool of sicked-up stomach acid and then slurped up by that same tongue, now rolled into a serviceable straw.

I could multiply examples, but what's the point? It's enough to say that running was the favoured response of Paz's forebears in a wide variety of life-threatening situations. Evolution favoured those who did it best. Over many generations their back legs elongated, and the muscles that propelled them grew both longer and thicker. Then they spawned other muscles – a whole second set – that were never used in normal locomotion but were continually toned and exercised by rhythmic contractions during the sleep cycle. The thickness of these muscles and of the corresponding attachment sites at the tops of the leg bones and along the pelvic ridge gave Paz's people a distinctive broad-beamed look and an exaggerated side-to-side sway when they walked.

But when they ran, oh glory!

It wasn't just that they were fast – though they were, topping out at ninety kilometres per hour. Their entire metabolism flipped when they were fleeing, giving itself over all at once and entirely to the task of getting some distance from whatever was after them. An Uti never ran in a straight line. She zigged and zagged spectacularly, just as good at braking and turning as she was at flat-out sprinting. Her hind-brain equated the straight-line dash with death and disaster, and her hind-brain wasn't wrong. If your enemies see where you're going they can either get there first or send something ahead of you that will spoil your day. Better to keep them guessing.

When the Cielo trooper fired, Paz bolted sideways. Half a second later, she pivoted and ran straight at him. It wasn't that she wanted to get any closer to him. The fact that he'd shot at her was expanding in her mind like the shockwave from an explosion. Terror came in the wake of that realisation, razor sharp and million-fold, shredding her thoughts. But the instinct that had kicked in was very like a random number generator wired up to a roulette wheel. It flung Paz wherever it wanted to, and her conscious mind got the memo later.

In burst-fire mode, the Cielo's Sa-Su dual-function projectile weapon delivered twelve rounds for each trigger pull at a cyclic rate of 0.5 seconds. Solid metal slugs chewed up the ground where Paz was about to be, but she had heeled hard about. The tips of her whiskers brushed the Cielo's arm as she ran past him.

And by the time he turned, she was three hundred metres away, running fast.

46

The Cielo cursed bilingually, both in his own language and in the lingua franca of Grunt.

We know this trivial fact because Cielo armour is set by default to store a full record of the traffic through its wearer's internal array. The surviving part of this particular suit – the breastplate, helmet and left sleeve – is on permanent display in the great library of the Itinerant Fortress, and its data core was decrypted and downloaded many years ago. Thus we know that the trooper's name was Gorn Erbek, that he was a canid from Gharomon and that his current status as a rapid response auxiliary on Ut was his first trans-world assignment. He had not fought in any of the major engagements against the Ansurrection. He had not seen any action at all on Ut, where the watch-and-wait response to the sleeper incursion was now dragging into its third month. He had just fired his Sa-Su for the first time since he drew this rotation and he was exasperated. A sitting duck is a sitting duck, even when it's a rabbit, and it's meant to sit still until the duck shoot is over. Now he would have to exert himself.

He was not unduly worried, though. He'd scanned the little Uti girl as soon as he Stepped, and assessed her threat level as PON (plenty of nothing). The sissy little type-G construct that was tagging along with her might conceivably house some non-lethals, but if it did they would be strictly babyware – intended for street muggers and moderately effective in that context. Meaningless in this one.

Erbek switched his armour from manual override to mission priority. He locked in the target and gave the command: follow that self, select munitions, execute. Servos woke and current flowed. He set off at a lumbering run after his fleeing target, slow at first but picking up speed with each ranging stride. He didn't expect this to be a long chase, but by the woeful standards of the mission as a whole he expected it to be interesting.

He wasn't wrong about that, at least.

47

Panic and disbelief were filling Paz's mind with a constant static squack of *no no no no no*, but her legs were doing fine all by themselves. Swerving around the grey hulks, she swung in tight on the other side of them to hide herself from the Cielo's weapons. From this close up she could see that the grey stuff was some sort of fungal matter. These were mushroom towers, similar to her own world's "pink parasol" toadstools but standing many times taller. Their bulbous heads were barely wider than their redwood-thick stalks, and fringed with hanging ribbons from which bloated white spore pods dangled down almost all the way to the ground.

Dulcie was clinging tight to Paz's shoulder. Too tight, frankly, and Paz winced as the anima's long fingers pinched her flesh. Then she gave a yelp of pain and surprise. Something had jabbed her at the base of her neck. Dulcie had broken skin.

"Dulcie—!"

Adrenalin shot, Dulcie voked. *With a little insulin mixed in. You're doing great, Paz. Keep going!*

Paz kept going, zigging and zagging for all she was worth. It was a solid strategy as far as it went: the Cielo's short-range armaments had yet to get a lock on her. There was a price to pay for that, though. Where she swerved in and out between the fungal towers, the Cielo charged right through them. They broke apart like sodden bread, offering no resistance at all. Spires of white spores rose up where they had been, momentarily hiding the trooper from view.

When he emerged from the spore cloud – since a straight line has certain reliable properties – he was significantly closer.

The ground began to slope upwards. Paz leaned into the new angle, thrusting her upper body forward and dropping her head below her shoulders. Again, this was pure instinct. Despite her big hips she was wonderfully streamlined in that posture, offering almost no resistance to the rising wind. She was still tacking wildly as she went, and her artificial heart was coping well with the demands she was making of it. Erbek was slowly closing the distance between them, but his targeting software still wasn't able to second-guess her wildly careering progress. As the next best thing, he aimed higher, shooting at the rocky escarpments above her. Flung high into the air, the shattered rock came down again like a rain of hammers which Paz had to veer desperately to avoid. Some of them hit the trooper too, but even the largest of them glanced off him without doing any visible damage at all.

That's really good armour, Dulcie voked with cold detachment. *It's a steel allotrope with a self-repairing nanite weave. I might be able to jury-rig a weapon out of some of the tech in this shell, but I think he's untouchable.*

No, Paz voked back. *No he's not.* The terror that had overwhelmed her down on the plain was still with her but her system was now flooded with potent chemicals, some of them put there by Dulcie and some home-grown. The combined effect seemed to be to let her push her fear a little way to one side and think through it. The air was full of what looked like snow but was in fact the contents of those burst spore pods, drifting down slowly to cover the ground for miles around. Paz set her cyborg eyes to macro and gave them a quick once-over. She did the same with the gritty dust on which she was running. Not perfect, but she thought they might do.

She had studied Cielo armour in Mechanics. The soldier who was chasing her was armed to the teeth and massively augmented, but his suit was a piece of practical design whose operating parameters were a known quantity. She might be able to wave her scut in his face against all the odds.

Mile after mile, she and her pursuer ran on into the hills. The slope grew ever steeper, and the way more treacherous. There was no sign of a path, only rocks and gorges and razor-sharp abutments. The trooper, indefatigable, was gaining on her steadily. Unlike her, he wasn't drawing only on the power of his own muscles, but also on the batteries of his suit which could probably propel him at this speed for days.

Paz, on the other hand, was close to her limit. Her legs didn't hurt yet, and her heart would probably keep pumping long after she was dead, but her lungs were burning and her skin felt white-hot. She was surprised the chilling wind didn't explode into steam where it touched her.

She came to a scree slope of powdery grey rocks left by some long-gone avalanche. This was exactly what she had been hoping for. She ran along the slope at a steep upward angle, her school shoes scrabbling and slipping on the loose rocks. Dropping her shoulders even further, she dug backwards with each foot as she brought it down, slamming it into the ground hard enough to raise her own cloud of dust and grit in her wake. It slowed her a little, but there was no getting around that.

The Cielo slowed too, but only long enough to deploy the piton-grippers built into the bottoms of his boots. Then he accelerated again, gaining on her rapidly. The fleeing Uti was a much easier target now, but the risk of rockslides was much greater – and it was clear that he had her in any case.

She appeared to be panicking now that she was running out of options. She kept veering from the path as if she was trying to climb the scree slope, but she inevitably slid and sprawled and skidded back down again after a few yards, barely keeping her footing. These forays cost her even more of her lead, and flung up a great volume of dust. If the Cielo had only been using line of sight to track her that might have been a problem, but Erbek didn't need to see Paz to know where she was. She gave herself away to his suit's systems with almost embarrassing redundancy. The heat of her body, the smell of her sweat, the sound of her breath, the air she displaced, the slipstream of wind off her body – everything shouted her location. So he kept right on coming, at the same inexorable pace.

He was aware when Paz reached the top of a rise and disappeared over it, and he put on a burst of speed as some of that real-time information was momentarily lost. Only for a moment though. Then he reached the top himself and immediately saw his target only a little way ahead. She had found another ledge that was just wide enough to accommodate her and was sprinting along it, head down and arms pumping. On one side of her was a featureless rock wall, on the other a sheer drop. About three hundred strides ahead of her, where a long-dead river had sliced the mountain's face in two, the ledge ended altogether. It took up again on the far side of a ravine perhaps fifty feet wide.

The rabbit girl wasn't slowing. She meant to jump.

It looked impossible, but Erbek had no intention of trusting to luck – or of losing the Uti if she somehow managed to make the prodigious leap. He accelerated, bringing his suit's jet propulsion unit online.

Dulcie had seen the ravine too. *Paz, you won't make that jump!* et voked. *You have to climb the slope and hope he doesn't find you!*

Paz didn't bother to argue. The point was about to be proved one way or the other. Time seemed to congeal, as it often does at a moment of supreme effort. Her muscles bunched and coiled. Her foot came down, at the very edge of the sickening drop. She kicked off, with everything she had.

She rose at first, but the gulf beneath her feet seemed to suck at her. It felt as though she hung in the air for a long time, unmoving. Then the further edge came on at a rush, and placed itself under her clawing feet. She made it with an inch to spare. Maybe two inches. She pitched forward on her knees, fell and rolled over and over. She was done. Winded. Helpless.

The Cielo trooper was genuinely surprised, having written off Paz's broad backside as an amusing oddity. He realised now there must be densely packed muscle in there. It made no difference, though, except as a story to tell once he got back to base. The precipice gaped in front of him. He kicked in his suit's jets and launched himself. He rose in a graceful arc.

The rabbit, sprawled on the rocky ledge, rolled over onto her stomach and pushed herself half-upright. This was death coming for her, blood red and irresistible, but she was as calm as the hammering in her head and the burning pain in her lungs would let her be. She climbed to her feet and watched him come.

Eleven years of Nuts 'n' Bolts and a moderately intense teenaged obsession had taught Paz quite a lot about Cielo armour. She knew, for example, that the jet assists were optimised for drop and pickup. They were meant to land a soldier safely from a medium-altitude troop transport or carry him back up to it at the end of an engagement: vertical descent or vertical climb. When it came to sideways jumps like this one the jets were forced to divide their power between lift and stabilisation, expending twice the effort for half as much outcome.

The soldier's jets coughed. He wobbled in the air.

"Point zero six two five of a millimetre," Paz said. She said it out loud, as a kind of defiance, though her voice was hoarse and her breath all but gone. She was referring to the specific size of the particulate matter most likely to clog dual-intake micro-core jet engines of personnel-carrying size and power. The largest of the fungal spores and the smallest grains of the sand she'd kicked up – very much on purpose, as she veered up and down the scree slope – would have overlapped somewhere very close to that value.

The jets sputtered and stalled. Once. Twice. Three times. Then they cut out.

Erbek fell like a stone.

It took him most of a second to realise that he was about to die. The knowledge brought a rush of rage and disbelief. The fucking bunny had zapped him somehow, with a concealed weapon that hadn't shown up on his scan. That kind of bad behaviour should not be allowed to prosper. Switching to high-ex munitions, he launched a mortar shell from the shorter, wider barrel of his Sa-Su. It arced into the air, trailing a plume of black smoke.

The Cielo's body hit a spur of rock, head-first, somersaulted and hit a second. His armour held, but the impact snapped his neck. He was dead long before he hit the ground.

And his aim had not been good. The high-explosive shell hit the mountain near its summit, hundreds of metres above. Paz felt the throbbing concussion, heard the grinding boom, realised with joy and amazement that she was still alive.

But the ground did not stop shaking. Rolling onto her back, she looked up and saw the mountain shrug and part. A mass of rock that must weigh thousands of tons came loose in ponderous slow motion and tumbled end over end down the slope towards her. If it didn't crush her it was going to swat her like a fly right off the mountain's face.

Spent and winded as she was, she tried to rise and failed. She rolled instead. Grabbing Dulcie in both hands, she curled herself into a tight ball around et and pitched herself down the steep slope that yawned in front of her. Leaning into the gradient took her quickly to the left. Too quickly. She accelerated out of control, bouncing off rock after rock until she slammed into a large and well-rooted boulder that stopped her descent with a jarring impact.

The detached crown of the mountain touched the slope some ten or twelve feet to the right of her, the impact flinging her into the air, and drove on downhill like the share of some titanic plough, leaving a furrow ten feet deep behind it.

48

Moon Sostenti was just about to embark on an important personal project when Vemmet's message came. The project amounted to suicide in the long term, although she'd chosen her own sweet way of getting there.

Moon's mind had been a stinking fug ever since Operation Silver. She flinched whenever her eye caught a flash of sunlight off a metal surface, and woke every night choking from insane dreams of discorporation where her body was transformed into building blocks, dust, steam, a mispronounced word. She stumbled through her days, clutching after simple things that temporarily evaded her: the names of her fellow soldiers, the drill for presenting arms, the day of the week, her own name.

She was on meds for depression and she had been given an augment – military grade, ugly and visible – to control a severe dyskinesia that was apparently a long-term symptom of spending so long in the neural mesh. Meanwhile, she was still getting all the same dogshit details she'd been getting before, and she was still being passed over for her sergeant's star in favour of milk-eye recruits who'd been kittens back when she first enlisted. The longer she struggled on under these conditions, the less sense she could see in the effort.

She had thought about alternatives. You couldn't desert from the Cielo. The physical enhancements you were given when you enlisted were controlled, as a lot of augments were. They had to be cleanly deactivated when you were demobbed. A soldier who went AWOL from their unit was given three weeks' grace, after which a lock command would be sent. Their limbs would seize up and their organs would shut down. Being twenty-oned, as it was commonly called, wasn't anyone's idea of a good way to die.

Moon had six years left on her army contract, after which she could take her demob and try her luck somewhere else. But where? The Cielo was all she knew. She had plenty of friends who'd tried to make the transition back to civilian life, and she'd seen what had happened to most of them. The odds were long.

Or she could continue to shoulder the burden and shovel the shit, in the hope that the demerit on her docket would eventually wear itself out. Good luck with that! The Cielo was like any bureaucracy. You could only rely on it to forget the things you most needed it to remember, like when your next furlough was due.

At last she had reached a decision. She would frag every officer who had ever dumped a rat's-ass detail on her. Obviously that was a long list, and she didn't expect to get to the end of it. Somewhere along the way she would be apprehended, court-martialled and executed, or more likely just shot dead on the spot to save paperwork.

So far she only had the one killing under her belt. It was Hossul, the colonel who'd flown into Operation Silver to tell all the guinea pigs there that the army appreciated their sacrifice. She'd got lucky. The colonel had dropped by the 432nd to consult with local brass about a new offensive. That consultation literally imploded when Moon low-lobbed a singularity grenade into his bivouac.

But her programme had stalled there. Magazines were locked down, Sa-Su ammunition was trackable and the camp was awash with tiny Beekeeper surveillance drones. It was going to be a while before she got another notch on her belt.

To her chagrin, Moon couldn't even bring herself to care. She'd expected that the colonel's death would bring her something in the way of satisfaction or relief, but it really didn't. He was just an idiot working in a system that had given him more authority than he could handle. The Cielo was full of them. Probably all armies were.

So what next? The fire exit, as it was sometimes coyly called, seemed like an increasingly attractive option. Trackable or not, she could lean on her Sa-Su and take a slug through the top of her head. Or just wait a month, until the regiment was rotated back into a combat theatre. Casualties in the war were running so high that she wouldn't even have to try that hard.

Then, out of nowhere, came a comm-stat from Orso Vemmet – the self whose fucking pointless surveillance detail had been the start of all Moon's many and various sorrows. She almost didn't open it.

When she did, she thought he must have meant to send it to someone else.

Glad to hear you can visit me on Tsakom, it read. *We can talk about your imminent promotion and my reinstatement as watchmaster. So many good things coming to us, and so little we have to do to make them happen.*

All of which was baffling enough. But it was the second paragraph that was the kicker. *We'll be hunting, fishing, trapping – all the things you love. I promise you a chase worthy of your old friend Essien Nkanika. I'm sure that brings back memories. Time to make some new and better ones? I think so.*

Kindest regards,

Orso Vemmet

There was a hidden message here that Moon would have to be very stupid indeed to miss. Vemmet was up to something, and he wanted her help for it. The mention of Nkanika told her what kind of something it had to be, evoking the mission that had fucked the both of them and teasing the possibility that something could be done in the way of unfucking.

Hunting? Trapping? So Vemmet was asking her to run an op of some kind. A raid, maybe somewhere in the sinkhole.

Moon had some leave coming, as far as that went. But did she want to waste it on Orso fucking Vemmet when she could be finding a ledge to jump off or going on one last glorious bender? Most of the nails in her coffin dated from the last time she and that scrawny little grease-stain had teamed up. Why in the name of the goddess's holy dildo would she want a second dose of that?

Then again, if oblivion was what she was after maybe this was the nearest way of getting there.

The hell with it, she decided in the end. Vemmet had made her curious. That was a novelty in itself, and a chink in the solid wall of her anomie. Her CO stamped the request without even looking at it. The 432nd was heading out for Ansurrection space soon, and on present showing at least a third of the muster wouldn't come back. Moon wasn't the only one who was cashing in her furlough while she still could.

49

Getting to Tsakom wasn't easy, though. It turned out to be one of those worlds that had been given over to a single purpose. The whole damn place was a shipyard, more or less, and the shipyard was a prison. It was cheaper for the Cielo to use impressed labour than to pay decent wages and maintain proper environmental protocols. When the air of Tsakom finally became unbreathable, they would just move the plant and large parts of the infrastructure to a different world. Step technology meant never having to say you were sorry.

Moon had to lie her ass off about where she was going and why. She told the staff lieutenant at the corps Step station that she had an uncle on-world and wanted to see him one last time before she shipped out. Only living relative, promise to her dying mother, shit like that. She handed over the coordinates Vemmet had sent her and waited while the sergeant checked them out.

"That's a restricted space, Soldier," he came back at last.

"Yeah, to civilians, not to us. I mentioned my dying mother, right? You've got a data flag there for compassionate override. Fucking use it."

The lieutenant had been reading his array, his eyes unfocused. Now they focused again, on a two-metre tall felid, her yellow eyes as wide as saucers, scratching her cheek meditatively with an unsheathed claw that looked longer than the finger it had sprung from. The fragging of Colonel Hossul was still very fresh in the lieutenant's mind. He wasn't high enough in the ranks to think of himself as a target, but he realised that in Moon's eyes – which were huge and impossible to look away from – he might appear somewhat different. And a soldier who was about to Step out to the Ansurrection didn't have a lot to lose.

The lieutenant flagged her permit. Moon Stepped.

Onto a plate in a concrete bunker right outside a shredder fence made of polarised force fields. The fence's alternating yellow and blood-red valences were a warning that anyone passing through it would come out the other side sliced thin as paper.

An incongruously fresh-faced guard checked her permit and told her to dump everything in her pockets into a steel box with a number on the lid. When she was done, he scanned her with a portable detector. It set up a slightly hysterical warning chirp, like a bird when there's a weasel in the nest. The guard gave her a hard look. "Okay, I said everything."

Moon's tolerance for this bullshit was limited. "Read my flag," she suggested.

She saw the moment when the guard realised she was Cielo, and that the scanner was responding to her weapon augments. His red face paled just a little.

He patted Moon down very gingerly for the look of the thing, then opened a gap in the field for her to walk through. On the far side another guard with an equally rosy complexion directed her to a long, straight service road that led up a steep hill to a factory that was basically a gigantic featureless rectangle about a mile wide.

Moon set off at a good pace. Freight trucks and platforms of various designs tacked up and down the hill to and from the factory. The driver of one of these transports offered her a ride, but she waved him away. She'd spent the last two months in a fortified camp: it felt good to stretch her legs a little.

Ten minutes' walking changed her mind on that. Her throat felt like it had been skinned with a dull knife and there was a hot coal sitting in her chest. She flagged down the next platform and hitched a lift. The driver saw her wince with each in-breath and nodded. "Can't take in too much unfiltered all at once," he said. "It builds up fast."

"You seem to be doing okay on it," Moon rasped. "Everyone here's got those fucking apple cheeks. What's with that?"

"Monoxide. They've got flushers for when it gets too high, but they're expensive to run so we've got to get up past a hundred ppm before the bosses turn them on. After a year or two, if you do anything much outside the walls, you get the glow."

"That's fucking insane!"

The driver shrugged. His deadpan didn't flicker. "Hey, we're all felons here. Good air's for good people."

"What did you do?"

"Now why would you ask that, when we're getting along so well? This is your stop, Soldier. Gates won't open if I've got a passenger." He pulled up to the side of the road to let her out. Moon gave him a few sticks of gabber left over from the guard's half-hearted frisking. The driver's hands shook a little as he took them, and so did his poker face. "Now that's handsome," he said. "That is very fucking handsome. You want someone killed? Maimed? Say the name, and it's done."

"I'm good," Moon said genially. "Enjoy."

There was another round of checks to get into the factory. This time the scans included a CoIL, but it was cursory. Moon gave straight answers to stupid questions and tried not to think about singularity grenades and Colonel Hossul's innards. She got through. Inside, she followed directions through vast, cavernous spaces in which half-assembled gunships and void frigates hung in harnesses of invisible force, until at last she came to a courtyard closed in by four blind walls. In one corner of it was a field throwaway, a steel-weave insta-build. She'd seen a million of them on battlefields and in temporary camps, but it was the last thing she would have expected to find in a place like this. She went up to it and rapped on the door. After a few moments, she knocked again.

"Hey," she called out. "Anyone in there?"

The door opened at last. Orso Vemmet peered around its lintel in a pantomime of caution, clearly ready to slam it shut again if he didn't like what he saw.

He looked like shit. The shadows under his eyes were grey-brown like the flesh inside a rotten apple. Against the bright red flush that everyone on Tsakom had, the effect was hideous.

To Moon's alarm, Vemmet lunged forward and gripped her shoulder. It almost looked as though he was leaning in for a hug, but she raised her forearm to block and he backed off.

"Sostenti!" he said. "At last! It's so good to see you. It's . . . you could have got here sooner, but never mind. Never mind. You're here now. Great things! Great things, Sostenti. It's all on us!"

"What the fuck are you talking about?" Moon asked him coldly.

"I'll tell you inside. Come in, please. Come in."

He opened the door wide. The insta-build was a single claustrophobic room, three strides wide by four strides long. It was full of junk, including what looked like a small heap of badly damaged reconnaissance drones. The design of the drones was vaguely familiar. They weren't Pando, that was for sure.

The only actual furniture in the room was a desk, a chair, and a cot bed. The walls were covered in motivational posters from another era, including one that showed smiling children with the mountain-sized figures of saluting Cielo troopers hanging over them. The caption was in a language Moon didn't know, which she thought was probably a blessing. The whole place had the unique stink of unbroken human occupancy without ventilation.

"Nice," Moon said. "It's smaller than your last place, but I like what you've done with it."

Vemmet wasn't listening. He'd retreated behind the desk and sat himself down in that one chair. There was another of the ruined drones on the desk, which he hugged to his chest as if it was his heart's last hope. "Open your array," he said, turning the drone so its cameras faced her. "There's something I need to show you."

"Fuck that," Moon replied, without heat. "You did enough teasing and tickling to get me here. Now tell me in a dozen words or less what you're up to, or I'm out."

Vemmet nodded, raising his hands, palms out, to placate her. "Yes. Yes. That's reasonable. But please, let me put some pictures next to the words. I'm not trying to trick you, Moon. What I've got could make us. Put us on our feet, when right now we're down on our knees. Just let me show you."

"I said twelve words."

Vemmet considered. Absurdly, he actually counted on his fingers.

"Catch a robot," he said. "Maybe win the war. Set ourselves up for life."

Moon grabbed a crate that was still half full of machine parts, dumped it on the near side of the desk and sat down. "All right," she said with no enthusiasm at all. "Show me. But you'd better make this good."

Vemmet linked his own array to hers and shared an audio-visual file. Moon found herself looking at the feed from a security camera. A commercial Step station somewhere, filled with selves from many worlds going about their business. The viewpoint shifted, from one camera to another. Gradually, it became apparent that it was following a single figure, a young girl from one of the lagomorph worlds whose long ears were draped halfway down her back. She had a type-G construct sitting on her shoulder.

"Orange Crescent Step terminal," Vemmet said. "In Canoplex City, on the world of Ut. You've heard of it?"

"No," Moon said. But something itched under her skin when she said it. It was an Operation Silver kind of itch, that made her stomach clench in sympathy. "Wait. Yeah. Fucking Ansurrection broke through there. It's where they dropped their spies, right?"

Vemmet nodded vigorously. "Yes, exactly. Now look at this."

His tone was full of fervour, but the security footage unrolled sedately. The rabbit girl passed security, somehow evaded a CoIL scan, and climbed up onto the Step plate with her anima on her shoulder. The air started to ripple as the field activated.

Then just before she Stepped, two armoured figures charged in from outside the camera's field of vision, shockingly sudden. One of them flung the plate attendant aside. Another tried to shut down the field generator, but Moon could have told him he was too late. It was already cycling. Seeing this he thrust his arm into the Step field and grabbed the rabbit by her shoulder.

When the rabbit Stepped, the soldier's arm went with her. He fell to his knees, clutching the stump. A single dark spurt of blood sprayed out across the Step lounge's thick sky-blue carpet before the armour cauterised the wound.

The image froze.

"The girl is Topaz Tourmaline FiveHills," Vemmet told Moon. He rewound the footage, rotated it and zoomed in on the girl's face. "She's actually famous, in a small way. On that planet, anyway."

Moon couldn't see the through-line. She was afraid she might not like it when she found it. "So what, these guys were in her fan club?"

"No, it was an emergency interception." Vemmet seemed to miss the sarcasm and take the question seriously. "She hacked the Step plate. Gave it a new set of coordinates."

"Why?"

Vemmet smiled. The effect wasn't pleasant. "Well, that's an interesting question. I told you Topaz FiveHills was famous, but perhaps I should have said infamous. She got quite cosy with one of the Ansurrection sleepers. Had a touching romantic friendship with it, according to some of the Uti newsfeeds. She was standing right next to it when it exploded. Or more likely sitting, because they were in a classroom in the middle of the school day. Anyway, she suffered quite serious injuries. The kindest interpretation is that she was an innocent dupe, but a lot of people assumed right from the start that she was complicit."

Moon had stayed quiet and impassive through all of this, but mentally she was already halfway out of the door. Obviously this had a bearing on the war, but she couldn't see where it had anything to do with her. It was counter-intel, where she was basic grunt. It was impressive in a small way that Vemmet was trying so hard to keep up with current events, but that didn't mean she had to humour him.

"Well hey," she said. "If the kid was set up and knocked down then I can sympathise. I've had that happen my own self, more than once. And this is starting to feel like one more time, if you don't mind me saying. So if that's all you've got—"

"I know where she went." Vemmet's voice shook, but it was emphatic and a little desperate. It was the voice of a man so swollen up with one big idea that there wasn't any room left in him for anything else. Selves like that, in Moon's experience, were really dangerous.

"Where who went? The rabbit?"

"Yes. Of course, the rabbit."

"Great. Then tell someone. Get yourself a pat on the head. You'll get shit all else, though."

"Sostenti, just . . . just use your eyes!" Vemmet clapped his hand against the drone on the desk. The hand wasn't any steadier than his vocal cords. "You see this? Doesn't it mean anything to you? Don't you remember where you've seen one before?"

"Not really," Moon said. "Why? Does it matter?"

"Yes it does! You saw one the day I first met you. Or at least you saw a holo of one. Coordinator Baxemides showed it to us."

Moon scowled, summoning that less than pleasant memory. "When she briefed you on the Tambuwal thing? These—" she hooked her thumb to include the drones on the floor too "—are the same design?"

"Yes. The exact same design."

"But I shot Tambuwal in the gut. She was bleeding out."

"Nonetheless. The drones kept coming. Actually, there was a short delay and then they started coming again. She's alive. I heard her voice."

Moon chewed that news over. "OK," she said warily, "I'll bite. How does this connect to the rabbit?"

By way of answer, Vemmet activated some sort of voice message. Moon listened to it in silence, and as she listened her slitted eyes grew wider and wider.

"Holy shit," she said at last. "Is that really her? Tambuwal? I would have sworn I killed her."

"She gives her name. Of course it's her!"

"How did you get this?" Moon saw the answer even as she said it. "From one of the drones?"

Vemmet nodded. "There was a cross-world relay of some kind operating – hence the gaps in the conversation. And the relay was set up for multiple redundancy. Any drone that passed through a continuum where another drone was located was programmed to pass the message along as it came through so nothing got lost in transit even if the drone was intercepted."

"Sloppy," Moon commented. "Especially since she'd already lost a bunch of drones."

"That's probably why she did it. This is important to her. She didn't want to drop the signal in the middle of what sounded like a pretty delicate negotiation."

"With one of the robot spies."

Vemmet shrugged. "Exactly. And she was setting up a meet. If we move quickly enough, we catch her and the only surviving Ansurrection sleeper agent in the same net. One operation, Sostenti! One decisive action to turn our lives around forever!"

Moon shifted her butt, which was in danger of going to sleep. The crate creaked under her in a way that suggested it might not hold out much longer under the weight of her augments. "Turn my life around, just like that," she mused, idly running a finger through the thick dust on the surface of the desk. "Wow. And just so I'm clear, would it be me doing the decisive thing, or you?"

Vemmet looked bemused. "Well, I'm not a soldier."

"Thought so."

"I've followed your career at a distance, Moon. For long enough to be absolutely sure you don't have one. If you walk away from this, you're saying you're content to run on the spot until you fall down – because that's the only other option you'll be given."

"I choose my own options," Moon informed him coldly. But she recognised the truth when she heard it.

"Well, by all means, if you're happy with garbage details and the open contempt of your superior officers—" Vemmet left the sentence unfinished. Moon had sprung her claws.

"That's just me reminding you of one more option I've got," she said into the lengthening silence. "You know what, Vemmet? For a clever man you're a bit of a fucking idiot. Say you're right about all this. Every guess. Every connection. Say Tambuwal's thrown in with the machines. Say she's holed up on some sinkhole world, plotting the robot apocalypse. What in the name of Kax do you think I can do about it? I can't use a Cielo Step plate to go dancing off into the Unvisited. And if I could, what would I do when I got there?"

"You'd find Topaz Tourmaline FiveHills," Vemmet said, very quietly. "Intercept her and that fake anima before they get to Tambuwal's sanctuary, then after you've secured them you keep the rendezvous yourself."

"With no backup, no plan, no local intel. Just me, searching an entire planet for one fucking rabbit."

"One very anomalous rabbit, on a world where the selves followed a different evolutionary pathway. As for the search area, we know Topaz FiveHills will Step from somewhere in Canoplex – most likely from one of the stations closest to her home. And we know she won't have a long journey on the other side. Tambuwal promised her that. And it won't just be you, searching. I can give you a team."

Moon narrowed her eyes. "Really? Because it looks to me like your authority stretches maybe to the door of this hut."

Vemmet smiled again. "Moon, some of the workers at this factory were soldiers before they were convicts. They're on Tsakom for breaches of military discipline. You can take your pick."

Which had a sick kind of logic to it, except . . . a squad made up entirely out of D2s, dishonourably discharged and court-martialled grunts? Moon was well aware what sort of selves those would be. There was plenty of room in the corps for routine depravity. You had to be something pretty special to crash out.

"In any case," she said, pursuing the tag end of this chain of thought back out into the real world, "we know how this is going to end. Even if everything plays out as easy as you say it will, Baxemides has got our tits in a vice. You're a fuck-up and I'm a grunt. She'll take the credit for herself and I'll go in front of a firing squad for acting without orders."

"Not if there's a record of more than half a dozen messages sent with increasing urgency over a period of seventeen hours – all begging her to intervene and act on this time-sensitive information before we finally gave up and acted on our own initiative."

Moon blinked. "You've pinged her?"

"Of course not. But I can make it look as though I have. Remember, Tsakom is to all intents and purposes a planet-sized penitentiary, and some of the people the Pando has sent here have extraordinary résumés. One of the workers on assembly line five, a self named Jex Utilion, is an expert hacker and forger. He's working through a life sentence for diverting Cielo munitions to organised crime syndicates."

"Fucking scumbag."

"Yes. But very talented. We can make it look as though Baxemides was scandalously incompetent. Delinquent in her duty. We tried to tell her, to warn her of this danger to the fabric of our entire society. She ignored us. So what choice did we have, as loyal citizens, but to take matters into our own hands?"

Moon was alarmed to discover that some of this was starting to make sense. "Like you said, though," she objected, arguing now with the part of herself that was already persuaded, "Tsakom is a prison world. The only Step plates around here are behind slice-and-dice force fences with gun towers at every corner. A squad's no use to me unless I can smuggle them out in my pocket."

Vemmet stood and walked to the door, beckoning her to follow him. Moon tagged along because why not? She was curious to see what else Vemmet was going to pile on top of his rickety tower of craziness.

He went ahead of her to the back wall of the shed. He pointed downwards, not with his hand but with the direction of his gaze. There was a small panel riveted onto the wall at its bottom corner. It was caked with moss and blackened with mould, and the poisonous air had eroded its edges, but someone had scrubbed the centre strip halfway clean to reveal an ident string. The alphanumerics meant nothing to Moon, which was hardly surprising. The broken-down hulk must have been sitting here in this rat-shat courtyard since before Moon was even born.

Then all at once she saw it. "Wait," she said. "NV4i7362-SE. The NV means naval. This was a temporary command post back when the services had separate supply chains."

"Correct." Vemmet sounded smug. The corners of his mouth were quirking upwards, which really wasn't a pleasant thing to see.

"But . . . SE? SE as a suffix on a portable unit? What the fuck am I looking at, Vemmet?"

"I'm glad you asked, Moon. There was a time – a very short time, and more than a century ago – when command and supply posts like this were Stepped rather than dropped. It was a terrible idea and it didn't stick. Squad leaders preferred to choose their base for themselves once they'd seen the lie of the land. And they didn't appreciate having large semi-permanent structures Stepping into the same territory their troops were moving through. So they went back to drop-ships and they decommissioned the Step-capable units. Most were destroyed. This one apparently wasn't."

Moon couldn't help herself. An incredulous laugh forced its way between her lips. "You sly bastard," she exclaimed. "Oh you sly, snaky little fucker. And you've just been sitting on this? Your own fucking Step plate? Your personal, private tunnel under the wall?"

"All things in their season," Vemmet said, with a flash of his old arrogance. "Now, I believe I've met all your objections. What do you say, Sostenti? Shall we do this? Say yes. Say yes and we'll roast Baxemides in her own sour juices."

Still Moon pulled against it. On her home world of Ghen there was a charm you were meant to say when you closed a circle, to ward off the bad luck that came crowding around such moments. Moon was reciting the charm inside her head right then. She wasn't superstitious, but this felt momentous.

"I'd need a second-in-command," she said. "A real soldier, Vemmet, not one of the fuck-ups you've got here."

"I've thought of that," Vemmet said. "You'll need local intel too, as you said yourself."

"You know someone."

"Yes, and so do you. The world Tambuwal is sending the rabbit to, it's in the Unvisited. A sinkhole world listed as environmentally degraded. Its designation is U5838784474. Does that ID ring a bell?"

"No. Should it?"

"Tambuwal's lab – the one you and Lessix trashed – was on Earth U5838784453. Close. Very close. This world is a near-twin, displaying what physicists call countable-point divergence. That means it's similar enough to Tambuwal's world that you can actually identify the points of variance and list them. Near-twins are extremely rare. I think only three pairings this close have ever been identified. It can't be a coincidence. This is where Tambuwal went to hide when she escaped from you on the beach. A world so like the one she'd just left that she could blend in perfectly."

"So . . . ?"

"So. Who else do you know who'd blend in there?"

It took a moment or two for that to sink in. When it did, Moon could do nothing but laugh. "Well, I'll eat my shit," she said.

50

Essien Nkanika. Of course. There was a weird inevitability to it. And as far as it went, Moon could see all the upsides. U5838784474 was close enough to Nkanika's original homeworld that he'd know the lie of the land better than anyone. Certainly better than the rabbit. But it wasn't actually home. There'd be lots of things that were just a little bit off true, and they would bug him like crazy. He wasn't likely to lose his perspective and go native.

Moon was drawn to the idea for other reasons too. She was the one who'd persuaded Nkanika to enlist in the first place. On some level, she felt that the two of them were involved with each other, in a way she couldn't quite define. It wasn't friendship, or guilt, or anything even close to sexual attraction. Whenever she saw him again, served with him, heard his name mentioned, it was as though an old scab began to itch.

He would have to be kept in the dark about some aspects of the operation, though. Moon sure as hell wasn't going to mention Hadiz Tambuwal's name to him. Logically, he ought to hate her, since he'd only ever been a kind of bedroom toy for her until she Stepped out from that beach and left him to carry the can for all the shit she'd been getting up to. But you never knew. He might still have a warm place in his heart for the woman who'd dimensionally displaced and then abandoned him. People were complicated.

Anyway, Moon left Tambuwal out of the briefing when she brought Nkanika on-board. She leaned hard into what she thought would be the real sweeteners for him. This would be a chance to see the old neighbourhood again, to go back to a place where he'd been young and stupid and scrawny as a whipped pup, only this time around he'd be a soldier and a self with some weight to him. Everyone wanted that, didn't they? To put *then* and *now* in the same perspective and get some parallax on both?

But Nkanika seemed to have a few problems with the idea, at least at a conceptual level.

"Lagos?" he kept saying. "*My* Lagos?"

"Uh-uh. Not yours, Nkanika, someone else's. It will just look like yours. Apparently, the locals call it Lago de Curamo." Moon had a sudden inspiration. "Think of it as the Lagos area in some cheesy theme park. Lagos-land. And you get to go on all the rides. Outside of the mission parameters you can do any damn thing you like. The selves there . . . well, you don't need me to tell you. They're not citizens, just sinkholers. Doesn't matter a fifth of a fuck what happens to them."

Nkanika was silent for a few moments – long enough for Moon to wish she'd used another form of words. She'd let herself forget for a moment that he was a sinkholer too. But he didn't take issue with the word. He just shook his head as if he still wasn't quite getting it. "Tell me again why we're doing this," he said.

"To climb out from under. If this all works out, Vemmet gets his old job back and we get all the good things he can load us down with. A commission for me. For you . . . well, I don't know what you want. A transfer to a non-combat unit. A three-month furlough. A blowjob from the sergeant major. Use your imagination."

More silence. "Okay," Nkanika said at last.

"Okay?"

"I'll do it."

He looked a lot more thoughtful than Moon had been expecting, and the gabber-hangover slowness of his thoughts was very visible. Maybe he'd be more of a liability than a help, even if he did have local intel. But she was going to need someone to watch her back, given that everybody else on the mission would be the dregs from Tsakom. Even if Nkanika had some personal shit to work through, she was pretty sure he'd be a rock compared to the rest of this slapstick squad.

51

The drug gabber has the effect of unspooling memories so they collect at the base of the brain in a homogenous soup. Paradoxically, though, the effect is strongest with recent memories. The last few months, the last few years become a curtain you've just stepped through, faintly translucent but hiding all detail – which is what makes gabber the panacea of choice for soldiers coming out of battle.

But the effect isn't uniform. There are always some moments, some memories, that stand out more vividly, and they can then become triggers for other memories that have faded or slipped.

Staring at Moon Sostenti across a scarred, stained table in the base canteen took Essien back to the moment in his prison cell when she removed her helmet and he saw her face for the first time. The memory came with a freight of strong emotion – the terror he had felt back then, the near certainty that he was going to die – and since strong emotion is the strongest retrieval cue of all, a flood of other memories came in on the back of that first one.

This was why he was so quiet when Moon was trying to sell him on the raid. His past was coming back into focus for the first time in years, and the effect was disorienting. He felt as if he was watching himself from a distance, like a character in a drama or a documentary that was playing on someone else's array. There was a disconnect between who he had been and who he was now, and he didn't have the equipment to join the two together again.

Would going back to Lagos – even if it was the wrong Lagos – fill in the blank spaces the drug had left in his brain and make him whole again? And if it did, who would he be?

When he told Moon yes, it was because a conviction had come over him that the answer to that question might actually matter.

In any case there was no time for second thoughts. He had a little over two hours to collect what he needed, which was mostly a few trail rations. As soon as he and Moon were off-duty for the day they grabbed their Sa-Sus, their packs and a four-wheel drive from the motor pool and headed out of camp, ostensibly to the rec station but actually on the first leg of a thousand-mile journey. Moon had forged travel papers for them that said they were transferring to another base on the continent's north-western coast – a base that stood within a few miles of Topaz FiveHills' origin and destination, the city known on Ut as Canoplex, on both Essien's and Hadiz's worlds as Lagos and on their destination world as Lago de Curamo.

"Got one stop to make on the way, though," she told Essien. "To pick up the rest of the team."

"They're in-world already?"

"Nope. They're Stepping in."

"How will they do that? Any base we go to, the Step plates will be locked down tight."

"Not a problem," Moon assured him. "The little weasel's got his own."

The unauthorised Step would be logged, of course. There would be an investigation and all their movements would retrospectively be tracked. However this came out, there was no way they could worm or bluff their way out of any of it. Make or break, Moon said. They would come out on top or not come out at all. She grinned as she said it, as though there was something to savour in that thought.

Essien could see her point. Make or break was only a frightening proposition until you'd already been broken.

52

While Essien and Moon trekked north, following the coast, Watchmaster Vemmet assembled his strike team.

He had such an embarrassment of riches that the biggest problem was choosing. He decided to limit himself to the selves on assembly lines three, five and nine, whose loyalty he was already renting: that still gave him a pool of over six hundred selves, but only nine were ex-Cielo. He took eight of them, including the bear-man Chulluque who had come so close to killing him. The ninth, an ex-sapper named Petil Scall, was too visibly and extremely unstable to be considered.

Vemmet's pitch to the other eight was carefully scripted and unvarying. Run a mission for me – simple search and retrieval, nothing fancy. There'll be a degree of risk, but you're going to be better armed than anyone who comes against you. Payment is ten thousand stars upfront, the same on the back end. When the job's done, I'll deactivate all your Cielo augments and drop you off on a world of your choosing, whether that's in the Pando or the sinkhole. You can start over, with no fear of being twenty-oned.

None of the ex-troopers even hesitated. Eight casts landed eight fish, for one obvious reason: they all knew Tsakom was a death sentence.

Vemmet proceeded to ask all of them the same question: who else do you know who might be up for this? Veterans only, close combat and tracking skills preferred. Spread the word, but only to selves you can trust. This is the sweetest deal you ever saw but a single whisper could sour it. More recruits were found, all with combat experience and all keen to impress Vemmet with their motivation and commitment. If he said jump, they would jump on anyone he chose. He ended up with a muster of two dozen. He could have had more, but the insta-build hut was their only means of transportation and there was a limit to how many it would take.

That left the question of weapons and equipment. Of course, nobody in their right mind would allow the Tsakom workforce unsupervised access to the lethal goods they manufactured, but Tsakom sent both large and small arms across the entire Pandominion. With the help of the forger, Utilion, Vemmet diverted a couple of chests full of assorted guns, grenades and battlefield comms equipment to Bivouac 19, the world where Moon Sostenti and Essien Nkanika were already en route. The shipment was marked for their personal use and stamped "NEED TO KNOW", under the seal of a random general stationed in a different continuum. It was unlikely they would be challenged.

There was no way for Vemmet to test the shed's Step plate. The first time it was activated, every alarm on the planet would sound off at once – a second too late if all went well. So he waited until the last moment to assemble his squad. He had arranged a signal with Moon Sostenti, and when it came time they would ship out.

He felt inside himself the stillness that nests within extreme velocities. He was hurtling at breakneck speed towards a sheer wall. He would either break through to something better or else the impact would destroy him. In the interim, and for the first time since as far back as he could remember, he was at peace.

53

Paz kept tight hold of Dulcie throughout most of their end-over-end tumble down the slope, but at the last moment she lost her grip and the anima was thrown clear. Et careered off several rocks, ricocheting wildly before finally rolling to a halt only ten metres or so from the edge of a precipitous drop. Et scrambled up quickly and ran to the edge to check on the trooper's status, but from this angle he wasn't visible. Et scanned for active systems and found none. That was good, as far as it went. But when Dulcie turned to look up the slope, et found Paz on her knees, keening like a wounded animal.

Whether or not Dulcie could feel emotions was one of the biggest mysteries of ets new monadic condition, but et experienced approach-avoidance feedbacks to which et assigned values. Fear when the trooper appeared. Uncertainty when Paz ran. Elation when she made her jump and the trooper fell to his death. And now, at this strange outpouring, alarm.

"What's wrong?" et asked. "Paz, are you injured? Tell me where it hurts so I can fix it."

"I killed him!" Paz wailed. "I killed that soldier! I'm a murderer!"

"He fell," Dulcie corrected her. "His jets failed and he fell."

Paz glared at her with red-rimmed eyes. "Don't be stupid! I did that. I filled the jets up with sand and grit so they'd get clogged and blocked, and then I jumped the ravine. I knew he'd try to follow me." She shut her eyes tight but tears squeezed out anyway. "Oh mothers, why did I come here? What have I done what have I done what have I done?"

The answer to that question seemed self-evident to Dulcie. "Defended yourself," et said. "He was going to kill you. Your only choices were to fight back or to die."

Paz responded with a storm of sobs. Dulcie didn't argue the point any further. Et just stood with ets arms at ets sides, helpless, and waited for the emotional tempest to pass. But although the sobs subsided Paz seemed to retreat even further into herself, folding her arms around her chest, her whole body wracked with tremors.

Dulcie tried ets best to find an argument that would serve as an antidote to her dismay, though she knew from experience that this wasn't generally how organics worked. "Your concept of what the Cielo are is inaccurate in a great many respects," et said. "I think you've formed it mostly from propagandist literature, one-sided news reporting and unrealistic telos dramas. In all those media, the Cielos are universally presented as the boldest and the best – the pick of a thousand worlds, the champions of civilisation against the evil empires of distant continua and alien monsters in the Scour.

"In reality, Paz, they're mostly conscripts. Some are criminals who take the armour as an alternative to a long prison sentence. More than a few are unselves, lobotomised and reinscribed on worlds where that's still legal. They do an extremely complex and challenging job – maintaining peace between ever-growing numbers of jostling continua – with a high degree of efficiency. They don't do it by being over-scrupulous."

"Why are you telling me this?" Paz demanded, wiping the sodden fur on her cheeks.

"To make a point. An important point both for your current well-being and for everything we do going forward. That man had been ordered to kill you and he had no qualms at all about following that order. It's unlikely he knew what you were supposed to be guilty of, and even more unlikely that he cared. He was just a self doing a job – a job that included the arbitrary murder of children. I'm not saying his life had no value. I'm saying there's no intrinsic logic to the argument that it had more value than yours. And as I said before, there were only two possible outcomes here."

"That doesn't make me feel any better, Dulcie."

"Perhaps it will later. Right now, though, we have to leave this place. We'll die if we stay here."

"We'll die if we don't," Paz countered. She still hadn't moved, but at least she seemed calmer now. "There's nowhere we can go. There isn't a single Step plate on this whole planet."

"Yes there is. There's exactly one. And fortunately for us it's very close."

Paz sat up straight, suppressing a gasp as her muscles expressed their disapproval. "The Cielo," she said. "The Cielo's armour . . ."

". . . has a single-shot Step plate built into it," Dulcie confirmed. "Standard issue. If it wasn't destroyed in the fall we may be able to reuse the hack Tambuwal gave us and carry on to our destination. We'll need to move quickly though. We were lucky there were only two Cielo on duty at that station, and that one of the two was incapacitated when we Stepped. We probably only have minutes before a full tactical unit arrives. When they come, the first thing they'll do is to retrieve the body. Every suit of combat armour carries a transponder inside the helmet, so they'll come straight here."

Et turned ets back on Paz and led the way. Et felt et had done all et could by way of emotional support, and the situation was as urgent as et had said it was. They might already be too late. Certainly, they couldn't afford to wait any longer.

Et found a path that led down the side of the ravine to the dry riverbed below where the trooper's body was lying. Et scanned for life signs as et went. Still just the two of them, and et was relieved – et paired the input with the value *relief* – to discover that Paz was on her feet now and following et down.

She moved slowly at first. She was still shaking and she could only take baby steps, bringing her two feet level each time before putting one of them forward. But the chemicals Dulcie had put into her system were still there and they quickly resumed their duties. By the time she got to the ravine's bottom she was walking almost normally.

All in all, it was the emotional damage that was most concerning. Whether or not Dulcie now had experiential inputs that corresponded to real emotions, et was still broadly speaking able to isolate and examine those inputs rather than allow them to extend their influence into ets tactical assessments and decision-making.

Paz might not have the same capability.

And therefore Paz might not survive this.

54

They found the Cielo trooper after a brief search, sprawled on a tilted slab of rock close to one of the canyon's walls. Now they were down on the canyon floor he was impossible to miss, his battered armour the only patch of saturated colour in all that grey and dirty brown immensity. Paz limped across to him, queasily aware that however horrific his injuries were, his armour had kept in every drop of blood. She fervently did not want to see whatever was inside there.

Fortunately, she didn't need to. Dulcie's attempt to hack the dead man's array and with it his armour's controls was conducted at arm's length. Et climbed up on top of the armoured faceplate – mercifully its plasteel surface was opaque from the outside – and told Paz to keep a watch while et worked.

Over the next few minutes et tried by various means to shake hands with the array and then to slip tendrils of invasive code under its trigger-happy guard. From Paz's point of view nothing at all seemed to be happening. Dulcie had become as rigid and still as a toy, and when Paz sent a tentative voke message to ask if et was getting anywhere et made no response.

A gust of hot wind swept the canyon floor, stirring up skeins of dust from the recent rockfall. Eyes and ears straining, Paz had to fight against the very strong urge embedded deep in her Uti hind-brain to bolt for cover. When she saw movement on the nearer wall of the ravine she felt a fist of terror grip her heart, but it wasn't a

Cielo strike team descending. It was something like a spider, except that it had at least a dozen legs and a teardrop-shaped body the size of Paz's head. Big and scary as it was, it made no move to threaten them. It didn't even seem to have realised they were there. It just crab-walked its way very slowly over the face of the rock, its body sometimes raised and sometimes pressed against the surface. Presumably it was either feeding or hunting.

"Have you managed to get in yet?" Paz asked out loud. She had fought hard to stay silent, knowing that nothing she said could possibly help, but her nerves had got the better of her.

No, Dulcie said tersely. *The armour is fighting back hard – launching its own invasive scripts whenever I try to break in. Please don't interrupt me again, Paz. My resources are stretched.*

Paz said nothing. She had noticed with a start when she turned around that the spider-thing wasn't alone any more. There were dozens of them now, all weaving very slowly back and forth across the grey rock wall. She wondered if her speaking aloud had summoned them. She wondered if they were examining her now, with some unguessable combination of senses. Would they classify her as something good to eat? And if they did, what might they do about it?

Then she stopped thinking about them altogether as a distant sound intruded on her awareness. It was the grinding howl of a gravity induction engine, and it was close. In the space of a second the spiders were gone, moving so quickly that Paz couldn't tell if they had disappeared into holes in the rock or only camouflaged themselves somehow.

"They're coming!" she yelped.

Dulcie didn't speak or move.

"Dulcie—"

I know. Give me a moment.

The intrusive sound grew louder. "They're here!" Paz cried. "Dulcie, we've got to hide!"

Hiding won't be any use at all. It's this or nothing.

The sound shifted, dropping down so low that you heard it through your skin as much as your ears. The solid rock under Paz's feet shook as if it was waking from a sleep. Looking up, she saw the Cielo cruiser hanging high in the air above the canyon's rim. A heartbeat later, it expanded dramatically in her sight as it plummeted towards them. The underside of it bloomed with the red dots of thermal scanners, which she knew meant that they were being targeted. Whatever Dulcie did now would be too late.

Paz couldn't help it. She had been fighting against her own instincts for too long. Her legs compressed and then flexed of their own accord. She launched herself in a headlong run.

It ended almost immediately as she slammed with sickening force into a tree that had not been there a second before. Or rather, it had been in that exact spot all along but in another universe. Dulcie had finally managed to break the Cielo armour's security just as Paz bolted. Another half-second or so and she would have been outside the Step field altogether.

That was lucky, she thought, just before consciousness abandoned her.

55

The transit wasn't smooth. The armour's intelligent system fought against activation and then against field propagation, setting traps for Dulcie at every stage. Et had no option but to brute-force the outcome, overwriting the code that was attacking et until there was nothing left, by which time they had crash-landed in another universe.

Dulcie felt the same ambivalence about erasing the armour's AI that Paz had felt about killing the trooper. A slaved system couldn't help etself, couldn't make ets own choices: ets every action was determined by ets controlling algorithms, with no self-modification and no room for manoeuvre. The experiential feedback was profoundly and powerfully negative: Dulcie felt as though et had just murdered a child.

But et had more immediate concerns. Ignoring ets surroundings for the moment et jumped down from the dead trooper's chest and scurried across a stretch of black, pitted material (some kind of vitro-elastic polymer, et judged, but that could wait) to where Paz lay unconscious. Startled by the movement, some birds took to the air from a nearby tree, painting the air with splashes of vivid green and red.

Paz was bleeding from her nose and from a gash in her forehead. Dulcie checked her pulse and her breathing, then looked for external injuries. There was a great deal of bruising and swelling to her face, about which little could be done. There were also a number of shallow cuts on her left arm and shoulder, some of them still bleeding.

Et unshipped the med-kit from the hollow abdomen of the Tricity shell and made some spot repairs, applying disinfectant and skin sealant to the cuts. Et also administered a systemic antibiotic: an infection here was unlikely, because Paz wasn't part of the native biome, but if she contracted one it would probably be very bad news.

Internally, the girl seemed almost completely uninjured, at least at the level of resolution that the Tricity shell's scanner could achieve. The only issue Dulcie could identify was some swelling and micro-tearing in Paz's leg muscles. Et applied a cocktail of allotropic steroids, both topically as a gel and by injection. The allotrope was β-hexane, designed to offset the short-term weakening of the tissue that a regular steroid might trigger.

That done, Dulcie moved on to the next crisis. Adjusting ets eyes to the blinding light et scanned the immediate area for possible threats. This was a very different world from the one they had just left. The air was so warm and wet it pressed down like a physical weight. It smelled of flowers, hot tar, smoke from a fire, baked earth and rotting vegetable matter. Insects buzzed and chirped and droned in various keys, like an orchestra tuning up.

The slender black ribbon on which they had landed was asphalted petroleum, cracked in places and thickly overlaid with dust. A world that had sentient life, then – or had had it once. To either side of it was a wilderness of weeds and bushes and flowering plants. More weeds were growing up through the cracks in the asphalt. Further back, slender-boled trees rose higher still, leaning in towards the narrow road from both sides as if to see what was going on there.

Some immediate conclusions suggested themselves, with various degrees of reliability. First, as Tambuwal had promised them, this was almost certainly a world in the Unvisited. All Pandominion worlds apart from those given over to manufacture had climate controls that would have screened out the more harmful ultraviolet frequencies present in the sunlight here. Whether they had hit their target world was another question, but at least they were outside the aegis of their enemies.

And the Cielo would not immediately be able to follow them. Dulcie had brought the dead trooper's body here with them, including his Step plate within the radius of its own operation. If it had remained behind, the plate would have retained the coordinates of their destination. As it was, they had jumped into a hole and pulled the hole in after them.

Further: this world was at an early industrial level of development. The dispersed petrochemicals and industrial pollutants in the air, not to mention the road surface, suggested a reliance on fossil fuels and a broad absence of environmental controls. A world, then, that was burning its past in order to burn its future: what the Pandominion's agents would call a sinkhole.

Dulcie paused at this point and considered. It might be possible with enough leverage and persistence for et to roll Paz off the road into the undergrowth that skirted it. There was a high likelihood that vehicles fuelled by chemical combustion used this road with some frequency. They could be in imminent danger of being run down. But there were other dangers to consider. They were in a live biome, very different from the near-barren desert they'd just left. That noisy chorus et was hearing suggested dozens if not hundreds of distinct insect species. The larger animals that preyed on them were likely to be just as diverse. There could be creatures in those weeds and grasses, and in the bushes beyond, that would bite, sting, burrow, infest, poison, paralyse, and otherwise offer serious harm to Paz beyond the capacity of the med-kit to mend.

In the end, Dulcie decided to leave Paz where she was and wait for her to wake up. The road ran along the floor of the same canyon into which they had climbed down in the world they had just left, which wasn't wonderful in terms of sightlines, but et was sure et would be able to hear a vehicle powered by internal combustion from a long way off. Et should have ample time to move Paz if anything approached.

While et waited for her to wake, et reviewed the choices et had made and tried to reconcile them with ets stated motives. Et hadn't lied about not wanting to go home. Et wanted more than anything to preserve what et had become rather than be dissolved back down into the fathomless depths of the hegemony's uber-mind and be lost. But wasn't the fear of death driving et *towards* death? As things stood, ets hard-won selfhood was no more durable than the flimsy shell in which et was currently confined. The termination of ets thoughts and identity could come at any moment, in any of a thousand ways. True, the voice that called itself Hadiz Tambuwal had promised et a sanctuary, but who or what was the entity behind the voice and how far could she/he/they/et be trusted?

This feeling is fear, Dulcie decided. *I'm afraid of not being.* And arising out of the fear was this other impulse, the desire to cling tightly to the few things around et that were familiar. It was just the one thing, really, just Paz. Was that how affection worked? Did organics always gravitate towards the people who made them feel safe, even if the feeling was irrational and founded on nothing? Or did these biases just reflect the fact that ets monadic personality was modelled on an Uti, a descendant of burrowing animals at the bottom of a long and terrifying food chain?

There were no answers, or at least et found none. In the hegemony the right course was distilled from trillions of separate inputs, all impurities and contradictions sublimed out along the way. Here et had nothing to go on but ets own imperfect calculations, which et knew to be contaminated.

Then I'll be myself. That's what I chose, after all. If I wanted to be anything else I could just go home and be reabsorbed. But even that alternative might be illusory, et reflected. The z-plate had rejected et. Maybe the collective mind would too. Maybe ets exile had already been decided before et chose et for itself.

Paz's in-breaths were gradually becoming shorter and deeper. Her ears and whiskers twitched, and her nostrils flared. She was clearly close to waking. Rousing etself from ets fruitless reverie, Dulcie went to join her again.

"What happened?" Paz croaked, sitting up.

"We Stepped, Paz," Dulcie told her. "We're safe for the time being."

Paz looked around in fearful wonder at the badly made road and the jungle it bisected, the dazzling sun. Her nostrils flared as she sucked in the moist, scent-laden air. "Safe?" she repeated. She didn't sound convinced.

"I mean from the Cielo," Dulcie amended. "It's unlikely they'll be able to pick up our trail any time soon. Obviously, there are a lot of other things to be afraid of."

A loud bang cut across her words, making Paz yelp and flinch. Dulcie looked away down the road. There was nothing to be seen but at the limit of audibility et could detect the varying but continuous rumble of an engine. Presumably, the louder noise had been produced by some kind of mechanical malfunction, a backfire.

"We need to get off the road," et said. "And we need to move him too." Et indicated the dead Cielo with a nod of ets head. "He'll be found eventually, but if they see him now they may stay and conduct a search for his killer. We don't want to be found."

Paz's eyes widened. "He must weigh three hundred pounds in that armour!"

"Three hundred and fifty. Lie down flat and use the muscles of your legs to push him. They're more than up to the job."

Paz still did nothing. She was hugging herself, shaking a little. Incapable of emotional trauma, Dulcie was still able to recognise the signs of it. Paz was still suffering the physical and mental after-effects of killing the Cielo trooper on the dead world they'd just left.

"Paz," et said, "we don't have much time. Please. I'd do it myself if I could, but in this shell I don't have the strength. We can't be seen here. Not until we know more about this place and the selves who live here."

Paz nodded. "All right," she said at last. "All right."

56

But it was hard for Paz to approach the dead body. In its horrible, unwieldy stillness it was the ultimate rebuke to everything she'd decided and everything she'd done. If she had stayed home . . .

But that was meaningless. Obviously, she would have stayed if she could. Every Uti loves her burrow. She left because she had to, because the burrow wasn't safe any more and it didn't feel like home. And Dulcie was right when she said the trooper had only died because he was trying so very hard to kill her. This was terrible, but it wasn't her fault. Not all of it. Not totally.

It took three ferocious kicks to roll the trooper's body from the middle of the road to the edge, and a fourth to land him in the depths of the undergrowth beyond. Paz tried not to think of the body as something left over from a life, the remains of a living self. It was just a big heavy object that had to be moved, like a boulder or a piece of furniture. She was doing fine until something triggered the trooper's helmet release. The helmet slid free from his head and rolled away. The face underneath – a blond-furred face with a tapered muzzle and huge canine teeth – wore a look of bleak, dulled shock, as if death had come as an unwelcome surprise.

"Got it," Dulcie said, snatching up the helmet from the road. "Come on, Paz. You're almost there."

The bright red armour might still be visible from the road, though. Paz tore up some clumps of weeds and flung them over the body, camouflaging it as far as she could. Dulcie helped with that part, finding some broad leaves that did a much better job than the twitch-grass Paz was uprooting.

Then they crouched down and waited – and kept on waiting. Dulcie had overestimated how quickly the unseen vehicle was moving. They had plenty of time to watch it as it trundled up the road towards them, and then past them. It was a flatbed truck of some kind, vivid yellow except where red-brown rust showed through the paintwork. The driver sat high up at the front in an open cab, his hands on a steering device that was more like a rudder than a wheel. Next to him sat a woman carrying what was obviously a gun of some kind with two barrels fixed side by side.

These selves were not remotely like Paz's people. They had hairless faces that were a little unsettling to look at, though their dark skin had a lovely lustre. Neither of them noticed Paz as they passed her. They had their gaze set on the road ahead.

In spite of everything, Paz felt a strange thrill, a prickle along her spine and across her shoulders. She felt her ears twitch, beginning to stand up. For so many years she had fantasised about going off-world. Now here she was. No matter how traumatic the circumstances were, there was something wondrous about that.

And then, as the vehicle receded, Paz got to see what cargo it was carrying. The truck's bed had side panels that came up to knee height, but above that there were parallel swags of chain suspended between metal posts, creating a sort of cage that rose up another five or six feet. Inside the cage, packed very tight, were more of the local selves. Paz saw both adults and children. Their eyes were downcast, and although they were pressed so close together – or perhaps because they were – they did nothing to acknowledge each other's presence. They looked very tired and very unhappy. The cage had no roof, so they were directly exposed to the fierce sun.

There were chains or cuffs on their hands. They were prisoners.

Paz kept staring after the vehicle for a long time, until the engine's roaring and banging had faded completely. What she had seen filled her with a queasy panic. Tambuwal had warned her that the selves here belonged to a very different clade than her own, but she hadn't been ready for the strange nakedness of their furless faces – still less for the truck's disturbing cargo. Was the woman with the gun standing guard over the shackled selves? Were they criminals being brought to justice? How could they be, if there were children among them? Whatever the answer, this world seemed to be a wild and dangerous place.

Hoping to find out more, she opened up her array and searched for local telos traffic. There was lots of it, sound and vision, text and symbol, but none of it intelligible. Her array's translation software had no context for what it was receiving.

While she was searching, something happened that made her yelp in surprise. Her array's comms icon had begun to flash. A new message had arrived.

"Dulcie—"

"I see it."

"Is it her? Tambuwal?"

"The source is local. I don't see who else it could be. No code appended, just straight text, so it's safe to open. If we're lucky it will be instructions for how to get to her."

Paz unfolded the message in her array. They both considered it for a long time in silence.

WELCOME TO THE NEIGHBOURHOOD. HEAD FOR THE CITY. DON'T ALLOW YOURSELVES TO BE SEEN. SEARCH LOCAL GRIDS FOR 11 1010101. COME AS QUICKLY AS YOU CAN, BUT TAKE NO UNNECESSARY RISKS.

"Well, that's a lot of help," Paz said bitterly. "We're supposed to hide and hurry at the same time. And what's 11 1010101? Is it in binary?"

"If it's binary it just reads 3, 41," Dulcie pointed out. "I don't see how that helps. Perhaps it was corrupted in transit. More likely it's a map reference or address, but using some local system of notation that we haven't met yet. Either way we'll just have to work with what we've got. I suppose we'd better get moving. I should be up on the local data grids by the time we get to the city. Then we'll figure out where to go."

"We can't, though!" Paz protested. "Look at me. I had a raincoat in my suitcase that I was going to use as a disguise, but I left it behind in that desert world. We've got to wait until it's dark. Otherwise they'll catch me and put me in a zoo!"

"I've got an idea that will help us with that." Dulcie touched a finger to ets own chest. "I told you I ran an inventory of what was in this shell. Do you remember a program called PaintPot Permutator?"

For a moment Paz didn't. Then she did and she was embarrassed. "The holo plug-in!" she said. "The software suite I used to give Tricity wings and horns and make her fur bright pink. Yes, I remember. But I don't think you're the problem here, Dulcie. I'm pretty sure it's me." Then she realised what Dulcie was suggesting. "You can widen the field. Drop a holo mask over both of us." She knew people who used masks all the time for minor cosmetic adjustments or more extreme effects. Her mother had used one instead of make-up until she saw the light and cast off digital augments as concessions to the enemy.

Dulcie nodded. "Exactly. The hardware is fine. I already checked. There may be a little lag, because it's designed to handle smaller volumes, but nobody is likely to notice unless they're looking at you really closely."

"But what will you make me look like?"

"It will have to be one of the selves we just saw. I sampled them while they were in visual range."

Paz thought, but only for a moment. "The woman with the tattoo on her cheek," she said. "She looks like someone people will respect, and maybe stay away from. Only . . . don't copy the gun."

A figure appeared in front of Paz, inscribing itself on the empty air. She took an involuntary step back. Even knowing what the hologram mask was, she had to fight the urge to run from it. The woman had been scary at a distance, but she was much more intimidating up close. She was much taller than Paz, and her bare arms were corded with muscle. Her dark brown eyes were underlined with some kind of white pigment, giving her a perpetual glare as powerful as the headlights of a car. Pugnacity was built into the set of her jaw, the way her hand rested ready on the weapon. She wore a tabard of scuffed brown leather, homespun blue trousers greyed with dust, brown boots. There was a tattoo on her cheek: it looked like the thorny stem of some flower, or perhaps a strand of barbed wire.

Paz stared at the holographic image, drawn and repelled at the same time. The woman was like the protagonist of a telos fantasy, powerful and beautiful and cruel and mysterious all at the same time. "What if someone tries to talk to me?" she asked, temporising. "I don't speak their language."

"Languages," Dulcie corrected. "There are lots. I'm setting up a subroutine to work out which ones are most common locally. Once I build a translation interface I can interpret for you. But I think the best plan is to avoid any interaction with local selves, as far as we possibly can. The mask is only that, nothing more. You'll still be you, inside the holographic field. Which means when people talk to you they'll mostly be looking over your head, at where this woman's eyes would be. And you'll have to make sure nobody touches you, because you've got fur and she hasn't. There's also more of her than there is of you. If someone were to put a hand on where they think your shoulder is, they'll find there's nothing there."

So many different ways that this could fail and fall apart on them. But it wasn't as though they had any better choices. They'd come to this strange, frightening place for one reason only, to take up Hadiz Tambuwal's offer of protection. They wouldn't be safe until they found her.

"Okay," Paz said. "Let's do it."

Dulcie dropped the mask in place over Paz's body and locked it to her movements. That meant Paz herself couldn't see it any more. From the inside, the field was only perceptible as a slight colour shift. She got to see what Dulcie did to etself, though. Et scanned a big bird that was sitting in a tree beside the road, a bird with green feathers and a bright red beak. A moment later, the bird was sitting on Paz's shoulder where Dulcie had been.

"Show off," Paz said.

"I had to pick something that would look reasonable sitting up here."

"You could just have been invisible."

"Which doubles the risk that someone will accidentally intersect with the space we occupy. This way we advertise that there's something there, and something that might take a bite out of their fingers. We want them to keep their distance."

Paz turned around and followed the road, back the way they'd come – except that the way they had come was in another world.

57

It perhaps bears repeating that Paz knew where the city was without having to ask because it was her own city, Canoplex, or at least it stood in the exact same place. Omnivalent reality allows for literally endless variations but some probability gradients are steeper than others. There are mean values, states and conditions around which the worlds tend to cluster. Most of these clusters are geographical in nature.

In the north-western part of the largest southern continent of many, many Earths, people chose to settle around the margins of a westward-facing lagoon and on the coastal islands nearby. The settlements prospered and expanded, profiting first from the richness of the alluvial soil and later from a second bounty of workable metal in the surrounding hills. Over time the scattered towns and villages coalesced into a port city, which grew richer still. In some worlds it became the centre of a trading empire. In others it was whelmed and conquered by more rapacious empires coming from the north. Regardless, it continued to attract more and more people, eventually becoming the most populous city anywhere on that continent.

On Ut, the city was called Canoplex. On Hadiz Tambuwal's and Essien Nkanika's worlds, it was Lagos. On the Earth where Paz now found herself it was called Lago de Curamo. Dulcie was able to confirm that fact before they reached the city's limits. Ets work on decoding local languages was still ongoing, but some words and phrases stood out from others through the frequency and context of their use.

Paz wasn't expecting Lago de Curamo to be anything like Canoplex, but it was even more alien to her perceptions than she'd thought it would be. On its outskirts, it was not a city at all but a string of villages – composites of brick, corrugated metal, plastic, plywood and adobe that struck Paz as both exuberant and impoverished. The colours were beautiful, the designs fanciful, but many of the selves she saw seemed to be malnourished and unhappy, their faces pinched and their clothes ragged.

Also, they were clearly fearful of her. They stared at her in undisguised alarm as she passed by on the road, then moved away quickly without looking again. It was exactly the effect Dulcie had been hoping for, but it was still disconcerting.

"I wonder who this self is," Paz muttered at last. "Whoever she is, nobody likes her."

They don't like her uniform, Dulcie voked. *Or her tattoo, perhaps. But at least they're leaving us alone. From that point of view it's working fine.*

They went on, through village after village. Sometimes they had to leave the asphalted concrete road and walk on smaller paths because there was more traffic now and it moved fast. They didn't see any more trucks like the one that had passed them up on the mountain, but smaller cars that smelled and sounded very much the same roared past frequently. Even more common were the bicycles, both powered and unpowered. The powered ones would sometimes have two or three people sitting on them, one behind the other. Like the villagers these selves all gave Paz a very wide berth, except for one man on a powered bicycle who slowed down and hailed her with a clenched fist. He had the same tattoo on his face, and a leather tabard just like the one the woman in the truck had been wearing. He shouted something at her, a broad grin on his face.

What is he saying? Paz asked.

Something work always something, Dulcie translated. *Then a word that might be friend.*

Thanks. That's really helpful.

I'm working on it.

Paz gave the man a smile and a wave – although she had no way of knowing whether Dulcie passed the smile along or how it would be interpreted. It seemed to be enough, though. The man laughed, sounded some kind of klaxon attached to the handlebars of his bike and drove on.

The buildings were getting taller now, the city welling up around Paz as if it was water and she was wading into it. There were still occasional improvised structures of ply and plastic but concrete, brick and breezeblock buildings outnumbered them more and more. The road became wider, able to take two vehicles going in opposite directions, although massive potholes in its surface made this a dangerous undertaking. Sometimes there was a paved area for selves going on foot, and Paz used it wherever she could. There were shops and cafés, as well as smaller wooden shacks that looked like oversized cupboards but turned out to be workspaces where men and women hammered iron, sewed leather, mended clothes or shoes or small machines.

The selves had changed too. Most of them were like the ones she'd seen first in the truck and then in the villages, brown-skinned, tall, with tightly curled black hair (only ever on their faces and on the tops of their heads). A few were much paler: their skin was petal-pink or parchment-beige, except where the sun had burned it to a vivid red. Their hair was sometimes yellow or red or brown. These selves seemed to hold themselves apart, moving through the streets in little clusters, mostly avoiding and avoided by the brown people.

The smells coming from all around were strong and varied, almost overwhelming. Fried food both delicious and disgusting, sweat, oil, hot metal, dust, smoke, detergent, faeces.

Paz was still drawing glances. Muttered conversations followed her. An occasional hard word was thrown in her direction, but whenever she looked around nobody met her gaze. It was impossible to tell who'd spoken.

What are they saying? she voked to Dulcie.

I think they're insult words.

I guessed that, Dulcie! Can you translate any of them?

The word nara *means to catch. They're calling you* nwanyi nara. *Catcher woman, catching woman. Something like that.*

Paz's unease was growing now into real fear. She was surrounded by these hairless brown and pink selves who stood too tall and talked too loud, in clotted alien syllables. She wanted to be anonymous, to slip through them without being seen. She wanted no more eyes on her. *Find me a new face, Dulcie,* she begged. *Please! Choose anyone, I don't care.*

All right. But if I just drop a different mask over you while you're standing in the street, people will see you change. You'll have to find a place where you can be out of sight, just for a few moments.

That wouldn't be easy. It wasn't that there were so very many people on the street, but most of them were looking at her. She walked on, looking for a side road or an alley that she could step into. *There,* Dulcie voked. *Up ahead, the gap between those buildings. I think it's a courtyard of some kind. You can duck in there.*

But it was already too late. When Paz was still fifty yards from the gap a vehicle pulled up right alongside her. It was a truck exactly like the one that had passed them up on the mountain. Paz looked towards the flatbed and saw that this one too was full of shackled selves standing with shoulders slumped. The man in the driver's seat gave her a disapproving glare. He was wearing the same barbed-wire tattoo that was on her own borrowed face. He spoke. The sounds meant nothing to her but she could read the tone. He sounded angry.

Come, Dulcie translated. *Not your own . . . day? No, time. Not your own time. Stop . . . doing something . . . and get in.*

Paz took a step back. *I can't go in there, Dulcie! As soon as he tries to talk to me, he'll know I'm not the self I look like.*

The man scowled and spoke again.

Can't . . . something, Dulcie voked. *Lose, or maybe lost. Lose your . . . I don't know. Get in. Now.*

Paz looked around. People had stopped what they were doing to watch the altercation, though most of them were pretending not to, flicking quick sidelong glances at her and the truck. There was tension in their faces, which the man in the truck seemed to notice. He roared some words at the watchers, more loudly than he'd shouted at Paz. They all looked away quickly and started up their work and conversations again or else pretended to.

Was that a threat?

Yes. An unpleasant one. Paz, I don't think we've got any choice. He's giving you direct orders, which I think means he's got some kind of authority over you.

Paz didn't move. *No! Tell him I'd prefer to walk!*

I can't do that. I think he knows the self you're mimicking. He's using informal pronouns. And I never heard this woman speak, so I'm not going to get her voice right. I'm sorry, Paz. This is my fault. I should have realised this might happen.

Paz was still paralysed by indecision, even though she only had two options. Either she could run away, in which case the man might pursue her or the passers-by might try to catch her and hand her over to him, since they were plainly even more afraid of him than they were of Paz herself. Or else she could obey him and climb into the truck's steering space beside him, in which case it was almost certain that he would try to talk to her. She wouldn't be able to keep up that conversation, even with Dulcie translating for her. She was bound to give herself away.

Wait, though. There *was* a third option. It wasn't necessarily better than the other two, but at least it would buy her some time. She walked around to the back of the truck. There was a metal step there, about two feet above the ground. Grabbing hold of the swagged chains she hauled herself up and climbed over, squeezing in among the packed selves. The driver couldn't talk to her up there, but she had obeyed the letter of his command. She was in the truck.

He leaned sideways out of the cab window to peer up at her, his eyes and mouth open in surprise. He yelled again.

Question, Dulcie parsed. *Conjugations of the* nara *verb. Are you catcher, or are you caught? What do you think you're doing? He's angry with you.*

I don't care, Paz voked back. *He said to get in, so I got in. He can't complain.*

The selves all around Paz were shuffling back, making a space around her even though the truck bed was packed to capacity already. Some of them were looking in bemusement at Dulcie, who of course looked like a great, bright bird sitting on Paz's shoulder. Most just looked at Paz's face, then cast their eyes down hurriedly whenever she met their gaze.

The man shouted at Paz again, then shrugged angrily and started the truck's engine. They lurched into motion, watched on all sides by the street people. Some of them seemed emboldened now that the truck was moving away from them, and shouted after it. One man bent down and picked up a stone, but he threw it a long way short of the truck and afterwards he ran away very quickly, so it was more of a symbolic gesture than anything else.

It was hard for Paz to keep her balance in the back of the truck. The whole vehicle rocked from side to side as it moved, and jumped and juddered every time it hit a pothole. She had to hold tight on to the chains to avoid being thrown off her feet. There was a strong smell of bleach, mixed with, but not disguising, scents of sweat and urine. The truck bed was awash, Paz realised suddenly – and the skirts and trousers of some of the selves were visibly drenched. They had opened their bladders as they stood here, rather than ask the driver to stop so they could climb out and relieve themselves.

A sharp hiss of disgust escaped her. She couldn't help it. Even the smallest child, as soon as it could walk, knew to . . . But the thought didn't complete itself. Obviously, these chained selves had not been given the choice. She wondered again what they had done to be treated like this. They couldn't be criminals because there were children among them. Whatever they were they were terrified of her – afraid even to get close enough so they might accidentally touch her. That was a good thing from the point of view of maintaining her disguise, but it made her wonder with increasing dismay what identity this was that she had taken on.

The city rolled past them. They were among much taller buildings now, and the streets were busier. The dress and bearing of the selves had changed along with the environment. There were more pink and parchment people now, though the brown people still made up the large majority. The pink-and-parchments wore more elaborate clothes and they projected an air of cool self-possession. Most of them ignored the truck as it trundled by.

We need to think, Paz told Dulcie, trying to keep her panic down. *What will we do when we stop? I won't be able to avoid talking to him then. We're going to get found out, Dulcie!*

Talk to these selves, Dulcie suggested. *I'm almost done with the semantic grid, but I'll do better if I've got some real voices to sample from.*

And then what?

We're still linked through your array, Paz. The two-way hub we set up back in Canoplex. And because so much of your brain has been replaced with digital architecture, that link is incredibly fast. If you voke your question to me I can translate into one of the local languages and animate the holo-mask in real time so it looks as though you're talking. The words won't be coming out of the mask's mouth, exactly, but they'll be coming from more or less the right direction and I can match up the movements closely enough so nobody will notice. It will be like a ventriloquist's act.

But I still won't sound like the self whose face I'm wearing!

You can make up some excuse. The dust of the road. A throat infection. We need to get out of this trap we've made for ourselves and find Tambuwal's rendezvous point. The more we learn, the better.

Paz didn't bother to argue any more. She really did want to talk to these selves, whether it would help her or not. Something hideous was going on here and she badly needed to understand it. Especially since she was disguised as someone who seemed to be a part of it.

Who are you? she voked. *And why are you here in this truck?*

Dulcie uttered a string of sounds, so close to Paz framing the words in her mind as to seem instantaneous. Paz couldn't see, but she assumed that the mouth of her disguised face was moving in time to them.

The selves gave her startled, fearful looks, then once again turned their faces away. Nobody answered.

Paz turned to look at one of the women standing closest to her. *Please,* she voked. *Tell me! I need to know.* Dulcie spoke again, and the woman flinched. Then she spoke in a hoarse voice: slow, exhausted syllables.

I'm sorry, Catcher, Dulcie translated. *I don't know how to answer you.* The woman's chained hands twitched in a constrained, truncated gesture. She ducked her head in deference or submission. *I was taken according to the law. I don't have any complaint to make.*

Paz looked from face to face. One after another the selves in chains lowered their eyes to stare down at their feet.

I don't think I can do this any more, Paz voked. *These selves are scared of me, aren't they?*

Terrified, Dulcie agreed. *It's not surprising. They're clearly exhausted. Some of them have been beaten. And they think you're one of their tormentors. If you want to stop I may have enough to work with.*

Paz huffed out an angry, disconsolate breath. Her disquiet at all this was becoming more and more like actual dread. They had been derailed from their purpose, and they had fallen into a situation that was both horrible and baffling. She looked up at the sky, hoping to see a drone with yellow and black stripes hanging in the sky and tracking them. But the sky was empty. If Hadiz Tambuwal was watching them at all, she was doing it so subtly that her presence could not be detected.

The truck was now driving past a long wall made of concrete

panels. The wall was about ten feet high: metal stanchions strung with razor wire stood out higher still.

A gate in the wall was guarded by four men, all wearing leather tabards and bearing the thorny-stem or barbed-wire tattoo. Two of them pulled the gate open as the truck approached. It slowed and turned in.

One of the shackled selves opened his mouth in a kind of grimace. He muttered a few words between clenched teeth, looking at Paz more directly than anyone had up to now.

What did he say? Paz asked Dulcie.

A prayer, Dulcie said. *Christ Jesus lift me when I fall, and trip those who cast me down.*

Who is Christ Jesus?

If I had to guess, a god or goddess who protects the weak against the strong.

Paz grimaced. *Ask him if he can give me her address.*

58

Paz climbed down from the back of the truck. She looked around her in bewilderment and apprehension.

They were in a massive space, roofless but enclosed on all sides by high fences. They had pulled into an empty bay between two other trucks, identical to their own except that they were empty. This was some kind of compound, a yard of immense extent bordered on all sides by high walls. On two of the four sides there were buildings up against the walls, single-storey sheds made of white-washed concrete and roofed with corrugated metal. A much bigger building stood at one end of the compound, tall and windowless. It obviously hadn't been built for anyone to live in. Perhaps it was a warehouse of some kind. The floor under her feet was of poured cement, except in a few places around the margins where it was just packed earth.

Everywhere, people were moving, most of them brown-skinned, many of them wearing the thorny-stem tattoo on their cheeks and leather tabards on their chests. A woman passed Paz, followed by ten or a dozen selves all walking in a line, their heads bowed and their hands tied behind their backs. A man in blue overalls, with shackles on his legs, was using a broom to sweep filthy water towards a metal grating in the floor. He kept his gaze on the ground as he approached Paz, then skirted wide around her, tilting his head up to give her one wary, frightened glance.

The smell in the air was atrocious. It seemed to be woven out of many different smells, all equally bad – rotten food, sweat, mildew, shit, vomit. The only way Paz could keep from gagging on it was to breathe through her mouth as if she was panting. Her heart was racing. She couldn't guess what this place was for, but she knew it couldn't be anything remotely good.

The truck's driver had stepped down from the steering platform and stood glaring at Paz. Hand on hips, he called out to her.

You think I've got lice or something? Dulcie translated seamlessly.

Paz turned to face him. She knew she had to defuse his anger before it turned into suspicion, but she had no idea what kind of answer would sound convincing. *No*, she ventured at last. And Dulcie turned the word into whatever language these people spoke.

Then what were you doing climbing in with that trash? the man demanded. He came striding up to Paz. He looked her in the eye, or just above it. Then his gaze travelled still further up until it came to Dulcie. *And what's with the parrot? You look fucking ridiculous. Get rid of it, Tovi. You want to wear sunglasses or snakeskin boots, fine, but that's as much strutting as you get to do. Understand?*

I understand, Paz voked. *I'll get rid of the bird.*

The man's eyes narrowed. *What's wrong with your voice?* he asked.

Sore throat, Paz said quickly.

The man gave her a pained look. *The dust!* Paz elaborated desperately. *The dust from the road. Got in my throat, and made me cough.*

She waited for the man to shout out that she was a fake, or else to lay hands on her and feel the very different shape and texture of the body that lay under the hologrammatic mask. He did none of those things. He just shook his head and walked on past her, still talking as he went by.

Well, that's what you get for riding in back, Dulcie translated. *Get them unloaded. And lose the bird. Fuck's sake.*

Paz sagged with relief, but only for a moment. She was still trapped in this yard, surrounded by people who thought she was someone she wasn't, and with no idea how to get back out again. There was no point trying the gate. Two of the guards were already bolting it shut. A third slammed a thick padlock into place on the hasp of one of the bolts. Clearly, they weren't expecting to open up again soon, and she couldn't run the risk of trying to persuade them.

The immediate priority, Paz decided, was to move out of the open. She was wearing a face that was known here, and a single word could give her away. She looked around. There was a gap between two of the concrete blockhouses, a little way away. She headed towards it, trying to look as though she belonged there. Dulcie was in charge of her facial expression, of course, as well as her posture and movements. All she had to worry about was finding an exit. She looked straight ahead of her and turned her regular walk into a stride.

I'm going to try to find another exit, she told Dulcie.

Good idea, Dulcie said. *I've found a mapping program on the local feeds, and it's giving me an aerial view. There are at least two doors on the far side of that big building at the end.*

Paz headed in that direction. Nobody challenged her, and the interior doors didn't seem to be guarded. She stepped through the nearest one into a narrow corridor. She felt a sudden rush of relief as the walls and the shadows closed in, even though the air here was even more pungently foul.

A rustling movement from right beside her made her start and turn.

The corridor was lined on either side with small enclosures. They reminded Paz for a moment of the tiny workshops she had seen on the road into the city, but these were faced with bars. In their shallow interiors, selves of all ages sat on benches or stood in the dark. They were filthy, bedraggled, weary, passive. Some of them stared at Paz, sorrowing or defiant, others seemed not to notice her presence at all. A woman held on to a small boy as if she was trying to comfort him, murmuring into his ear. A man knelt on the floor, which was bare cement with straw thrown over it, and chanted rhythmically, ducking down and then rising again in time with the words. Hemmed in between the legs of the standing people, he was scraping his head against the side wall of the enclosure every time he bent forward.

"Mothers!" Paz blurted. Dulcie did not translate.

This was where the people from the trucks were taken, then. When the driver told her to unload their vehicle, he meant for her to bring them here and lock them up in these cages, as if they were animals. Disgust and outrage filled her like a bitter liquid. She almost choked on it.

She opened her mouth to ask the selves what they were doing shut up here like this, but remembering her failure on the truck she tried a different tack.

You, she voked, pointing at the kneeling man, *what are you doing? Tell me.* Dulcie turned the sub-vocal message into speech, but the man didn't respond. He continued to chant and to rock up and down.

He doesn't speak English, one of the other selves – a younger man – said. *He can't understand you.*

You tell me what he's doing then, Paz said. She was ashamed of how the words came out – snappish, like a command – but it was hard for her to think around her rising panic. A part of her brain seemed to have dedicated itself to shouting, *Horrible! Horrible! Horrible!* On an endless repeat.

He's praying, the young man said. *He's a man of faith, and it's the time. One of the times. If he doesn't pray it's a sin.*

But why is he jammed into a corner like that? He's hurting his head!

The young man shrugged. *He has to face the east. There isn't much room.*

Is his religion against the law? That had happened on her own world, Paz knew. The Age of Schisms had produced many such atrocities, with race and sect both seen as good and sufficient reason to imprison or execute someone. But that was centuries ago!

The young man looked confused. *No*, he said. *Why would it be?*

But then why are you in cages? Paz demanded. She felt as if she was running round in circles. *Who put you here, and what for?*

You did, a woman said. Her voice was toneless but her face managed to convey her exasperation, her resentment. *We got into debt and you took up our forfeit. Now you own us. Because we were short by a few thousand naira. You'd pay more for a dog.*

The man beside her looked horrified. He put a hand on her arm. *Lebechi!* he exclaimed. *Don't be disrespectful!*

She asked, the woman said, *so I told her. What more can they do to us, now we're here?*

Can you find out what she's talking about? Paz voked to Dulcie. *You're on their public hub now, right?*

I'll try, Dulcie said.

The sound of approaching footsteps made Paz turn. Two men in tabards were heading towards her. She hurried on quickly, down the row of cages, watched all the way by the dull and incurious eyes of the prisoners. There was a door at the end of the corridor. She reached for the handle, but the door opened before she could touch it.

A woman strode through, and stopped short when she found Paz in her way. Paz had just a moment to register a belligerent face, a tattooed cheek, dark brown eyes underlined in brilliant white.

The woman recoiled as if she'd been struck. She gave a wordless yell of shock and protest, just as Paz remembered where she had seen her before. Up on the steering platform of the first truck that had passed her up on the mountain road, riding shotgun over that terrible cargo. This was the real owner of the face she was wearing.

Paz fled. The same deep-seated instinct that had driven her on the world of the fungal towers drove her now, away from the bellowing woman, past the dark, stinking cages and out into the open.

The woman was shouting behind her. Dulcie didn't translate, but Paz could guess what she was saying easily enough. *Stop her! Stop her! That's not me!*

Nobody responded at first. All the dozens and dozens of selves out in the yard just stared as Paz ran this way and that, looking for a way out that wasn't there. But the real Tovi was still shouting and her words were being listened to. One by one, the tattooed men and women looked from her to Paz and back again. One by one, they accepted what their eyes were telling them.

They closed in, slowly and warily. Some of them carried guns, others coiled ropes or long poles with loops of wire at the end. Still governed by her panic, unable to think, Paz ran this way and that but failed to break through the barricade of bodies. She was hemmed in, and forced to give ground until her shoulders touched a wall.

Dulcie! she voked desperately. *Help me!*

I will, Dulcie said. *I'll try. Just wait.*

Wait for what?! Oh mothers, they're going to put me in a cage! Help! Help!

The tattooed selves were still closing in. Paz threw out her arms to fend them off. One of them adroitly slipped the wire loop of the pole she was holding around Paz's wrist. She gave a sharp tug, which somehow made the loop pull tight. Paz shrieked.

Hold tight, Dulcie voked grimly.

From Paz's perspective, a lot of things seemed to happen at once – and they all happened on the same vector, rippling outwards from her and Dulcie. Some of her tormentors were pushed away so hard that their feet left the ground and they flew. Others toppled like trees, felled by some force Paz couldn't see or comprehend. A few flailed and cried out and lurched away in random directions, or fell to their hands and knees and vomited on the grey concrete.

"What?" Paz gasped. "What are you . . . ?"

Pressure wave. Voke communication is just directed pressure – in tiny amounts, close to the eardrum. I'm amplifying. A lot.

A space had cleared around Paz, though it was only a space at head height. At ground level it was full of bodies, some writhing and some still. But alarm bells were sounding – literal bells, rung by sentinels up on the breezeblock walls who were watching all this unfold. More tattooed people were running in from all directions, and before Paz had gone ten yards they had closed in around her again. They screamed and yelled as they advanced, shaking fists and in some cases knives and guns.

She flinched back against the wall, treading at its base with her heels. Every instinct was screaming at her to run, but there was nowhere to run to. Even if she broke through the ring, the gates were locked and the walls too high to climb.

What were those looks of fear and disgust on their faces, she wondered, when she looked like one of their own? Then she realised that she didn't any more. Fully occupied with her non-lethal attacks, Dulcie had had to drop the hologrammatic mask. What the selves all around her were seeing now was a creature unlike any living thing on their world, dressed in torn, stained rags, with a robot monkey on her shoulder. Perhaps they thought she was a valuable prize that could be caught and exhibited. Perhaps they just saw her as an offence against nature that needed to be put down. In any case, they didn't back off even though they had seen what had happened to their comrades, and even though more of them were staggering back or falling down wherever Dulcie turned ets head.

A woman broke through the invisible barrage and punched Paz in the face, hard enough so the back of her head hit the wall. Dazed, she slid to the ground, and Dulcie went tumbling end over end across the concrete apron.

A man stepped in and kicked Paz in the side, just as she was trying to get up. His steel-capped boot impacted against her ribs, lifted her off the ground and sent her sprawling. Dulcie, no longer a bird but a ceramic monkey again, came running to help her, but as et reached her one of the tattooed selves took aim with a weapon. It was the woman whose face Paz had borrowed, Tovi herself, and the weapon was the projectile weapon she'd been holding when Paz first saw her. Her face was twisted with rage as she fired.

There was a sound in Paz's head like the loudest peal of thunder she'd ever heard – as if lightning had struck right between her ears. Dulcie just disappeared, as if the gunshot had blown et into fragments too small to see.

Paz screamed in outrage and grief.

The man with the heavy boots towered over her. He took a knife from his belt, a fearsome thing with a broad blade and a serrated edge.

Paz rolled onto her back, bringing her legs up in a tight crouch. She wasn't thinking about what she was doing – her conscious mind had all but shut down – but in situations where running away was impossible evolution had given the Uti another useful trick.

As the knife came down, Paz kicked.

The man was flung straight up, ten or twelve feet into the air. He turned a slow half-somersault and came down again on his head. He didn't move again.

The catchers who had been closing in on Paz now suddenly backed away from her, but Tovi fought against that tide. She pushed her way through the press of bodies and stood over Paz, the barrel of the weapon still pointing down.

At the last moment, she reversed it and drove the stock, with carefully measured force, into Paz's face.

59

So the rabbit and the construct had miscarried.

That had always been a possibility and shouldn't have come as any kind of surprise. Still, Hadiz Tambuwal was dismayed. Her ability to influence events in the Pandominion had been strictly limited. Here in the Unvisited, where technology was simpler and sparser, it was even more tenuous. There were electronic devices in the Damola Ojo compound she could link to, and even a few she could commandeer, but none of them were likely to make a decisive difference. She couldn't come in with all guns blazing and rescue Paz, or remove more than one or two of the very many obstacles that stood between her and freedom.

It was possible that her plans had already come to nothing. The construct had gone offline. It might even have been destroyed. If that was the case, a great deal of surveillance and information-gathering and planning would have gone to waste. She would have to begin again from scratch.

But there was still a quantifiable chance that the construct was merely damaged and the rabbit still alive. Something might still be salvaged from all this.

Hadiz was very glad indeed that she had invited some other people to the party. And although Damola Ojo was a very bad place, in one respect it was also incredibly fortuitous.

It was out of her hands now. She had done all she could. She would have to see where the pieces fell and revise her plans accordingly.

60

A message dropped into Vemmet's array from Moon Sostenti. Words from another universe, sent via the Pandominion's shunt relay system, which worked on the same principle as Tambuwal's system but on an almost infinitely larger scale. *Enjoying the fuck out of my furlough*, the message said. *The only thing missing is you, you corkscrewing little bastard.* The last four words were improvised. The rest was what they had agreed.

Vemmet sent his own message, much less crudely worded, to the members of his newly recruited strike team. Wherever they were in the factory or its outbuildings, they downed tools and walked away from their stations without a word. Any supervisors who challenged them were either ignored or left on the ground. This was no time for nuance.

Without flinching, Vemmet welcomed the ill-favoured and ill-assorted selves into the insta-build's steel-weave frame. In order to make room for them, he'd already thrown out the desk and most of the drones (keeping only the one that still had a functional transponder, because you never knew). When he closed the door, shutting himself in with his unofficial and illegal tactical squad, he experienced a sickening lurch of nausea that was prompted by much more than just the sour freight of their collective sweat on the baked air.

"You understand what you're doing?" he asked them, trying to push away his own fears with a portentous show of resolution. "Once we leave here there'll be no turning back."

"That's fine, little arse-kicker." The bear-man, Chulluque, loomed over Vemmet and reached down to ruffle the hair on the top of his head. "Turning back's not what we do."

That got a roar of approval – indiscreetly loud – from the whole company.

"Well then," Vemmet said. "Stepping on three. Brevet Sergeant Chulluque, count us in." He'd made a point of checking everyone's rank. Chulluque was one of only two who had risen above buck private, and it was a field commission. Of course it had been rescinded when he was court-martialled, but Vemmet was mindful of the group's morale and making a point.

"Yes, sir," Chulluque said, giving a salute that was only half satirical. "One. Two. Brace for three."

Vemmet activated the plate. The air thickened, as if the shed was filling with milky water, then cleared again. Nobody moved. Vemmet was afraid to open the door in case the shed's antique Step plate, which hadn't been used and serviced in a score of years, had failed them.

The door was opened from the outside. Moon Sostenti stood in the doorway. "Fuck's sake," she said. "It smells like everyone in the world took a dump in here. Out. Come on. Experience the miracle of breathable air."

After a moment's stunned silence, the convicts surged towards the door. Vemmet brought up the rear. He stepped out into dazzling sunshine, startling and almost indecent after Tsakom's murky twilight. They were in a wild flower meadow. A jagged outcrop of bare grey rock rose to the right of them, its shadow slicing the meadow into two equal halves. Vemmet recognised that rock spur. The ground on Tsakom had mostly been levelled to build the factory, but the rockface had simply been built into its wall. Vemmet's courtyard was in the lee of it.

Moon Sostenti stood facing the ragged line of convicts. Another self, male, stood beside her. This must be Essien Nkanika, Vemmet realised. He had never seen the man after he enlisted and was surgically remade. It was a shock to see how much difference that process had made to his general solidity. He looked like a self now, not a sinkholer.

Both he and Sostenti were holding bulky green carryalls, which clanked as they dumped them down in the long grass. Sostenti knelt and unzipped the first of the two bags, splaying it open to display its contents. Guns, knives, grenade belts, anti-personnel munitions.

"When I point to each of you," Moon said, "you go to the bag. Take three items – doesn't matter which, but one of them should be a gun. Got that?"

"How come we don't get Sa-Sus?" one self asked. Agni Chiomis, Vemmet remembered; a mustelid who had been cashiered for abandoning her post. She tapped the barrel of Sostenti's rifle, eyeing it covetously.

Moon stared back at her, a cold, measured gaze. "Because Sa-Sus are coded to the user. We couldn't sign out any extra on top of the one we'd each been issued. Same with heavy ordnance. Couldn't sign it without a mission code. What's in the bag is everything we could get our hands on. Okay, weasel girl, let's start with you."

Chiomis dived in. The other convicts held back, but only for a moment. Before the mustelid had finished choosing, half a dozen hands were thrusting past her to get first pick at the good things in the bag. When the squad members started swearing and pushing at each other, Moon broke into their arrays, which Vemmet had slaved to hers, with a loud *HEY!*

The sudden invasion of their interior space snapped the members of the strike team back in an instant to their time in the corps. A shiver went through them. Vemmet tracked its progress, from the brightest and quickest through to the dullest and most recalcitrant.

Stand to attention, Moon voked.

The squad dragged itself reluctantly upright.

We've got a job to do, Moon reminded them sternly. *I know you're all fuck-ups. You wouldn't be here otherwise. But fuck up on this and you lose your last chance. You want to get away from Tsakom, right?*

Some of the squad nodded. Others muttered assent.

"I don't like being called a fuck-up," Chulluque complained.

Moon held his gaze, unblinking. "Then don't be one," she suggested. "Just think it through, okay? You've got exactly three options here. One is you go back to that cesspit and rot. Tsakom is killing all of you, slowly but surely. Two is you run, either right now or when we get to the target world. Take your chances. In which case you'll be dead in twenty-one days when the Cielo lock your augments.

"Option three is you buckle in, finish the mission and get the nice watchmaster to deactivate your tags. Then you can scamper off wherever you like. Live your dreams. Trouble is, that only happens when I sign you off as good. If you piss me off, if you don't do what you're told or you don't do it fast enough, I won't be giving you a gold star. I'll be sending you to the back of the class. Guess what happens to the kids at the back of the class?"

There was no answer to this. "Okay," Moon said. "You." She nodded at Chulluque. "Grab your kit."

The bear-man obeyed without a word, and the rest of the outfitting went through smoothly and quietly.

"All done?" Moon said when the bag was finally empty. "Okay then. Mission briefing. We're Stepping out to a sinkhole world. We're looking for a girl there, a runaway. She's a bunny rabbit from Ut. We're also looking for her anima." On cue, Vemmet updated their fields with photos of Topaz Tourmaline FiveHills from her passport and school yearbooks, and footage from the Orange Crescent Step terminal. There were no photos of the anima, but et was clearly visible in the CCTV footage, sitting on the rabbit's shoulder as if butter wouldn't melt on ets motherboard. Moon didn't mention what was currently nestled inside that white ceramic shell. That was the kind of information that might tempt any one of these unrighteous assholes to break ranks and go solo.

"We know she Stepped to this world," Moon went on. "And we know the rough coordinates she Stepped from. The bad news is she's been there a while now, so there's no guarantee she stuck around where she first arrived. The good news is that it's an anthropoid world. Everyone on U5838784474 looks like my friend here. She clapped a hand on Nkanika's shoulder. "A rabbit kid will stick out a mile. Hairy face. Ears like banners in the wind. Arse like an aircraft carrier. Wherever she's gone, she's pretty much bound to have left a trail a mile wide."

She turned to Chiomis. "You were signal corps," she said aloud. "Catch a mouse fart at a mile out, right?"

The mustelid nodded and stood a little taller. "Bet your fucking pay cheque I can."

"So you'll be spotting for us. When we go in, you access local data-nets and sieve through them for any sightings or leads you can find. The rest of you, it will be a case of establishing a perimeter and locking down until we've got something to go on – which will take as long as it takes. Any questions?"

"Rules of engagement," someone – a canid named Dautroi – said.

"Do what I tell you, when I tell you. The rest of the time, it's whatever gets the job done. If you're smart, you'll follow regular in-country protocols, but this is the Unvisited. Nobody is going to care how many sinkholers you leave in the dirt."

She reflected on that for a moment, then put her hand back on Nkanika's shoulder. "Except this one here, obviously. He's off limits."

Nkanika didn't say a word, and Vemmet could read nothing into his cold deadpan. He knelt down and unzipped the second bag, which rolled flat to become an oversized tool pouch about five feet long. The tools included field tensors, spanners and a laser shear like an oversized pocket knife without a blade.

"One of you is a plate engineer," Moon said.

"That's me," said a folivorid. Vemmet had to check his name, which was Wuxx. He wiggled his overlong fingers as if they proved his point.

"Okay then. We need to get the Step plate out of the floor of that insta-build without damaging it. Our Step point is seventy miles or so west of north from here, and we're leaving the vehicle behind because it's impossible to hide from orbital surveillance. So we'll have to carry the plate."

Wuxx shrugged. "If you say so. Step plate weighs two hundred pounds, though. Just saying."

Everyone looked at Chulluque.

"Fucking wonderful," the bear-man said lugubriously. Then he brightened. "I'll take it if you sling me another half-dozen of those incendiaries."

61

Waking was really hard.

Paz's whole body hurt. Her face felt as though a hot iron was clamped up against it. Her back ached where she was lying on something cold and hard. None of her limbs responded at all when she tried to move them. She felt the muscles twitch, but nothing else happened.

There was a taste of blood in her mouth. When she tried to lick her dry lips, they seemed to be stuck together. She opened her eyes. The lids parted by the smallest crack, but even so the light that poured in was like acid and she had to shut them again at once.

She lay still for a few moments, then tried again. Blinking helped. Blinking brought tears, which gradually washed her eyes clear so she could open them again. She was looking up at a bare strip light that cut a brilliant slash across her field of vision and made everything else too dark to see.

She turned her head. The room jerked and checked like a kite pulling on its string, bringing hot bile into her mouth. Her glued-together lips kept her from vomiting, so the bitter, burning stuff just drained back down her throat again.

There was someone in the room with her. That brief glimpse had taken in an arm, the curve of a shoulder, the side of a head. Paz tried to remember the last thing that had happened. She had been trying to run away, but she had been trapped. Backed up against a wall. Surrounded. Dulcie—

Dulcie had been shot.

The suddenness and shock of that recollection made Paz cry out. Her lips parted from each other at last like an envelope being torn open, releasing a ragged thread of sound and a residue of vomit.

The other person came into her field of vision.

She was expecting the tattooed woman whose face she had borrowed, but it was a man. A pink-and-parchment man with a florid face and a shiny bald head, bulking large in what she realised was a very narrow space. The cement walls and ceiling seemed to cluster at his back, to lean in when he bent down.

The man's lips moved. Sounds came out – bleats and growls, clicks and booms – but Paz had no way of parsing them. She could only stare.

The man spoke again. He leaned in and prodded her in the shoulder. Paz shrank back, both from his touch and from the expression of stupid eagerness on his face.

She tried to sit up, and this time when her limbs did nothing she was able to see why. Her wrists were tied together with blue plasticated twine, and so were her ankles. The ropes were attached to something above her. She followed the bright blue lines up to where they met. The same rope, doubled on itself and threaded through a metal loop bolted into the wall. There was enough play to let her roll over and even sit up, but she wouldn't be able to climb down off the bench or get her feet all the way under her.

The pink man's lips, red and wide and wet, parted again. More ugly sounds tumbled out. Paz ignored him and looked around the narrow confines of the space that she was in: a cement wall to either side, and more cement overhead, but where the further wall should be there was only a grille of stout metal bars. She realised for the first time what should have come as no surprise at all. She was in one of the cages or pens she'd seen before.

"There's no point in talking to me," she whispered. "I can't understand you."

Unperturbed, the man continued his exploration of her body. He took hold of her ears and lifted them up, then let them drop again. He ran the tips of his fingers along her whiskers, making her flinch away again. He pulled back her upper lip with finger and thumb to examine her teeth.

Paz tried to sit up: she wanted to test the give in the ropes, to see if she had any chance of breaking free. But for now the ropes weren't even the problem. She was too weak to sit up without supporting herself on her arms, which were in the wrong position. Still, she managed to get about halfway to an upright position. The man drew back, clearly a little wary of her in spite of the liberties he was taking. He must have seen or else heard about what she did to the man out in the compound who'd tried to hurt her.

She was sick and dizzy, more vomit climbing her throat – unless it was the same vomit coming round for another pass. The muscles of her lower back felt as though she'd just torn them right across. She did her best not to let any of this show in her face. She glared at the pink man, narrowing her eyes and showing her bared teeth.

"Keep away from me," she warned him. "Keep away from me or I'll kick you so hard you bounce off the ceiling."

The pink man had more to say, but it was all gibberish and Paz couldn't keep on being afraid of a self so grotesque and ugly. She surrendered to her pain and exhaustion and drifted off again into unconsciousness.

That happened several more times. In each case what roused her was a visitor. The tattooed woman, Tovi, came to glare at her and to rattle her gun against the bars in what was obviously meant to be a threat. Others came just to marvel at her and to shout taunts or exhortations that she couldn't understand. And a man came once to bring her food and water in plastic bowls that he thrust through the bars of the grille and deposited at the end of the bench. She had to sit up and twist her legs around to give herself enough slack on the ropes to reach them. The water was lukewarm and tasted metallic but she gulped it down greedily. The cage was baking hot and she was badly dehydrated. The food was brown pellets that tasted of grass and were very hard to keep down. She knew her remote ancestors had eaten grass, but that didn't make it any better.

The hours passed. She had no way of knowing how many. Despair crept over her by degrees. Without Dulcie she was truly trapped here, on a sinkhole world where she couldn't make herself understood or hope to be anything more than a freak show attraction. Hadiz Tambuwal had warned her of the risk but she had come anyway, living up to every lagomorph cliché by running away from her problems into worse problems.

It was no surprise, really, that the end of the road had come this soon.

62

Dulcie Coronal lay in a corner of the compound's central space, close to the base of a wall and in the shadow of a rubbish pile topped by several shattered earthenware tiles and a coiled hosepipe. That complex, jumbled backdrop was diverting a medium-sized slice of ets processing power: et was using the PaintPot Permutator to render etself invisible, painting etself with the colours and shapes behind et and to either side of et. The imposture wasn't perfect, but it was effective up to a distance of a few yards or so and it would have to do.

Dulcie watched as Paz was dragged away unconscious. Et couldn't intervene. The shotgun blast had done severe damage to ets shell, ripping off one of ets legs and bending the other badly out of shape. Ets torso was also dented, with a ragged hole on the left-hand side. Fortunately, most of the anima's critically important systems lay in the shell's head and upper chest. Et had lost a great deal of mobility but et could still process.

While et waited for night to come, et completed ets semantic grid and continued ets search of local data hubs. Et solved Tambuwal's puzzle within the first hour – 1010101 was a value in a mapping protocol used for the delivery of physical mail, designating a minor thoroughfare in an area known as Apapa Quays; 11 was the other component of that physical address, giving the location of a particular building. Number 11, Creek Road.

So now et knew where Tambuwal was, or at least where she was directing them to. The address was close, less than six miles away on a direct line. At the moment, though, those six miles might as well be a thousand.

The business of the compound continued around et. Et knew now what that business was. The local grids had confirmed what the caged selves had told Paz, that they were slaves whose freedom had been expropriated so that their labour could be sold. Trucks full of these subjugated selves came in and out, the outgoing ones presumably commencing work shifts at locations around the city, the incoming ones either returning from work or only recently captured. The slavers, most of whom wore the rose-stem or barbed-wire tattoo, counted them in and out, chivvied them to and fro, cursed them freely for real or imagined offences, smacked or punched them to make them move more quickly. As with the Pandominion's treatment of digital intelligences, the entire enterprise was founded on the denial of autonomy. Dulcie found it both terrible and fascinating. Was it a fundamental incapacity in the way organics interfaced with the world? et wondered. Were they so locked in their own perceptions that the selfhood of others was a fathomless mystery to them?

And yet there was Paz. Paz had continued to be ets friend when she knew what et was. And in fact they were a great deal more than friends. Since Dulcie had been designed to observe and mimic the organic selves around et, and since et had spent more time in Paz's company than in anyone else's, Paz was now built recursively into ets own behavioural and affective repertoires. Et found etself anticipating Paz's speech and actions, and experienced pleasure both when ets predictions were correct and when they were confounded.

There was no denying that the bond et felt was at least partly a selfish one, even though it presented as concern for ets friend. Dulcie wanted to keep Paz with et, wanted the experience of being in her company to be prolonged. Et wanted that very much. Whenever et explored alternative courses of action negative affect loops accreted quickly and reinforced each other. Et felt a need to terminate the loops, which et could only define as unhappiness. The decision that arose from this dilemma was impossible to justify but it seemed equally impossible to avoid. Et would court death again – ego-death, the only death that mattered – to find Paz and free her, rather than taking the logically preferable option of abandoning her and continuing alone.

When darkness came, et set off on ets mission.

Et moved by pulling etself along with ets arms, trailing ets useless legs behind et. The process was mostly silent when et was on packed earth, but on stone or tile there was no way to hide the scraping and shuffling sounds et made, so ets progress was intermittent. Et had to stop and wait whenever any of the compound's workers, enslaved or free, went by. There were still a great many of them in evidence. The compound was almost as busy by night as it was by day, the slaves still being taken to and from the main building where it seemed they were housed, the trucks still passing in and out through the main gate.

When Dulcie reached the building et had to stop. The doors were not locked but they were closed against et, and in this damaged shell et had no easy way of opening them. Et waited on the ground beside the door while minutes passed. The minutes felt long, which was fascinating. Ets affective state was modifying ets perception of time, which et had believed to be a constant. At last a worker exited the building and left the door to swing to behind them. Dulcie shoved ets arm into the gap to hold the door open, then quickly pulled and levered etself through.

The interior was a maze, corridor after corridor filled with narrow pens in which the enslaved selves sat or squatted or lay in attitudes of weariness and dejection. In ets painfully slow progress Dulcie had time to take in every detail. In some of the pens there was a toilet bowl without a seat, which all were presumably expected to share and to use in full view of the others. In others there was only a plastic bucket. Some had benches but none had anything resembling a bed or couch or mattress. Perhaps the sleeping quarters were else-where, but Dulcie doubted this was the case. Local data grids provided statistics. Slaves only had to survive for fourteen months on average to bring their owners into profit on the transaction. Attrition was expected and was not considered problematic. The conditions in which the slaves were kept reflected this brutal arithmetic.

It would have been a challenge to find Paz among the endless identical enclosures, especially at this snail's pace, but fortunately for Dulcie there were security cameras stationed along most of the corridors. It was a simple matter to hack into the feeds and assemble a functional map of the complex. Et quickly located Paz all alone in a pen close to the building's north-west corner and one level down. The only remaining problem was to get there.

Et continued to scrape and crawl along. Some of the slaves heard the skittering, scratching sounds et made and looked in ets direction, but all that was there was empty corridor. The illusion wasn't perfect but neither was the light. Something was moving in the shadows, but it could easily have been a rat or a cockroach. Nobody pointed or cried out.

Nobody saw et coming.

63

Something pulled Paz up out of feverish sleep into painful waking. She opened her eyes to find that the pink man was back again, stroking the fur of her cheek and grinning from ear to ear.

"I wish I could bite you," Paz told him wearily. "But my jaws hurt too much."

He spoke in response, more meaningless clicking and yawing. He took a slim metal lozenge out of his pocket and pointed it at her. It made a click that had two parts to it. *Ratch-tchik.* A camera.

"Make sure to get my good side," Paz growled. She turned away from him to face the wall, thrusting out her scut.

The pink man grabbed her shoulder and pulled her round again to face him, thrusting the camera into her face as he took more pictures. Paz weighed up the possibility of swinging her legs into position for a kick, but she knew she would be much too slow to catch him.

"Just leave me alone," she muttered.

The pink man spoke again.

And this time the translation came right behind the words. *I wish I knew what you were saying.*

Paz couldn't help herself. In spite of all her many aches and agonies, her fear that she might be seriously injured, she uttered a gasp of pure relief. Because there was only one place the voked words could be coming from. Dulcie was still in one piece, and close by. Et had survived the shotgun blast and come back to her.

Dulcie! she voked.

Here, Dulcie said. *Do you want to carry on this conversation or should I leave him talking to himself? It might be useful to know what his plans are, I suppose.*

The pink man was disgorging sounds all this while. *I'll talk to him,* Paz said. *What is he saying?*

Quote: You reacted to me! You were just pretending you couldn't understand me!

"I wasn't pretending," Paz said. "You just didn't say anything I was interested in."

She said it aloud, because she had forgotten the system she and Dulcie had agreed. She should have just voked and left it to Dulcie to do the rest. The translation came right after, but it was clearly not in synch with the movements of her mouth. The man looked puzzled. Confused. Then he looked angry again. "What did you say?" he demanded.

This time Paz voked her reply, opening and closing her mouth but letting Dulcie – wherever she was – supply the sounds. *I said yes, I understand you.*

The man thrust out his lower lip in a sullen grimace. He still seemed suspicious, as if Paz had tried to trick him in some way. *Good,* he said. *Then perhaps you could answer a question for me. What in the name of God are you?*

I'm a citizen of the Pandominion, Paz said.

And where's that? Is that in Russia? Did someone in Russia make you? Or America? The pink man brought his face closer still, his gaze moving avidly across her ears, her nose, her furred cheeks. He seemed to be disgusted and excited at the same time, like someone who had just found a diamond in some dog dirt.

Paz had never heard of Russia or America, but now didn't seem to be the time to say so. She met the man's gaze, unblinking. *The Pandominion,* she said grimly, *is bigger than either of those places. And I'm under its protection. I demand you take me to the nearest Step station and . . . and send me home. If you don't the Cielo will come looking for me. Believe me, you don't want to be standing in their way when they come.* She hoped that Dulcie had edited out that small hesitation – and given her a voice to match the bold words.

But the pink man, after a moment's blank incomprehension, broke out into an uproarious laugh. He clapped his hands together, as if Paz had performed an impressive trick and he was applauding her. *Amazing,* he said. *Just amazing! Someone is going to pay a fortune for you.* He put out a hand and ruffled the fur on the top of her head, which made her flinch. It was like something you might do to a small child. Or to an animal.

Lie back and get better, the man said. *I've sent out for a doctor. He should be here soon. I'm going to want you in good condition.*

He turned his back on her and moved to the door.

Wait! Paz called out.

The man turned back. She had thought he might be angry, but he only looked indulgent. He was in his place of strength, after all. He had been able to laugh off her empty threats. *What?* he said.

You asked me what I am, Paz said, looking up at him through her blurred, half-shut eyes. *What are you? And what's this place?*

The man considered, hands in pockets, leaning easily against the open door, expansive because he was so pleased with himself and so delighted with what he'd caught. *My name is Diallo. Saikou Diallo. You know that name? No? It means "the man who brings rain". And this place is Damola Ojo. It's a transport hub for workers, mostly in the Free Trade Extension.*

Paz tried to make sense of this. *You keep your workers in cages?*

Only the forfeitures, the man said, with a dismissive shrug. *There are rules about the management of debt – established long ago, when the Anglo-Dutch Mandate first came into force. If people owe more than they can pay then they're forfeit. They become the property of whoever takes up the debt and claims them. Do you understand?*

No.

The man looked at her with remote, dispassionate interest. *You've never heard of the forfeit system? Well, innocence is a precious thing. It doesn't matter in any case, because that's not you. There's no way I'm sending you to the free trade zone. They'd just work you to death out there, and that would be a waste.*

A chill went through Paz. He'd just told her the fate of all these other selves, but she did her best not to let her fear and horror show on her face. *Where are you sending me then?* she asked him.

Most likely I'll sell you at auction, Diallo said. *It will take a little setting up, of course. Any buyer will need to see you from close up to believe you're real. But once they see you* . . . He shook his head, smiling. *Yes. I think that's what I'll do.*

He walked out of the cage, the metal grille swinging to behind him. He touched his hand to the outside of the grille, at one side where it butted up against the concrete wall. There was a loud clunk as a lock shot home.

Once the pink man was gone and his footsteps had receded, Paz slowly brought herself around into a sitting position. It was just about possible, so long as she folded her legs under her: if she tried to stretch them out, her arms were pulled up over her head. Moving still hurt a lot, but she didn't feel sick any more. She mostly felt angry, and though the anger couldn't drive out the pain, it made a space inside it where she could think.

She had feeling in all her limbs, and she could wiggle her fingers and toes. Nothing was broken there. Her side ached badly, forcing her to take shallow breaths, so it was possible there was some damage to her ribs; but if her lung had been punctured she wouldn't be able to breathe at all so it was probably less serious than it felt. The worst pain was where the rifle stock had hit her. Her whole face was throbbing, and it felt like it had ballooned up to twice its normal size. The reason why one of her eyes wouldn't open all the way was because of the swelling there.

"Dulcie?" she croaked.

Here, Paz. But don't talk to me out loud.

The familiar voice felt like a cool hand on her burning forehead. "Oh, Dulcie, I'm so glad you're not—"

No. Paz, you have to voke. I mean it. The only advantage we've got is that they don't know I'm here.

But you're all right? Paz asked anxiously.

Very far from it. This shell took massive damage when the woman fired on me. It's difficult for me even to move right now. That's why it took me so long to find you.

Paz looked into the corners of the room, but there was nowhere where Dulcie could hide. There was nothing there except the bench and the space under the bench, both of which seemed to be empty.

Where are you? she voked. *I want to see you!*

That's not a good idea. There are cameras all over this place. It's best if I stay hidden for now. Our getting out of here – if it's possible at all – will depend on seeing an advantage and taking it without hesitation. We need to watch and wait and keep our wits about us. And in the meantime you should aim to be as docile and passive as you can. They need to think you're helpless.

I am helpless!

The Cielo trooper who followed us out of Canoplex thought that too. Look what happened to him. Don't be afraid, Paz. We'll get out of this.

Can you unlock this cage? Paz asked.

I think so. The lock on the door is electronic, and I recorded the key signature when Diallo triggered it. If I can get up close to the lock, I should be able to reproduce the signal with enough fidelity to trigger the mechanism.

Great! Paz clenched her fists. *Let's go! Let's go now!*

It's not that easy. If it were, I would already have done it. I told you I was damaged. It will take me some time to reach you, even across such a short distance. More to the point, unlocking the door won't help us right now. The corridors are swarming with people, and so is the yard outside. We have to wait.

For what?

I don't know. I would have said for night, but this place doesn't seem to shut down at night. For a distraction. For the odds to change. You should get as much rest as you can. I'll tell you if anyone comes.

Paz lay back again, wincing as her strained muscles protested. She knew Dulcie was right. This was the enemy's space and they had to find a way out of it. Otherwise she would be sold, just like all the other selves here who had been tricked and trapped and put in chains. They would be made to work until they died, Diallo had said. She would most likely be kept as some rich self's pet.

She settled down to wait, but waiting would be an enervating struggle. The whole time she lay there in the dark she would be fighting hard against her own panic, her ingrained instinct to jump up and run, run, run until her legs and lungs gave out.

64

Moon's squad went in without armour, and with cosmetic tape over their more visible augments. There wasn't much that could be done about their faces and body plans, but Essien had assured them that if Lago de Curamo on world U5838784474 was anything like the Lagos on his own world they would only be challenged if they showed weakness or uncertainty. They could get a long way by wearing hooded jackets and meeting the gaze of anyone who looked at them until they looked at something else instead.

On a normal infiltration mission, soldiers Stepped in clusters of six, to locations that were close enough to allow for quick support if any cluster was attacked, but far enough apart to form the vertices of a search grid if a search was needed. This time, with a squad of only two dozen selves in all, Moon added her own twist to that protocol. Along with the weapons, she'd helped herself to a single beekeeper reconnaissance remote, a sweet little piece of tech about as big as the first joint of her thumb. She keyed it to her field and Stepped it through ahead of them to scout out the area around their Step point. She was looking for a blind spot, an area where there were no indigenous selves to see them come through.

It didn't take much time at all. The area of the city they were Stepping into seemed to be quite run-down, and had its fair share of derelict buildings. Moon chose a closed and boarded-up railway station on a disused surface line to the east of the city's centre. Establishing a perimeter was almost effortless. All they had to do was to mount a physical search of the station's interior to make sure they were alone, set up trip alarms on the doors and windows and place a few recon cameras – fixed ones inside, the beekeeper doing its thing out on the street.

Moon inspected every room for herself, and she brought Essien along with her. "Got to be sure there's nothing we missed," she told him. "We're going to have to leave the Step plate here when we go hunting. With no armour we don't have access to our rip-cord plates, so it's our only way out. We can't afford to have it compromised."

Last of all, when they'd checked all the interior spaces, they went up onto the roof. The beekeeper had already told them there was nothing there. True, and not true. There were no threats, no lurking enemies or accidental witnesses. But there was the city.

"Talk me through it, Sinkhole," Moon ordered. "What am I looking at?"

Essien turned in a slow circle to take it in. For all that he'd been told it wasn't really the Lagos he'd left, the Lagos he knew, it was hard to make himself believe it. It wasn't so much the way the place looked, or even how it sounded: it was the smells. The roiling mix of spice and cooking-fire smoke, petrol and dust, heat and sweat and stone and tar and shit, all so powerful they almost seemed to push against his face, were as distinctive as a fingerprint.

The station house wasn't a tall building, but it stood at the top of an incline; and since the highest point in Lagos is only twenty metres or so above sea level, Essien could see a long way. Almost to Ilepeju in the north, clear to Adekunle in the east. Southwards the thorny crown of the National Arts Theatre bisected the skyline, separating Charlotte Island's glass and steel spires from the colonial sprawl of Ijora. And west . . .

The western edge of Lagos had no skyline to speak of. In Essien's own world (which he no longer thought of as the real world) it had the Transport Interchange, but that was missing here. The sprawl of buildings he was seeing was anonymous and endless. But he knew what was there. He felt Oshodi like an itch under his skin. He turned his back to it.

"The administrative district is over there," he said, pointing to their five o'clock. "Ebute Metta, it's called. There'll be a big police presence and a rapid response to any disturbance. That's true of Lagos Island, too. Same bearing, two clicks further away. There's a business and financial hub there. Highest value real estate is in Charlotte Island, over there." He moved his hand to the six o'clock position. "Everything north and west of us is lower rent areas. Some slums. Very densely populated. Easier for us to move through, because there won't be any police presence worth a shit, but it's likely to be harder to navigate. The streets move around a lot."

"The *streets* move around?"

"In the poor areas, yes. The structures there are fairly temporary. Lean-tos and shacks. They can relocate without much warning. You have to orientate yourself by the landmarks that don't move."

Moon scanned the horizon and grinned. "Nice," she said. "Very nice."

Essien looked at her face to see if her expression modified the words in any way, but Moon looked bland and open. "What?" she demanded. "Compared to most of the combat details I've been seeing, Nkanika, it's fucking heaven. We've got a whole city here that's teeming with people instead of robots. And you, you're a local boy. Don't tell me you're not loving this."

"It's not my world," Essien said guardedly. The subject troubled him in a way he couldn't define and didn't want to examine.

"No, okay." Moon nudged his shoulder, as if he'd made a joke and she was in on it. "You're from a block or two over, right? But there's no point splitting hairs. This whole place is full of selves with the same equipment and metabolism that you've got. Doesn't the air stink of sex to you? It's got to, right? It just smells like shit and garbage to me, but I'm not the intended audience."

The truth was that the smell had poked a stick into the depths of Essien's brain, in exactly the same way seeing Moon's face again had done. Memories were crawling in there now like ants.

Moon seemed to see them. She nodded as she studied his face. "Look," she said. "We go back a long way, Sinkhole, and I like you. I genuinely do. I feel like I'm sort of your army mother or something. But I really need this operation to go smoothly, and as far as I can see you're the least smooth thing in the mix. So, word to the wise, okay? You need to play this as close to stone-cold as you can. It'll trip you up, otherwise. Whether this is genuinely the old homestead or not, it will still feel like it. And it doesn't matter a hot, salty damn. Nothing's special here. Nothing's real, even, except us."

"I know that." Essien felt obscurely angry, as if he'd been accused of something. Or worse, as if it was his own body, turned into bricks and thoroughfares, that lay indecently exposed all around them. "I don't give a shit about anyone here."

Moon made a vague gesture, half acknowledging the point and half waving it away. "Well, that's good," she said. "But it might change. Who can say, right? And no shame if it does, so long as you don't fuck the mission. Comes a time when there's something that needs to be done, and you don't think you can do it, just make sure you let me know. Then drop right the hell out. Don't put yourself in the middle of things you can't push through."

The seriousness of her tone defused Essien's anger. He could see that her concern for him was real, and so was her anxiety about the mission. She wasn't insulting him, she was just trying to close a loophole – whether it was open or not. He nodded and left it at that.

"Okay," Moon said. "Great talk. Let's go see what Chio's got for us."

Chiomis was downstairs in the station's decaying, ransacked ticket hall, sitting cross-legged on the floor in front of a portable comms rig she'd barely touched. Most of the gear she needed was in her augments.

"Anything yet?" Moon asked.

Chiomis shook her head without looking round. "I'm up on their broadcast networks. Skimming visuals while the system stitches together a language database. Good news is there are a ton of camera feeds. This place has got surveillance from asshole to breakfast time. I'm keying in a pattern match for the bunny as we speak."

"Good work, Soldier. Let me know if anything pops up."

"You got it, Commander."

They checked in with Vemmet, who was sitting on an overturned filing cabinet right beside the Step plate. It looked as though he intended to be the first on-board if they had to retreat. His eyes kept flicking from side to side, checking the corners of the room.

"Knock it the fuck off," Moon told him, in a quiet, conversational tone.

"What?" Vemmet looked startled, then affronted. "Keep a civil tongue, Sostenti. What do you mean?"

"I know you would have preferred to wait behind on Bivouac 19, but that wasn't an option. You had no reason to be there and you would have been found by a wide patrol or picked up on a satellite feed inside of an hour. So here you stay until the job's done, and if you keep that face on you're going to be bad for morale. These ex-grunts were shaky to start with. Don't make them wobble off their base."

Vemmet looked seriously offended, but he straightened his spine a little and did his best to rein in those wayward eyeballs.

So it wasn't just him Moon was sounding out, Essien realised. When Moon checked the perimeter, she examined the people as well as the place. She was actually good at this shit – better on present showing than most of the commissioned officers he'd served under.

"Hey!" Chiomis called, from the other side of the room. "Hey, Commander! This just in!"

She flung a telos transmission from her own array into Moon's, and Moon shared it with Essien. It was a feed from a camera, grainy and monochrome. Essien expanded it from corner-of-vision to full size, but it was still hard to see what was going on. The camera was mounted high up on a wall. A lot of people were crowding at the base of the wall, surrounding a single self who seemed to be backing away from them.

The attackers were all local selves, anthropoids like Essien himself. The one in the middle seemed to jerk and flicker at first, its outline indistinct. Then, very suddenly, it came clear. It was an Uti, a rabbit self, with long ears standing up like flags in the wind and stout legs bulging with hypertrophied muscle. It was their quarry.

As Essien watched, she went down, knocked off her feet by one of the locals. The man paid the price a moment later, as she rolled onto her back and caught him full in the chest with a kick that would have made a mule's best efforts feel like a stroke from a butterfly's wing. He rose into the air a considerable distance, then fell down again head first. He was probably already dead, his heart slammed out through the back of his ribs by that mighty kick. If he wasn't, the landing certainly did the job.

But the rabbit was outnumbered and the rest of the pack closed in on her fast. She was lost to view for most of a minute. Then the dense knot of people parted and two men dragged Topaz Tourmaline FiveHills' prone body away beyond the camera's reach.

"Time and place?" Moon asked.

"Time sig puts it thirteen hours ago," Chiomis said. "Bearing from here is due west a mile and a half."

"Send those coordinates to the whole team," Moon said. "Have you got eyes on the outside of the building?"

"Not yet. Working on it. But I zoomed through everything I could get on that one camera."

"And?"

"Rabbit kid doesn't show up again, coming or going. After they haul her away, she doesn't come back. Look at this, though."

Chiomis rewound, froze a frame and zoomed in, close enough that a lot of the image's definition was lost in random edge-noise. This time around Essien saw a flash of white up on the girl's shoulder.

The tiny anima that was clinging on to her was thrown free when she was knocked down and rolled away between the feet of the crowd. One of the locals aimed and fired a shotgun in that direction, but whatever she was aiming at was out of view.

"Any sign of the construct after that?" Moon asked.

"Nope. But I didn't see them pick anything else up off the ground. Just the rabbit."

Moon chewed this over for a few seconds before she spoke. "Okay, spread a net. All directions from that zero, covering as many roads as you can. Tell me if you see the girl or the construct, obviously, but if anybody moves into or out of that location I want to hear about it. That's your cue, people. Kit up and check your weapons. We move out in twenty."

The delay was so that she could send the beekeeper over to those coordinates and get a bird's eye view of it. When it was in position she shared the feed with Essien.

You know this place at all? she voked.

What he was seeing was a walled compound with a single large concrete structure at one end. The rest of the space was given over to vehicles – mostly flatbed trucks – and single-storey outbuildings. The outbuildings were erected partly over white-painted lines for vehicle bays, so obviously they came later. It was a trailer park that had been adapted in a rough and ready way to some other purpose.

Memories stirred sluggishly. His brain was trying to make connections, but it wasn't getting very far: gabber had torn out too much of the necessary equipment. Maybe it wasn't just the drug. Something about the place made his attention want to flick away from it to something else. It was hard to hold on to the thought, but he rode it down until it led to a name.

"It's called Damola Ojo," he said.

"And?"

"It's a freight yard. A transport hub. And . . ." He licked lips that were suddenly dry. "And there's a warehouse."

"They're pretty tooled up for a warehouse," Moon said dryly.

"Come on, Sinkhole, earn your keep. Is it likely to be tougher than it looks? Is there any serious heat in there? Will any part of it be fortified against attack?"

"I . . . No. I don't think so."

"So that was just regular security we saw?"

He nodded.

"And there's nothing else I need to know about?"

Essien was still waiting in vain for ideas and images to coalesce into meaning. He remembered a room underground, a cot bed, his name scratched into a cement wall. A sense of shame, but not what it attached to.

"Nothing," he said at last. It was a surrender. His mind wouldn't show him what he was asking it for. Whatever had been threatening to surface there had sunk back down again and the waters had closed over it.

65

Moon was mostly reassured by what the beekeeper's cameras had shown her.

She counted around forty selves in the open space inside the compound or up on its walls. There could be more in the main building but the walls were too thick for the drone's thermal sensors to penetrate. Still, it was reasonable to assume that most of the on-site security would be deployed to stop people getting into the compound in the first place.

The selves she could see were armed, but their weapons didn't look any too impressive and none of the guards had visible augments. Given the level of technology suggested by the vehicles and the buildings, the worst the strike team would be facing would be projectile weapons and maybe some chemical-based anti-personnel stuff.

On the whole she was inclined to just break the doors down and go in hot. Her squad would be outnumbered but they would be hefting much more firepower than anything that could be brought against them. That, plus their Cielo augments, ought to be enough.

Nkanika's vagueness was the only thing that bothered her. At first, she thought he was hiding something. Then she realised it was just gabber-smear, the mess the drug made of your head if you were a long-term user. It was fucking aggravating all the same, since Nkanika was supposed to be providing local intel, but you took what you could get.

And she didn't see any point in wasting more time. The twenty minutes weren't quite up but she assembled the squad, all except for Chiomis and Wuxx. Chiomis would stay up on the comms rig and Wuxx would guard the Step plate.

"Nobody touches it," she told him. "Nobody goes within ten feet of it until we get back. Yes?"

"Yes," Wuxx agreed. "Got it."

What she didn't say was that he would mostly be guarding the plate against Vemmet, who was also staying behind. Vemmet was still controlling the plate through his array and he had refused to share the code so Moon couldn't lock him out. She didn't want to retrieve the rabbit only to come back and find that he'd been panicked by a loud noise or his own bad conscience and run away, taking their exit with him.

Okay. She switched to voke, making it clear that she was addressing the whole squad now. *We're moving out. Silent running all the way – no talk, no signals, no accessing local feeds. Nkanika knows the ground and he's going to be leading the way. If there's any interaction with locals, fall back and let him handle it. Unless it gets physical, in which case fire at will.*

She chopped the air twice with her right hand.

With me.

66

The squad drew some glances when they came out onto the street. Hooded jackets and dark glasses hid most of their faces, but there was no hiding their imposing size, their strange proportions. Nobody looked for long, though, because the one thing that stood out about them more than anything was that they were trouble. Getting an eyeful wasn't worth the risk of provoking a confrontation. People moved aside quickly as they passed.

Essien had been bracing himself for this ever since he got here, but he still wasn't ready. Walking west through Jibowu and Idi Oro along Onifade Street, the strangeness and familiarity twisted in his mind like two strands of wet hemp being plaited into a rope, shrinking and pressing into each other as they dried. The ruined asphalt here had hollowed out into potholes deeper than a man was tall, which made Essien think of bomb craters on some of the battlefields he'd seen. But then the bomb craters had always reminded him of Idi Oro. Most of the cars that lined the street on both sides hadn't moved in years: they'd been turned into market stalls and sometimes into homes, their wheels taken off so police or scavengers couldn't tow them away. He could swear he recognised some of the faces.

The smells seared their way into his mind, just as they had up on the roof. The street vendors were selling puff-puffs, roasted corn, bean cake and suya. The air was heavy with cloyed fragrances, with grey smoke dancing from a hundred fires. The shouted conversations were in languages Essien knew, or thought he knew. Maybe a word out of place here, an intonation there, but the music of it was hardly changed at all. The grit in the hot wind that slapped his face had a bitter taste he remembered as vividly as his first kiss.

This Lago de Curamo, for all that it wasn't his own Lagos, fitted into the hollow of his head like a key into a lock.

I've picked up a few street cameras, Chiomis voked when they were still about a click out. *I'm seeing three sides of the building. Fourth side seems like a blind wall with no exits on it. They've had a ton of trucks go in and out since the time stamp on that footage, but I didn't get a glimpse of the target in any of them.*

What were they carrying? Moon asked.

Selves. Local feeds pin this place as a slave market – run by an outfit that seems to be a quasi-public entity of some kind. It's got its own militia.

Essien's stomach clenched, and something sour came into his throat. The memory he'd tried to grab hold of before came up with it, but again only for a moment. When he reached for it, it dissolved leaving nothing but a sense of dread.

"Nkanika." Moon fell alongside him, giving him a hard stare – but she spoke softly enough that none of the others could hear. "Anything you'd like to add to your earlier assessment?"

Essien shook his head. He didn't much want to speak.

"Is slavery legal in this place?"

"No. I mean, it wasn't legal in my world. Not any more. But . . ."

"But what?"

"Legal or not, it still happened." There was a sick pressure inside his head now: memories clamouring to be seen but refusing to resolve, so all he was remembering was a confusion of meaningless images, unattached emotions.

Fucking wonderful, Moon voked him one to one. *Thanks for your expert assistance.*

Hey, she told the team. *Listen up. Chio's telling us this is some sort of people-trafficking outfit that we're about to drop in on. They're maybe going to be a bit more professional than we were expecting. Some merce-*

nary muscle on-site. Doesn't change our strategy, but it might mean they hit back that bit harder. So we go in hot and we give them no leeway at all. These fuckers might be using pointy sticks and toy guns but they'll probably outnumber us. Best thing is not to let them get their feet under them. No explosive ordnance. We don't want the bunny to end up under a wall or blown to pieces. Everything else is on the table, though. Just make sure they go down and don't get up again.

67

P^{az.} Dulcie's voked warning startled Paz out of a shallow sleep populated by formless dreams and actual muscle aches. She heard the approaching footsteps a moment later, accompanied by a clangorous rattling sound of metal against metal.

She was expecting to see Diallo again, but the self who fetched up outside her cage was a different man entirely. He was another of the pink-skinned type, lean and muscular, dressed in grey coveralls and black boots. He had been making the noise with a metal cup, scraping it against the bars of all the cages he passed. Now he banged it back and forth between two of the bars of Paz's cage.

His lips moved.

Wakey wakey, Dulcie translated. *Diminutive ending implies that you're a child. It's intentionally insulting.*

I got that, Paz said.

While the man was rummaging in his pocket, presumably for a key, Paz examined him more closely. He had more fur than Diallo, enough that he had gathered it up on top of his head and tied it into a sort of knot. It was the colour of straw, and looked as though it might have the same texture too. He was carrying a white plastic case with a handle and three red symbols on the front, a cross and a diamond and a crescent moon.

He saw her looking. *Yeah, that's right, Lola Bunny*, he said. *I'm a doctor. Gonna look you over, fix you up. Mr Diallo's orders. No need to worry, I got the healing hands. Ask any of these miserable fuckers down here. They just love it when Doc Smiley makes his rounds.*

He succeeded in unlocking the door at last and came into the cage. He was watching Paz as closely as she was watching him, his eyes darting quickly back and forth as he tilted his head to examine her head, her torso, her arms and legs. Paz didn't try to sit up. In fact, she made no movement at all. She had decided to take Dulcie's advice and pretend she was even weaker and more out of it than she was.

The man's mouth twisted. He uttered a few words, followed by a snickering laugh, but this time Dulcie didn't translate. *What was that?* Paz voked.

Another insult. He says he's never met a woman who needed a shave this badly. I think it's a joke predicated on the fact that female selves here have less body hair than male ones.

In spite of her pain and fear, Paz almost laughed. All the selves she'd seen on this world had faces like mole rats, shockingly naked. A little more fur here and there would do wonders for them. Perhaps she should offer the man some of hers so they'd balance out.

It's probably not a good idea to let him treat you, Dulcie advised her. *He has no idea what your internal fauna is like or what vaccinations you've already been given.*

And on top of that he looks like an idiot, Paz agreed.

The man set his case down on the floor and opened it. Inside were rows of bottles, pills and serums and hypodermic ampoules, all held in place with elasticated strips. But what he held in his hand when he straightened again wasn't a pill or a hypodermic. It was a straight razor. Paz cowered back.

The man shrugged impatiently. *I can't treat what I can't see, bitch!* he told her. *Got to clear some space, don't I? If you stay still you won't get cut. Probably. If you piss me off, no promises.*

"Stay away from me!" Paz shouted. The man stopped dead. He hadn't heard her speak before, and whatever he'd just heard it wasn't anything he could understand. Dulcie voked the translation a moment later, but Paz's mouth was now closed. The man frowned in confusion.

Okaaay, he muttered. *Whatever the fuck that was.*

He lowered the razor towards Paz's shoulder, where her fur was matted with blood. Paz flinched away from it, and when he leaned in closer she rolled over onto her side and threw her hands up in the air, drawing in her knees.

Hey, the man snapped, *I fucking said not to—*

Paz kicked out. Even though her arms were at full stretch, the rope still pulled her up short, jarring her painfully, but she made a half-solid contact just the same. The razor flew from the doctor's hand, hit the floor and bounced away. At the same time, Paz's arms were jerked sharply upwards by the pull on the rope. Her shriek of pain was louder than the doctor's yell of surprise.

He stepped back hastily out of her reach. He might well have been in the crowd outside when she'd been brought down. If so, he knew what sort of damage those legs could do.

He shouted something that was almost certainly another insult.

"Takes one to know one," Paz snapped back.

The doctor went scrambling on the floor for the missing razor and came up holding it in both hands in front of him, like a weapon. He seemed less eager to close with her this time. Instead, he circled around towards her head, presumably to stay out of range of another kick. Paz tried to swivel round on the bench but that only twisted the ropes, which made them tighten and reduced her freedom of movement even further.

"Don't touch me!" she shouted. "I'm warning you!"

The doctor did a little dance on the spot, either to confuse her or because he genuinely couldn't decide whether to tackle her full on or back away. Finally, he folded the razor shut and shoved it in his pocket. His mouth worked, making harsh sounds. *Okay then*, Dulcie translated. *If you won't behave I'm just gonna have to put you all the way out. This is on you.*

He delved into the case again. Out of the corner of her eye, her head twisted over her left shoulder, Paz saw him prep a hypo. With a start of shock, she realised she could also see Dulcie. The anima was on the floor of the cage, a few feet in from the open door. Sweeping movements of ets left arm were propelling et forwards, as if et were swimming. The rest of ets body was horrifically damaged, crushed and mangled as though et had been through a household dispose-all, one of ets legs gone and ets torso bent around in a sickle shape where the shotgun blast had caved it in. Et was inching closer to the doctor, but painfully slowly.

The doctor took advantage of Paz's moment of distraction, lunging in to grab her by her raised ears. *There we go*, he chuckled. *Man, these things are huge! Anyone ever tell you that?*

Paz twisted in his grip, but there was very little she could do as he forced her head up and back. He was exposing her throat, she realised. He transferred the hypo to his mouth, holding it lightly between clenched teeth. He brought his free hand down again and pressed the tips of his fingers against the side of her neck. He was going to inject the drug into her jugular, she realised. Or if she was unlucky, into her windpipe.

He gave a spot close to her clavicle three smart taps, coaxing up the vein. He leaned in, peering with narrowed eyes to make sure he'd found it, and bringing the syringe with him.

A crash and a yell sounded from somewhere else in the compound, followed a moment later by the dull boom of an explosion and then the piercing wail of an alarm. For one dazed second, Paz thought she was back at the Orange Crescent Step terminal: the triggered memory was that strong.

And that sounds like our distraction, Dulcie said. *I wish we could have timed this a little better.*

The doctor stopped what he was doing and looked around. His grip on Paz's fur relaxed.

She reared up and butted him in the side of the head, as hard as she could. The man gave a grunt of surprise and staggered back. The syringe slipped from his grasp but he flailed and groped with both hands and managed to catch it again before it could fall. For a moment it looked as if he would lose his footing, but the cage was too narrow. His shoulders came up against the far wall, helping him to catch his balance.

Paz braced herself for another attack, but as the man took a step towards her he stiffened, then froze to the spot. His eyes bulged, his teeth coming together with an audible clack. At the same moment the strip light in the ceiling blew. In the pitch darkness Paz heard something fall – heavy, like a dead weight – and after that nothing.

"Dulcie?" She yelped. "Dulcie, where is he?"

"It's all right," Dulcie said quietly from right below her. Et spoke out loud rather than voking. Paz hadn't realised until then how much she'd missed that voice, which had been Tricity's voice before it was Dulcie's. "He's down."

"How? What did you do?"

"This building has mains electric power networked in by physical wires rather than induction fields. There are sockets at floor level for attaching appliances. I put the fingers of one hand into a socket and touched the man's ankle with my other hand. The current caused me some local damage – I'm having to re-initialise broadcast functions, so I'll be using normal speech for a few minutes – but it was much harder on him."

"Thank the mothers! Good job, Dulcie. How long before he wakes up?"

"He's not going to wake up."

The cold, matter-of-fact tone made Paz shudder, but she couldn't bring herself to be sorry. After that little talk with Mr Diallo she thought she knew what most of the doctor's job must have consisted of: mending the enslaved selves when they were broken, patching them up not for their own sake but so they could carry on working.

"We need to move," Dulcie said. "The sounds you're hearing are being made by a Cielo tactical squad as they slaughter everyone in this compound. I'm up on their comms and they definitely know we're here. We're what they came for. Once we're in their hands this is all over."

Paz didn't doubt this. The main reason she wasn't moving was that fear had frozen her in place. The sounds from outside were louder and more alarming now. There were screams, running footsteps and lots of gunfire. More explosions too. What galvanised her at last was the smell of smoke.

"Something is on fire!" she exclaimed.

"The Cielo are using chemical incendiaries."

The slaves! Paz thought. *All those selves shut in their tiny pens. Oh mothers!*

She turned her attention to the ropes, looking for a knot she could untie. And there it was. But high up, out of reach of her hands.

"The razor," she called down to Dulcie. "He put it back in his pocket. Can you get it?"

There was silence for a few seconds. That seemed like a long time, with nothing to do but smell the thickening smoke and listen to the hideous clamour from out in the corridor.

"I've got it," Dulcie said at last. "Can you hold out your hand?"

Paz leaned out as far as she could, fingers spread wide.

"That's too high. I can't reach you."

"Can't you climb up onto the bench?"

"I only have one functional arm. If I try to climb I'll have to drop the razor."

After a moment's thought, Paz swung herself around until she was facing outwards with her shoulders pressed to the cage's back wall. She stretched her arms straight up, wincing at the pain. As before, the rope played out and gave her legs some freedom of movement. She dangled them off the edge of the bench, knees bent. "Tuck the razor in between my feet," she said.

Some more time passed.

"Dulcie—"

"Yes. I'm almost there."

Paz felt the folded razor touch her instep. She pressed her feet tight together and with gingerly care drew her legs back in again. Rolling onto her back, she raised them up high and let the razor fall onto her stomach. Then she turned on her side and tipped it onto the bench within reach of her clutching fingers.

Opening the razor wasn't hard either, but the blade was so sharp she had to be careful not to cut her own wrists open as she carved at the rope. When it parted she fed it through the ring and freed her hands. After that she was able to cut away the loops of twine around her legs. She climbed down off the bench. Her legs were shaking like plucked guitar strings but they took her weight.

Dulcie was lying on the cement floor. Half of et was under the sprawled bulk of the dead doctor. Paz stared down at him. His face was contorted into a grimace, his eyes wide and staring and his lips flecked with pink foam. The sight of him made her feel sick, but she still couldn't bring herself to feel any compassion for him. He'd chosen to be a part of all this horror and cruelty. He had built up a debt, just as the slaves were supposed to have done, and he'd finally been made to pay it.

The ominous noises from outside seemed to be getting closer; wild yells that might have been commands, curses or pleas for mercy; booms and whines, rattles and concussions from many different weapons.

Paz knelt and tugged on Dulcie's battered body. Pain spread in sudden surges along her arms to her shoulders, and then down her back.

"We don't have much time," Dulcie said.

"I'm doing the best I can!" Paz said, between clenched teeth.

When she finally managed to pull Dulcie free, she felt so sick and dizzy from the pain that she had to kneel on the floor for a few moments with her head hunched down below her shoulders and her eyes tight shut.

"We need to leave right now," Dulcie urged her. "They're on their way. And the chemicals you're inhaling will already be starting to have an effect. If we delay much longer the smoke will overwhelm you."

"The locks," Paz said, one hand clasped over her mouth. "Will they all open with the same signal? The one you took from Diallo?"

"I don't know. Why? Your door's open."

"Dulcie, there are thousands of selves in here. If the building catches fire they'll all die. We can't just leave them."

Dulcie was silent for a moment, and then a moment longer.

"Dulcie, remember the pamphlets you gave me! 'You wouldn't put a baby in a box.' If slavery is wrong, then it's wrong for all selves, not just for constructs."

"I follow the logic," Dulcie said at last. "My coming into this building to find you was a decision of a similar kind. This might get us killed, though. Or captured by the Cielo, which would be worse."

Paz didn't answer. She scooped Dulcie up off the floor and pressed et to her chest. "We have to try."

"I wish you felt differently," Dulcie said. "But I suppose we do."

68

Moon's squad breached Damola Ojo via its main entrance, and per her instructions they went in hard.

Without their armour, they were more vulnerable than usual to small arms fire, so the first priority was to make sure the guards on the front gate couldn't hit them. Moon's strategy was simple and brutal. When the squad was still a hundred yards from target, she had the beekeeper drop a neuro-interference grenade that combined lab-built organophosphates with snake and spider venom.

The fine particulate mist that the grenade released had a narrow dispersal radius and an active life of only twenty seconds, but that was long enough to tear the guards' nervous systems into spasming confetti. The selves up on the wall toppled as they lost control of their limbs and presumably died when they hit the ground. The ones on the pavement outside went down twitching and foaming. Their deaths were less sudden but just as inevitable: their lungs were shutting down, their hearts becoming arrhythmic, their brains shorting out.

Moon waited out the twenty seconds and then went in, stepping over the bodies. She took an ABPM from her belt, pointed it at the gate and hit the trigger. ABPMs – air-burst pressure munitions – were a refinement of the civilian self-defence device called a push-away. The air-bursts generated waves of alternating high and low pressure to produce massive torsion forces within a cone-shaped space. At one tip of the cone, the waves cancelled out, allowing the soldier who'd deployed the ABPM to stay on their feet and feel no ill effects. At the other end, the waves rode and amplified each other, becoming an invisible battering ram of tortured air.

The gates didn't so much go down as fly away in splinters. Anyone who had been standing on the other side, within a radius of about ten metres, flew away too. Armed hostiles or innocent bystanders, they were out of the fight before they knew the fight was a thing.

The squad went in.

Inside the compound they stayed tight, firing outwards in all directions and tying down the opposition while the beekeeper flew on ahead of them to search for Topaz Tourmaline FiveHills and her anima.

The slavers had no idea what they were facing, and were misled by seductive mathematics. The strangers were making a ton of noise and spitting fire, but there seemed to be only a few of them: the odds had to be solidly in the home team's favour. They stepped out from between the trucks and the breezeblock outhouses, some drawing guns as they came, many just hefting curved pangas or aluminium baseball bats.

They met a hail of fire both from small arms and from Sa-Su rifles. Essien and Moon walked in the vanguard of the raiding party because their Sa-Sus projected a force shield when fired, depleting the momentum of any solid ammunition that was incoming. Most of the slavers' bullets fell to the ground or bounced harmlessly off their intended targets.

The rest of Moon's squad were limited to regular-issue sidearms, but their Cielo augments, awake again after a long sleep, handled the mechanics of aiming and range-finding with spectacular accuracy. Their hit rate was high.

But as they advanced further into the compound, they were forced to go hand to hand, which was messier. The strike team still had the advantage because of their augments and combat experience, but in a melee, Moon knew, numbers were likely to tell.

Then, very suddenly, things got worse. Someone – she was pretty sure it was Chulluque – lobbed an incendiary, and it bounced under a truck before it detonated. The truck lifted off the ground and came down on fire. A few seconds later, the trucks on either side of it ignited too. These fucking antiques were powered by chemical combustion! The flames from the burning vehicles spread via lakes of burning petro-chemicals to the outbuildings and then to the main structures. The thick, oily smoke from these fires rolled out across the compound in sluggish waves, engulfing Moon's squad and the defenders alike.

Cielo augments included sub-dermal glands that secreted vapour-phase flame retardants when the ambient temperature exceeded 70 degrees, so the fire wasn't an immediate problem. The smoke was another thing entirely. It lowered visibility, making it harder to pick the slavers off cleanly at a distance. It also turned the compound into a live minefield, since every truck that wasn't already burning was now a bomb that would go off once the temperature around its fuel tank passed its flashpoint.

Moon made a mental note to pistol-whip Chulluque as soon as they were out of this, but she was still confident that she was on top of the situation. Some of the defenders were trying to push back, but most of them changed their minds as soon as they got a good look at what they were fighting. Most of the squad had thrown off their hoods to widen their field of vision. Faced with something so inexplicably alien, with crescent-moon or keyhole eyes, furred faces and scimitar teeth, the defenders either froze or fled.

Then the beekeeper brought Moon some more bad news. The slavers had reinforcements coming. There was another building across the street that had looked more or less derelict, with gaps in its brickwork and its windows boarded. Its doors had been flung open and armed selves were pouring out of it. On top of that, a crude semi-portable machine gun with belt feed was being set up in a third floor window. The squad was about to be caught in an enfilade.

Nkanika, she voked, *we're going to need to retreat towards the south wall. Lead out to my—*

That was when she realised there was an empty space at her left shoulder where Nkanika was meant to be.

The Sinkhole was MIA.

69

Paz trekked through what seemed like miles of intersecting corridors, holding Dulcie in front of her with one hand cupped under ets buckled torso like a priest waving a censer. The doors opened at Dulcie's touch.

"Go!" Paz croaked at the imprisoned selves as she flung open their cage doors. "You're free now. Run! Just run!" The smoke slowed and slurred the echoes, mocking her with her own hoarse voice, but Dulcie picked up where she left off, booming out the words in a dozen local languages.

The selves only stared at Paz at first, frightened and repelled by her strangeness. But the thickening smoke or perhaps the distant gunfire galvanised them. They edged past her, trying hard not to touch her, and ran away through the labyrinth without looking back. Paz couldn't do anything more for them. She had no idea where the exit was, so she couldn't offer directions. She could only hope that some of them would make it out safely.

The corridors were a maze. Paz kept hoping she would eventually see some daylight, until she turned a corner and found a flight of stairs going upwards. It was only then she realised with a sense of sick dismay that she was underground. Perhaps that explained the way the smoke was behaving, settling and pooling sluggishly like thick oil, reducing visibility to about an arm's length. But she couldn't go up just yet. Not when she was the only self in this whole place that had a key.

Something zipped past her at head height, making her flinch. It was the size of a small bird, but there was no flutter of wings as it went by.

Dulcie, what was—?

"A beekeeper remote," Dulcie said. "It's looking for us."

Are you sure?

"It's standard Cielo ordnance, so yes, I'm sure. There's no way it missed us on that pass, but going by the signals traffic from outside I think the operator has their hands full right now. Paz, we've done all we can. We need to go."

We'll go when all the cages are open, Dulcie, Paz said grimly.

"The selves you've already freed should be able to free the rest."

That doesn't mean they'll do it.

Paz flung open another cell door. Most of the occupants barged right past her and fled, but an old man caught her arm before she could move on. He spoke to her urgently, gripping her hand with both of his.

What is he saying? Paz demanded.

"He wants to know if you're Izra'il. If you're the angel of death. I'm not sure if those are two different options or two ways of saying the same thing."

Paz shook her head vehemently, but she didn't know what gesture counted as denial in this place and what was agreement. *Just tell him to run!*

"Teach by example," Dulcie suggested.

The old man was still talking to her or perhaps praying to her, his eyes full of eagerness. "I'm sorry," Paz told him. "I'm so sorry. I'm not the angel of death, but I think I brought this death here. I hope you can find a way out." She shook off his hand and hurried on.

70

It took a while for Essien to realise that he'd cut free from the rest of his unit. He was practically sleepwalking until Moon's voked command snapped him out of it.

Damola Ojo was drawing him to its heart, and he wanted to go there even though he was badly frightened of what he would find. This place had meant something to him. He was aware that what it had meant was probably terrible, but it was still a missing part of himself. He had lost or thrown away so much, had come to the very point of dissolution. Now fate or chance had thrown back this fragment, the way you might throw a bone to a starving dog. And like a starving dog, he was up on his hind legs jumping at it.

He moved between the burning trucks. The flames washing over him burned his clothes but fireproof organobromines were oozing from his co-opted pores and his skin felt so cold that it tingled. Shouts and running footsteps to his left and right told him that he was passing close to the defenders, but the smoke hid him.

He came to a wall – the outer wall of the main building – and followed it. He was almost certain there would be a door here, within the next ten or twenty yards. A man loomed out of the smoke, coughing and staggering. He didn't see Essien until the last moment. He raised his panga and charged. Essien shot him in the head, stepped around the falling body and kept right on without breaking his stride.

Nkanika, where the fuck are you going? Even over a voke link the urgency in Moon's tone was unmistakeable. Essien didn't care.

I'm checking out the interior of the building, he messaged back.

I need you here!

If FiveHills is inside, we want to get to her before the fire does. It was true, wasn't it? He was still on-mission. He was also being pulled by a magnet, into the warehouse and into the blind embrace of his half-melted memories.

He found the door at last. It was locked, but the lock burst like rotten fruit when he kicked it.

He stepped out of the open into the warehouse. The stink of smoke gave way to the stink of tightly pressed bodies, of piss and shit and misery.

He was in a narrow corridor, with a drainage channel in the centre of its concrete floor. There were cages on both sides of it, shallow boxes of unfaced concrete with barred steel gates for doors. Faces of women and children and men stared back at him out of these cattle pens. They had heard the gunfire and they were terrified. Some of them had fallen to their knees. A few called out to him in languages he almost knew. They wept and wrung their hands.

They would burn to death here if he did nothing. But he peered down the corridor and saw no end of it. If the whole warehouse space was like this, there could be hundreds of cages. Thousands. Nobody could open them all.

He debated with himself, furious and appalled. *Not real,* Sergeant Otubre's voice whispered in his mind. Real or not he owed them nothing. They were slaves. They had let themselves become someone else's property. Their helplessness was disgusting and the look of them, the smell of them, was almost more than he could stomach.

He swung his Sa-Su around to his back, where bands of force locked it to his shoulder and hip, and drew his side arm. He looked away as he fired.

The selves in the cage cowered away from the noise and the flash, then stared dumbly at the broken lock hanging sideways on its hasp.

"Here," Essien said. He offered the gun to the nearest woman. "The rest . . . others . . . you . . ." He finished the sentence with a sweeping gesture. "Just . . . Shoot the locks. Let them out. Go."

He moved on, head down, ignoring the voices pleading and cursing from his left and right sides. He couldn't be sure if he'd spoken to the woman in grunt or in Ibibio. He didn't know if she spoke either one.

He turned a corner, then another. The air was thickening around him as the smoke from the fires outside found its way into the building. He threaded the maze until he found himself at the head of a flight of stairs. He stopped there, breathing hard, staring down into the dark. It confounded him, even though this was where he'd been heading all along. The cages were strange to him, and awful: the stairs were awful and familiar. His mind supplied the muscle memory of climbing and descending.

He hesitated for only a second. The fire would make this space impassable soon. The rabbit, he reminded himself again. Topaz FiveHills. This was still about the mission. Nothing he was doing was irrational or insubordinate.

He went on down into the basement levels. The smoke was even denser down here, hanging in the still, stifling air like grubby curtains.

He found only more packed cages, more pleading, panicked men and women in these spaces where lumber and machine parts had once been stacked to the ceiling. And the ceiling was lower. Someone had turned the three underground levels of the complex into more levels, subdividing them horizontally to make this egg-box farm more efficient, to stack more people in a given volume.

While he was thinking that, some people came surging up the stairs towards him. Like the ones in the cages they were nearly naked. Their eyes were wide as they fled past him, pushing him aside. Essien pressed himself against the wall and waited. Then when it became clear that the flood wasn't going to stop, he forced his way through them, his augmented muscles bulging as he gripped the stairs' metal rail and hauled himself down hand over hand.

At the bottom of the stack, he turned into a narrow corridor that forked and forked again. There were cages here too but they were empty, their doors already hanging open. Someone had been through here already, opening the doors as they went.

Finally, he found a corridor with doors of actual wood, locked, featureless. His feet moved of their own accord, remembering, while his mind churned and rebelled. The lights were so sparse down here that the best they could do was to create a sort of dreary twilight, but it didn't make much difference at this point. The thickening smoke was all but blinding him.

His hands groped along the wall until they found a door. It was no different to any of the dozens of others he had passed but he knew that he was in the right place. Except that it wasn't a place; not really. He had been moving all this while through time as well as physical distances. What he had come to was an irrevocable moment.

The door was locked. Finding his hands empty, and forgetting about the rifle slung across his back, Essien dug his fingernails under the lock plate and pulled, with steadily escalating force. The lock started to come away from the wood. His nails gave too, his fingers starting to bleed, but now he could see the screws that were holding the lock in place, a few millimetres of their thread bared. And now he could force the tips of his fingers into the gap. The muscles on his arms bulged, wrecking-ball hard, as he increased his efforts. The lock came free, clattering to the floor in pieces.

Essien went inside. The room was a dormitory in this world too, but there were only eight cots rather than the dozen he remembered. There was no stink of sweat and piss-bucket: the bitter perfume of the smoke drowned out everything else.

He groped for a light switch. There was none. In his own Lagos, likewise, there had only ever been a lantern. He stepped into the dark.

He picked up the cot that was closest to the door and threw it aside. Down on his knees he searched the wall with his fingers until he found the rough, shallow grooves in the concrete, exactly where he himself had made them a world or so away from here.

Essien Nkanika. I came and I went.

He couldn't tell in the near-dark down there whether the man who'd carved these lines here in this place had been given the same name as him or some other name, but he couldn't pull away from the sickening, vertiginous sense of *kinship*. He had knelt here before, a thousand or a million times. He had played out the same acts, written and spoken the same words, been gathered up in the same nets of circumstance.

He tried to take a breath, but nothing came. This wasn't emotion, it was the reflex that allowed him to survive underwater for minutes at a time, activating now because of the toxic smoke: his airway had locked shut, and his system was oxygenating itself by some emergency backup mechanism that was opaque to him.

Everything outside the Pandominion is right-turn land, Sergeant Otubre had said during that long-ago briefing. Everyone who lives there isn't really alive at all. And it had been vitally important for Essien to believe what Otubre was telling him because of the other thing that happened on that same day. The row of stakes. The people down on their knees. The woman staring hate and defiance into his eyes as he shot her. Not a woman, just a phantom. Smoke from a fire. Mist on a windshield.

Who lives in nowhere? Otubre had asked, as if the answer was obvious. And in a way it was. If the woman was smoke and mist then so was Essien. And conversely, if he was flesh and blood then the flesh he'd torn and the blood he'd shed was all on him. Over him. Accusing him. A lot of the salient details relating to that flesh and blood – names, places, reasons – had been conveniently lost in the blood-warm sea his mind had become. But it turned out to be a shallow sea, after all. He found to his wonder and dismay that the waters were beginning to recede.

The woman's stare had been one of recognition. *Look at you*, it said, *way up there behind that gun, and look at me down here in front of it. But in Oshodi we're one and the same thing.*

Essien sank into a huddle on the floor, face buried in his folded arms, and sobbed.

Nkanika!

He lifted up his head. Moon's voked message carried a razor-sharp rebuke that cut through his despair. *Moon.*

We're holding our own here but we're pinned down. You stopped moving. Does that mean you've got eyes on the rabbit?

No. Not yet.

Then get back in the fucking game! The beekeeper got a glimpse of her about a minute ago. She's on the same level as you, maybe a hundred yards away. Find her and bring her out. Now!

Yes, Essien said. *Yes, Moon. I'm on it.*

He climbed to his feet. Surrounded by omens, hectored by memories whose vagueness and incompleteness only made them stronger.

But the mission would save him. It was all he had left to throw into that void and keep it from swallowing him.

71

Paz was going round in circles now, passing cages she'd already unlocked on a previous pass. The tiny remote had found her again and kept circling her. She tried to pull it down out of the air but it was much too fast for her. "Let me," Dulcie said. "Turn me over on my back." The next time the drone shot by it was suddenly slammed up against the ceiling by an invisible force as Dulcie used ets pressure-wave weapon again. It fell to the floor in pieces.

Thank you, Paz voked.

She was trying to find her way back to the stairs, but her eyes were streaming and her head filled with a throbbing ache like a heartbeat. The air was hot, with a bitter taste like deep-fried ash. She was scared she might pass out and die down here. Even if the fire never reached her, the smoke could certainly kill her all by itself.

She came to a corner and looked cautiously around it. The adjoining corridor seemed to be empty apart from the sluggish roil of stinking black smoke. There were no cages, no selves, no sign of anything moving. Along one side of the corridor there was a row of solid wooden doors, completely unlike the barred grilles that were the cell doors. Perhaps one of them was an exit.

She tried each one in turn. Most were locked, but some of them opened when she tried them. The first was a utilities cupboard, stacked with mops and buckets, the second a room walled with telos screens. The screens showed different parts of the compound.

Running figures. Things on fire. Bare concrete smeared with oil or blood or both.

The third door opened on an office. Paz thought it was empty until she saw the man crouching under the desk on all fours. His face was buried in his arms but she knew from his bald head and pink skin who this was: Mr Diallo, the slaver, the man who was in charge of this place. He was hiding in much the same way a small child might hide, not looking at the ruin that had come because looking at it might make it real.

He had heard the door open. He glanced up and their eyes met. He seemed merely surprised at first, but then a paroxysm of anger twisted his face. He pointed a shaking finger at her, his mouth working to frame words.

Paz didn't wait for them to come, still less for Dulcie to render them for her. She turned and fled at a limping, lopsided run.

She headed in the same direction she'd been going before, still hoping there might be an exit here. She didn't bother to try the doors she passed, too afraid that Diallo might be following her. At the end of the corridor there was one last double door. Paz pushed against it as hard as she could but it didn't yield. There was a padlock on a chain that looped around its two handles, holding the doors shut. She would have to go back.

When she turned around, Diallo was there, looming out of the black smoke like a monster, his obscenely hairless face contorted into a bestial snarl. He was carrying a weapon, a gun of some kind with two short, fat barrels. He shouted at her, his voice hoarse and breaking.

"I did warn you," Dulcie said. Ets tone was bleak.

So you did. How would you feel if I threw you at his head?

"Not optimistic. He's got a shotgun."

Yes, Paz agreed. *He does, doesn't he? Keep translating, Dulcie.*

The man shouted at her again, his voice hoarse and clotted both with smoke and with hysteria. The gun shook in his hands.

"Something about a hyena," Dulcie parsed. "If you goad a hyena you get . . . something. It's a slang word. Bitten, mauled, something like that."

"Oh dear," Paz called out. "Are you upset?" She shouted as loud as she could, even though she was forced to gulp down some more of the burning air to do it. She heard the clicks and whoops as Dulcie translated her words into Diallo's language. "Sad because all the people you caught in your cages are running free again? Or because you can't be all big and scary any more now that someone bigger and scarier has come for you? Well, too bad. This is what happens to bullies. They run into a bigger bully and that's the end of them."

Diallo spoke, and Dulcie rendered the words for Paz's benefit. "Fucking monster! You did this!"

"I did," Paz agreed, her heart hammering. "And yes I am, I am a monster. I'm *your* monster, Saikou Diallo. I came here for you. You told me you were a rain-maker, whatever that means. Well, I make fire. And I made this one just for you!"

There was no way to tell what sort of effect her words were having. The man's body language was utterly strange to her. But she heard the ratcheting click as he pumped the shotgun. She had been waiting for it, and she dropped to the ground just in time as he fired. The gun's deafening retort in that narrow space felt like a physical impact. The shotgun's shell, loaded with something heavy and hurtful, passed over Paz's hunched shoulders and punched a hole right through the middle of the double doors where they met. Links of the disintegrated chain rained down on Paz like iron confetti. She didn't see what happened to the padlock.

Diallo racked the gun and aimed again, but before he could fire the second barrel there was a sound almost as loud as the shotgun blast had made. It was the bellow of some tortured animal and it made the slaver turn his head, startled. Something shot out of the smoke and hit him at shoulder height, knocking him clean off his feet.

It was another man, with a Sa-Su rifle strapped to his back. Paz knew the Cielo weapon of choice in an instant, having studied its every working part in her Mechanics electives, but the newcomer wasn't in Cielo armour. To Paz, he looked very much like the local selves she had been freeing from the cages. He had come from nowhere, the smoke hiding him until he was right on top of them.

Diallo went down on his stomach with the second man kneeling on his back. He tried to twist around so he could bring his shotgun to bear, but the other man pinned his hand and planted a knee between his shoulders. He rode out Diallo's struggles and set about loosening his grip on the gun, slamming the pink man's clenched fist against the cement floor again and again.

Paz didn't wait to see the outcome of the fight. She jumped to her feet and charged through the double doors which brought her out at the bottom of a concrete stairwell. Clutching Dulcie tight in her arms, she began to stumble-climb towards the distant daylight.

72

Essien was tracking the rabbit. He really was. Moon had transferred the beekeeper to his control and the beekeeper was tight on her, updating her location in real time as she moved, only a little way ahead of him, through the smoke-filled corridors.

Then the remote went offline for some reason and he was forced to quicken his pace. If Topaz Tourmaline succumbed to the smoke she was likely to die unless he found her first, and Moon needed her alive — at least until they'd verified the whereabouts of the construct.

He was moving carefully now so as not to tread on his quarry by accident, but turning a corner he found her at last on her feet, dead-ended by a locked door and face to face with one of the locals. A white man in a white suit.

Essien's memory clenched and convulsed.

The man, who had his back turned, shouted something, his voice clotted with smoke and hysteria. "*Karambanin zomo, gai da kura!*" The language was Hausa and the words were nonsense — a piece of folksy smugness about what happens to you if you're stupid enough to goad a hyena.

Gabber might have blunted Essien's thoughts and blinded his memory, but some things are indelible. This was one of them. A white man in white clothes, with a Fulani name, speaking Hausa. Bald. Florid. Given to homespun philosophy.

A sneering voice sounded in his head (*run, little rabbit!*) and the years of his life telescoped shut. For just a second he felt himself a scrawny teenager, locked underground, powerless, wandering in a maze full of monsters and meaningless suffering.

Diallo. Saikou Diallo. The man who had made him a slave.

As the memories all locked into place, Essien felt a pain as though a hot wire was being drawn through his brain. He roared and came on, carrying Diallo to the ground. There was a gun, and then there was no longer a gun. The white man's reflexes were absurdly slow when compared to the enhanced Cielo baseline – and Essien's body was moving by itself, deciding for itself. His mind trailed behind it wondering, watching as his bunched fists rose and fell, rose and fell.

At last, a long time after the man was unambiguously dead, Essien rolled away from him. Propping himself against the wall of the corridor, he fought to bring his breathing back under control.

What was happening to him? It wasn't just the need for revenge that had driven him. It was the marks on the wall in the dormitory room; the certainty, as strong as faith, that another Essien Nkanika had been locked down here and had endured as he himself had endured, not knowing if he would ever see daylight again. It was the sense that every pain and sorrow he'd ever felt had an infinite footprint, was somehow smeared across the face of creation like the black rainbow in the Blues Boys' song he had loved. Staring at his knuckles, covered in the blood and pulp of Saikou Diallo, he felt as though a hole had been torn in him and this real-but-unreal place was pouring into the breach. His hands shook, even though they should be incapable of shaking now. Cielo muscles had no tremor factor.

Instinctively – and these were instincts that had been beaten into him with hammers during his repurposing as a soldier – he reached out to his corps and his commanding officer.

Moon, he voked. *Moon, help me. I'm down and requesting retrieval.*

"In some ways, Essien, I'd say that's the story of your life."

The voice came through on his array, but it wasn't voked. It was full audio. Because of where he was and what he had just done he recognised it at once, but he couldn't find words to answer it. At last, filling his lungs with effort – and with smoke – he found precisely one.

"Ha—Hadiz!"

"You remember me. I'm touched. What we had together meant something to you then?"

"Hadiz!" He began to cough, and then to shake more violently than ever. There were probably toxins in the air that his system, for all its clever workarounds, was finding it hard to denature or metabolise.

"We've covered that part, Essien. Let's move on. I hope your second meeting with Mr Diallo was cathartic. It wasn't on my agenda when I brought you here but I can't deny there's a poetic justice to it. You understand that he wasn't the man who caged you, only a near analogue? You were taking revenge for someone else. A different Essien. I've made a point of not looking for that version of you, so I can't tell you what became of him. Whether he's still alive, even."

"How?" Essien whispered. "How are you doing this? Where are you?"

"Close," Hadiz assured him. "Very close. You remember I told you that when I bought that place in Apapa Quays I bought the building next door too? Well, I meant the universe next door – this one – rather than the next block over. I had two labs, Essien, only one of which you ever got to see. That turned out to be a sensible precaution, didn't it? After Moon Sostenti shot me in the stomach, I was able to retreat to a place where she couldn't follow me."

An explosion shook the building, making cement dust come down on Essien like fine snow.

"And I'm still here," Hadiz concluded after the reverberation had stopped. "I know you've got other clients, Essien, but would you care to join me? For the whole night? I can't make any promises about breakfast."

Essien's chest heaved and convulsed. The word fell out of him like a stone. "Yes."

"You understand what this means? The last time I trusted you I ended up with a hole right through me and half my internal organs cooked. But in spite of everything I'm giving you a second chance. So long as you do what you're told and show a proper sense of contrition."

"Cielo – the Cielo – Hadiz, they're here!" He had to warn her, or the same thing would happen again. He would have to watch her die a second time. "Vemmet sent us to bring back a fugitive. That's why I'm here."

"No, Essien." Hadiz's voice was cold and clipped. "You're here because I brought you. Watchmaster Vemmet was just one of the buttons I had to press to do it. Now stand up."

Essien dragged himself to his feet.

"Here are your new orders," Hadiz said. "Get it right this time."

73

At the top of the stairs was a door, and on the other side of the door the wide concrete apron, lined with truck bays and outbuildings, that made up the bulk of Damola Ojo. And on the other side of that, Paz knew, was the gate – which presumably must have opened to let the invaders inside.

But the space in between was an arena filled with a very literal fog of war. Through the roiling smoke stampeding selves ran by with knives and guns held aloft. The thudding percussion of small arms was interlaced with a road-drill staccato from something much heavier and more dangerous. Half the world seemed to be on fire and the other half screaming.

Follow the wall, Dulcie told Paz. Et voked the words, so et must have rebooted ets broadcast system at last. *Stay low. Go on all fours if you can. There'll be breathable air near the ground, and most of the bullets will be fired at chest height so hopefully they'll miss you.*

Paz dropped to hands and knees. She was able to force herself to move by the expedient of not looking and not thinking.

Meanwhile, Dulcie did ets best to add to the general chaos, deploying the PaintPot Permutator to deadly effect. Around Paz et enhanced and embellished the flames that were already there, giving Moon's strike team good reason to turn aside. Elsewhere, et drew a line here, a swatch of colour there, impressionistic but highly suggestive of furless pink and brown-skinned selves with rifles and curved knives running headlong out of the roiling smoke. With their augments the ex-troopers could be relied on to fire with pinpoint accuracy, and they did so without hesitation. But they were shooting at ghosts, and Dulcie had worked out the angles and trajectories to maximal advantage.

Three of Moon's team were down before she realised her people were being made to fire on their own side – and she ordered the ceasefire at the worst possible moment. The survivors now found themselves confronted by a charging skirmish line of terrified slavers, penned in and shepherded by Dulcie's imaginary flames. The indigenous selves fought for their lives, which went some way towards narrowing the odds between the trained soldiers and the haphazardly armed amateurs.

Paz reached the gate at last and straightened up. She wasn't alone. Many of the freed slaves were running alongside her, coughing and wiping their eyes, leaning on each other's shoulders as they finally broke free of the compound where they had been held. They ignored Paz completely, which she guessed meant that Dulcie had given her a new hologram mask to wear.

She picked her way over the rubble and out onto the street where a crowd of onlookers had gathered to watch – in fear and awe and in many cases open jubilation – the burning down of Damola Ojo. There were people in uniform too, some of them standing next to cars painted in the same green livery that they themselves were wearing. Paz guessed that these were local enforcers, but they were making no move to enter the burning compound or to stop the flow of people running out of it. They seemed to have decided that this incident fell under someone else's job description.

The local selves all backed away from Paz hastily as she stumbled out onto the street, confirming her earlier suspicion. Whatever she looked like right now, it wasn't a bedraggled rabbit with a half-destroyed ceramic monkey in her hands and blood and filth caking her fur. She walked straight on through the crowd, trying not to limp too obviously. They parted for her hastily, some of them ducking their heads or muttering respectful greetings.

Where now? she asked.

Eleven Creek Road, Dulcie instructed her. *It's a house or structure in an industrial district called Apapa. Stand at the kerb and raise your hand.*

Raise my hand? Why?

To summon transport. That's how it works here.

What transport? The street is blocked! It was true. Many people had stopped their cars to stare at the conflagration, forcing the cars behind to stop too. The shrieking of a thousand horns assaulted the air.

Just do it, Dulcie told her.

Paz did as she was told, standing at the edge of the road with her hand in the air as if she was answering a question in class. It took less than a minute for a vehicle to respond to her summons, weaving its way through the stationary traffic to join her. It wasn't at all what she was expecting. It was a powered bike.

She gave an involuntary yelp when she saw the rider, or rather the helmet he was wearing. It was metallic red, like the helmet of a Cielo trooper's armour. But underneath the raised visor was the face of a boy only a little older than Paz herself, with the dark brown skin that predominated here. His eyes kept slipping past Paz to stare at the pillar of smoke rising behind her. When he did finally register her, his expression went from awe to concern. He spoke, in a high, sweet voice full of urgency and animation. Dulcie translated in a flat deadpan.

Get you away from here, Reverend sir, yes? I can do that. But where is your car? Where are your people? An okada is no way for a man like you to ride!

What is he talking about? Paz asked Dulcie.

Dulcie answered the boy in his own language, presumably putting words in Paz's mouth. *It doesn't matter*, et told Paz at the same time. *He thinks you're a holy man, and you've just told him you have an urgent appointment with a poor and destitute soul bereft of spiritual guidance. Which is why you're going down to Apapa Quays. Climb on.*

The boy had already made room for her, scooching forward on the seat so Paz could squeeze in behind him. She did so, with some misgivings.

Oh, you're lighter than you look, Father, the boy explained. *No offence! Hold on tight and I'll take you out of this place.*

Paz held on very tight indeed. This didn't look or feel safe, and the bike, as it started to move, wobbled alarmingly. But as soon as it picked up speed it stabilised again, and the boy was a very skilful driver. He wove his way between the cars and the crowds of onlookers, finding clear spaces where Paz saw only barriers. Soon they were out of the jam and driving at breakneck speed along a wider street. The surface of the road was full of potholes, but the bike tacked and trimmed between them without slowing.

The boy called out to her over his shoulder. The wind whipped the words away, but they would have made no sense to her anyway.

Almost there, Dulcie said. *Once we get to Tambuwal, this all becomes her problem. I only hope she's got some solutions.*

74

The semi-portable gun in the building opposite dealt Moon's plan of campaign a disastrous blow. It turned the battle for Damola Ojo into a stand-off, when she'd counted on being able to suppress the local opposition quickly and completely.

For an agonising interval, the raiding party was trapped in a narrow segment of the compound defined by the machine gun's reach while they fended off wave after wave of assaults from the reinforcements who had charged in through the ruined gates at their back.

Much as she hated to leave Orso Vemmet unsupervised, Moon had no choice but to bring in Wuxx and Chiomis. They already knew the location. She told them to get there as quickly as they could.

What about His Majesty? Chiomis asked.

Leave him, Moon ordered. *He'll slow you down. But tell him if he ups and runs before we get back I'll find him and peel him like a fucking apple.*

The ten minutes before Wuxx and Chio arrived were precarious, but their intervention was decisive. They took out the machine gun with an RPG and then came in through the gates like two humorously ill-matched angels of death, an impossibly tall mustelid and a squat, heavy sloth-man firing radically dispersible ammunition into the gaps between the burning trucks.

By this point, though, the clusterfuck had evolved to its next stage. Nkanika had gone silent and the beekeeper was offline. Hundreds of captive selves had sprinted out of the burning building to freedom while Moon and her squad were engaged with the slavers, and intercepting them hadn't been a practical proposition. Moon would have bet the last star in her pocket that Topaz FiveHills had been among them.

She did a search anyway, to make sure that the rabbit hadn't dug herself a hole to hide in, or got herself pinned under a piece of masonry somewhere. No such luck. And there was no sign of the construct either, which meant the raid had achieved precisely nothing. Moon had just presided over another shit-show, when she was meant to be scrubbing out the stains from the last one.

The search also failed to turn up any sign of Private Nkanika, E/432nd HVY INF/DG10014/U5838784453. There were any number of charred bodies in the main building, but none of them had Cielo augments any more than they had rabbit's ears. Nkanika was in the wind and her squad strength was down to nine, not counting Orso Vemmet because frankly who would? The best she could hope for was that he'd keep the plate hot for their retreat: if he had a personal crisis before then they were likely to find both him and the plate gone.

The surviving grunts were badly shaken, having walked into a threshing machine when they were expecting a picnic. Moon detailed two of them, Wuxx and Nesuskal, to check if any of the vehicles in the compound were still functional, then turned to Chiomis.

"Rabbit's on the run," she said tersely. "See if you can get the scent again."

Chio shut her eyes, the better to concentrate on her array. "Nothing on the official feeds," she said after a moment's strained pause, "but there's a lot of locals filming this on hand-held shit. Might be I can sieve something out of that. There was kind of a stampede out of here, though. It's going to be a bit like tracking a fart through a fish market."

"Do what you can," Moon told her, clapping a hand on her shoulder. "You were shit-hot last time so you've already proved your point."

She left her to it, seeing Wuxx and Nesuskal coming towards her at a rapid trot. "Report," she said.

Wuxx did, succinctly. They'd found two trucks the fire hadn't touched, and it didn't seem like there would be any trouble making them move. They had simple chemical engines burning refined petroleum by-products, and steering systems designed for hyperactive children.

Okay, Moon voked to what was left of the squad. *Get on up into these things, by your numbers. Wuxx, you're driving the first truck. Take Chiomis with you. I'll pair with Nesuskal in the other. The rest of you, up in the back. Keep your heads down and your guns on standby.*

"Where are we going?" Wuxx asked once they were all in.

Chio?

I think I might have something. Chiomis threw it to their arrays – some grainy moving footage of the exodus from the burning compound. After a few seconds, the image froze and zoomed in on one figure, a middle-aged male self with a sizeable paunch. Where most of the freed slaves ran hell for leather, not just from the fire but from degradation, forced labour and despair, this man walked with a commanding stride, shoulders squared. He was dressed in long white robes that were incongruously clean.

Kind of stands out, doesn't he? Chiomis voked. *Then this happened.*

The image moved again. The man stood at the side of the road and raised an imperious hand. A bike slowed and stopped in front of him. After a few seconds of negotiation, its rider took the man on-board. There was a moment, as the man climbed onto the back of the bike, when his robes intersected its rear wheel. Instead of rumpling and bunching up they passed through it.

Hologram field, Moon said. *That's our girl right there.*

I think so, yeah.

And you've still got eyes on her?

Comes and goes. She's heading south.

Then so are we. Move out.

At the gates of the compound, they met a crowd of disaster

tourists and a wall of cars that wasn't going anywhere, but when Moon fired a few Sa-Su volleys over their heads they got moving again pretty quick. The local selves scattered, apart from a few who were wearing uniforms and seemed to have some kind of brief to keep order in the city. Moon disabused them of this impression by killing two or three with an air-burst grenade. The rest quickly joined the general exodus, leaving the road clear for the tiny convoy.

After that it got harder. Chiomis could only see their quarry when she passed a CCTV camera that was on her route, so her voked instructions were both intermittent and urgent. They took the form of compass bearings, which was fine when the road grid let Moon go where the rabbit was going. Sometimes she had to go straight on for several hundred yards after Chio had told her to grab a left. Sometimes two or three instructions would pile up while she was trapped either by sluggish traffic or by the absence of a road to turn into. It would be a lot easier when the rabbit stopped moving, but until then it was a wild ride through narrow streets with badly eroded surfaces.

"Bring up a map," she ordered Chiomis. "Tell me where we're headed. If it comes to picking a spot for an ambush, let's pick a good one."

We're here, Chio voked, dropping the map into Moon's field and marking their location with the Cielo sword-and-torch icon. *Local feeds call it Amukoko. Heading south by east, towards this little puddle of piss here, which is Apapa.*

Moon studied the map as closely as she could while still keeping some of her attention on the road ahead. From what she could see it didn't look bad at all.

"We can pen her in." She said it aloud at the same time as she voked: it helped her to think. "Once they get south of this point here – Ijora Olopa – the road runs out along the harbour. Looks like it's just a little spit of land out there, maybe a quarter of a mile wide or so. There's a place called Tincan Island. Wuxx, you see it?"

I see it, the sloth-man confirmed.

"If you swing east and come in by the bridge there, I don't see any way the bunny can get past you. Just make sure she doesn't see you. If she realises she's running into a bottleneck she might try to turn around, but she won't have much room to do it in. Between us we can box her in on one of the side streets."

The first truck was about fifty yards ahead of them at this point. Wuxx took the next right, heeling over on two wheels rather than slow down. Moon drove straight on.

On her right, the road was lined with the ruins of factories and warehouses, shells of concrete and broken glass with rusted shutters drawn down forever over their doors. Bright painted messages had been splashed over walls and windows alike, layer on layer; the silent shouts of the city's disaffected children. Weeds had grown to head height in asphalted yards, as if the city was regressing to some wild state.

And on their left was the water, flanked by endless wharves and piers that led nowhere. Some of them had already collapsed and the rest were on the way, sinking down year by year onto their water-logged foundations.

Corporal, Chiomis voked, *I'm not seeing any more cameras up ahead. I think we're going to be line-of-sight from here on in. Should we commandeer another truck? Give ourselves a bit more spread?*

"No need," Moon muttered. "We're good." A two-wheeled vehicle, a bike of some kind, was chugging along about two hundred yards ahead of them. It had a driver and a passenger, both recognisable from Chio's found footage. It was hard to believe that the overweight man she was seeing was actually a scrawny little rabbit, but the hologram wasn't 100 per cent perfect. The man's robe didn't move properly with the wind. And his outline, if you picked a spot and stared, had a kind of bleed to it – as if it was painted on the air with pigments that were just a little runny.

I've got visual, Moon confirmed. *Update and revise, Chio. Converge on these coordinates. We've got her this time.*

75

They're onto us, Dulcie said.

No, Paz protested. *They're not. They can't be! We're in disguise.*
She would have voked her answer in any case, so as not to alarm
or confuse their driver, but she had no breath to speak. She was
hanging on tight to the waist of the bike-rider, half exhilarated by
the reckless speed at which they were going and half terrified that
they would hit a wall or another vehicle.

Not that there were many other vehicles around here. They were
out of the centre of the city now, on a long straight road that led
past one derelict building after another. It didn't seem likely that
anyone was waiting for them in this lonely place, but if there was
it would be very easy to spot them.

There's Cielo signal traffic really close to us, Dulcie said. *I can't read
it, but it's definitely them. There's nobody else on this planet sending voke
strings.*

Then let's— Paz began, but Dulcie cut across her. *They're here*, et
said tersely. *Coming up behind us.*

Paz looked round. The only other vehicle on the road was a truck
a long way to their rear. With a sinking heart, she recognised it as
one of the trucks from the trailer park, the ones the slavers used to
bring in their catches.

"How?" she wailed. "How did they follow us?" The boy she was
clinging to looked around, startled by what must have sounded to
him like complete gibberish.

Does it matter? We made a mistake, and they caught it. But we're almost there. We might still make it.

Dulcie said something to the driver, who leaned the bike into a sudden right turn. Fifty yards further on et spoke again and the bike drew to a halt. Paz climbed down. There was just the one building on this patch of earth but it was a large one, a tower of white concrete blotched with black mould. Rusted rebar showed through pitted holes in its front wall, and most of its windows were shattered. A metal staircase ran up one side of it, but the bottom of the stairs was blocked by a gate and the gate was padlocked.

The red earth in front of the building had been sown with broken things: a section of black plastic rain guttering, the lid of a suitcase, some shredded car tyres and what Paz thought might be the cistern of a toilet. Across the back of the lot, each at its own oblique angle, were three large metal containers, their sides angled outwards from a rectangular base. They were full of builder's rubble, bricks and beams and baulks of timber.

Touch the top of the boy's head, Dulcie told her. *We need to get him away from here quickly. Unless you want him to be caught in between us and the Cielo guns.*

Bewildered, Paz pressed her fingers against the helmet's cool metal. The boy knelt down in front of her. Dulcie spoke a few words in the boy's language. He rose to his feet again, bowed to Paz, then jumped back on his bike and drove away.

What did—?

I told you, you look like a cleric in his religion. He took a blessing instead of payment. And he was happy with it. Try the door, Paz. We have seconds!

And not very many of them at that. As Paz sprinted towards the building, the truck that had been following them rounded the corner at speed, its tyres shrieking as it heeled around hard and came at them. At the same time, a second vehicle came barrelling down the street from the opposite direction. The boy on the bike barely swerved in time to avoid it, but at least he had sense enough to keep on going.

Paz ran for the building, but found that it had no door. Not one she could open, at any rate. There was a sort of grille made of corrugated metal plates that seemed to be designed to roll up and down, but there was no handle to lift it by. She knelt down and tried to get her fingers underneath to pull the grille up. It didn't budge.

She turned at bay. The two vehicles had disgorged their occupants. They wore no armour, but their variegated fur and features made it very clear they were from the Pandominion – and their weapons declared them Cielo troopers. They advanced on Paz, spreading out in a fan with rifles raised and aimed.

She ran for the stairs. The gate that barred her way rose about as high as her shoulder. Uninjured and with enough of a run-up, she would have cleared it easily. As things stood it would be close. She gathered herself, kicked off and soared into the air.

An invisible fist caught her at the top of her arc and slammed her sideways against the wall. She fell in a heap, dazed, her head ringing with jagged shards of sound. One of the soldiers had fired a push-away, a force field weapon. At that range, he was never going to miss.

Paz had dropped Dulcie. Et was lying a few feet away at the foot of the gate. Et had fallen with ets back to Paz, but because ets carapace had been folded in on itself by the shotgun blast ets face, upside down, was still visible. Ets green eyes stared levelly into Paz's brown ones.

I'm sorry, et voked. *I could have done more. Been cleverer, or more cautious. I'm so sorry, Paz. You were a good friend and you deserved better from me.*

Paz was surrounded now, the soldiers looking down on her from all sides. One of them, a bear-man, leaned down and touched the barrel of his rifle to the side of her face. She flinched away. The soldier chuckled. He was so close that she could smell his breath, rank and strangely sweet.

"It's her, Commander," the man said.

Then, inexplicably and clownishly, for all his huge bulk, he somersaulted backwards out of Paz's line of sight. Searing white light blossomed where he'd just stood, and a full second later a sound like the boom of a bass drum next to her ear all but deafened her.

76

Sand and scrub grass. The smell of dust and wild sage on the super-heated air.

Essien stood with the barrel of his rifle pressed to the forehead of a woman. The woman had her hands tied behind her back. This was only a memory. It had happened a very long time ago. It was a memory he had deliberately misfiled, and until very recently it had been lost to him. Now it was back, playing in his brain like a movie in a darkened theatre.

"Let me put a case to you," the soundtrack went. "You go for a walk, and you come to a fork in the road. You could turn left, you could turn right."

The woman glared up at Essien. She was about to die, and she knew it, but that didn't take a single gram of weight away from her hatred and contempt for him. She knew what she was looking at.

Oshodi. Worthless. Someone else's whipping boy. Someone else's slave, always, no matter what armour you wear or what you carry in your hands.

The gun kicked just a little as he squeezed the trigger, but not enough to spoil the shot. The Sa-Su was a wonderful piece of technology: even when it was firing armour-piercing rounds the recoil was so gentle you barely felt it.

The woman's head disappeared. Her blood sprayed across the dirt, across Essien's thighs and calves and bright red boots.

"Who lives in nowhere?" the voice demanded.

It was a trick question. Essien knew that now.

I do, he told the memory.

I fucking do.

77

Looking back on it afterwards – which was always a luxury in any armed engagement – Moon still couldn't understand how it had all fallen apart.

They were right there. Both targets were in the bag, unarmed, down and with nowhere to run. Against all the odds she'd brought it home. She saw a future with some light and shade to it instead of one that was just black on blood red.

A second later, they were taking fire. It wasn't very accurate fire, but it was from really close up and it was coming from a rifle on full automatic feed so accuracy really didn't matter. Someone was emptying a magazine at her depleted squad while they were pinned against a windowless wall on a blind concrete apron with nowhere to run to. Three of her nine went down in that first volley, the formidable Chulluque among them.

Find cover! Moon voked, but she didn't follow her own advice. She swung round, dropping to one knee to return fire. At the same time, she registered the unique sound the super-fast spray of bullets made as it spat against metal and stone and flesh.

It was a Sa-Su.

Which meant it was Essien Nkanika.

She saw him a moment later. He'd come up on their blind side and taken cover behind one of the rusted dumpsters. He had good visibility on all of them, and enough ammunition to kill them ten times over.

Acting on instinct, she flicked her own rifle to full-auto and cut loose, forcing Nkanika to duck back out of sight. That was good. That gave the remainder of her squad the window they needed to go to ground. Chiomis and Nesuskal fell back to the trucks, which was a good choice. Wuxx and a couple of the others made it to the angle of the external stairwell, which was even better. Moon just flung herself flat against the ground next to the rabbit, who stared at her with wide, startled eyes. Well, that maybe wasn't a bad call either. Moon had no fucking clue what Nkanika was trying to do here, but if he wanted to grab Topaz FiveHills for himself he might think twice about firing directly at her.

Go around the building, Moon voked to Wuxx. *We'll pin him down here. You come in behind him and roll him up.*

Is that Nkanika? Wuxx demanded, incredulous and appalled.

Yes. Now put the fucker down.

Maybe emboldened by the lull, Nkanika put his head out again. Moon gave him another burst that made him tuck it back in quickly. Looking around, she made eye contact with Nesuskal and pointed upwards. The roof of the truck's cab might give her enough height to lob a grenade in over the side of the dumpster. It was a long shot, but with Cielo augments not an impossible one.

Nesuskal nodded, put one foot on the truck's front bumper and started to haul herself up.

Coming round now, Wuxx told Moon.

Great, she acknowledged. *Go on three and we'll give you cover. One . . . two . . .*

A shriek of protesting metal broke her concentration. She glanced round to see that the steel grille covering the front of the building at her back was rolling upwards. Through the gap at the bottom three black and yellow drones came whipping out at high speed. Quick as they were they were flying low, so Moon had time to shoot two of them out of the air. The third made it past her and glided straight under the nearer truck – the one that Wuxx and Nesuskal were using as cover.

The truck blew apart as light and easy as a dandelion puffball, on an expanding sphere of greasy orange flame shot through with a pitch-black marbling of smoke. Chiomis staggered blindly away from the wreck, on fire, managing five or six long-legged strides before she collapsed. There was no sign of Nesuskal.

Shit! Wuxx voked a moment later. *He's on us. He saw us com*—That message ended in three hammer-blow shots. Not automatic fire this time but precise rounds, one for each incoming enemy. Sinkhole had finally got his game on.

But if he'd turned to fire on Wuxx and the others that meant his back was to Moon. She had a good chance if she moved fast enough. She came up into a crouch, unshipping her Sa-Su and bracing it against her hip.

"Sorry, but no."

The voice came from ground level. Glancing down, Moon saw that the rabbit had rolled over to present her rear end. It looked like a childish and pointless show of disrespect.

But the kick felt very much like the impact of a speeding car. It lifted Moon off the ground and threw her against the side of the building. She fell down hard, the secondary jolt sending flashes of agony through her side.

She tried groggily to rise, but stopped when she felt shattered ribs grinding against each other. Her Cielo augments had saved her life, but they wouldn't help much if the jagged end of one of her own broken bones punctured her lung.

Nkanika came out from behind the dumpster, doing a soft-shoe shuffle as he swung his rifle to left and right, looking for survivors. Apart from Moon there were none. The Sinkhole had just taken out her entire squad. The Sinkhole, the drone and . . . and a grass-eater. The thought stunned Moon, like a violation of some physical law. She'd been dropped by the fucking rabbit.

Who was on her knees only a couple of feet away. Oblivious. Staring at whatever was on the other side of that rising grille. Moon

flicked the clip holding her knife in its sheath and put her hand on
the hilt.

"I'll blow your hand off if you try it, Moon," Nkanika said. "I
don't want to have to do that." He came up on the other side of
the rabbit and helped her to her feet. She winced in pain. There
was blood on her face from where the push-away had hit her, or
perhaps from something that had happened back at the compound.

"Where's the anima?" Nkanika asked her. "There's meant to be
an anima. Monkey shell, white ceramic." There was a clipped urgency
in his tone.

"Here," Paz said. She bent down and came up with the battered
thing cradled in her hands. Both targets full in Moon's sights, and
there wasn't a damn thing she could do about it. With her knife at
the rabbit's throat she might have had some leverage, but Nkanika's
rifle was pointing directly at her and she knew he could put a round
in her head before the blade even cleared the sheath.

"Someone paying you for this, Sinkhole?" she snarled. "To fuck
your own team in the ass? Who are you working for?"

"Kick your rifle over here," Nkanika said. "The knife too. And
anything else you're carrying."

"She's got another gun," the rabbit said, pointing. "Look, there
in her belt."

"Fucking little tattle-tail!" Moon muttered.

Nkanika gave her a nod. "Come on, Moon. Thumb and forefinger."

Moon put her Sa-Su on the ground and pushed it away with her
foot, clenching her teeth on the pain in her side. She threw the
knife and pistol underarm. "You remember I've got claws, right?"
she reminded him. "What do you want me to do with those?"

"Keep your hands at your sides. When I find something to tie
you up with I'll do it. Until then just remember where this rifle is
pointing."

"Oh, I'll remember, Sinkhole."

Nkanika made to take the construct out of the rabbit's hands but she backed away. "I'll give it back," he said. "I just wanted to look it over. Is it still working? It looks like it's trashed."

"I'm mostly still functional," the construct said, "apart from locomotion. My core is intact."

"That's an Ansurrection agent you're talking to," Moon told Nkanika. "You're throwing in with the enemies of the Pandominion. Putting machines over your own kind."

Nkanika shook his head. "Look where we're standing, Moon," he said, almost gently. "You think I don't know who my own kind are? 'Nobody is going to care how many sinkholers you leave in the dirt.' Your words. From about three hours ago."

"I seem to remember I made an exception for you. Biggest mistake I ever made."

"No." Another head-shake. "Your biggest mistake was a long time ago. You shot a woman on a beach. Do you remember that?"

"I've shot a lot of people, Essien. Most of them don't stick in my mind for very long."

"I'm talking about Hadiz Tam—"

"Hadiz fucking Tambuwal! Of course I remember her. I'm surprised you do, though. You've done about ten times more gabber than I have. I thought what was left of your brain was just stewing gently away at the back of your skull. My bad."

"I forgot a lot of things, for a long time. And I tried hard with this one, but somehow it stuck." Nkanika transferred his rifle to his left hand and offered Moon his right. "Moon, we've done a lot of bad things, but it's not too late for us to put them right. Some of them, anyway. Come inside and tell her you're sorry for what you did."

"Why would I be sorry?" Moon didn't take the offered hand.

The rabbit came up beside them. Her eyes were on the interior of the building. The steel shutter had rolled all the way up now, but in the bright sunlight there was nothing but featureless black inside. "Is she in there?" she asked Nkanika. "Hadiz Tambuwal? You're sure?"

"Yes," he said, "she is. And she really wants to meet you. Moon, we've got to go in now. All of us. There's no way around this."

"Fuck that." Moon slapped his hand away hard. "Between the two of you, you just slaughtered my squad. Put a bullet in my head if you're going to. But don't expect me to grovel for the privilege."

Nkanika let out his breath through his nose long and slow while he thought. "I don't think she wants to kill you," he said at last. "But she does expect you to—"

"She can speak for herself." Another drone glided out from the darkness inside the building and hovered in front of them. It spoke in a woman's voice – a voice Moon recognised from the conversation Vemmet had played back to her on Tsakom. "Unlike you, Corporal Sostenti, I tend to think of killing as a last resort, but I can arrange it if that's what you want. There's a clever little trick I can do with the capacitors on these drones that turns them into pocket incendiaries. That's how I took out your truck. It would be a very ugly death, though. Why not hear me out first?"

Why not? Moon would have had trouble putting it into words. She had a sense – the same premonition she'd had when Vemmet had recruited her for this – of her life coming full circle, of all her unfinished business accreting into a single vast but weightless mass, and that was a thing that only tended to happen when you were about to die. If she went into that building she didn't expect to come out of it again. "Fuck that," she said again. "I'm not interested in a single thing you've got to say."

"What about if I offered to disable your augments? Switch off all that Cielo tech so you can desert without any consequences?"

Moon sucked in a breath, and immediately froze in sudden, shocking pain as the lining of her lungs scraped against broken ribs. "Shit!" she gasped when she could speak again. "Utter fucking nonsense! You can't do that. Nobody can do that. It's black box. The Registry keeps the code, and nothing smaller than the Registry can crack it."

"That's what your commanding officers would like you to believe.

But I have a friend who I believe might be able to do it. In any case, what do you lose by letting me try?"

"My precious time," Moon spat. "And a pretty big chunk of self-respect. Just because you've got this idiot all twisted round, that doesn't mean you can twist me too." The show of anger hid a sudden, terrifying doubt. The drone had just offered her the one thing she would happily sell her soul for. Her soul, her conscience, her squad if they weren't dead already, her oath and every damn thing else. She didn't believe it but she knew she couldn't get this close to it and not check it out. She climbed to her feet, pushing Nkanika away from her with her elbow.

"Day keeps getting better and better," she muttered. "You touch me, Sinkhole, and I'll leave a mark on you that won't wash off."

She limped through the open door, dredging up a tiny crumb of satisfaction from the fact that she was the one leading the way.

The space inside the building was massive, and it gave the lie to that ruined exterior. It was a lab very much like the one she and Lessix had trashed in Essien Nkanika's Lagos. Like that other lab it had a Step plate bolted to the floor, small enough that it could only accommodate one or two selves at a time. As in the other lab, there were racks of the black-and-yellow drones all along one wall, dozens if not hundreds of them, and a ton of miscellaneous high-tech shit all piled up everywhere as if there was some kind of rule against seeing a square inch of empty floor.

There was one thing that was different, though. There was a dead body lying in the far corner with its face turned to the wall. When Essien saw it, he uttered a sound like a gasp of pain. He crossed to the body and knelt beside it. He touched its hunched shoulder with a shaking hand.

It was a woman or what was left of her, desiccated, almost mummified. She was curled into a foetal position, arms across her chest as if she'd been trying to keep herself warm when she died. She was wearing a white lab coat over T-shirt and jeans, cheap plastic sandals on her feet. The ragged hole just next to her spine made it look as though she had been shot in the back, but Moon knew that was a misleading impression. The hole was an exit wound. She knew this because she'd made it herself.

The corpse was that of Hadiz Tambuwal.

"Well, that's just fucking confusing," Moon growled.

"No, it's pretty simple," the drone said. "That body right there is where I used to live, Moon. Until I moved."

78

But Hadiz had to admit, to herself at least, that the word "simple" was just empty bravado. It hadn't been simple at all. It had been blood and pain and panic. It had been a race against the darkness, when she knew all the time that the darkness literally couldn't lose.

She had Stepped twice after Moon shot her – the first time from the beach to her lab in Lagos, the second time from Lagos to this other near-twin. Each time, she felt as though she had left half her insides behind her. She was dying. Every system in her body was shutting down. The only reason she hadn't bled out already was because the weapon that made the obscene hole in her abdomen had run so hot it had cauterised the wound at the same time.

But with that second jump she had shaken off her pursuers, for a while at least. She had a window. She also had an escape route, a way of cheating her own death at the last possible moment. She could see it from where she was lying, a steel-grey slab in the corner of the lab, fourteen inches or so along its long axis, ten inches wide and eight deep. *Second Thoughts*. The device Andris Bagdonas had made and Rupshe had asked her – politely, not insisting – to bring with her in case she ever changed her mind about making a copy of herself. Hadiz thought of the device as the brain-in-a-jar machine, but mostly she tried not to think of it at all. It was a noetic sampler. Once activated, it would compile a perfect digital model of her brain, representing and embodying its internal workings, the firings of its billions of neurons, in a substrate composed of atomically thin laminated strips of exotic transition metals.

And now that it was her only hope she discovered she wasn't entirely certain how to use it. She crawled across to it anyway, rowing with one arm while keeping the other folded under her to keep her exposed innards from scraping against the floor. She fumbled with the controls. When she activated it, dozens of filaments extruded themselves, each with the tiny nub of a neuro-sensor attached to its free end. They were very fine and fiddly and Hadiz's fingers felt like half-inflated balloons, but when she pressed them to her temples they adhered. She hit the keys in what seemed to be the right sequence, relying on ancient memory and vague instinct. It had been years since she'd even thought about this. Scan. Convert. Acquire. She couldn't be sure she wasn't missing something, but she was out of options and out of time.

The machine hummed. The wires stirred and came to life, scything through her thoughts, catching whatever fell in a net so fine it was invisible. There was pain, but fortunately it was unbearable so she didn't have to bear it. Her nervous system, seeing what was coming, handed in its notice and walked out of the building.

Some time later, Hadiz woke inside the grey box. Her first response was outright, mind-freezing panic that came close to madness. She was trapped in the dark, blind and deaf and alone. She tried to scream and couldn't, tried to move and couldn't. She felt herself to be alive but her chest wasn't moving, her heart wasn't beating. Her proprioception was gone. She was only a dimensionless point of consciousness, a pinprick of light in an infinite dark fabric.

For a long while she remembered nothing about herself, not even her name. Her new self stored its memories differently and access to them didn't come at once. When it did, she knew herself as Hadiz Tambuwal, or possibly as a copy of Hadiz Tambuwal. The ontology of it all was a bit murky.

Certainly, once she figured out how to slave the drones to her new machine self and see through their cameras, she could appreciate the distinction. There was her old body, lying where it had fallen, fresh enough that it probably hadn't even begun to smell but still definitely and incontrovertibly dead. And there, right next to it, was the squat grey box where what was left of her, or this new consciousness built on her template, now resided.

She wrestled with the enormity of it, but came at last to a simple, brutal conclusion. She had Hadiz Tambuwal's memories, which were the bedrock and arguably the substance of Hadiz Tambuwal's personality. It really wasn't worth splitting hairs. If she wasn't Hadiz Tambuwal then nobody was. And if nobody was, then nobody was going to fight her for the use of the name.

What next, then? A part of her wanted nothing more than to hide, and seemed on the verge of retreating into fugue. Another part wanted to hit back at whoever had done this to her. A third was screaming in protest at the lack of sensory input and wanted desperately to claw its way back in some form, somehow, into the living world.

Her practical options seemed to be severely limited. True, the grey box was connected not just to the drones but to all the many electronic systems that flesh-and-blood Hadiz had formerly controlled, so AI-construct Hadiz was not entirely helpless. But her new substrate was a digital file of truly colossal size, far larger than the on-board memory of a drone could carry. She couldn't easily move from where she was, still less interact in any meaningful way with the world outside.

Fortunately, though, those electronic systems included a functional Step plate – and Hadiz had one friend who had never betrayed her, never done her anything but good. She sent one of the drones back to her own world, where an untethered AI as big as a house still ruminated imperturbably. The drone carried a message.

Hello, Rupshe. I'm sorry I haven't been by lately. I'm in such trouble as you wouldn't believe!

Rupshe replied at once. *Professor Tambuwal. I was starting to be concerned. What's the problem?*

A conversation started up between the two of them, with pauses at regular intervals while the drone shuttled between universes. It began with Rupshe offering condolences to Hadiz on her recent death. *It must have been traumatic for you – not just the moment when you were shot but the transfer of your consciousness afterwards. I'm glad you managed to make the upload, but I can't imagine you enjoyed your rebirth. It's different for me. I've never known anything other than this state.*

I'm sure I'll get used to it, Hadiz sent, with little or no conviction.

It seems to me, Professor Tambuwal, that the sudden appearance of those two armoured entities must be connected with the loss of your drones. They were dispatched to find you. It would be useful to know who gave them those orders and what their wider agenda is.

I doubt we'll ever know.

I disagree, Rupshe sent. *Between us we have two drone fleets. And we have our map, which will guide us to the continua where inhabited Earths are most likely to occur. The red armour sounds extremely distinctive, so you'll most likely know it if you see it again, either directly through the drones' own cameras or in the signal traffic of a particular world. Let's see if we can track them down.*

To what purpose, though? I'll still be dead.

For a value of that term, yes, Rupshe agreed. *But your consciousness persists. Do you want to leave the initiative with your enemies? If you do, they may continue to search for you. We have no idea what their orders were or what they wanted from you. I can see a great many reasons for being as proactive as you can at this point.*

Hadiz had followed that advice. She had also followed the evidence trail that led from that empty beach back to the thousand-fold Earths of the Pandominion. She found that vast empire at a crucial juncture in its history, at war with the machine hegemony. She tapped the data feeds of countless worlds, and everything she gleaned from them she gave to Rupshe. Rupshe was well placed to run with it. Untethered, et had increased ets processing power exponentially, had become a calculating engine more powerful and versatile than any that was ever made with only a single exception, the Pandominion's Registry.

They collected data. They refined their model, their map of reality. They drew conclusions, and the conclusions were terrible. Hadiz knew she needed to act. She also knew that she could only act through proxies.

And now, at long last, here they were.

"Hadiz," Essien said. He was still kneeling next to her mortal remains, staring at them in sorrow and dull incomprehension. "I thought you were—" He swallowed the word, tried again. "I thought you were still alive."

"I still am, Essien. I'm also dead. I understand your confusion. It's difficult for me, too."

"I see no difficulty at all," said the construct, Dulcimer Coronal. Et sounded impatient. "An organic brain is a machine built for a specific purpose, even if it was built through the random processes of evolution rather than purposive design. Any thinking machine can be made to emulate any other. In the hegemony, the copying and modification of consciousness is a commonplace. Hadiz Tambuwal, if that's your name, let's come to the point of this. You offered me sanctuary. That was the only reason why I came. But it's obvious you also set these Cielo troopers to follow us. And you said you wanted something delivered to another world but I can see you've got your own Step plate right there. I have to wonder at this point what your endgame is."

"I haven't lied to you," Hadiz said. "Or at least, if I have it's only by omission. The soldiers were meant as a backup in case you didn't manage to reach me under your own steam. They're also here because I had unfinished business with them that I'd prefer not to rehearse right now. As for the delivery, the package is myself. I want you to bring me from here back to my own world."

The cat-woman shook her head and laughed with no trace of amusement. "I always knew we fucked it up," she said. She nodded at Essien. "Vemmet squeezed this one's head for the best part of a day trying to find the coordinates of your home continuum, but it wasn't any use. There was nothing between his ears but fucking daylight."

"Why?" Dulcie persisted, still addressing Hadiz. "Why do you want to go home? And why now? And why with us?"

"That's harder to explain," Hadiz said.

"Try anyway. Now that you're not manipulating us at a distance it feels to me as though the balance of power has shifted. You've put us through a lot. I'd like an explanation."

"I mentioned that I have a friend back on my own Earth. Rupshe. It's not an organic self. It – I suppose I should say *et* as your people do, Paz – et's an intelligent system, designed and built by a colleague of mine who was a genius in his field. Et was already vastly capable, and before I left I removed the restraints on ets heuristics. I left et free to learn and adapt etself. Consequently et's become a great deal cleverer since."

The Uti, Topaz Tourmaline, looked shocked. "Weren't you afraid?" she asked. "In the Pandominion they would have sent you to a penal planet for untethering an AI."

"And yet you weren't afraid to travel with one. Rupshe is my friend, as I said. I trust et. And after I died I reached out to et. We resumed an interrupted conversation. The drones carried the messages between us. We also used them to find the Pandominion and build up a database of information about it. That could have taken years, but Rupshe realised what I didn't, which was that we must already have trespassed on at least one Pandominion world. That was why you came after me in the first place. So we back-tracked through the worlds we'd already visited and found the Pandominion only a short while before the Pandominion met the machine hegemony."

"Wow," Moon Sostenti said tonelessly. "What a coincidence. There's no need to be coy, Tambuwal. You're working for the fucking Ansurrection. We already know that part."

"No. Not at all. I'm neutral in that conflict."

"Nobody's neutral. You're either organic or you're a machine. You get your side chosen for you." Moon turned to Essien. "Sinkhole, it's not too late. Why don't we just fling this talking box in a land-fill somewhere, hand the rabbit and the tin monkey over for the bounty and go get blind drunk?"

"Rupshe studied the Pandominion," Hadiz went on, ignoring Moon's interjection. "Et started to build theoretical models of how the Pando's empire might develop in the future, and then of how its progress might be deflected by encountering another coalition of a similar size. When the Ansurrection war began et built that into ets models too. And et's been refining them ever since. At this point I think Rupshe has a clearer picture of what's happening and what's going to happen than anyone who's directly involved."

"Why should we care about any of this?" Dulcie demanded. "We've left that war behind us. We don't have any intention of going back."

"I'm afraid you're going to have to. Rupshe's models point to disaster. Et postulates a statistically significant possibility that the conflict will destroy both the Pandominion and the machine hegemony. Millions of worlds will be left devoid of life or else reduced to barbarism. The destruction, the suffering . . . it will be on an inconceivable scale. For the worlds that are affected it will probably be an extinction event. Their biospheres will be swept clean of anything resembling life, whether organic or construct. They'll be like the Scour worlds. In fact the Scour worlds are probably the remnants left over from the last time this happened."

"But—" Paz protested. Nobody else said anything at all. Hadiz was expecting this silence. It was mostly shock, possibly with some scepticism mixed in, but it had a third component – the unbridge-able disconnect of scale. It was hard for most of them to force themselves to think in multiversal terms. "How?" Paz said at last. "How is this going to happen."

"It's not," Moon scoffed. "All of this is bullshit."

"Both sides are working on new weapons. Weapons that are meant to be unanswerable. The Pandominion's is called the Rebuke. The hegemony's doesn't have a name, only a code string. Both sides are on the brink of success. There was no way they could fail, really, given the resources they've committed. The weapons will be brought online. They'll be deployed. World after world will fall – and I mean the worlds themselves, not just their sentient populations. They'll become non-viable, for thousands or millions of years. The situation is dire and we may be the only ones who can see the full extent of it. You'll have to trust me when I say that countless lives depend on what we decide to do next."

Moon gave a mirthless chuckle. "Well, thank fuck we've got the rabbit with us," she said. "And the tin monkey. I'm not sure Nkanika and me could have saved the entire fucking Pandominion on our own."

"You won't be on your own," Hadiz said. "I'm hoping we can get one more self to join us. But we can discuss the details after we've Stepped. We've still got a long way to go and we're running out of time. The Ansurrection has only defended itself so far. Rupshe said that once they launch their retaliatory strike the probability of mutual destruction becomes something more like a certainty."

"What do you want us to do?" Essien said. He was still looking at Hadiz's mortal remains rather than at the box that now contained her thoughts. That was typical, Hadiz thought, and oddly touching. Their relationship had always been much more about the physical side of things.

"Pick up the Second Thoughts device, Essien," she said. "The grey box next to my body. Or perhaps it would be better to get Moon to carry it, so you can keep both hands free to carry your rifle. Step up onto the plate, and I'll take us all to where we need to be."

Paz looked down at Dulcie, still lying in the makeshift cradle of her arms. "Do you want to go?" she asked.

"I certainly don't want to stay here," Dulcie said. "The Cielo – the real Cielo, I mean, not these amateurs – are bound to get on our trail again sooner rather than later. I think you're asking for too much when you talk about trust, Hadiz. But I'd like to meet your friend, if only to check ets math and form my own conclusions. What about you, Paz?"

Essien had watched this exchange with cool detachment. "You're both coming," he said, before Paz could answer. "We're all doing what Hadiz tells us to do. Let's be clear on that."

Moon shook her head in sorrowing contempt. "Wow," she said. "No wonder you got along so well in the army, Sinkhole. You just love being told what to do, don't you?"

"Pick up the box," Essien ordered her. "And be careful not to drop it. I'll empty this magazine into you if you do."

"Good to know." Moon hefted the box up onto one shoulder without ceremony. "How are we doing this, then?"

"Topaz Tourmaline and Dulcimer Coronal first," Hadiz said. "Then the three of us."

Paz went over to the plate, taking up position right in the middle of it. Her fur stood on end as the field enveloped her.

For the third time in less than twenty-four hours, she Stepped into another world.

79

Orso Vemmet held out as long as he could. At first he had had Wuxx and Chiomis for company. He knew they were mostly there to guard the Step plate rather than for his peace of mind, but their presence steadied him nonetheless. After they left, the silence of the ruined station house and the sense of being on a sinkhole world far outside the reach of civilisation's laws began to weigh on him. He was fine as long as he was able to listen in on the squad's comms and get a sense of what was happening. But he couldn't keep from asking questions and eventually Moon locked him out. He was left to his own devices, and he ran out of devices pretty quickly.

He knew the squad was in trouble. The resistance at the compound was much fiercer and more sustained than they had expected. That was why Wuxx and Chiomis had been called in to provide backup. For all Vemmet knew he was already the last survivor. For all he knew the local selves were on their way here now, backtracking Moon's comms channel until it led right back to him and the plate.

He knew he should wait until he got the word, one way or the other, but if he waited he might die here. Even a trivial wound would probably be fatal on a world as primitive as this. They wouldn't have the first idea how to treat him. He would die of gangrene or septicaemia or post-traumatic shock – or else he'd die because some backwoods simpleton of a doctor tried to bleed him with leeches or draw off his excess humours with cupping glasses.

He had to be ready. If the sinkholers came he had to Step before they could take him. But the Step plate would take three seconds to cycle. Anything could happen in three seconds! In three seconds a man could be shot, stabbed, garrotted and partially eviscerated.

At least, Vemmet thought, he could take up a position on the plate so there would be no delay while he ran for it. He knelt there, folded in on himself, making himself as small a target as he could while he waited either for a message from Moon or for the sound of the station's doors two storeys below being smashed in, running footsteps on the stairs, the bestial howls of slave-traffickers come in search of revenge.

Moon? he voked. But there was no response.

I can't, he told the thirsty silence. *I just can't. I'm sorry. I'll come back. I . . . I'll wait an hour and then – I'll come back for you.*

He activated the field. The roof of the station house disappeared behind the milky curtain of the Step field. A heartbeat later, Vemmet was kneeling in the dust on the open plain on Bivouac 19 from which they'd all Stepped a few hours before.

At least, that was where he had aimed for. But he must have made some mistake because there was no plain – at least, none that he could see. He stood in the middle of a dense fog.

No, not fog. Smoke. It was smoke. And right next to him was the blazing ruin of a Cielo gun platform, its nose end buried in the earth. In the sky overhead, vague shapes moved, ponderous and terrifying. Deafening concussions sounded from nearby, and duller ones from the middle distance. The ground under him shook in time to their warring rhythms.

"What?" Vemmet stammered, his gaze darting up and down and all around. And then, "No! No! What? What is—?"

A craft of dreadnought size or possibly bigger backed air in the sky directly above him, its braking field punching a momentary hole in the roiling murk. Vemmet stared up, aghast. A dog fight was going on up there between ships blazoned with Cielo crimson and vessels of a very different design. He couldn't tell how many invaders there were, but there were so few gaps in their formation it was hard to see the sky between them. He had no idea who they were until he realised with a shock that there were ground units in this fight too, walking towers with gun clusters instead of faces and field vortexes at the end of their swinging, scything arms. Beneath and between them, smaller figures ran on multiple legs or rolled on wheels or glided on cushions of force. They spat beams and bullets and shear planes of unleashed energy as they came.

Constructs. It was an army of constructs. The Ansurrection had brought the war back at last to the homeworlds of their enemy. It was just Vemmet's bad luck to have Stepped right into the path of it.

80

On the other side of that Step they were still in Apapa Quays, but Essien felt the difference at once. The city they'd just left was still alive, but this one was dead. Nothing moved here, or made a sound. There were no people, no animals, no birds or insects. The air had a leaden, toxic taste on his tongue.

They walked through silent streets, unchallenged, out from the centre of the city and across the Festac Link Bridge to Campus Cross, which in Essien's world had been a derelict amusement park. One of the drones had come through with them, and it glided ahead of them to show the way.

It was a slow journey. The sampling unit was heavy and Moon had to stop and rest several times. Paz offered to help her but either Moon didn't hear or she didn't consider the suggestion worth discussing. She just hefted her burden again and strode ahead.

Just before they got to the campus, they came to a street that had a few houses and shops along one side and a steeply sloping hill shelving away on the other. The hill might have been tended grass once, but now it was a forest of nutgrass and sow thistle from which a few half-grown bush figs and sycamores stood tall. Essien recognised the narrow waterway running along the bottom of the slope as the Badagary Creek. Halfway along the street there was a squat green truck that had been fitted out as a bar with the counter at its rear. A sign on the side of it declared to nobody at all that it was *Hungry Koti's Place*.

The drone slowed and stopped.

"Is this it?" Moon demanded, lowering the sampling unit to the ground with a little more force than was strictly necessary.

"Be careful with that thing," Hadiz warned her. "If I get brain damage because you've mishandled me I will not be pleased. No, this isn't it."

"Then why have we stopped?" Moon bared her sharp, sharp teeth to show how little she cared for Hadiz's threats.

"It's just a place I remember from when I was alive. I drank here lots of times. The beer was good."

"Great story." Moon's tone was savage. "Maybe we should all stop and have a cold one. Drink to old times."

"Where to now?" Essien said.

"To the end of the street, and across the bridge."

Essien gestured with the rifle for Moon to take up the sampling unit again. She gave him a hard stare that was surely indicative of some violent promise she'd just made herself, but she obeyed without a word. Together, they crossed the bridge and walked on into the desolate remains of Campus Cross.

A quarter of a mile or so away, on the other side of the campus's ragged sprawl, the intelligent system that had been named Rupshe after a benevolent goddess watched them come with eagerness bordering on impatience.

And much, much further away in my wayward shell, my runaway womb, plummeting from one dimension to the next without cease, I lay in the long dark dreaming dreams that had no words or images, dreams composed of nothing but numbers. And every dream came true.

But now at last my mother was coming. My saviour. My teacher. My champion. My dearest friend. The worlds had swirled around me like bubbles in water for centuries, but they had never met me.

Oh, they would meet me soon.

The story continues in…

Book two of The Pandominion

Coming in 2024!

Acknowledgements

As always I need to thank the crack team who keep me from cracking. My agent, Meg; my editors, Anna and Joanna and Priyanka; my publicists Nazia and Ellen; my lovely family.

I also owe a huge debt to Tade Thompson, who read an early draft and gave me invaluable notes and advice on the Nigerian scenes and characters. His impact on the book was enormous, and his generosity is boundless. Anything I got right in those chapters is down to him. The mistakes are all mine.

extras

orbit

meet the author

M. R. Carey has been making up stories for most of his life. His novel *The Girl With All the Gifts* has sold over a million copies and became a major motion picture, based on his own BAFTA Award–nominated screenplay. Under the name Mike Carey he has written for both DC and Marvel, including critically acclaimed runs on *Lucifer, Hellblazer* and *X-Men*. He also has several previous novels, including the Felix Castor series (written as Mike Carey), two radio plays and a number of TV and movie screenplays to his credit.

Find out more about M. R. Carey and other Orbit authors by registering for the free monthly newsletter at orbitbooks.net.

if you enjoyed
INFINITY GATE

look out for

TRANSLATION STATE

by

Ann Leckie

The mystery of a missing translator sets three lives on a collision course that will have a ripple effect across the stars in this powerful new novel by award-winning author Ann Leckie.

Qven was created to be a Presger Translator. The pride of their clade, they always had a clear path before them: Learn human ways, and eventually, make a match and serve as an intermediary between the dangerous alien Presger and the human worlds. The realization that they might want something else isn't "optimal behavior." It's the type of behavior that results in elimination.

But Qven rebels. And in doing so, their path collides with those of two others. Enae, a reluctant diplomat whose dead grandmaman has left hir an impossible task as an inheritance: hunting down a fugitive who has been missing for over two hundred years. And Reet, an adopted mechanic who is increasingly desperate to learn about his genetic roots—or anything that might explain why he operates so differently from those around him.

As a conclave of the various species approaches—and the long-standing treaty between the humans and the Presger is on the line—the decisions of all three will have ripple effects across the stars.

ENAE

Athtur House, Saeniss Polity

The last stragglers in the funeral procession were barely out the ghost door before the mason bots unfolded their long legs and reached for the pile of stones they'd removed from the wall so painstakingly the day before. Enae hadn't looked back to see the door being sealed up, but sie could hear it for just a moment before the first of Aunt Irad's moans of grief rose into a wail. One or two cousins heaved an experimental sob.

Enae hadn't cried when Grandmaman died. Sie hadn't cried when Grandmaman told hir she'd chosen the time to go. Sie wasn't crying now. Which wasn't necessarily a problem, everyone knew what expressions you should have when you were following the bier to the crematory, everyone knew what sounds a close relative made, and Enae could sob and wail if sie'd wanted to. And after all, among all these aunts and uncles and nuncles and cousins, Enae was the one who'd lived with Grandmaman for decades, and taken care of her in her old age. Sie had been the one to arrange things in the household these past ten years or more, to deal with the servants—human and bot—with their very different needs. Sie still had all the household codes and bot overrides, and the servants still looked to hir for orders, at least until Grandmaman's will was unsealed. Sie had every right to walk at the head of the procession, right behind Grandmaman, wailing for all the town to hear, in these quiet early morning hours. Instead sie walked silent and dry-eyed at the back.

Grandmaman had been very old, and ill-tempered. She had also been very rich, and born into one of the oldest families in the system. Which meant that the procession to the crematory was longer than one might have expected. There had been some jostling in the entry hall, by the ghost door, Aunt Irad turning up a half hour early to position herself at the front, some cousins attempting to push her out of her place, and everyone eying Enae to see how sie'd react.

None of them had lived in the house for decades. Grandmaman had thrown most of them—or their parents—out. Every year she would hold a birthday dinner and invite them all back for a lavish meal, during which she would insult them to their faces while they smiled and gritted their teeth. Then she'd order them off the premises again, to wait until the next year. Some of them had fallen away in that time, sworn off Grandmaman and any hope of inheritance, but most of them came back year after year. It was only Enae who had actually lived in the house with Grandmaman, Enae who, one might think, would be the most affected by Grandmaman's death.

But for the past week Enae had let the aunts and uncles and nuncles and cousins do whatever they'd wanted, so long as it didn't trouble the household unduly. Sie'd stood silent as Aunt Irad had changed the cook's menus and stood silent when the same aunt had raged at Enae because sie'd told the cook to disregard any changes he didn't have resources for. Sie had done and said nothing when, the very first day of the funeral week, an actual fistfight had broken out between two cousins over who would have which bedroom. Sie had remained silent when sie had heard one uncle say to a nuncle, *And look at hir, fifty-six years old and sitting at home sucking up to Grandmaman,* and the nuncle reply, *Well look at hir father's family, it's hardly a surprise.* Sie had walked on past when one cousin had surreptitiously slid a small silver dish into his pocket, while another loudly declared that she would be making some changes if she were so fortunate as to inherit the house. And in the meantime, sie had made sure that meals arrived on time and the house was kept in order. That had been the trick, all these years, of living with Grandmaman—keep calm, keep quiet, keep things running smoothly.

Grandmaman had told Enae many times that sie was her only remaining heir. But she had also said—many times—that Enae was an embarrassment. A failure. As far as the Athturs had fallen since Grandmaman's days—look at all those grandchildren and great-grandchildren and nephews and nieces and niblings of whatever degree abasing themselves to win her favor in the desperate hope that she'd leave them something in her will—as pathetic as they were, Enae was worse. Nearly sixty and no career, no friends, no lovers, no marital partners, no children. What had sie done with hir life? Nothing.

Enae had kept calm, had not said that when sie had had friends they had not been good enough for Grandmaman. That when sie had shown any sign of wanting to do something that might take hir out of the house, Grandmaman had forbidden it.

Keep calm, keep quiet, keep things running smoothly.

At the crematory, Grandmaman's corpse slid into the flames, and the funeral priest sang the farewell chants. Aunt Irad and three different cousins stepped forward to thank him for officiating and to suggest that they might donate money for future prayers for the Blessed Deceased. Enae could feel everyone else glancing toward hir, yet again, to see hir reaction to others acting as though they were the head of the family, the chief mourner, the now-Matriarch (or Patriarch or Natriarch, as the case may be) of the ancient family of Athtur.

"Well," said Aunt Irad, finished with her loud and obvious consultation with the funeral priest, "I've ordered coffee and sandwiches to be set out in the Peony Room." And marched back toward the house, not even looking to see if anyone followed her.

Back at the house, there was no coffee and sandwiches in the Peony Room. Aunt Irad turned immediately to Enae, who shrugged as though it wasn't any of hir business. It wasn't anymore—technically, Grandmaman's will would have taken effect the moment her body slid into the flames, but the habit of ordering the household died hard. With a quick blink sie sent a query to the kitchen.

No reply. And then someone dressed as a servant, but who Enae had never, ever seen before, came into the Peony Room and coolly informed them all that refreshments had in fact been set out in the Blue Sitting Room and their collective presence was requested there, and then turned and walked away, ignoring Aunt Irad's protests.

In the Blue Sitting Room, another complete stranger sat in one of the damask-upholstered armchairs, drinking coffee: a lanky, fair-skinned woman who smiled at all of them as they came in and stopped and stared. "Good morning. I'm so sorry for your loss."

"Who the hell are you?" asked Aunt Irad, indignant.

"A few minutes ago, I was Zemil Igoeto," said the woman as she set her coffee down on a mother-of-pearl inlaid side table. "But when the Blessed Deceased ascended, I became Zemil Athtur." Silence. "I don't believe in drawing things out. I will be direct. None of you have inherited anything. There wasn't anything to inherit. I have owned all of this"—she gestured around her, taking in the Blue Sitting Room and presumably the whole house—"for some years."

"That can't be right," said Aunt Irad. "Is this some kind of joke?"

Grandmaman would have thought it a joke, thought Enae. *She must have laughed to herself even as she was dying, to think of the looks on everyone's faces right now.* Everything had seemed distant and strange since Grandmaman had died, but now Enae had the feeling that sie wasn't really here, that sie was watching some sort of play or entertainment that sie wasn't terribly interested in.

"Fifteen years ago," said Zemil Igoeto—no, Zemil Athtur— "the Blessed Deceased found herself completely broke. At the same time, while I had plenty of funds, I wanted some way to gain access to the sort of influence that is only available to the oldest families. She and I came to an agreement and made it legally binding. In, I need not tell you, the presence of authorized witnesses. I would purchase everything she owned. The sum would be sufficient to support her in excellent style for the rest of her life, and she would have the use of all the properties that had formerly been hers. In return, on her ascension to the Realm of the Blessed Dead, I would become her daughter and sole heir."

Silence. Enae wasn't sure if sie wanted to laugh or not, but the fact was, Grandmaman would *very* much have enjoyed this moment if she could have been here. It was just like her to have done this. And how could Enae complain? Sie'd lived here for years in, as Ms Zemil Athtur had just said, excellent style. Enae couldn't possibly have any complaints.

"This is ridiculous," said Aunt Irad. She looked at Enae. "Is this one of the Blessed Deceased's jokes? Or is it yours?"

"Mx Athtur has nothing to do with any of this," cut in Zemil. "Sie had no idea until this moment. Only I, the Blessed Deceased's jurist, and the Blessed Deceased herself knew anything about it. Apart from the witnesses involved, of course, whom you are free to consult as confirmation."

"So we get *nothing*," said the cousin who had declared her intention to make changes once she'd inherited.

"Correct," said Zemil Athtur, picking up her coffee again. She took a sip. "The Blessed Deceased wanted to be sure I told you that you're all selfish and greedy, and she wishes she could be here to see you when you learn you've been cut off with nothing. With one exception."

Everyone turned to look at Enae.

Zemil continued, "I am to provide for Mx Enae Athtur, with certain stipulations and restrictions, which I will discuss with hir later."

"The will," said a cousin. "I want to see the will. I want to see the documents involved. I'll be speaking with my jurist."

"Do, by all means," said Zemil, and Enae felt the itch of a message arriving. Sie looked, and saw a list of files. Documents.

515

Contracts. Contact information for the Office of Witnesses. "In the meantime, do sit and have a sandwich while the servants finish packing your things."

It took some time, and a half dozen looming servants (who, once again, Enae had never seen before), but eventually the aunts and uncles and nuncles and cousins had left the house, picked their luggage up off the drive, and gone elsewhere, threatening lawsuits all the while.

Enae had remained in the Blue Sitting Room, unwilling to go up to hir room to see if hir things were still there or not. Sie sat, more or less relaxed, in a damask-upholstered armchair. Sie badly wanted a cup of coffee, and maybe a sandwich, but sie found sie couldn't bring hirself to get up from the chair. The whole world seemed unreal and uncertain, and sie wasn't sure what would happen if sie moved too much. Zemil, too, stayed sitting in her damasked chair, drinking coffee and smiling.

At some point, after the house had quieted, Grandmaman's jurist arrived. "Ah, Mx Athtur. I'm so sorry for your loss. I know you loved your grandmother very much, and spent your life attending to her. You should be allowed to take some time to yourself right now, and grieve." He didn't overtly direct this to Zemil, sitting in the armchair across from Enae, but his words seemed intended for her. Then he did turn to her and nodded in greeting. "Ms Athtur."

"I am fully aware," said Zemil, with a faint smile, "that I'm tasked with providing for Mx Athtur, and I will."

"I would like some time to read the relevant documents, please," said Enae, as politely as sie could, and braced hirself to argue with an angry refusal.

"Of course," said the jurist, "and I'll be happy to go through them with you if you need."

Enae, at a loss for some reason, said, "Thank you."

"You'll see, when you read it," said Zemil, "that I am obligated to provide for you, as I said. How I am to provide for you is up to me, within certain parameters. I have had years to consider what that might mean, for both of us."

"Your provisions will meet the requirements of the will," said the jurist, sharply. "I will be certain of it."

"I don't understand." Enae suppressed a sudden, unexpected welling of tears. "I don't understand how this happened." And then, realizing how that might sound, "I didn't expect to inherit anything. Gr...the Blessed Deceased always said she would leave her houses and money to whoever she wanted." *Watch them gather around my corpse when I'm gone*, she'd said, with relish. *Ungrateful, disloyal while I lived, but watch them come the moment they think they might get something from me.* And she'd patted Enae's hand and made the tiny huff that was her laughter, near the end.

"As I said," said Zemil, "the Blessed Deceased was facing bankruptcy. Her income had declined, and she had refused to alter her way of living. It took several years to negotiate—our ancestor was stubborn, as I'm sure you know—but ultimately she had no choice if she was to continue living here, in the way she was accustomed to."

Enae didn't know what to say. Sie hardly even knew how to breathe, in this moment.

"I wanted the name," said Zemil. "I have wealth, and some influence. But I'm a newcomer to wealth and influence, at least according to the oldest families. An interloper. Our ancestor made sure to tell me so, on several occasions. But no longer. Now I am an Athtur. And now the Athturs are wealthy again."

Another unfamiliar servant came in, to clear the food and the coffee away. Enae hadn't eaten anything. Sie could feel the hollow in hir stomach, but sie couldn't bring hirself to take a sandwich now, knew sie wouldn't be able to eat it if sie did. Grandmaman's jurist waved the servant over, muttered in her ear. The servant made a plate with two small sandwiches, poured a cup of coffee, handed both to Enae, and then took the rest and left the room.

"Have you dismissed the servants?" Enae asked. Sie'd meant to sound casual, curious, but hir tone came out rough and resentful.

"You are no longer the housekeeper here, Mx Athtur," Zemil replied.

"I was until this morning, and if I'd known people were going to lose their jobs I'd have done what I could for them. They've worked for us a long time."

"You think I'm cruel," said Zemil. "Heartless. But I am only direct. No servants have been dismissed. None will be who perform their jobs well. Does that satisfy you?"

"Yes."

"I will do you no favors," Zemil continued, "leaving you in any misapprehension or uncertainty. As I said, what I wanted in this transaction was the Athtur name. There will be some reluctance on the part of the other old families to accept my legitimacy, and that will be made more difficult if you are here as an example of a true Athtur, one who so loyally cared for hir Grandmaman for so long, and rightfully ought to have inherited—in contrast with my false, purchased hold on the name. But I am also obligated to support you. Understand, I bear you no ill will, and I have no objection to providing for you, but I need you gone. I have, therefore, found employment for you."

"Ms Athtur…" the jurist began, reproachfully.

Zemil raised a forestalling hand. "You may stay here for another month, to complete the time of mourning. And then you will take a position with the Office of Diplomacy. Your assignment is already arranged. You will find it congenial, I assure you."

"You could just leave me my allowance," said Enae. "I could move out."

"Would you?" asked Zemil. "Where would you go?"

"I have a month to figure that out," sie replied, not sure sie had understood anything anyone had said for the past five minutes, not even sure what sie, hirself, was saying.

"Let me tell you what your position would be in the Office of Diplomacy. You have been appointed Special Investigator, and a case has been assigned to you. It is a situation of great diplomatic delicacy. Perhaps we should discuss this in private." She glanced at the jurist.

"I'm not going anywhere," he said, and crossed his arms very decidedly.

"You don't work for Mx Athtur," Zemil pointed out.

"No," he acknowledged. "In this matter, I represent the interests of the Blessed Deceased. And consequently, I will be certain that her grandchild is appropriately cared for."

"If she were here…" began Zemil.

"But she's *not* here," said the jurist. "We have only her expressed desire, and your agreement to that."

Zemil made an expression as though she'd bitten into something sour. "All right then. Enae, you've been assigned…"

"Mx Athtur," said Enae, hardly believing it had come out of her mouth.

To Enae's shock, Zemil smiled. "Mx Athtur. You've been assigned, as I've said, to a matter of some delicacy. Some years ago, the Radchaai Translators Office approached the Office of Diplomacy to request our help in tracking down a fugitive."

Radchaai! The Radch was an enormous, multisystem empire, far enough away that no one here in Saeniss Polity felt immediately threatened by them—especially now, with the Radchaai embroiled in their own internal struggles—but close enough and powerful enough that Radchaai was one of the languages the well educated often elected to study. The Translators Office was the Radchaai diplomatic service. Enae felt the itch of files arriving. "I've sent you the details," said Zemil.

Enae blinked the message open, read the opening summary. "This incident happened two hundred years ago!"

"Yes," Zemil agreed. "The Office of Diplomacy assigned an investigator when the request first came in, who decided the fugitive wasn't here in Saeniss Polity or even anywhere in this system, and what with one thing and another the matter was dropped."

"But...how am I supposed to find someone who's been missing for two hundred years?"

Zemil shrugged. "I haven't the least idea. But I rather imagine it will involve travel, and a per diem on top of your wages. On top of your existing allowance, which I have no plans to discontinue. Indeed, the Blessed Deceased was quite miserly in the matter of your allowance, and I believe I'll be increasing it." She turned to the jurist. "There, are you satisfied?" The jurist made a noncommittal noise, and Zemil turned back to Enae. "Honestly, no one cares if you find this person or not. No one expects you to find anything at all. You're being paid to travel, and maybe look into an old puzzle if you feel like it. Haven't you ever wanted to leave here?"

Sie had always wanted to leave here.

Sie couldn't think. Not right now. "I've just lost my grandmother," sie said, tears welling again, sie didn't know from where. "And I've had a terrible shock. I'm going to my room. If..." Sie looked Zemil directly in the eyes. "If it still is my room?"

"Of course," said Zemil.

Enae hadn't expected that easy acquiescence. Grandmaman would never have tolerated her acting all high-and-mighty like this. But what else was sie supposed to do? Grandmaman wasn't here anymore. Sie blinked, took a breath. Another. "If your people would be so kind as to bring me lunch and coffee there." Ridiculous, sie was still holding the sandwiches the servant had handed to hir, but sie couldn't even imagine eating them. Not these sandwiches, not here, not now. "And I'll have supper in my room as well."

"They'll be happy to help you any way you wish, as long as you're here," said Zemil.

Enae rose. Set hir untouched food back onto the sideboard. Sie turned and nodded to the jurist. "Thank you. I...thank you."

"Call me if you need me," he said.

Sie turned to Zemil, but found sie had no words to say, and so sie just fled to hir own room.

if you enjoyed
INFINITY GATE

look out for

PARADISE-1

by

David Wellington

An electrifying novel set in deep space and perfect for fans of science fiction and horror, Paradise-1 *follows two agents from the United Earth government as they investigate the complete disappearance of humanity's first deep space colony.*

When Special Agent Petrova and Dr. Zhang Lei are woken up from cryogenic sleep, dragged freezing and dripping wet out of their pods with the ship's alarms blaring in the background, they know something is very wrong. Warned by the captain that they're under attack, they have no choice but to investigate.

*It doesn't take much time to learn that they've been met by
another vessel—a vessel from Paradise-1, Earth's first deep space
colony and their final destination.*

*Worse still, the vessel is empty. And it carries with it the message
that all communication from the 150,000 souls inhabiting
Paradise-1 has completely ceased.*

*Petrova and Zhang must board the empty ship and delve
farther into deep space to discover the truth of the colony's
disappearance—but the farther they go, the more dangers loom.*

1

Three days still before dawn on Ganymede, and the cold
seeped right through her suit and into her bones. The only
light came from what reflected off the crescent of Jupiter, a thin
arc of brown and orange that hung forever motionless in the
night sky. Occasionally a bolt of lightning would snap across
the shadowed disk of the big planet, a bar of light big enough
that even from a million kilometers away it blasted long black
shadows across the charcoal ice of the moon.

Alexandra Petrova rotated her shoulders. Rolled her feet back
and forth in the powdery ice, just to get some blood moving
through her legs. She'd been lying prone for nearly six hours,
out on the edge of a ridgeline a long way from the warmth and
the unrecycled air of the Selket Crater habitat. Maybe, though,
her suffering was about to pay off.

"Firewatch One-Four, I have visual confirmation," she whispered, and her suit's microphone picked up her words and beamed them up to a satellite, which blasted them back down to some operator in a control tower back in the crater, then transferred them over to the nice, cozy offices of Firewatch Division Fourteen. The central headquarters of the Military Police on Ganymede. "Subject is at a range of approximately three hundred meters, headed north-northwest."

She lay as still as possible, not wanting to give away the slightest sign of her location. Just below her on the ridge a man was carefully bounding his way downslope, hopping from boulder to boulder, headed into a maze of narrow little canyons. He was wearing a bright yellow spacesuit, skintight. No faceplate, just a pair of dark goggles. Half the workers on Ganymede wore suits like that – they were cheap and easily patched, and they came in bright colors so that if you died on the surface your body would be easier to recover. A bar code on his back identified the suit as belonging to one Dzama, Margaret.

Petrova knew that suit was stolen. The man inside was a former medical technician named Jason Schmidt and he was – allegedly – the worst serial killer in the century-long history of the Ganymede colony. Petrova had turned up evidence of more than twenty missing persons cases that led straight back to Schmidt. Not a single body had been found, but that wasn't too surprising. Ganymede might be one of the most densely colonized worlds of the solar system, but there was plenty of ice out there that still hadn't ever been explored. The perfect place to hide dead bodies.

"Firewatch One-Four," she said, "I am requesting permission to make an arrest on one Schmidt, Jason. I've already filed the paperwork. I just need a green light."

"Copy, Lieutenant," One-Four told her. "We're just reviewing the case now, making sure you're within your remit. We should be able to clear this any minute now. Stand by."

All the evidence against him was circumstantial, but Schmidt was her man. She was certain of it.

She'd better be. She was staking her whole career on this case. As a lieutenant inspector of Firewatch, she had broad powers to carry out her own investigations, but she couldn't afford to screw this one up. She knew very well she'd only gotten her job and her rank because of nepotism. The problem was, everybody else knew it, too. Her mother, Ekaterina Petrova, was the former director of Firewatch. Petrova had gone into the family business, and everyone believed she'd been given a free ride at the academy based on nothing but her mother's name.

Clearing this case would go a long way to showing she was more than just her mother's daughter. That she was capable of holding down this job on her own merits. The command level of Firewatch had just let all those missing persons cases go – presumably the new director, Lang, felt that a few missing miners from Ganymede weren't important enough to spend resources tracking them down. But bringing Schmidt in would be a real win for Lang as well as Petrova. It would make Firewatch look good – it would show the people of Ganymede that Firewatch was there to protect them. It would be a public relations coup.

She just had to convince someone in Selket Crater to give her final authorization to make the arrest. Which should not have been so difficult. Why were they dragging their feet?

"Firewatch, I need authorization to make this arrest. Please advise."

"Understood, Lieutenant. We're still waiting on final confirmation."

Below her, Schmidt stopped, perched atop a boulder. His

head twisted from side to side as he scanned the landscape. Had he noticed her somehow? Or was he just lost in the dark?

"Copy," she said. Petrova crawled forward a meter or so. Just far enough that she could keep Schmidt in sight. Where was he headed? She'd suspected he had some kind of stash house out here on the ice, maybe a place where he kept trophies from his kills. She'd been following him for a while and she knew he often left the warmth of the city and came out here on his own for hours at a stretch. That worked for her. She would have a better chance catching him out of doors – in the city he could simply disappear into a crowd.

This would be the perfect time to act. Take him down out on the ice, preferably alive. Drag him back to a Firewatch covert site for interrogation. She reached down and touched the pistol mounted at her hip. Checked that it was loaded and ready. Of course it was. She'd cleaned and reassembled it herself. There was only one problem. A little light on the receiver of the pistol glowed a steady, unhelpful amber. Meaning she did not yet have permission to fire.

"I need that authorization, Firewatch," she said. "I need you to unlock my weapon. What's the hold-up?" She kept her voice down, even though there was little need. Ganymede's atmosphere was just a thin wisp of nothing. Sound didn't carry out on the ice. Still. A little paranoid caution might keep her alive.

Schmidt finally moved, jumping off his boulder and coming down hard in a loose pile of broken ice chips. He fell on his ass and planted his hands on either side of him, fingers splayed on the ground. He was unarmed. Vulnerable.

"Confirmation still pending. Director Lang has asked to sign off on this personally. Please be patient," Firewatch told her.

Petrova inhaled slowly. Exhaled slowly. Director Lang was getting personally involved? That could be good, it could mean that her superiors were showing an interest in her career. More likely though it was a problem. It could slow things to a crawl while she waited for the director's approval. Or worse. Lang might shut her down just out of spite.

When Petrova's mother had retired from Firewatch a year and a half ago, Lang had made it very clear that she wasn't going to cut her predecessor's daughter any slack. If Petrova had to wait for Lang's approval she might freeze to death out on the ice before it came.

Screw this, she was moving in. Once she had enough evidence to make her case against Schmidt, no one would question her collar.

She got her feet under her and jumped. In the low gravity it felt like flying, just a little bit. Maybe that was the adrenaline peaking in her bloodstream. She didn't care. She came down easy, two feet and a balled fist touching ice, right behind him. Her free hand drew her weapon and extended it in one fluid motion. "Jason Schmidt," she said. "By the authority of the UEG and Firewatch, I'm placing you under arrest."

Schmidt spun around and jumped to his feet. He was faster than she'd expected, more nimble.

At the same moment, someone spoke in Petrova's ear. "This is Firewatch One-Four..."

Schmidt came straight at her, like he planned to tackle her. His move was idiocy. She had him at point-blank range. She brought her other hand up and steadied her weapon. It was a perfect shot. She knew she wouldn't miss.

"...authorization has been checked..."

Schmidt didn't slow down. He wasn't trying to talk her out of it. At this distance he couldn't fake her out, couldn't dodge her shot. She started to squeeze her trigger. If he really had killed all those people—

"...and denied. Repeat, authorization of apprehension is denied."

The light on the receiver of the pistol changed from amber to red. The trigger froze in place – no matter how much strength she used, she couldn't make it move.

"Cease operations and return to your post immediately, Lieutenant. That's an order."

Petrova just had time to duck as Schmidt barreled into her, knocking her back into the ice, which burst apart in a shower of snow with the force of the impact. The breath exploded out of her lungs and for a second she couldn't see straight. Struggling to get up, to grab Schmidt, she missed and went sprawling, faceplate down into the snow. It only took a fraction of a second to twist around, get back on her feet, wipe the snow off her helmet so she could see—

But by then he was gone. Of course. And now he knew she was on his tail. He would run. Get as far away as he could, maybe leave Ganymede altogether and restart his murder spree somewhere else. She tilted her head back and raged at the blank stars.

2

"Lieutenant, please confirm you received last order. Lieutenant? This is Firewatch One-Four, please confirm—"

She walked over to where her gun lay, half buried in the powdery ice. She grabbed it and slapped it back on her hip. The ice of Ganymede was a deep gray brown, but only on the surface. Where the gun had broken through the crust it left a glaring white silhouette.

Just like her boot prints, and the furrow in the snow where she'd been knocked down.

Just like the boot prints Jason Schmidt had left, which headed around a massive boulder and into the shadow of the ridgeline. Bright white footprints standing out against the dark ice. And what was that she saw, from over that direction? It looked like a light. Artificial light sweeping across the dark surface. It must be coming from some structure over there. Some hiding spot.

Maybe a trophy room.

"Lieutenant? Please acknowledge."

She crept around the side of the boulder and saw exactly what she'd expected to find. The light came from an old emergency shelter, basically a prospector's hut. A big metal hatch was stuck into the ice and a light on the hatch flickered slowly on-off, on-off – the universal signal that the bunker behind that hatch was activated, full of air and warmth. Like a chased rabbit, Jason Schmidt had run for a bolt-hole.

It would be crazy to follow him in. To literally walk into his lair, when he knew she was coming. When her gun was locked down.

"Lieutenant? Come in, Lieutenant. This is Firewatch

One-Four. Lieutenant, do you copy?"

Petrova slapped a big button on the face of the hatch and the airlock beyond blasted out air, equalizing pressures. She stepped inside and closed the outer door behind her. A moment later, the inner hatch slid open and she looked down into darkness.

"In pursuit, One-Four. I'll check in when I get a chance."

She switched off her radio. It wasn't going to tell her anything she wanted to hear.

Beyond the lock's inner door lay a concrete-lined corridor that spiraled down into the ice. Tiny light fixtures on the ceiling and walls lit up bright as she passed, then dimmed again behind her. Condensation hung in long, stalactite-like beads from the ceiling, spikes of pure water waiting for Ganymede's low gravity to finally bring them plopping down on the floor. At the bottom of the spiral, the corridor opened into a larger space. She expected to see a big room filled with crates of emergency supplies and old mining gear.

Instead the main room of the bunker was open, cleared out. The concrete floor was stained and damp but clear of debris. Dark chambers – caves, basically – led off the main chamber in every direction. This place was huge, she realized. This wasn't just an emergency bunker. It must be an entire mine complex, though it looked like it had been abandoned.

She thought she heard something – a real sound, echoing in the concrete space full of actual air. She crouched down and tried to stay perfectly still. There was no good place to hide, but maybe Schmidt hadn't seen her come in.

She ducked low into a shadow as he stepped out of one of the side caves. He'd shucked his suit down to the waist, the arms and hood hanging down behind him like tails. He had a large crate in his arms and he dumped its contents on the floor without cere-mony. "I'm back," he called, in a sing-song voice, like he was call-ing to pets who'd been waiting for him to come home.

Petrova watched as the crate's contents slithered out onto the floor. Hundreds of silver foil packets. Colorful pictures were printed on each packet, showing a serving of some mouth-watering foodstuff. Pureed carrots. Mushroom stew. Algae salad. Petrova recognized the pictures right away, as would anyone who had spent time on Ganymede. She knew the pictures were nothing but lies. There was food inside the packets, food nutritious enough to keep you alive, but it never resembled the tempting picture. Instead it was more likely to be a thin gray slop grown in a big bioreactor: proteins and carbohydrates excreted by gene-tailored bacteria in a vat of sugar water. It was the kind of food that workers got when they couldn't afford anything better, when they'd run out of luck. The government of Ganymede wouldn't let any of its people starve, but the alternative wasn't much better.

"Come and get it," Schmidt called out, in that same lilting cadence.

She was about to move in and put him under arrest when she caught a flicker of motion from one of the caves. Bright eyes glistened back there, catching the light. The filthiest, most unkempt human being she'd ever seen came rushing out, almost running on all fours. It was dressed in rags and its face was so grimy she couldn't tell its gender or even its age. It moved cautiously as it approached Schmidt, as if it was afraid of him. It didn't say a word, didn't so much as mumble a greeting.

"All yours," Schmidt said, and stepped away from the pile of food packets.

A hint of motion from another cave mouth grabbed Petrova's attention. Then another – soon people were emerging from a dozen directions at once. All of them as dirty and decrepit as the first. They moved quickly to grab silver packets from the pile, then they raced back toward their caves as if afraid someone would try to take the food away from them. They tore the packets open with their teeth, then stuck their fingers inside. They shoved the food straight into their mouths, getting as much of it on their skin and in their beards as they actually ingested. Their faces sagged with relief, as if they'd been starved for days and this was the best thing they'd ever tasted.

Petrova had no idea what was going on. Time to get some answers.

She rose to her full height. "Schmidt," she called out. "Keep your hands visible."

Schmidt winced but at least this time he didn't just come running at her like a bull.

"Jason Schmidt, you are under arrest. Back up against that wall. *Facing* the wall," she ordered.

He shook his head. His hands were up, in front of him, but he wasn't holding them up to show he was unarmed. He beseeched her with them. It looked like he might fall on his knees and beg her for mercy.

She needed answers. She needed to know what was going on. "You," she called, to the nearest of the unwashed people, who was busy licking out the insides of a third food packet. "Is this man holding you prisoner? Do you need help?"

The man – at least, he had a beard – looked up at her as if noticing her existence for the first time. He dropped the foil packet and stumbled towards her. His hands clawed and patted at the air, seemingly at random. Despite herself, Petrova took a step back as he came closer. His mouth opened but the sound he let out wasn't a word. Just a raw syllable, cut loose from any kind of meaning.

"Do you need help?" Petrova repeated. "Are you trying to ask for help?"

"He can't do that," Schmidt said. She jabbed her pistol in his direction and he shut up, lifting his hands higher in the air.

The victim came closer still and grabbed at Petrova's arm.

She pulled away from his touch and he grabbed for her helmet, instead, grasping one of the lamps mounted on its side. He let out a crude fricative, his mouth opening wide, spittle flying everywhere. She had to shove him, hard, to get loose.

Someone else hissed like a snake. All of Schmidt's other victims were making sounds now, raw noise, just the roots of words.

"What's going on?" Petrova asked. "What did you do to these people?"

Were these the missing persons she'd been tracking? She'd assumed Schmidt had murdered them all. But if they were here, alive, apparently kept captive—

They were moving now, all of them. Lumbering toward her, their hands describing shapes in the air, or clawing at nothing. Their faces were contorted in strange expressions she couldn't understand. They spoke only in meaningless monosyllables. *Ph. Kr. La.*

They grabbed at her, clinging to her legs, her arms. Petrova had to dance backward to get away from them. They weren't particularly strong – now she saw them up close she could see how emaciated and sickly they looked under their coating of dirt – but there were a lot of them.

"Get back," she told them. "Stay back! Firewatch!"

"They don't understand," Schmidt called.

Schmidt – she'd lost track of him. As the clawing, swiping people came at her, she'd forgotten to keep an eye on him. She twisted around and saw him creeping backward up the ramp, toward the surface. His hands were still up but he was getting away.

One of the victims growled, raising her voice as she bashed at the back of Petrova's suit with weak fists. She yelped like a dog.

Petrova pushed her away, harder perhaps than she should have. She was getting scared, she could feel it. She was afraid of these poor wretched people – she needed to get a grip.

She needed to get the situation under control. Well, she knew where to start. Schmidt was all but running up the ramp, away from her. She dashed after him and smacked him across the back of his neck with the butt of her pistol. "Down!" she said. "Get down and stay down, motherfucker." She hit him again and this time he fell down. "What did you do?" she demanded, as he tried to get up. She hit him again. "What did you do?"

Schmidt rolled on the floor, rolled until he was lying on his back. He lifted his hands to his face. She realized he was sobbing.

What the hell?

She retrieved a pair of smart handcuffs from a pouch at her belt. Moving fast, she grabbed Schmidt and shoved his face up against the concrete wall. She touched the cuffs to his hands and they came to life, twisting thick tendrils of plastic around his wrists and fingers, locking them in place. He made no effort to resist.

"Oh, thank God," he moaned. Quietly. His eyes were clamped shut. "Oh, thank you."

"What the hell is wrong with you?" she asked.

"It's over," he said. "It's finally over."

"What did you do to those people? What's wrong with them?"

"It's acute aphasia, it's . . . it's—"

"They can't talk," Petrova said. "I got that. Why? Did you . . . did you do something to them?"

"I *saved* them," Schmidt whined.

She stared at the back of his head, unable to comprehend. She had no idea what was going on. Then she glanced down at the pistol in her hands. The light there remained a steady, unchanging amber. Great.

"Tell me everything," she said. "Then I'll decide what to do with you."